Seducing the Enemy

YVONNE LINDSAY

O MILLS

First Published in Great Britain 2017
By Mills & Boon, an imprint of HarperCollins*Publishers*
1 London Bridge Street, London, SE1 9GF

SEDUCING THE ENEMY © 2017 Harlequin Books S. A.

The Wayward Son, *A Forbidden Affair* and *The High Price Of Secrets* were first published in Great Britain by Harlequin (UK) Limited.

The Wayward Son © 2012 Dolce Vita Trust
A Forbidden Affair © 2012 Dolce Vita Trust
The High Price Of Secrets © 2013 Dolce Vita Trust

ISBN: 978-0-263-92964-5

05-0517

Printed and bound in Spain
by CPI, Barcelona

New Zealand born, to Dutch immigrant parents, **Yvonne Lindsay** became an avid romance reader at the age of thirteen. Now, married to her "blind date" and with two fabulous children, she remains a firm believer in the power of romance. Yvonne feels privileged to be able to bring to her readers the stories of her heart. In her spare time, when not writing, she can be found with her nose firmly in a book, reliving the power of love in all walks of life. She can be contacted via her website, www.yvonnelindsay.com.

THE WAYWARD SON

BY
YVONNE LINDSAY

To E.M.
—In the immortal words of Casper, "Can I keep you?"

One

She hadn't seen anything quite this beautiful in forever. The exquisitely colored autumnal landscape aside, the figure of the man chopping wood in the distance, shirt off, muscles rippling in the still-warm Adelaide Hills sunshine, was quite enough to remind Anna of every hormonal response her body was capable of. And then some.

Never averse to indulging in appreciation of the male form—even if her busy work-filled schedule meant she rarely did anything about it—she walked a little closer. A tingle of awareness skimmed across her skin, raising goose bumps on the surface, which had nothing to do with the hint of evening breeze that rolled through the hills. It was only when she was about twenty meters from him that recognition hit her with all the subtlety of a bucket of ice water.

Judd Wilson.

Her entire reason for being in Australia.

Although they'd never met, there was no mistaking Charles Wilson's son. Obviously tall, Judd had dark hair and warmly tanned skin stretched over a physique that was the epitome of every woman's fantasy. His sharply sculpted features hinted at a resemblance to his father. She'd hazard a guess his eyes were the same piercing blue, as well.

Anna was surprised when her inner muscles clenched on a purely instinctive female reaction and her heart stuttered a little in her chest. She hadn't responded this strongly to anyone in a while, and she sure as hell never expected to feel so drawn to the son of the man who was not only her employer, but practically a father to her. She drew in a deep breath and forced back the flood of attraction that threatened to swamp her anew—reminding herself that she was here on business. She'd made a promise to Charles—a promise she fully intended to keep.

His instructions had been painfully clear. Somehow she had to persuade Judd Wilson to come home to New Zealand, before the father he hadn't seen in more than two decades died.

Anna took a few more tentative steps through the pathway designated amongst the rows and rows of grapevines that striated the land. Her eyes were fixed on the male figure working ahead of her—the man completely oblivious to the bombshell she was about to drop on his world. She paused for a moment, sudden nerves weakening her resolve.

Judd had been only six years old when his parents' divorce resulted in his and his mother's leaving New Zealand—not to mention leaving Charles, and Judd's baby sister, Nicole—behind for good. Did he even remember his father? Would he be pleased at the chance to reconcile, or would he be bitter over all the lost years?

Anxiety over Judd's potential reaction was swiftly followed by a swirl of familiar anger and defensiveness on Charles's behalf. If it hadn't been for Cynthia Masters-Wilson's deceptions, Charles would never have been separated from his son in the first place. Anna hadn't yet met the woman who had torn apart Charles's very reasons for existence, and she certainly wasn't looking forward to it. No doubt it would prove to be a necessary evil at some stage, but for now her focus was on meeting Charles's son and on gauging what his response to his father's contact would be. Her intense physical reaction to him now promised to make that a little more complicated than Anna had anticipated.

She was here with a job to do, she reminded herself sternly, even as her eyes flicked back toward Judd's sun-kissed torso one more time. She couldn't afford to let herself get distracted. Perhaps right now was not the best time to meet him and try to broach the topic. This was a matter that would require good timing and not a small amount of finesse if she was to be successful, and she owed it to Charles to be successful. Lord only knew he'd done more than enough for her family over the years. The least she could do in return was bring some peace of mind to the man who had supported Anna and her late mother for most of Anna's life. She couldn't just barge in and potentially destroy her one opportunity to bring Judd Wilson home.

She took a turn in a different direction, determined now to create some distance between herself and the very man she'd flown almost five hours to see. There would be time enough during her stay here at The Masters' Vineyard and Accommodation, she reasoned with herself. She had to tread this road very carefully if she was going to succeed.

Despite her best intentions, she didn't get very far.

"Hi, there," a voice as rich and sensual as a classic Shiraz called out from behind her. "It's a beautiful evening, isn't it?"

She couldn't ignore him now—not when it was vital she make a good impression. Anna braced herself as she turned around to face her boss's son.

Must be the new guest for the accommodation side of the business, Judd thought to himself as he watched the woman come closer. His cousin Tamsyn sent an update to all staff at the vineyard at the beginning of each week as to which of the luxurious cottages on the property would be accommodating guests for the coming days. She certainly hadn't mentioned that their newest visitor was so stunning.

Judd narrowed his eyes and tracked the movements of the woman in the blue dress as she approached. She walked with a gracefulness that belied the uneven ground she strolled along, and there was a sensual sway to her hips that sent a jolt of pure male appreciation rocketing through his body.

"Judd Wilson, welcome to The Masters'." Judd shifted the ax to his left hand so he could reach out his right to shake. She smiled in response, a slow movement of her lips that made his groin tighten almost imperceptibly, but the effect when she placed her hand in his was unmistakable. Raw need, hot and greedy, unfurled with latent intent. Interesting. Very interesting. Perhaps he'd found a solution to the boredom that had been plaguing him for weeks. He smiled back and clasped her hand firmly.

"Hi, I'm Anna Garrick," she said, her voice husky.

Her eyes searched his face keenly. As if she was looking for something. Perhaps some spark of recognition from him? No, the instant he thought of it, he eschewed the idea. If he'd ever met Anna Garrick before, he had no doubt he'd have remembered her.

From the top of her burnished dark chestnut-colored hair to her perfectly proportioned body and the tips of her painted toenails, she was his every fantasy. Even her voice—slightly soft, slightly rough—stroked his senses in a way he could never forget.

"Lovely to meet you, Anna. Did you arrive today?"

Her eyes flicked away, as if she was suddenly nervous—or hiding something. Judd felt his instincts go on alert.

"Yes, I did. It's wonderful here. You're so lucky to live in such a beautiful area. Have you…worked here long?" The question was innocent, but he'd caught the slight hesitation, as if she'd started out with the intention of asking something else.

"You could say that," Judd replied, his smile tightening. "It's something of a Masters family business—I grew up here."

"But your name…"

Ah, yes, his name. The reminder of the father who cast him aside all those years ago—and the reason why, even as the very successful head of The Masters' far-flung interests, some of his cousins still never quite treated him like he belonged.

"My mother is Cynthia Masters-Wilson," he replied. No need to go into details. Not when there were so many more pleasurable things he'd like to discuss with this woman.

"And do all Masters chop wood for the winery fireplaces?" she teased.

"But of course," he replied in kind. "Anything at all we can do to make your stay more…pleasurable." That certainly sounded better than admitting that he'd needed the tension release after an incredibly frustrating day of work.

Some days were like that. Bashing at the keys on a laptop didn't quite cut it when you just needed to get physical. And when his choices were either to chop wood or to resort to physical violence against his cousin Ethan, Judd had, reluctantly, chosen chopping wood.

Of course, Ethan really did need someone to knock his head straight. The man might run the winemaking side of the business with undeniable skill—their stock of award-winning wines was proof enough of that—but he was so stuck in his ways, he might as well be cemented in place. Ethan was devoted to maintaining the integrity and superiority of the wines that were synonymous with The Masters' brand. With the current glut of certain wine varieties on the local market, Judd was equally adamant that Ethan needed to diversify. He'd been suggesting it from the day the first projections about the excesses had arisen some years ago. His cousin was like a bear with a sore head on the issue and even more stubborn with it.

Yes, he definitely needed the distraction Ms. Garrick provided.

"And I do hope you'll let me know if there's anything at all *I* can do for you," he added.

"I'll keep that in mind," she replied. "But I can't think of anything I need at the moment. My plan for now is just to enjoy a ramble through these lovely grounds before it gets too dark."

"Then I'll let you return to it. But I'll be seeing you at dinner tonight?"

"Dinner?"

"Yes, we have a family dinner to welcome the new guests every week. There would have been an invitation in your welcome pack when you checked in. It begins with drinks in the formal sitting room of the main house at seven o'clock." Judd stepped closer, taking hold of her hand again. "You will be there, won't you?"

"Yes, I'd like that."

"Excellent," he murmured. "Until then." He lifted her hand, brushing his lips against the back in a soft kiss. She seemed taken aback for a moment, but then she gave him another slow, delicious smile before walking away. Judd leaned on the ax handle and watched her go. Shadows were beginning to creep along the foothills. He looked up to the ruins of the gothic mansion that crowned the nearby peak.

The charred remains were all that was left of the original Masters home. Years after its destruction, it remained a symbol of the family's past glory and their fight to rebuild a world that had been burned to the ground in a devastating sweep of ravenous bushfire. You had to admire a family that had had every marker of their wealth laid to waste, but who had fought back, tooth and nail, to be where they were today.

He was proud to be a part of that heritage. Despite his name, he was as much a Masters as any one of his many cousins and had just as much right to be here. Even so, he'd always felt as if he was an outsider. It had made him work twice as hard to prove his worth, and that work ethic had pushed The Masters' forward and onto a global platform beyond the family's expectations since he'd taken over as head of operations.

But perhaps he'd been too work-focused lately. It had been a while since he'd let loose. His duties here had consumed him for months now. Today, he'd finally admitted to himself that, no matter how hard he pushed himself, he was bored. Life, work, everything lacked the challenge he craved. A little light flirtation with the lovely Anna Garrick could be the perfect antithesis to the frustrations he was facing.

Judd methodically stacked the pile of logs he'd split and put away his tools before heading for his suite of rooms and having a much-needed shower. The prospect of another evening with his family suddenly held a great deal more appeal than it had after his latest altercation with Ethan's inflexible attitude.

Perhaps he'd found the challenge he was seeking after all.

Judd's hair was still slightly damp when he made his way into the formal sitting room, where whichever members of the Masters clan who were resident gathered for drinks with the guests before dinner. It was an old-fashioned habit, one that had its roots firmly linked to the ruins on the hill and a lifestyle long since gone, but one which still held a certain charm and which had no doubt been integral in keeping the family so firmly knit together.

Sunset brought a deeper chill to the air outside, which was offset by the crackling fire in the large stone fireplace.

He cast a glance around the room, giving a grim-lipped nod briefly in Ethan's direction before smiling at his mother, who sat, with her usual supreme elegance, on one of the chairs near the fireplace. No sign of the new guest yet.

He crossed to the sideboard and poured himself a half glass of The Masters' pinot noir. As he did so, he saw the object of his intentions hover in the doorway. He moved toward her immediately, but his mother—ever vigilant—beat him there. As he approached, he could hear her questioning Anna.

"Excuse me for being so forward, but you do look familiar to me. Have you stayed here before?" Cynthia asked.

To his surprise, a swiftly masked look of shock flitted across Anna's face.

"N-no," she replied. "This is my first visit to South Australia, although I hope it won't be my last."

She smiled, but her eyes still held a shadow of the shock he'd seen earlier. Was she lying? His instincts honed to a sharper edge. Ms. Garrick was becoming very interesting indeed.

"Perhaps you have a double out there. They say we all do." Cynthia glossed over any awkwardness with an arch of one expertly plucked brow. "Tell me, what can Judd get you to drink, my dear?"

"A glass of sauvignon blanc would be lovely, thank you. I hear you recently were awarded two golds for your sauvs."

"Yes, we were. We're very proud of Ethan and what he's doing with the wines," Cynthia said with a pointed look toward her son that told Judd his cousin had probably already apprised her of their earlier dispute. "Aren't we, Judd?"

"He's a master, that's for sure," Judd agreed.

His double entendre didn't go unnoticed by his mother, who flung him a silent rebuke with her expressive eyes, before apparently deciding it would be a suitable punishment to him to lead Anna away and introduce her to the other members of the family. Judd was forced to admit that his mother had chosen her chastisement well—Anna was the only one in the room whose company he truly wanted tonight.

He stood with one hand in his trouser pocket and observed Anna's movements as she was introduced to Cynthia's two older brothers and then Ethan. The instant his cousin stood to welcome the newcomer, Judd's hackles rose and every feral instinct inside of him leaped to the fore.

Something must have shown on his face, because he didn't miss the spark of interest in Ethan's eye before his cousin leaned forward to say something to Anna. Something which made her laugh. The sound itself was enough to send his blood humming along his veins, but knowing it was Ethan who had brought that laugh to her delectable lips set his teeth on edge.

Determined not to give his cousin the satisfaction of knowing just how much, and how surprisingly, his action had riled him, Judd turned to welcome Ethan's sister, Tamsyn, as she appeared in the door.

"I see you've already met our latest guest," she commented, removing his untouched pinot noir from his hands and taking a sip. Her brand-new engagement ring flashed brilliantly in the overhead lights. "Mmm, good. Can you pour me one?"

"Have this one, I haven't touched it."

"Thanks," Tamsyn answered with a smile.

"That fiancé of yours not here with you tonight?"

"No, he's still in the city—working." Her warm brown eyes searched his face. "You look tense. Is everything okay?"

Judd forced a smile to his lips. Tamsyn always had the unerring ability to sense when something was wrong with him.

"Nothing that won't be sorted when your brother learns to pay as much attention to market trends as he does to our guests," he commented.

Tamsyn laughed. "Oh, well, good luck with that, cuz. You

know market trends are the last thing Ethan concerns himself with. But I wouldn't growl too much about that." She nodded in Anna's direction. "You know Ethan's partial to blondes. And this particular brunette keeps sneaking glances at you, anyway. Have you met her yet?"

Judd nodded, letting his gaze track back to Anna's slender form and drinking in the smooth lines of her body, allowing a satisfaction-filled smile to cross his face when he realized his cousin was right—Anna's attention wandered in his direction several times. "Did she say what she was doing here in Adelaide?"

"No, I just assumed it was a short vacation. She didn't say much when she rang to make the booking."

"A short vacation?"

"I'm sure you'll have plenty of time to get to know her," Tamsyn teased. "But yeah, she's only here four days."

"I'd better not let her waste any more of her time here, then," he replied. "If you'll excuse me."

Without waiting for Tamsyn's reply he made his way across the room and to Anna's side. She turned and gave him a smile.

"It must be lovely being able to work with your extended family like this," she said. "Ethan's been filling me in on what you all do."

"It has its benefits, certainly," Judd agreed. "Tell me, have you planned any extended sightseeing while you're here? As luck would have it, I find myself with a couple of days with little to do and I'd love to show you around if you're keen."

Anna told herself to remain calm. This was exactly the opportunity she needed. Time alone with Judd Wilson would help her to better find out what he was like. She knew Charles had expected her to simply make an appointment with him and to give him the letter that even now burned a hole in her evening bag, but despite Charles's directive, she wanted to understand her boss's son just a little more before she took that step. God only knew that Charles had borne his fair share of disappointment in his lifetime and, if she had her way, his last years would be quite the opposite.

As much as Charles longed to be reunited with Judd, Anna knew that Charles was braced for his son's refusal. That was why he'd told no one but Anna how crucial it was to him to bring Judd back into the fold. Charles had sworn her to complete secrecy, not allowing her to tell even his daughter, Nicole, who had subtly taken up the reins of the company when Charles first got sick, any of the details of this trip. The cone of silence rankled, especially when Nicole was her best friend and they all not only worked together, but lived under the same roof, as well. Anna couldn't help but feel that she was betraying Nicole by doing all of this behind her back.

It was for Charles's sake, she reminded herself. And Charles deserved her very best efforts to convince his son to come home. If only she knew what the best approach was for her to take!

Instinct told her that Judd might be more receptive if she hid her true purpose for a little while longer and got him to open up to her more before she revealed the truth of her visit. But the purely female part of her worried that the longer she put off her business, the harder it would be for her to resist the powerful draw pulling her toward him. She chose her response to Judd Wilson's suggestion carefully.

"Are you sure? I wouldn't want to impose on you. It's my first visit to the region and I can already tell I haven't left myself enough time to enjoy it fully."

Judd leaned in closer. "Maybe we can entice you to come back again."

His words sent a shiver of anticipation across her skin. If the man got any more enticing she'd need a chillingly cold shower before the night was through. This visceral reaction to Judd Wilson was an unexpected complication she wasn't quite sure how to handle. But at least his reply showed her one thing—he was *definitely* willing to let her get to know *him* better…at least for as long as she hid the truth.

A dinner bell sounded down the hall, saving her from making a response. Judd offered her his arm.

"May I escort you to the table?"

Anna hesitated a moment before tucking her hand in the crook of his arm. "Are you always this formal?" she asked.

He shot her a look, a fierce blue blaze of fire in his eyes that let her know in no uncertain terms that he himself could be very informal, indeed. Her body reacted on an unconscious level. Her nipples tightened, her breasts suddenly full and aching with a desire to be touched. Everything in her body tensed, drawing her into a heightened state of awareness.

"When I need to be," he responded with a smile that was pure wicked intent from the curve of his lips to the light that gleamed in his eyes.

Anna forced herself to break eye contact. The compelling power of his male beauty was quite enough to take her breath away and to addle her wits along with it. Maybe getting to know Judd Wilson wasn't such a good idea after all. As Charles's assistant, she had the opportunity to interact with many powerful and compelling men, but never before had she dealt with a man with such effortless charisma.

The next few days suddenly took on an edge of uncertainty. What on earth had she let herself in for?

Two

The long wooden table in the formal dining room had been set with a dazzling array of china, crystal and cutlery. Anna sent a silent prayer of thanks that her upbringing in Charles Wilson's home meant that such a setting didn't faze her. Charles had insisted she have all the same social advantages Nicole enjoyed, even if—with her mother's position as Charles's housekeeper and companion—she hadn't had anywhere near the same financial background.

Seated near the top of the table, at Judd's right, Anna could observe the family dynamics in action. It was clear that Cynthia was very much the female head of the household. If Judd Wilson physically resembled his father, his estranged sister, Nicole, was her mother personified.

Anna studied Cynthia from her vantage point at the table. This was what her friend would look like in another twenty-five years—without, perhaps, the faint lines of bitterness that bracketed the older woman's mouth. That said, and despite the swish of gray at her temples that contrasted to her thick, dark hair, Cynthia Masters-Wilson was still a striking woman.

She carried herself with an almost regal air—expecting everyone to defer to her wishes and not holding back her disapproval if those wishes were not observed. Anna wondered briefly what Cynthia had been like early in her marriage to Charles, and found herself caught by the older woman's very intent gaze. Giving her hostess a smile, Anna tore her eyes away, mildly horrified that she'd been caught staring. The last thing she wanted to do was attract attention to herself.

There was a strong bond between Cynthia and her son, too, Anna observed. Judd, it seemed, was the only one capable of defusing his mother's rather autocratic attitude and bringing a genuine smile of warmth to her fine features. So why then, when her son was obviously so important to her, had Cynthia left behind her one-year-old daughter, Nicole, when she'd returned to Australia? Had she ever taken a moment to think about the baby girl she'd left behind and what impact her abandonment would have on that infant's life?

Anna had come to Australia full of sympathy for Charles, who had been so hurt by Cynthia's actions during their marriage. But seeing the woman now just brought home how badly Nicole had been cheated, as well.

"You're looking serious. Is everything okay with your meal?" Judd asked softly in her ear.

The gentle caress of his warm breath made her skin tingle, and she forced her concentration back from where she'd let it lead her. Anna shook her head.

"No, everything is wonderful, thank you."

"Is it something else that's bothering you?" he pressed, reaching across the table in front of him to lift a bottle of wine to top off her glass.

Just you, she thought before giving her head a shake.

"I'm perhaps a little tired, that's all."

"We can be a bit overwhelming, can't we?" he commented.

"No, it's not that. Actually, I envy you this. I'm an only child, as were both my parents. To have so many family members all in one place… Well, you're lucky."

"Yes, we are lucky—and equally cursed at the same time," he said with a charming wink that took the sting out of the latter part of his statement.

And Nicole should have had the chance to be a part of this, too, Anna added silently. Not for the first time, she wondered what had happened to drive Charles and Cynthia, and their children, apart. Whatever it was, Charles had flatly refused to discuss it, aside from saying that Cynthia had betrayed his trust—something she knew that Charles considered unforgivable. Whatever it was, Anna knew that it had not only ruined his marriage, but it had led to a major rift between himself and his business partner also. So many lives altered. And here she was, trying to mend a fence. Boy, was she ever out of her depth.

By the time the meal had progressed to coffee and dessert, Anna asked to be excused from the table, pleading tiredness. The gentlemen at the table stood as she moved her chair back, and she found herself completely charmed by the effortless old-world manners.

"Thank you all so much for your company tonight, and for dinner," she said.

"You're very welcome, Anna. Just let housekeeping know tomorrow if you'll be joining us again during your stay," Cynthia said graciously. "Do you have anything special planned for tomorrow?"

"We'll be doing some sightseeing and then I'm taking her into Hahndorf for lunch," Judd interjected.

"Oh?"

Cynthia hid her surprise but not before giving her son a sharp look that gave Anna no doubt that his mother would be grilling him on his choice of companion the minute she left the room. Cynthia composed her features into a bland smile. "Well, then, I hope you enjoy our little taste of Germany. Sleep well."

"Thank you," Anna replied and turned to leave the room.

To her surprise, Judd followed her. As they reached the front door she stopped.

"Why did you tell your mother you're taking me out tomorrow?"

"Because I am," he said confidently. "You can't visit the Adelaide Hills without stopping at Hahndorf, as well. It would be culturally insensitive."

"Culturally insensitive or not, I got the impression she wasn't too pleased about it."

"She thinks I don't work hard enough, but that's my problem, not yours."

He opened the front door and gestured for her to precede him. Out on the narrow road that led to the restored pioneer's cottage where she was staying, Anna felt the night air close in around her with its frigid arms. She shivered, wishing she'd thought to bring her pashmina with her when she'd come across to the house earlier.

"At the risk of being cliché," Judd said, removing his dinner jacket and dropping it over her shoulders, "I think you need this more than I do."

"Thank you," she said softly.

He wasn't kidding. Judging by the heat of his body still held in the lining of his jacket, he certainly had no need of the garment. She instantly felt warmed by it. A faint waft of spice, blended intrinsically with a hint of vanilla and woody notes, enveloped her. She recognized the scent as Judd's cologne and felt her bones begin to melt.

"The nights can be quite cool here from now on. The staff will have lit the fire in your cottage for you. It should be lovely and warm compared to out here."

Anna had an instant and vivid flashback to watching Judd

chopping wood this afternoon. Did he accomplish everything with that much vigor?

"It's still a beautiful night," she said, looking upward at the inky darkness of the sky peppered with dots of light— anything to distract her from the influence of what he did to her.

"Certainly is."

There was something about his voice that made her drop her gaze and meet his. He was looking straight at her. Despite the fact that at least a meter separated them, she felt as if he'd reached out and touched her. Anna swallowed against the sudden dryness that parched her throat. This man was sensuality personified. With only one look, he had her virtually a quivering mess of longing.

She barely knew him and yet she was already on the verge of casting all her careful self-imposed rules to the four corners of the earth and inviting him to explore this overwhelming attraction between them. And she knew her feelings were reciprocated. She could feel the energy and tension fairly vibrating off him. What would he be like when he lost control, she wondered, allowing herself to dwell for only a moment on the idea before slamming it back behind her all too weak defenses.

She broke eye contact before she could do something totally out of character, and began to walk a little more briskly along the path. Judd silently kept pace with her. At the cottage, he waited as she opened the front door. She shrugged off his coat and handed it to him.

"Thank you again."

"You're welcome," he replied.

Why didn't he just turn and go? She felt a flush rise in her cheeks. Did he expect her to invite him in? The cottage came with both a well-stocked kitchen and wet bar complete with a wine chiller, she'd noticed on checking in earlier today. But what kind of message would that send, she wondered, if she asked him to join her for coffee, or a drink? One thing she knew for certain was where it would *lead*—straight to the luxuriously appointed bedroom, and a steamier, wilder night than any she'd had in years.

The thought aroused her as much as it scared her. She wasn't the kind of woman who hopped in bed with a man she'd barely met, and she'd never mixed business and pleasure before in her life. If she gave in to Judd's advances now, where would it leave her when she had to tell him the truth about why she was here?

"You're thinking again," Judd said, his lips twitching with a barest hint of a smile.

"I do that a lot," she admitted.

"Here, think on this, then."

Somehow he'd closed the distance between them without her noticing. His hand snaked around the back of her neck—his fingers warm against her cooler skin. Her face automatically tilted up toward his, her lips parting on a silent protest. She knew the protest was futile. She wanted this as much as he did, and she was helpless to ignore the demand.

His mouth, when it captured hers, was gentle, coaxing, and Anna felt as if he'd lit a fire that ran through her veins. A small part of her had hoped his kiss would be disappointing—something that would make it easier to refuse his attentions. In all honesty, she had known to the depths of her soul that his touch would be like this—*magic*—and she wanted that magic with every cell in her body.

She fisted her hands at her sides in an effort to prevent herself from reaching out and touching him. It would be too much, too difficult to step away from, but the way his lips teased hers invited her closer, and before she knew it, her hands were pressed against his chest, the fiery warmth of his skin burning through the expensive cotton of his shirt and letting her know that he could set other hidden parts of her aflame if only she'd let him.

His chest muscles shifted beneath her hands as he lifted his other arm to curve around her waist, drawing her closer to him. Hip to hip, there was no denying he was as powerfully aroused as she. Tension built in her body, coiling tight as he deepened their kiss and coaxed her lips open with his probing tongue.

He tasted of fine wine and illicit, unspoken promises. Promises that made her clench her thighs together against the swell of desire that rippled through her body before centering at the core of her belly. She rocked her pelvis against him, the movement a futile attempt to assuage the pressure building inside of her. Instead, it only incited her further. Anna kissed him back with a passion she'd never unleashed before, meeting his tongue with her own, letting him know that she was no innocent bystander in this assault on her senses.

She lifted her hands from his chest, sliding them upward, over his shoulders and the strong column of his neck, and burrowed her fingers in his dark hair, holding him to her as his lips devoured hers, as hers did his. She pressed her body against him, her nipples taut and sensitive against the lace of her bra, her breasts aching for his touch.

The call of a night bird punctuated the air, its unfamiliar sound bringing Anna back to her surroundings. Bringing her mind back to the task she'd been sent here to execute.

She untangled her fingers from Judd's hair, and let her hands drop to her sides once more. Their kiss, when it ended, was more bittersweet than she'd imagined, the loss of his caress felt deep inside. Judd rested his forehead against hers, his eyes still closed, his lips moist and slightly parted on an uneven breath. It would be so easy to kiss him again but she knew that if she did, it wouldn't stop there. Not with this conflagration that had ignited between them.

A kiss, a good-night kiss, was all it should have been and yet it had escalated into so very much more. She wasn't in a

position to let that happen. She didn't dare explore this further, not without some truths between them, and she wasn't
ready to tell Judd exactly what she was here for just yet.

The atmosphere between them was filled with possibili-
ties, yet Anna knew she could choose only one. To say good-
night and to let Judd go back to the main house.

"Is this how you say good-night to all your guests?" she
asked, in an attempt to lighten the mood that swirled around
them.

His lips quirked in a half smile and he lifted his head. "No,
only you."

Three words. So simply spoken. The expression in his eyes
so honest it went straight to her heart. She clamped down on
the feeling, fighting it back so she wouldn't succumb to the
lure of the invitation in his gaze. Or to the physical plea that
thrummed through every particle of her body.

Her mouth dried. She had no idea of how to respond to
him without it sounding careless and glib.

"It's okay, Anna," he said, as if sensing her quandary. "It
was only meant to be a simple good-night, nothing more.
Unless you want it to be?"

"I…I can't. I—"

"Don't worry," he interrupted. "I'm nothing if not a patient man. And you're worth waiting for. But I promise you
this—sooner or later we will make love, and when we do, it
will be unforgettable."

His words left her speechless. Unforgettable? Oh, she had
no doubt that sex with him would be off the Richter scale.
She'd never been into casual encounters, not that anything
about Judd Wilson was casual. For him, though, she might
have considered it if he hadn't been Charles's son.

Judd pressed his lips against her cheek, almost at the
corner of her mouth. All she had to do was turn her head
ever so slightly and she could let this lead to its natural and,

no doubt, very satisfying conclusion. But she held firm and felt Judd's unspoken acceptance of her refusal.

"I'll pick you up in the morning about nine," he said, letting her go and taking a step away. "Sleep well."

She watched him leave, his long legs eating up the distance along the wide track that led back to the main house. When he was out of sight, she finally let her body sag against the door frame.

Just hours ago, she'd arrived in Australia with one goal in mind—to convince Judd to come with her to New Zealand and reunite with his father. She still wanted—needed—to achieve that goal, but another need was taking over. A need to make the most of her time with Judd, to follow through on the attraction between them and see where it led.

But she knew she couldn't give in. So much rested on how Judd reacted when he learned why she'd come. If things between them got out of hand and he learned the truth too soon, she could inadvertently ruin all of Charles's hopes for reconciliation. She couldn't bear the thought of letting him down like that. Even if it meant closing the door on any chance to explore the sizzling attraction between her and Judd.

Her fingers fluttered to her lips. She could still feel him, still taste him. And God, she still wanted him. How on earth was she going to get through an entire day in his presence without giving in?

Three

The V8 engine of his Aston Martin Vantage roadster purred as Judd drove slowly along the private road that led toward Anna's cottage. A quiet smile of satisfaction played across his face—a total contrast to the frustration that even now held his body deliciously taut with expectation.

He hadn't felt this depth of attraction to a woman in a very long time. Actually, to be completely truthful, he'd never felt quite this level of need in relation to anyone else before.

Today was going to be interesting, very interesting indeed. And tonight? Well, that had the potential to be even better.

The faint burr of his cell phone distracted him. A quick look at the caller ID saw him ease his car to a halt and press a button on his hands-free kit to respond.

"Good morning, Mother. I didn't expect to hear from you this early."

Cynthia didn't waste any time on pleasantries. "I know where she's from."

"Who? Anna?"

"Who else? I was certain she looked familiar, and now I know why. I knew her mother. She worked at Wilson Wines. She was just an office dolly back then—flirted outrageously with the traveling reps. She left when she married one of them, pregnant of course, but I always suspected your father had his eye on her. About three years after we got here I heard that when her husband died, Charles employed her as his *housekeeper*—like anyone expected that was the truth."

Judd tensed. Every time Cynthia mentioned Charles Wilson there was a tone to her voice that set his teeth on edge.

"Did you hear me, Judd?"

"Yes, I heard you. What do you expect me to do about it?"

"Well, confront her, obviously. Her mother was living with Charles, ergo, so was Anna. Find out what she's doing here, because I'd wager she isn't here on holiday. It has to be something to do with your father."

He hated to admit it, but his mother could be right. Ever since they'd met, he'd suspected that Anna was hiding something. And the way she'd looked at him right at their first meeting was as if she was searching his face for a resemblance to someone. Had she been comparing him to his father? He stilled the curl of anger at that thought and at the possibility that his family might be being used by Charles Wilson again. Instead, he channeled his heated emotions into a tool to hone his thinking.

"I'll deal with it. Don't worry."

"I knew she was trouble the second I laid eyes on her," his mother continued. "She's probably working for him, you know. In fact, I wouldn't be surprised, if she's anything like her mother, if she is warming his bed. He always did prefer younger women."

His mother's words were acid in his ears. Cynthia had never let go of the bitterness she felt toward the man she'd left behind in New Zealand. He could still remember the first day he and Cynthia had arrived at The Masters' and she'd pointed to the shell of the mansion up on the hill.

Their house in New Zealand had been an identical replica of the original Masters home—a wedding present built under Charles's orders for his beautiful bride. Seeing a wrecked, charred ruin of a house that looked so very much like the one he'd always known had been a deeply unsettling experience for Judd, especially when Cynthia told him that the ruin would be a constant reminder of what they'd all lost when his father had rejected them both and banished them back to Australia. And it was to be a constant target for all that he should strive to regain.

His six-year-old mind had been unable to fully understand what she was saying, hadn't grasped the depth of her obsession with the home she'd lost not once, but twice, and every day at The Masters' he'd learned what it meant to be rejected by the man who'd fathered him. Whether it was the pitying gaze of his uncles and their sometimes overzealous attempts to be a father figure in his life, or the overheard remarks made by the staff from time to time when they didn't know he was listening, he knew exactly what it felt like to be a castoff. He snapped his mind back to the present.

"I said I'll deal with it, Mother. By the end of today we'll know exactly what she's up to."

"Good. I know I can rely on you, Judd. Be careful, my darling."

Careful? Oh, he'd be more than careful. He disconnected the call and guided his car once more toward Anna's cottage. He'd be so careful that Anna Garrick would hardly know what had hit her.

Anna stood waiting for him on the patio of the cottage. She looked deceptively fresh and innocent, dressed in layers of light clothing. He knew she was anything but innocent, especially if her response to him last night had been anything to go by. He hoped she was up to a little heat, because today promised to be warm in more ways than one.

She walked toward his car as he got out and opened the passenger door for her.

"Nice wheels," she commented.

"I was always a James Bond fanatic as a kid." He smiled. "Some things never get old."

She laughed and settled in the red leather bucket seat, its color a perfect foil for her chestnut-brown hair, he thought as he swung her door closed. As he got back behind the wheel she rummaged in her handbag, pulling out a long bamboo hairpin before twisting her long hair into a knot and securing it at the back of her head.

"I can put the top up if you'd rather," he said, his eyes caught on the elegant line of her neck, the perfection of her jaw.

"No, it's a beautiful day. Let's make the most of it," she answered with a smile that hit him fair and square in the gut and reminded him of just how uncomfortable it had been to walk back to the main house last night.

"Good idea," he agreed and maneuvered the high-performance sports car onto the driveway that led off the property. "You mentioned yesterday that it's your first time in Adelaide," he probed. "What made you decide to come here for a break?"

She remained silent for a moment. From the corner of his eye he could see her press her lips together, as if she was holding back her instinctive answer and taking the time to formulate another.

"It was suggested to me," she said, averting her gaze out the side window.

Oh, he'd put money on the fact it was suggested to her, and by whom. Even without the insight his mother had offered, it was Anna's evasiveness that gave her away. He'd known that she had something to hide, and now that he suspected it involved his father, he was absolutely determined to find out what it was before the day was out. In the meantime, there was nothing, absolutely nothing, stopping him from having a good time along the way.

As they turned out the driveway that led from the vineyard and out onto the main road heading toward the hills, he saw her gaze pulled up onto the ridge and to the silhouette of the devastated building that stood there. He waited for her to say something, to ask about what had happened. Everyone did, eventually. But she remained silent. The expression on her face was pensive. Some devil of mischief prompted him to comment.

"It was magnificent in its day, you know."

"I beg your pardon?" She turned to face him.

"Masters' Rise, the house up there." He let go of the steering wheel with one hand and gestured up toward the hills.

"It was your family home?"

Did she really not realize, or was she just bluffing? "Not that one, although I lived briefly in a replica of it back in New Zealand when I was young." When she didn't comment on that, he pointed back up the hill. "Masters' Rise was destroyed before my time. My mother and uncles lived there as youngsters, though. I don't think the family pride ever quite recovered from its loss. I know for a fact that my mother's didn't. And it wasn't just losing the house—a good bit of the vineyard was destroyed, as well."

"It wasn't as if they could have done anything to stop it, though, was there?"

"Done anything?"

"Well, it was a bushfire, wasn't it?"

He shot her a piercing glance.

"At least that's what I think I read somewhere," she added hastily.

Oh, good cover, he thought before slowly nodding.

"They were lucky to escape with their lives," he said. "Unfortunately, they didn't have much else—well, not much else but the Masters' tenacity. Rebuilding the house wasn't an option—not when they had to recreate their entire livelihood, as well. It would have taken everything they had left and they were forced to choose between rebuilding their home or re-establishing the vineyards and winery."

"Tough choices. It's a shame they couldn't do both."

"Yeah."

Judd lapsed into silence. Wondering, not for the first time, how different life might have been if the Masters family hadn't been forced into that decision. It couldn't have been easy for his mother and her brothers, starting over from scratch, seeing the life of ease and plenty they'd enjoyed vanishing in a flash. Was that why it had been so easy for Charles Wilson to sweep Cynthia off her feet? Was the life of wealth and luxury he offered truly impossible for a girl, who'd spent so long struggling, to resist?

"So, what's on the agenda for today?" Anna asked, her voice artificially bright. "Last night you mentioned Hahndorf, right? Where and what is it?"

Judd flashed her a smile before transferring his attention back to the road in front of them.

"It was originally a German settlement, established in the early eighteen hundreds. Much of the original architecture still survives and is used today. It's not far from here, but I thought I'd take you a couple of other places first and then we'll head back into Hahndorf for lunch."

"Sounds lovely, thanks. Really, I appreciate you taking time out of your schedule for me."

Judd reached out and caught her hand in his, giving her fingers a gentle squeeze.

"I want to get to know you better, Anna. Can't do that stuck in my office, now, can I?"

To his surprise, a flush of color spread across her cheeks. She blushed? The ingenuousness of the act was totally at odds with the wanton he'd held in his arms last night. Yeah, there was no doubt about it. Anna Garrick intrigued him, and he liked being intrigued—even if it was by someone with a hidden agenda.

Her fingers tingled beneath his touch and Anna felt heat surge through her body, staining her cheeks. God, this effect he had on her would be her undoing. She gently withdrew her hand, distracting herself by poking about in her handbag for a tissue. Her fingertips brushed against the envelope holding the letter from Charles and she pulled her hand out of the bag so rapidly she elicited another one of those piercing looks from Judd.

"So," she said, forcing her heartbeat to resume a more normal rate with a few calming breaths, "where are you taking me first?"

He gestured to the highest peak ahead of them.

"Mount Lofty. From there you'll see the whole of Adelaide spread out before you."

Judd proved himself to be a very efficient tour guide. That he knew the area like the back of his hand was obvious, as was his love and appreciation of his surroundings. By the time they'd taken in the panoramic views of the city and beyond from the peak of Mount Lofty and then strolled through the exquisitely beautiful botanic gardens below, Anna was having a hard time reminding herself that this was no pleasure jaunt.

Judd's fingers were loosely linked in hers as they walked, and every nerve in her body went on high alert, focusing intently on the scant physical connection they shared. Wishing against everything that the connection could be deepened and intensified.

She fought to regain control of her senses. She'd be crazy to embark on anything physical with Judd Wilson. Totally and utterly crazy. But no matter what her head told her, her body demanded something else entirely.

In her bag, she felt her cell phone discreetly vibrate. The only person who would be calling her would be Charles. Her stomach lurched. Was he okay? He hadn't looked well when she'd left Auckland yesterday. Extracting her fingers from Judd's light clasp, she reached into her bag.

"Excuse me, I need to take this," she said, putting the phone to her ear and turning to walk a few steps away from him.

"Have you met him yet?" Charles's voice sounded strong and healthy.

"Yes, I have," she said guardedly, wishing she'd let the call go to her message service and then phoned Charles back when she had a little more privacy.

"Well, what's he like? Have you given him the letter yet? What did he say?"

Charles's questions fired at her with the less-than-subtle force of a battering ram and she created a little more distance between herself and the subject of those questions.

"It's hard to say at the moment. No, and nothing yet," she answered each question in turn.

"You're with him now, aren't you?"

"Yes," she replied. "Look, it's really not a good time to talk. Can I get back to you later?"

Please say "yes," she silently begged. In response, Charles's hearty chuckle filled her ear.

"Not a good time, eh? Okay, then, I'll leave you to it. But make sure you call me back later today."

"Yes, certainly. I'll do that. Goodbye."

"Anna, don't hang up!"

She sighed. "Yes?"

"I'm counting on you. I *need* my son with me."

"I'll do my best."

"Thank you, darling girl."

He disconnected the call and Anna felt her shoulders sag with the reminder of what he expected of her.

"Bad news?" Judd asked.

"No, not really," Anna hedged.

"Anything I can help with?"

She fought back the strangled laugh that rose in her throat. If only he knew. But no, the last thing she could do was divulge the details of that phone call. Not yet, anyway. She shook her head and pushed her phone back in her bag.

"It was just work, I can deal with it later. I'm starving," she said, trying to shift the conversation onto safer ground. "How about that lunch you promised me?"

"Your wish is my command," Judd said, taking her hand again and lifting it to his lips.

His blue eyes gleamed, letting Anna know in no uncertain terms that he was definitely open to more than just lunch. Again that surge of heat swirled deep inside her, making her body tighten in anticipation. She fought to paint a smile on her lips. This was all going to be so much harder than she had ever imagined.

On the short drive to Hahndorf, Charles's words kept echoing around in her head, *I need my son with me.* An unexpected flash of anger rose within her. Charles was so bent on reuniting with his long-lost son that he'd completely forgotten he had a daughter right by his side. A daughter who understood his wine importation and distribution business better, almost, than her own father. A daughter who'd spent her whole life stepping up in an attempt to fill the near insurmountable gap left when Cynthia had taken Judd to Australia.

Anna wondered again about the contents of the letter that weighed so heavily in her handbag. She knew Charles was planning on offering Judd an incentive to return, but he hadn't shared the details with her. Whatever carrot he'd chosen to dangle, what would it mean to the sister who didn't even remember Judd? The one who worked so hard to please her father, for no reward other than his love and hard-won approval? Anna adored Charles with every breath in her body. He'd been the only father figure she'd ever known, but she worried that he'd overstepped the mark with this obsession with Judd and that he'd damage his relationship with Nicole irrevocably.

"What sort of work do you do that they need to call you when you're on vacation?"

Judd's voice interrupted her thoughts and made her start. She'd been dreading this question and had already decided that a vague response would be her best bet.

"Oh, I'm a P.A."

"You must be pretty important to your boss if he can't keep from calling you."

Anna forced her features to relax into a smile. "I've worked for him since I left school. We're probably closer than most boss/employee relationships."

She caught Judd's piercing look before his eyes resumed their surveillance of the road in front of them. He began to slow the car as they approached a township, and Anna let out an involuntary exclamation of delight as they entered the main road. Lined with massive trees and with quaint tin-roofed buildings, she'd have thought she'd stepped back in time if it hadn't been for the bustle of people and modern vehicles that lined the street.

Judd expertly backed the Aston Martin into a car space and came around to open Anna's door.

"I'm surprised he let you out of his sight, if you're so *close*," he said, his words weighted with something that Anna couldn't quite put her finger on.

"I'm my own woman," she answered.

"I'm pleased to hear it," Judd said in return, taking her hand and tucking it firmly in the crook of his elbow. "Because I don't like to share."

"I've heard that trait was reserved for only children," Anna said with a soft laugh, trying to defuse the heady rush of excitement his words stimulated inside her.

"What makes you think I'm not an only child?"

Oh, Lord, she'd nearly stepped right in it. She scoured her memory quickly, although deep down she knew that no one here in Adelaide had mentioned his estranged family to her.

"Oh, I don't know. I just assumed, since you grew up here surrounded by your cousins, that sharing was a natural part of your life."

She held her breath, hoping he'd be satisfied with her reply. To her surprise, he let out a short laugh.

"Yeah, I suppose that'd be a natural assumption."

"So, are you?" she probed, wanting some insight into how he might feel about the sister he hadn't seen in years.

"An only child?" He shrugged. "It's complicated. My parents divorced when I was young, and they split my sister and me up at the same time. I was six, she was just one year old."

"Isn't that unusual? That your father kept your sister?"

"He didn't want me—my mother did."

Judd's words, so simply spoken, hinted strongly at the hurt that had to lie behind them. Anna wanted to protest. To tell him that his father wanted him very much indeed, but they weren't her words to say.

"Have you ever wanted to see your sister? Get to know her?" she pressed, taking a different tack.

"Why the sudden interest?"

"Oh, nothing. It's just that, as I told you last night, I *am* an only child and I always wanted siblings."

"The human condition, huh? Always wanting what we can't have."

"I suppose so," Anna admitted, sorry that he'd so deftly avoided answering her question.

They walked along the shady sidewalk, stopping every now and then to wander into one of the many galleries before they crossed the road to take an umbrella-covered table outside an obviously very popular inn. Anna pulled the pin from her hair and shook it loose from its temporary restraint. She didn't miss the glow of pure male appreciation in Judd's eyes as she did so and felt her body warm in response.

"Would you like a menu, or would you like me to choose for you?" Judd asked.

"Go ahead and order for me. I eat just about everything."

"What would you like to drink? A glass of wine?"

Anna eyed a nearby patron swigging at a foam-topped beer. "One of those," she said, pointing.

"Beer?"

"Sure. Don't tell me you're one of those people who don't think women should drink beer."

"Not at all." He laughed. "In fact, I plan to join you."

When the waitress came over he ordered their meals and two beers. They didn't have to wait long before the food and drinks arrived. Anna gasped when she saw the size of the platter placed before them.

"It's their Taste of Germany. You couldn't come here without trying it," Judd said.

"I'll take your word for it. I sure hope *you're* hungry, too," Anna replied, taking a sip of her chilled beer. "Mmm, that's good."

She grew so engrossed in the meal and their surroundings that she didn't notice when a family with several children raced by their table. One of the kids lost his balance when his foot hooked into the handle of her bag, which she'd placed on the ground by the table leg. Anna's hands flew to stabilize the beer mugs on the table as it rocked under the impact of the youngster's clumsiness.

"Oh, no! I'm so sorry," his harried mother said, rushing to pick up the belongings that had scattered from Anna's bag.

"Don't worry, it's okay," Anna assured her, reaching for the items the woman had so far gathered and shoving them back in her bag. "Really, it's my fault. I shouldn't have left the strap hanging out like that."

Judd had risen from his chair and was helping to collect Anna's things. Too late she saw the stark-white envelope that had been ejected from its hiding place. His long-fingered hand hovered over it and her heart sank to the soles of her feet as she registered the exact moment he identified the name on the front.

He settled back in his chair, handing most of her things back to her, but holding the envelope between his fingers as if it contained something dangerous inside. The mother and her son moved on, rejoining the rest of their family, but Anna didn't even notice. All she could do was stare at Judd and the flat packet in his hands.

"Care to explain this?" he said, his voice suddenly devoid of the warmth it had contained only moments ago.

Anna took a deep breath. "It's a letter."

"I can see that. It looks like a letter to *me*."

She couldn't maintain eye contact and instead dropped her gaze to her lap, where her fingers knotted in anxiety. This was all wrong. She'd wanted to give him the letter when she was ready, when she was in control and when she could better gauge what his reaction would be. Not in a public place like this, with no warning and no chance to prepare him for the letter's contents.

"It is," she said softly.

She flinched as she heard the envelope tear open. Her stomach tied in a knot of unbelievable proportions as the sound of a single sheet of paper being unfolded overwhelmed the noise of the diners and sightseers around them.

Anna finally lifted her gaze and watched as Judd read the letter his father had written. The letter that had the capacity to change all their lives. When he'd finished, he neatly refolded the sheet and put it back in the envelope. Still he said nothing. A shiver of fear danced down her spine. He was calm, too calm. She'd seen Charles get like this and she knew that it was only the quiet before the storm. What was coming could only be cataclysmic.

She reached across the table, touching his forearm. He shook off her touch as if she were nothing more than an annoying insect.

"Judd—" she started, but whatever she'd been about to say died in her throat when he met her eyes and she felt the full fury of the glacial fire reflected there.

"Who the hell are you and why are you really here?"

Four

Across the table Anna stared at him in shock. She felt all color drain from her face and a numb coldness settle in the pit of her stomach. She'd done this all wrong. She should have just followed Charles's orders right from the start to make an appointment to see Judd and tell him from the outset why she was there. She took a deep breath before speaking.

"I…I've told you who I am. I'm Anna Garrick. And…" Her mouth dried, forcing her to pause for a moment, and swallow, before continuing, "And I'm here because your father desperately wants to make amends for the past."

"If he's so keen to make amends, why isn't he here himself?" Judd demanded.

His skin had gone taut across his features, lending an implacable hardness to his face, and his eyes burned with a hard blue intensity.

"He didn't tell you in the letter?"

"I want to hear it from you. Why did he not come here himself? Was he too ashamed to face up to me, to face up to the truth that his own pride and his stupid accusations are responsible for having torn our family apart in the first place?"

Anna made a small noise of protest. It wasn't like that. Sure, she'd heard that Charles hadn't been an angel at the time his marriage to Cynthia had fallen irrevocably apart—who ever was when under extreme pressure?—but from what her mother had told her, she knew that Cynthia had done plenty of damage, as well. Charles definitely hadn't been solely responsible for what had happened, no matter what Judd's mother might have told him.

"Well?" Judd demanded.

"He's unwell. His doctor wouldn't clear him to travel." The diabetes that had plagued Charles for so many years had worsened, in part due to his late diagnosis and subsequent reluctance to follow medical recommendations to prevent further damage to his body. His kidneys were showing signs that renal failure could be just around the corner.

"How convenient."

Judd lifted his stein and took a healthy swig of its contents, and Anna felt the initial stirrings of her own anger rise in response to his derision.

"It isn't convenient at all, actually. Look, I'm not privy to exactly what he said in his letter to you, but I have a pretty good idea of what he's asking. He wants to see you again. To get to know you before he—" Suddenly overwhelmed with emotion, her voice broke.

"Before he what?"

"Before he dies," she said shakily.

"You care about him?" Judd's voice was devoid of emotion.

"More than you could ever understand," she said, forcing herself to pull it together. "He is not a well man, Judd. Please, this could be your last chance to get to know him. He's your father, surely you owe him that."

"Owe him?" He snorted a laugh. "That's rich. I don't owe

him anything and I haven't exactly missed out on having him in my life. I don't see why that should change, although he has certainly attempted to sweeten the pot to entice me back to New Zealand."

"Sweeten the pot?" She felt a building sense of dread. Just what kind of incentive had Charles offered?

"You really don't know?"

"If I knew, would I be asking?" she snapped.

"Strange, given that you're his valued *employee,* and given—by your own admission—how *close* you are and how much you care about him, that he didn't see the need to apprise you of his intentions."

She didn't like his unspoken insinuation that there was something unsavory between her and Charles. Sure, she loved him—like a father. But how could she explain that to Judd now? He'd never believe her.

Judd leaned back in his chair and fixed her with his intense gaze. "It seems that your esteemed employer wishes to offer me a controlling interest in the family business."

"He what?"

A controlling interest? Just like that? Black spots swam before Anna's eyes and she gulped at the air. How could Charles do that to Nicole? How could *she* have done that to Nicole? Anna knew her best friend had standards just as high as Charles's when it came to loyalty and honesty. When she found out that Anna had been the messenger who had gone behind Nicole's back to practically hand deliver Charles's company to Judd, would Nicole ever forgive her?

"And that's not all. Apparently, he wants to assign the family home to me, as well." He casually waved the letter in the air. "All to do with whatever I please."

Anna couldn't believe her ears. "He wouldn't do something like that. You have no loyalty to Charles, no loyalty to Wilson Wines. For all we know, you'd just sell off your share to someone who didn't give a damn. Charles would never do something so rash."

Would he? Had he become so desperate to mend the vast chasm between father and son that he was prepared to offer the world on a platter? This would destroy Nicole. She'd grown up in the New Zealand house—it was still her home. And she'd poured her heart and soul into the business— surely not to simply see half of it handed over to her brother? Charles couldn't be so cruel.

But Anna knew full well that Charles was capable of doing such a thing. Single-minded to a fault, his aim was to return his son to his side before he died. When his doctors had confirmed that time might be running out, he'd gone after his goal to bring Judd back into his life with every weapon at his disposal. He'd do whatever it took, even if it meant hurting the daughter who loved him so very much.

Ever since the posthumous delivery of a letter from his former partner and biggest business rival, Thomas Jackson, he'd become obsessed with Judd, with somehow rebuilding a bond between them. Anna hadn't been privy to the contents of the letter but she'd wager her very generous salary that it had to do with the rift between the business partners and Cynthia and Judd leaving New Zealand very shortly after. She'd often wondered if Thomas Jackson and Cynthia had been lovers.

Which begged the question—had Charles believed Judd was not his son?

Judd passed the letter across to her.

"Read it for yourself."

The words blurred before her eyes and she blinked to clear them. It was true. There, in Charles's scrawling black hand- writing, was his desperate appeal to the son he'd turned his back on twenty-five years ago. She knew what it must have cost the older man to put his emotions in words like this. Never a demonstrative man, it shocked her to see him pour his heart out onto the page. Ever hedging his bets, though, he'd insisted on Judd undergoing DNA testing to prove he was, without a shadow of a doubt, Charles's child. Ah, so there had been some doubt. Now everything began to make sense.

She finished scanning the letter and neatly folded it before handing it back to Judd.

"I had no idea he had planned this. Will you accept his offer?" she asked.

"He insults my mother, even after all this time, and you think I'm going to leap at his offer?"

"Insults Cynthia?" She didn't follow his reasoning.

"The DNA test. He wants proof she didn't cheat on him when I was conceived. It's obvious, no matter what he says in that letter, he hasn't changed a bit. He still expects to call all the shots. And then there's you."

"Me?"

"What's your role in all this? Did he expect you to also sweeten the deal?"

Anna felt a flush rise in her cheeks. "I don't think I like what you're suggesting."

"Well, you can't blame me. You come to my family's home, you fail to identify yourself or your reasons for being here and you show yourself to be very receptive to attention from me. You certainly didn't object last night when I kissed you."

"That was…"

Words failed her.

"It was what, Anna? Going over and above the call of duty?"

Anna bit back the retort that sprang so readily to her lips and forced herself to calm down.

"I did what I came to do, you have the letter, you've read it. Now the ball is in your court."

And she'd failed Charles, she admitted to herself. The

knowledge lodged like a heavy ball of painful regret knotted tight within her chest. The most important thing he'd ever asked of her and she'd screwed it up.

"Please, I beg of you, don't let what I've done influence your decision in any way. Charles wanted me to be upfront with you. It was my choice to hold back my real reasons for being here."

"Why?"

"I knew he wanted to extend an olive branch, but I was concerned about how you might feel about him and whether you would take advantage of him. He's an old man, old before his time because of his illness. He doesn't deserve any more misery in his life."

"And that's your considered opinion?"

"Of course it is. Look, you don't know him. You probably barely remember him. Whatever happened in the past is past. It can't be undone. Can't you put it aside and consider what it would mean to him to make amends with you now?"

Judd stared at her for a moment, his expression not giving any sign of what he might be thinking. The knot of dread tightened even further.

Put the past behind him? Did she have even the faintest idea what she was asking? Of course she didn't. She hadn't been torn from the father who had adored him one minute and then refused to look at him the next. She hadn't been transplanted into another family, another world, and been told to "man up" because his mother expected him to be strong. He'd lost count of the number of times he'd watched cars arrive at The Masters' and hoped against hope that his father would alight from one of them. That he'd come to say it had all been a mistake.

But what his six-year-old heart had wished for had never happened and, in time, he'd learned not to scan the parents' faces at school events for the man whose features he'd always been told were an older version of his own. He'd learned to inure himself from the hope that one day his life would return to what it had been before.

And it had made him a stronger man. A man who knew that the only person he could, or should, rely upon was himself.

His first instinct on reading his father's entreaty was to ball it up and to tell Anna to take it back to Charles-bloody-Wilson and to tell the old man to put it where the sun doesn't shine. But then rationality overrode the deviation into emotionalism.

Without realizing it, his long-estranged father had actually given Judd the opportunity he'd quietly dreamed of for many a year—payback. Not only for rejecting the son who'd so earnestly idolized him, but for what he'd done to Cynthia.

Judd had heard the story from his mother more times than he could count—after pulling her away from her home and her family, Charles had neglected her. Ignored her. Prioritized every concern over and above his relationship with his wife. And when Cynthia, in her loneliness and frustration, had started spending more time away from home, trying to find friends and activities to fill the void left by her husband's absence, Charles had turned into a possessive monster, constantly jealous and utterly convinced she was cheating on him.

It had all culminated in the fight that had led Charles to kick Judd and his mother out of the house. And that was the last Judd had seen of his father. There had been no phone calls. No letters. No visits. Charles had clearly washed his hands of both of them for the past twenty-five years.

And now, this was Judd's chance to pay him back in kind for all the pain he and his mother had suffered. With the controlling interest in the company, Charles was placing the weapons right into his hands. Everything his mother had told him about the past had shown Charles up for a man who'd always put his business before his family. Judd knew exactly where to strike to cause the most pain, to exact the deepest satisfaction.

He needed time to think, to consolidate the plans burgeoning in his mind, but he had no doubt that he'd shortly be accepting his father's offer. No doubt at all.

He looked over at Anna—his eyes raking over her and taking in the lustrous length of her hair, her exquisite beauty, her enticing feminine curves. She was all woman from the top of her head to the tips of her toes. Even now, as angry as he was, she still had the capacity to excite him, to incite within him the desire to possess her in every manner of the word.

A tug of regret pulled deep inside. His mother's warning had done little to dim his attraction to Anna, but the letter had cast a whole new light on things. Maybe her reluctance to deliver it to him had its basis in something other than what she'd admitted. Maybe she was worried about what his entry back into his father's life would do to affect her position there and what she stood to gain from Charles Wilson after his death. Charles had chosen her as his ambassador in his attempt at reunion, so he obviously trusted her implicitly. By her own admission she said she and the old man were close—that she cared for him *deeply*. How close, exactly? Were they lovers, as his mother suspected? If that was true, it would no doubt give him a double-edged sense of satisfaction when he eventually seduced her.

But as with everything else, it would wait until the time was perfectly right. For now, he wanted her away from The Masters' and somewhere else, where she could do no harm.

He gestured to the food before them.

"Are you going to eat that?"

She shook her head. "I couldn't, not now."

"Let's go, then."

"Back to the vineyard?"

"To get your things, yes, and then to take you into the city."

"The city?"

"To a hotel. It may surprise you, but funnily enough, I don't want you around my family right now. My mother's been through quite enough over the years without adding the insult of your presence."

She flinched beneath his words, her face paling even more.

"Fine," she replied tightly. "When will you let me know your decision about Charles?"

"In good time. You aren't due to return to Auckland for another few days, is that correct?"

"Yes, on Friday morning."

"I'll let you know by then."

Anna paced the terrace of her hotel room, her cell phone to her ear.

"I'm sorry, Charles. I screwed up. I should have just done what you told me to do."

Charles was surprisingly philosophical.

"What's done is done. It's certainly no worse or better than what's gone on before this. Let's just hope he comes to his senses and comes home before it's too late."

Before it's too late. Her heart squeezed. It wasn't like Charles to be melodramatic. She knew he was deteriorating, but had he kept something from her? Was his health worse than even she suspected?

"I still can't believe you're prepared to go to those lengths to bring him home."

"It's his birthright, Anna. You know that as much as I do."

"But what about Nicole? Have you talked to her about this yet?"

"I wasn't going to say anything to her until he's back and we know for certain he's mine. Until then, it's a moot point.

And you're not to say a word, either. You promised me, Anna."

She sighed. "Yes, I know. I won't say a word, but keeping the truth away from her is only going to hurt all of us."

"Let me be the judge of that."

"And the house, Charles. Why the house, too? You're talking about taking Nicole's home right out from under her feet."

"Yours, too," he reminded her with a surprisingly curt note in his voice. "But I will have to trust him to do the right thing and to continue to provide the two of you with a roof over your heads. If I don't do that, if I don't prove to him that I'm prepared to accept him fully, it will never work. Besides, he grew up with the Masters—I know how they feel about the house. Judd is already running their company, so offering him mine might not be enough of a draw. But no one else can give him that house."

"What makes you so sure you have to take such drastic steps?"

"Because that's what it would take to lure me back if someone had done the same thing to me."

If Nicole ever spoke to her again after this it would be a miracle. Anna felt a chill run the length of her spine. She stepped inside her hotel room and slid the glass door closed, but even so, she continued to feel cold. What Charles was doing was wrong, she knew it to the soles of her feet. But it was too late now. The offer had been made. She could only hope against hope that Judd would be man enough to turn it down. That he'd accept his father for who he was without the added enticement of half of Wilson Wines and the home that Charles had built for Cynthia all those years ago.

"So you're not going to give her any prior warning. You're just going to present her with a brother and say this is how it's going to be from now on?"

"They are my children, it's my company and my home, so this is my decision. Don't overstep your boundaries, Anna."

His words stung.

"Of course," she said in reply, even as other more impassioned words filled her mind.

"He said he'll give you his decision by Friday?"

"Yes, he did."

"Let's hope it's the right one. Let me know as soon as you've spoken to him."

"I will."

"Good. I'll look forward to it."

His business done, the call was over, leaving Anna alone to stare at the darkening hills in the distance and to wonder just how all of this was going to end.

Five

"I told you I was right." Cynthia's eyes gleamed triumphantly.

Judd merely nodded. He'd spent the latter part of the afternoon locked in his office, looking at his schedule and seeing where, and to whom, he could apportion his workload. It was one advantage of having several cousins all working within the same family business, he conceded. There were plenty of people just as invested as he was in making sure The Masters' continued to run smoothly. Between his cousins and the well-trained staff they also employed, Judd felt confident he could leave the company in good hands.

Once he had everything worked out to his satisfaction, he asked his mother for a private meeting. Her delight at the enticement Charles was offering was palpable. He hadn't seen her this animated, ever.

"When will you let them know your decision?" his mother pressed.

"On Friday morning. I'll be too busy tomorrow bringing

everyone up to speed with their additional duties to be talking to Anna Garrick."

As soon as he said her name he felt the now-familiar tug of desire. He'd made some inquiries. She lived with Charles Wilson, which confirmed she was indeed far, far more than simply his father's P.A. Stealing her away from him, right under the old man's roof, was undeniably appealing but something he'd have to approach very carefully.

"Do you know how long the DNA testing will take?"

"I believe establishing paternity is a relatively simple process. A few days to a week for the results."

"You know, I cannot believe he would stoop to that. He only needs to look at you to know I never betrayed him."

She injected a note of pathos in her voice, but Judd had heard it all before. When she didn't elicit the response from her son that she obviously wanted, she continued.

"We'll finally have back what should have been ours all along," she said, her voice now stronger, showing her true mettle.

"The house?"

He should have known that would be the most important thing to her. He had to admit to a certain curiosity himself to go back to the place that had been his home for the first six years of his life. But where his mother seemed to want to reclaim the building, Judd was far more inclined to go after it with a wrecking ball...just as he planned to do with Wilson Wines. He'd take his father's legacy apart bit by bit, and when he was done, he'd be back here at The Masters', picking up the reins of his job once again. At that point, his mother could have the darn house for all he cared.

"I'll have to redecorate it, you know. Restore it to its former glory."

"How do you know it's not perfect just the way it is?"

She rolled her eyes at him. "Judd, darling, it's been twenty-five years since I've set foot in there. There will be work to do, I'm sure. I poured my heart into that house—no one loved it more than I did."

"Let's not put the cart before the horse, hmm?"

"Of course. We have to satisfy your father's ridiculous demands first. How long do you think you'll be away?"

"I don't see this taking more than a month."

"That long?"

He thought of his plans for the delectable Miss Garrick. A month? Maybe longer would be better. He wanted to savor this victory.

"Maybe longer. We'll see how it pans out."

After his mother left his office, he sat back in his leather chair and stared out the window at the vineyard and winery that occupied his immediate view. He enjoyed his work here, there was no doubt about that, and he was good at it. But he had become bored in recent months, feeling stifled by the lack of opportunity to make changes. Now, perhaps, even if only for a short time, he'd have the chance to really stretch his mind as he implemented his plans. Plans to dismantle his father's empire and steal his mistress right out from under his nose.

Anna woke on Friday morning in a state of nerves and automatically reached for her cell phone, as she had several times throughout last night. Still nothing from Judd Wilson. Just how fine was he going to cut this? She looked at the time on her phone and raced for the bathroom—the broken night's rest having made her sleep past the time she'd wanted to rise. A car was coming to pick her up and take her to the airport for her flight in about half an hour. She'd already packed her things the night before. All she needed to do was shower and dress in the clothes she'd left out for the journey home.

She was down in the lobby of the hotel and signing off her hotel account when a trickle of awareness filtered through the parting words of the hotel receptionist. He was here. Did that mean she'd succeeded? Was he accompanying her back to New Zealand, or maybe he was merely here to tell her in person that her quest on Charles's behalf had failed.

She knew she had to turn around. Had to face him. It took every ounce of strength in her body to paste a smile on her face and turn away from the reception desk. The moment her eyes lighted upon him she felt the excruciating pull of attraction. How could she still be so drawn to him when he'd been so awful to her? She'd asked herself that question over and over the past two nights, especially each time she'd woken from yet another tormented dream explicitly featuring the man standing directly opposite her.

He'd be a formidable poker player, she thought irrationally. He let nothing show in his expression as to what he was thinking, or whatever decision he'd reached.

"Are you ready?" he said coolly.

"What? No good morning?" she said, unable to keep the acerbity from her voice.

He merely raised one dark brow. Anna grabbed the handle of her wheeled suitcase and headed for the front door.

"Let me take that for you," Judd said, blocking her way and collapsing the extended handle and swinging the case up in one hand.

She'd packed for only three and a half days, and she hadn't packed light, yet he carried the bag as if it weighed nothing. Realizing he was headed for the automatic opening doors and to the dark limousine outside, she propelled herself after him.

"Wait, I've ordered a taxi."

"And I've canceled it. We'll travel together to the airport."

"And then?" she asked, suddenly tired of the game.

Was he coming back to Auckland with her or not? The not knowing was playing havoc with her stomach.

"And then we'll check in to our flight."

"So you're accepting Charles's offer?"

He handed her case to the waiting driver and then opened

the rear door, gesturing for her to be seated inside the dark, leather-filled interior. She halted at the door, not wanting to get inside until she knew exactly where things stood.

"I've consented to undergoing the tests and when my father is satisfied, yes, I will be accepting his offer."

Anna didn't know whether to feel elated or devastated. A hollow emptiness filled her heart. Unable to speak, she nodded in acknowledgment of his words and settled herself in the car. She was grateful when Judd took the passenger seat in the front of the vehicle. She needed some time to gather her thoughts, to prepare herself for what was to come.

The journey to the airport was short, and before she alighted she asked for a moment to call Charles.

"That won't be necessary," Judd said smoothly, offering her his hand to help her from the car.

"Why not?" she asked, reluctantly putting her hand in his and bracing herself for the jolt of electricity she knew would come next.

Sure enough, the merest touch of his fingers was enough to set her heart beating faster. Arousal flared deep inside. Not the type she was used to—the slow, gentle warming of mutual attraction. No, this was far more primal than that. Sharper, more instinctive, and it made her body ache in response. She pulled her hand from his, but the sensation still lingered.

"Because I've already spoken with him."

"You spoke with him?" Anna fought to keep the incredulity from her voice.

"Is that so strange?"

"Well, yes. Especially considering your reaction to his letter."

"As you said on Wednesday, the past *is* past."

She looked at him in disbelief, hardly daring to believe that he actually meant it. A man like Judd Wilson was too intense, too driven to simply put the past in a time capsule and lock it away. He had to have an ulterior motive.

"What? No comment?" Judd gently goaded.

"How was he?"

"He sounded fine. Surprised to hear from me, but I'd say he's cautiously optimistic."

So this thing would play out after all, Anna thought as the driver hefted their cases from the trunk of the car and went to procure a luggage cart. Not waiting for the man to return, she pulled the handle up on her case and headed for the departure check-in area, but within seconds Judd walked at her side, pushing his own much larger cases on the cart in front of him. Basically, everything was out of her hands from here on in. She could only hope that Nicole would forgive her for her part in the machinations of her father. But somehow Anna doubted any of what was to come would be that easy.

Charles's driver and handyman, Patrick Evans, collected them from Auckland International Airport. They were nearly home. Evans drove slowly and inexorably toward the massive gothic mansion Charles had built from the original plans of Masters' Rise—the headlights of the car sweeping the camellia-lined driveway in Auckland's premier suburb of Remuera. Anna had to admit she was relieved to see the house.

Back in Australia, it had shocked her to see the ruins on the hill overlooking the vineyard. Suddenly the home that had always provided her with security didn't seem so permanent after all. Of course, bushfires were nonexistent in the city, virtually nonexistent in New Zealand, really, and nowadays Charles had a state-of-the-art fire detection and sprinkler system throughout the house. But there were plenty of things other than bushfires that could tear a house—and a family—apart.

With the time distance between Adelaide and Auckland, and the flight time in between, it was already dark as they pulled up in front of the house, but clever external lighting showed the property off to its glorious advantage. Anna observed Judd, sitting opposite her in the limousine, and watched his reaction.

"So that's what it looked like," he said solemnly, his eyes raking the two-storied, pinkish-red brick building. "My memories from before we left were…incomplete."

"Apparently it's very true to the original, with extensive modernization, of course. Despite its size, it's still very much a home."

The car rolled to a stop outside the front portico, prominently marked by an ivy-covered, three-storied turret complete with a green-aged copper cupola.

"It's your home."

He made it a statement, rather than a question. A statement she chose to ignore as she stepped from the car and assisted Patrick in removing the luggage from the spacious trunk of the limousine.

The front doors opened and Anna turned, expecting to see Charles, but instead it was Nicole who stood there. Elegant and tall in her well-cut black suit and with her long dark hair pulled back into a ponytail that exposed her pale face, Nicole stared at the man who was her brother.

"I didn't believe him when he told me you were coming," she said, her voice flat—devoid of emotion.

Instantly Anna's defensive instincts went on full alert. Nicole was usually very outgoing, impulsive and generous to a fault. This frozen pale facsimile of her best friend was something she'd never seen before.

Nicole came down the steps and halted near Anna.

"Why didn't you tell me?"

Even as Anna flinched at the question, she found herself internally debating what Nicole was really asking. There was no way to know how much Charles had told her. Had he only announced that Judd was coming back to them—or had he explained all the rest of it, too, all the things Charles had promised to bring his son home?

Either way, her answer was the same. "He asked me not to."

"And your loyalty to him is greater than to me?" Nicole said softly, the hurt in her words flaying Anna like cold winter rain.

"That's not fair, Nicole."

"No, you're right. But there's a lot that's not fair about all this, isn't there?"

Pain reflected in her friend's large brown eyes. Anna put a hand on Nicole's arm and squeezed gently.

"You know I would have spoken to you if I could."

Nicole nodded and turned back to Judd, who'd remained silent as a statue.

"So, brother, I suppose I should welcome you home."

She held out her arms and to Anna's surprise he stepped into her embrace, holding her gently before releasing her and stepping back.

Judd was shocked at the depth of emotion he felt when he saw his sister at the top of the stairs to the house. She'd been a year old when he'd left, and in his mind he'd never imagined her fully grown. Another mark against his father, he thought savagely. All those years wasted.

"We have some catching up to do," he said.

To his surprise, Nicole laughed. "Well, if that's not the understatement of the century. Come inside. Dad's waiting for you."

Judd turned to Anna, who'd watched his reunion with his sister with a solemn expression on her face. "Are you coming?"

"I think this should be just for the three of you. I'll catch up with you all at dinner."

Nicole made a sound of protest. "Don't be silly, Anna. You know Dad will expect you there, too."

Anna looked at him, as if waiting for his approval.

"Sure," he said.

If the stiltedness between her and his sister was any indication, perhaps Nicole didn't entirely approve of Anna and their father's closeness.

Nicole hooked her arm in his. In her three-inch heels they were almost of a height and together they walked up the stairs and into the house that was shortly to become all his. One thing was clear to Judd—Charles hadn't gotten any better about showing consideration to the women in his life. It was obvious Nicole wasn't aware of the full extent of Charles's plans for him. He doubted she'd be this friendly if she knew. That would have to be a bridge to cross at a later date. First, he had to go face-to-face with the man who'd cast him from his home and his country twenty-five years ago, and he had to do it with a civil tongue in his head.

Judd's memories of his father had been of a vital man who exuded energy and bonhomie the moment he stepped in a room. The man who shakily rose to his feet as they entered a large salon was a mere shadow of whom he'd been. Despite Charles's unmistakable frailty, Judd's long-harbored anger at his father's abandonment did not lessen.

"Here he is, Dad," Nicole said.

"Judd—"

"Sir," Judd said, stepping forward and offering his hand.

He watched his father, searching for the man he remembered but seeing little of the vibrancy of his memories. Charles's hair was now steel-gray instead of the black Judd remembered, and his posture was less erect, his figure more portly than fit. But even though his father was obviously unwell, there was a keen intelligence that still gleamed in his eyes as they stood face-to-face. Those blue eyes, very like his own, scoured his features as silence stretched out between them. Something in his appearance must have satisfied the older man, because he gave a short nod and gestured to Judd to sit down.

Anna crossed the room and took the seat on the sofa next to Charles, her hand on his forearm as she leaned closer to whisper something in his ear. A fierce wave of something not unlike jealousy rose from deep inside Judd. Her body language shouted a familiarity between Anna and Charles that screamed loud and clear. A familiarity that Judd silently promised would soon change.

"Don't fuss, Anna. I'm fine," Charles protested, taking her hand and holding it in his for a moment before releasing it. "Now, let's not beat around the bush. You know I want proof you're my son."

Judd felt his hackles rise. "I know I'm your son. I couldn't be anyone else's."

"I'm sure that's what your mother told you," Charles commented, "but you must understand I need to be one hundred percent certain."

"I told you I'm prepared to be tested," Judd said, holding on to his temper by the merest edge.

His mother was no angel, but he knew she told the truth when she said he was Charles Wilson's son. She wouldn't lie about something as vital as that. Not to him.

"Good, good. We can attend to that on Monday and courier the samples to the lab here in Auckland. They offer an express service and promise paternity results within forty-eight hours. It's a shame Anna didn't get you back earlier and that we have to wait out the weekend before we can complete the tests."

He couldn't help it. He had to ask. "Why the sudden urgency? You've waited twenty-five years, surely another two days won't be a problem."

Charles shot him a glance and then smiled proudly. "Well, you certainly sound like me. Straight to the point, hmm?"

"I find it doesn't pay to beat around the bush in important matters."

"No, it never does."

Judd merely looked at him, waiting for him to stop hedging and get to the point. The air in the room became uncomfortable, and in his periphery Judd saw Nicole glance from him to their father.

"I'd like to know, too," she blurted, a tremor in her voice. "Why now, Dad?"

Charles looked at his daughter, a frown of censure on his forehead. "Don't go getting all emotional, Nicole. It's no secret that I'm not getting any younger or any healthier. It's time for me to get everything in order."

"Why did you drag Anna into this? Why send her to do your dirty work?" Nicole persisted.

"That's enough, young lady. I'm still the head of this household and I'm still the head of Wilson Wines. Don't question me."

Nicole slumped in her chair, all the fight gone out of her in a flash. Judd felt a momentary pang of regret for what she must be going through. He'd make it up to her somehow, he promised silently. She deserved something for having put up with the old man all these years without anyone to stand up for her. It was something he'd have done, if given half a chance.

A movement at the door caught everyone's attention.

"Excuse me, sir, but dinner is served in the dining room," a uniformed middle-aged woman said.

"Thank you, Mrs. Evans," Charles said, dismissing the housekeeper and turning back to Judd. "We keep regular hours here for mealtimes—my diabetes, you know."

Charles rose to his feet, refusing Anna's offer of assistance, and led the way through to the dining room. Each room Judd set foot in gave him a weird sense of déjà vu. Although his memories of living here were faded and sketchy, the old

photos of Masters' Rise that had been passed on by friends
after the fire were imprinted in his mind. This house truly
was a complete replica of his mother's old home. No wonder
she was so bitter about being made to leave.

He made a silent promise—Cynthia would return to triumph over all this again.

They'd been back one day short of a week. Anna sat at her
desk, finding it nearly impossible to concentrate on the work
ahead of her. Judd had traveled into the office with Charles
this morning, and the two of them had been closeted together
for a couple of hours now. Every time Nicole had ventured
out from her office, she'd sent a baleful glare toward her father's closed door and the atmosphere had become so tense
it was almost palpable.

The arrival of the junior receptionist from downstairs,
bearing the morning's mail and courier deliveries, was a
welcome distraction. Anna swiftly sorted the mail and then
turned to the courier packages. One in particular, slimmer
than the rest, stood out. She lifted it and checked the return
address. Her stomach instantly knotted. Marked Private and
Confidential and addressed to Charles, it had come from the
lab he'd engaged to conduct the DNA testing.

She dropped it on the stack of mail she'd already opened
for him, as if it burned her fingers. While he'd authorized her,
long ago, to attend to all his correspondence, both personal
and relating to the business, she had no doubt he'd want to
open this particular item himself.

The door to Charles's office opened and she jumped, feeling as if she'd been caught doing something wrong. Judd's
ever-intense gaze swept her body and, obviously noticing her
reaction, one dark brow lifted slightly in query. She ignored
him, something that she'd wished she'd become more capable of in the past few days. Back in Australia, she'd tried to
resist her attraction to him because she'd worried about the

backlash when he learned the truth. She'd never realized that there was part of the story that even *she* didn't know—that Charles intended for Judd to take over the company. Once the DNA test results verified what they all already knew, Judd would become her boss.

That *should* make him absolutely off-limits. Her brain was sure of it. Her body, though, was much harder to convince.

Just thinking about him was enough to make her body heat with arousal. Being in the same room as him, even under the same roof, was absolute torture. For the past week, work had been her refuge away from him, but it looked like that wouldn't be the case any longer.

"Anna, I want you to take Judd on a tour of our biggest Auckland stockists, introduce him to the store and chain managers. No need for appointments, hmm? Let's catch them on the hop and see how we're faring against the competition."

"Wouldn't you rather do that yourself?"

Anna couldn't think of anything worse than having to spend the balance of the day solely in Judd's company. While she hadn't been able to fault his behavior toward her since their return to New Zealand, there was an undercurrent that remained ever present between them. An undercurrent that kept her nerves wound so tight she was beginning to wonder if she shouldn't request a leave of absence and head away for a couple of weeks, just to be able to breathe again without constantly thinking of Judd Wilson.

"You know I can't drive myself and we can hardly expect Judd to find his way around on his own just yet."

"It's okay," Judd interceded smoothly. "I'm sure that with a GPS I'll be fine."

"No," Charles insisted, his color rising slightly. "I've asked Anna to take you and she will. Everyone knows her already and it will make the introductions much smoother. Isn't that right, Anna?"

Anna pushed her chair away from her desk and stood,

gathering her handbag from the locked drawer at the bottom of her desk as she did so.

"Sure, Charles. Whatever you want."

"Right, then, that's settled." Charles looked at the pile of newly opened mail on her desk. "Is that lot for me?"

"Yes, I was about to bring it through to you."

She saw his eyes light on the courier package and the ruddy color that had begun to suffuse his cheeks faded rapidly.

"Charles? Are you okay?"

"Stop fussing, woman," he blustered. "Of course I'm fine. You two had better get going. And take Judd somewhere nice for lunch, too. I don't expect to see the two of you back here this afternoon. You have a lot of ground to cover."

Resigning herself to Judd's company for the rest of the day, she passed the mail to Charles and took her car keys from her handbag. She watched Charles head back into his office and slam the door closed behind him. So, they weren't to discover the contents of the courier pack until he was ready to share it with them.

"You really don't have to take me around today if you don't want to," Judd said from close by.

"No, it's okay. Charles wants you to have personal introductions, I understand that." *I may not like it, but I do understand it,* she amended silently.

"Do you always do exactly as he says?"

"Why wouldn't I?" she answered, wondering where Judd was leading with his question.

"No reason, I just thought you might stand up to him a bit more."

"He'd never ask me to do something I truly objected to, if that's what you're aiming at," Anna said defensively.

"That's good, then. You don't object to being with me today. Shall we go?"

He smoothly reached out and placed a hand at the small

of her back, guiding her toward the door. She felt its imprint as if she was naked and hastened to create some distance between them. As his hand fell away, her body instantly mourned his touch and she castigated herself soundly for her ridiculous reaction.

Judd didn't speak again until they drove out from the underground staff car park in her shiny dark red Lexus IS 250 F-Sport.

"Nice car," he commented.

"It's a company car, it has four wheels and gets me where I need to go."

"Kind of pricey for a company car for a P.A. You must be *very* good at your job."

There was an insinuation that hung in the air between them that she really didn't like. But she wouldn't give him the satisfaction of biting back.

"Charles likes to show his appreciation to all his valued staff," she replied, choosing her words carefully.

"Some more than others, I imagine."

Again that prick at her relationship with Charles. She knew many people didn't understand it and she'd learned to shield herself from speculation and unkind comments. It was a skill she'd had to develop early when the children at the private school Charles had paid for had discovered she was his housekeeper/companion's daughter.

Growing up with the stigma of her mother's relationship with Charles hanging over her, and the sly innuendo that had accompanied it, had made her a great deal tougher than she looked. It didn't mean that such comments didn't hurt, not at all, but there was no way she would give the person inflicting it any satisfaction at all, nor would she divulge more information than she absolutely needed to. And never, ever would she let herself be a woman who got physically involved with her boss.

She started giving Judd a rundown on the major chains

that Wilson Wines supplied with imported wines as she drove toward their head office. But he interrupted her almost immediately.

"Who is Wilson Wines' greatest competition?"

"Jackson Importers. Why do you ask?"

"In any venture, it always pays to know who you're up against. Tell me about them."

"They were set up just over twenty-five years ago by Thomas Jackson. He died about a year ago and the company is now headed by Nate Hunter. He's about your age and he's been with Jackson since graduating with a business degree from Auckland Uni. That's pretty much all we know about him. He's been working out of one of their overseas offices for most of his career and has only recently come to New Zealand to take the reins from the interim CEO. No one's really too sure what he's like personally. What we do know is that he has a very competitive business head on his shoulders and he works hard to give us fierce competition. He's run their European operations superbly for the past few years."

"Thomas Jackson…I think I remember someone with that name from when I was a kid."

"That would probably be right," Anna commented. "Thomas Jackson and your father were business partners and best friends. They had a disagreement and Charles bought him out."

"Must have been a helluva disagreement."

"I wouldn't know." Anna shrugged, trying to keep her face expressionless. "It was before my time and my mother never spoke about it." True, her mother hadn't spoken about it, and neither had Charles—but Anna had drawn her own conclusions from the rumors that still persisted even years later, and it wasn't difficult to do the math. Charles's divorce from Cynthia and his falling-out with Thomas Jackson had happened at exactly the same time. Those incidents coupled with Charles's insistence on Judd being DNA tested—well, the writing was very clearly on the wall.

Judd sat in his seat, a contemplative expression on his face. Anna wondered what on earth was going through his mind.

"Charles has never said anything to you about it?" he eventually said.

"Not a word, and it's not really something I'd raise with him, anyway. If you want to know more, you'll have to speak to him yourself," she said a little sharply.

Judd chuckled. "And so I'm duly put firmly in my place."

"I didn't mean—"

"Don't worry, Anna. You're right. I should do my own background checks if I want to know things. And I will."

His words made her nervous. Why was it so important for him to dig into the past? Surely it was enough that his father wanted to mend the broken bridges between them. She knew that the death of Thomas Jackson had hit Charles hard. She'd always thought Charles had thrived on the challenge and competition his past colleague presented to him on a regular basis, but now she wondered whether, once the heat and anger had died down, Charles hadn't been suffering regret for the way their friendship had ended.

Either way, the topic wasn't open for discussion as far as she was concerned. She swung her car into a space in the car park at the premises of Wilson Wines' largest customer, grateful for the opportunity to put some space between them. Knowing his opinion of her had done nothing to calm her ever-present awareness of him—of the way her body warmed every time he was in the vicinity, of her hyperawareness of his alluring cologne as it wreathed her senses in forbidden enticement. She resolutely cleared her mind of anything else but what Charles had asked her to do today. She'd get through this, even if it was the last thing she wanted to do.

Six

The minute they set foot back in the house Anna could sense something in the air. There was an energy thrumming through the place that hadn't been there this morning and when she went through to the kitchen for a chilled glass of water, the cook and housekeeper were working flat out on what looked to be very elaborate meal preparations.

"Did I miss something?" she asked the cook, who was busily checking pots on the commercial-size stove top.

"No, dear. Just himself making requests for something very special for dinner tonight—says he has an important announcement to make, and he wants you all to dress up, too. Can you let Miss Nicole know when she gets in?"

Clearly the courier pack he'd received this morning had borne the news Charles had wanted so very much. A vague numbness permeated Anna's body, leaving her confused about how she felt about the news. It was what Charles had wanted, there was no doubt about that. But she knew he hadn't said a word yet to Nicole about his plans. If he had, she knew Nicole would have discussed it with her. Still, Nicole had been avoiding her lately, still stung, Anna was sure, over her not disclosing the reason for her trip to Adelaide. Worried she might miss Nicole, she sent her a text message.

Don't be late tonight. Your dad wants us all dressed up for dinner. He has an announcement to make. —A.

Nicole was quick to reply; a series of question marks flashed across Anna's screen. She swallowed against the knot of disloyalty that tightened in her throat as she texted back.

No idea what it's about, sorry.

On the way to her room she passed by Charles's suite, knocking softly on the door before letting herself in. He wasn't in his private sitting room, so she figured he must be resting. It had become a regular habit of his after a half day at the office—late starts, early finishes and plenty of rest in between. She was reluctant to disturb his nap, but she needed to talk to him about Nicole. Deciding to wait until she heard him up and about in the bedroom, she settled on one of the comfortable sofas he had in the sitting room and popped her feet up beside her.

Some time later Anna stirred at the sound of running water coming from the other room. She blinked to clear her eyes, realizing it had grown full dark outside. She dragged a hand through her hair. It was sticking every which way. Darn, she knew she should have tied it up today. A quick glance at her watch revealed how close it was to the dinner hour. There was no way she'd be able to be ready and talk to Charles this side of dinner. As it was, she'd be pushing it to get ready on time.

She shrugged out of her jacket, tucking it under one arm, and untucked then started to unbutton her blouse as she headed for the door. She opened it and slipped outside into the hallway, only to come face-to-face with Judd. Her nostrils flared, taking in the freshly showered scent of him.

"If you'll excuse me," she said, trying to sidestep past him and get to her room, "I'm running late."

Judd's expression, usually distinctly unreadable, reflected a look of surprise, before a cold, calculating look appeared in his eyes.

"So I see," he said, stepping to one side to let her by.

Understanding dawned with the drenching effect of sub-Antarctic waters. "It's not—"

"Didn't you say you were running late?" he reminded her with that arch to his brow that he used with such great effect.

Without another word she stalked past him to her room a little farther down the hall. She closed the door behind her and leaned against the solid wooden surface, realizing that she was shaking. There was no question that Judd thought he'd caught her *in flagrante delicto*. Anna pushed herself away from the door and forced herself to walk through to her en suite bathroom, peeling the rest of her clothes off on the way. What should it matter what Judd Wilson thought? It wasn't the truth, so as far as she was concerned it shouldn't matter one iota. Even so, as she stepped beneath the spray of her shower, she couldn't help wishing she hadn't put that look of disapproval on his face.

By the time she'd dressed, reapplied her makeup and swept her hair up into an elegant chignon, she'd missed predinner drinks. She joined Charles, Judd and Nicole as they walked through to the dining room. Despite her text to Nicole, her friend obviously hadn't had time to change out of her work clothes—or perhaps had chosen not to, knowing it would rile her father.

"Sorry I'm late," Anna said breathlessly as she entered the dining room.

"You're here in time for the important news," Charles said with a thread of emotion in his voice that put Anna's nerves on edge.

She took her seat, opposite Judd, feeling the blue fire of his gaze upon her as she did so.

"What important news?" Nicole asked.

Anna felt her throat close and her chest tighten. This wasn't going to be pretty. As dependable as Nicole was in a business setting, she wasn't known for deliberation or contemplation when it came to her private affairs. Impulsiveness and impetuosity were more her mark in trade. She wasn't going to take the news of her father's plans happily. Especially not when she'd worked so hard at his side all these years, striving constantly to be everything he needed in business and in family.

Charles seemed oblivious to Anna's distress and to the storm that was brewing. He was puffed up with pride. Anna hadn't seen him this animated in some time. He picked up his glass and gestured in Judd's direction.

"I'd like to propose a toast. To my son, Judd. Welcome home, where you truly belong."

Anna hazarded a look at Judd, watching to see if this open declaration that he was definitely Charles's son would have an effect on him at all. She was disappointed. He merely nodded toward his father and raised his own glass in response.

"Aren't you repeating yourself, Dad?" Nicole asked. "Didn't we already go through this last Friday when Judd arrived?"

"No, I'm not repeating things at all. It is a relief to an old man to be able to acknowledge his family, *all* his family, now that the results have come in. And to that end I have a small presentation to make."

Charles patted a long, narrow envelope that sat on the tablecloth next to his place setting. He picked it up and handed it to Judd.

"You'll find it all in there, son. Exactly as I promised."

Even though he knew there had never been any doubt about his paternity, Judd felt a thrill of exhilaration surge through him. Here it was, the moment he'd been waiting for,

for most of his adult life. His father handing him the tools with which to pay him back for what he'd done to Judd and his mother all those years ago. Tomorrow he would have a solicitor draw up the share-transfer papers in order for him to present Nate Hunter with an offer that the man could not refuse. The controlling interest in Wilson Wines for the princely sum of one dollar. Judd took the proffered envelope.

"Thank you, sir."

"Oh, surely you don't have to call me 'sir,'" Charles blustered. "If you can't call me Dad, then at least call me Charles."

"Thank you, Charles."

He saw the hope in his father's eyes dim a little. There was no way he could call this man "Dad," not after all these years. He scanned the two women at the table. Anna sat there, frozen, as if she was expecting something terrible to happen and she was totally helpless to prevent it. He began to get some understanding of the reason why when he saw his sister's face.

Confusion battled with irritation across her features and it didn't take long before she was demanding some clarity about what had just been passed over to him.

"What did you promise, Dad?" she asked, a fine tremor in her voice betraying her heightened nerves.

"Only what Judd has always been due, Nicole."

She flung a dark-eyed glare at Judd. "And that would be?"

"The deed to the house and a controlling interest in Wilson Wines. The rest will go to you on my death, as you well know," Charles interjected. "Now, shall we have another toast and get down to the business of enjoying the wonderful meal I know Mrs. Evans has prepared?"

"A controlling interest in Wilson Wines?" Nicole's voice rose on a note of incredulity. "Dad, what are you doing? He doesn't know the first thing about the business."

"He has experience with the wine industry in Australia.

And now that he's home, he has time to learn how we do things here," Charles said, as if that was the end of the matter.

"That's not fair. I've given everything to Wilson Wines, to *you*. And you just go and give it all away, just like that. To a stranger?"

"He's your brother, he's not a stranger," Charles snapped back, the color in his cheeks an unhealthy ruddy red.

"He may as well be."

Judd felt he should say something, but he held back. When he followed through on his plans for Wilson Wines, his sister would be glad she didn't know him better and would probably never even want to see him again, anyway. The knowledge gave him a sharp pang of regret. They'd both been cheated of so much by their father's dictatorial decisions. Maybe he'd be able to find her something to do within The Masters'.

Across the table, Nicole laughed, but the sound held no humor in it. Anna reached out and took Nicole's hand in hers, squeezing it tight, but Nicole shook her off, turning on her instead.

"You're just as bad. I suppose you knew about this?"

Anna's expression told his sister all she needed to know.

"I can't believe it. Betrayed by the only two people in the entire world that I love." She pushed her chair back from the table and rose. "I can't stay here and listen to any more of this. It's just wrong."

"Nicole, calm yourself and sit down," Charles interjected. "This is how things should have been all along. You know it as well as I do. I never made you any promises about Wilson Wines. Just you wait, you'll find some young man who'll sweep you off your feet and before I know it you will be married and raising a family. Wilson Wines will just be a hobby for you."

Judd might not know his sister well, but even he could tell that that had been the dead-wrong thing to say. "A hobby?" Nicole's voice rose steadily. "I can't believe this. You can't be serious. Wilson Wines is everything to me. I love the business, love the industry—everything I learned was so I could run the company one day. I've lived under the same roof as you all my life, worked beside you every day I possibly could to try and earn your respect, and yet you don't know me at all."

She made for the door. Anna rose and went after her.

"No, let me go!" Nicole said, tears tracking down her cheeks as she held up her hands as if to ward Anna off.

Judd could see the hurt in Anna's eyes, the guilt she clearly felt for not having given Nicole any warning of what her father had been about to do. Even he felt sick to his stomach that his father could so cavalierly shrug off Nicole's contribution to Wilson Wines in the past few years and denigrate it as a hobby. Another black mark in the increasing collection against Charles Wilson.

"She always was a little high-strung," Charles commented as Nicole slammed the dining room door behind her. "She'll come around, you'll see. She doesn't have it in her to stay angry for long."

"Charles," Anna said, "this is more than a tantrum. Can't you see? You've hurt her deeply."

"Do you think so?" Charles cast her a look of genuine surprise. "No, she's just being overemotional, that's all. She'll calm down soon and see this is all for the best. I've always had her best interests at heart, you know that."

"Do I?" Anna pressed. "Don't you think she sees it as her position within Wilson Wines being undermined, let alone her position here in her home?"

Judd had to admire the way she stuck up for his sister.

"Don't be ridiculous. She'll always be my daughter. In fact, I've probably spoiled her over the years. She'll just have to get used to the idea of sharing with Judd now, is all. Now, come and settle back down. Mrs. Evans is waiting to serve."

"I need to make a call—to make sure she's okay," Anna insisted.

Charles waved a hand. "Fine, then, go ahead. Do what you must."

When Anna returned, Charles rang the small crystal-and-silver bell that stood beside his water glass. Judd watched as Anna resumed her seat, her body vibrating with tension and her distress clear on her features. The call to his sister can't have gone well.

Anna excused herself from the table immediately after dessert, leaving Charles and Judd to talk, but it wasn't long before Charles showed signs of weariness and also left to go upstairs to bed.

Alone? Judd wondered, his mind uncomfortably casting back to when he'd surprised Anna coming from the older man's suite of rooms. She'd clearly been in the process of putting her clothes back on in case someone saw her in the hallway. And someone had. Judd's hand tightened on the stem of the Waterford crystal goblet in his hand, the glowing red wine within it barely touched.

Well, he could certainly find out if she had gone ahead to warm his father's sheets. All it would take would be an inquiry at her door.

Judd barely realized he'd made the decision to check on Anna until he found himself outside of her bedroom. He raised his hand and rapped softly on the door, leaning one shoulder against the jamb as he waited for it to open. To his surprise, it did.

"What do you want? To gloat?" Anna asked him.

For a moment, he was taken aback but he soon recovered his usual equilibrium and took a moment to savor the scrubbed freshness of her face and her hair loose in a well-brushed tumble across satin-covered shoulders. The shadows cast by the soft lighting in her room showed she wore very little beneath her robe. If anything. Instantly he was rock hard, his body clamoring with an urgent need to possess her. He stamped down on the sensation. So she wasn't with Charles now, but she had been earlier this evening. The image of her, fresh from his father's room, still burned in his memory, and he fought the urge to create a new memory— one of his making.

He gathered his thoughts together and expelled a harsh breath before speaking. "Not at all. It should have been handled differently."

She made a sound, a cross between derision and a cynical laugh. "You think? You know you could have asked him to consider Nicole's feelings before making that stupid announcement."

"Mea culpa," he said, straightening from the door frame and holding his hands wide. "It didn't occur to me that he wouldn't have told her privately."

"Well, it's too late now. Hopefully we can sort things out at the office tomorrow, if she's talking to me again by then. What did you come to see me for, anyway?"

"I wanted to make sure that you were okay. You looked upset at dinner."

She looked at him in surprise. "Upset? In being loyal to Charles I betrayed my best friend since I was five years old. Of course I'm upset."

"Why did you do it? Why does he have such an influence over you?" Judd persisted.

"You would never understand," Anna said and started to close the door.

Judd put out a hand to halt its traverse across the plush carpet.

"Try me."

"Look, it's late. I don't want to talk about this now. What's done is done." She stared pointedly at his hand and then back at his face. "Good night, Judd."

He took the hint and removed his hand from the door.

"Sweet dreams, Anna."

But he was talking to a plank of painted wood. So, he thought as he walked back to his room, she didn't want to discuss her relationship with his father. How surprising, not. He was prepared to leave it—for now—but eventually he'd get the truth from her. In the meantime, he'd do his best to imprint his own influence. Whatever her feelings for Charles, the attraction between Anna and himself was mutual—her capitulation would be a sweet success.

The next morning, Anna waited patiently for Nicole to come into the office, but she didn't show. Repeated calls to her cell phone resulted in no response. Charles hadn't come into the office today, either, and according to the household staff, Judd had remained closeted with him back at the house. Anna didn't like the way this was panning out.

She stifled a yawn and decided to take her morning break a little earlier than usual. Maybe a shot of caffeine would help her get through to lunchtime. In the staff lunch room she grabbed her favorite cup from the shelf and headed for the coffee machine. One of the office staff sat at the table, nursing her own cup of coffee and scanning her laptop screen. As Anna passed by she caught a glimpse of the page the girl was on and smiled. The anonymous celebrity-gossip column in the print and online newspaper usually made for a humorous read.

"Anything good in there today?" she asked, sitting down at the table with the other girl.

"The usual, mostly. Oh, wait. Look at this!"

She swiveled the computer around so they could both view the screen. Anna scanned the text, when her eyes were suddenly arrested by a name—Nicole Wilson. The comments about Nicole focused mostly on her being seen letting her hair down in one of the city's bright spots the night before and, in particular, with a certain extremely eligible and wealthy

Auckland businessman who was newly returned to town to take over control of a major company. While his name wasn't mentioned, there was only one person that Anna knew fitted the carefully worded description. Nate Hunter. A photo accompanied the article. While her partner's back was to the camera, there was no mistaking Nicole in fine form on the dance floor.

Somehow Anna managed to say the right things to the other girl and made her way back to her office, her rapidly cooling coffee clutched in her hand.

What on earth should she do? she wondered. She had to get a hold of Nicole and find out what she was up to—but how? She did a quick search online, and found the number for Jackson Importers. Maybe Nate Hunter might be able to shed some light on where Nicole was.

Five frustrating minutes of being stonewalled later, Anna replaced the receiver on her phone. Mr. Hunter was unavailable until further notice. What that meant, exactly, Anna had no idea, but she had the sinking feeling that wherever Nicole was, it was very possibly with him. And given her mood last night and her tendency to be outrageously impulsive, it didn't augur well.

Darn Judd Wilson, she thought, and darn Charles, too. This was all their fault. Anna clenched her hands into fists and fought back the urge to scream. One by one she uncurled her fingers and released her fury on a pent-up breath, then reached for her phone and dialed Judd's number. They needed to swing into damage control before all this blew up in their faces. He'd know what to do.

Seven

"It's preposterous. What on earth is she thinking?"

Anna winced as Charles raged through the office on Monday afternoon after what had been an exceptionally stressful and long weekend waiting for his prodigal daughter to return home. She knew all the anger and tension couldn't be good for him, but there was nothing she could do to calm him down when the bad news about Nicole kept pouring in. The latest update—that she'd turned up for work at the offices of Jackson Importers late that morning—had gone down like a lead balloon.

He continued his rant. "She isn't thinking, that's what. And she wonders why I gave the controlling interest in Wilson Wines to Judd."

"She's hurting, Charles. Give her time, she'll come back." Anna tried to soothe his anger but it was useless.

"Come back? I wouldn't have her back. Not now that she's working for that insufferable miscreant! I've a good mind to cut her out of my will completely after this." Anna wanted to believe he was just blowing off steam, but she had a sinking feeling that he meant every word. Nothing made Charles angrier than what he perceived as disloyalty. No matter what excuse she offered, Anna was pretty sure that Charles wouldn't be forgiving Nicole in a hurry.

"And what are we supposed to do in the meantime, hmm?" Charles continued. "We needed her here to help transition Judd into his duties. Now he's dropped in at the deep end."

"I'm sure I'll cope." Judd interrupted his father's tirade. "I'm not completely unaware of how a business should be run nor am I unfamiliar with the wine industry."

Anna looked at him and felt that familiar tug of attraction she'd fought all weekend to ignore. It was hard enough to resist him under normal circumstances, but over the past weekend, when Anna had felt that her whole world was collapsing around her, Judd had been a rock—stepping right in to make sure everything was taken care of. While Anna had been busy keeping Charles reined in and ensuring that his riled temper didn't prevent him from keeping up with his medical treatments, Judd was the one who'd handled the reporters' phone calls, coordinated with the company's PR team and ensured that all Wilson Wines employees, particularly those who reported directly to Nicole, were reminded of the nondisclosure agreements they had signed.

He'd single-handedly kept the disaster from spiraling out of control. While Anna couldn't help but be grateful to him, she was forced to admit to herself that it was entirely unfair how attractive he was when he was coolly, competently in charge.

Today he looked every inch the high-powered executive, wearing a navy suit and crisp white shirt with a patterned tie. He could have stepped off the pages of a men's fashion magazine, and yet despite the polish, there was still that edge of visceral male that hovered about him.

"Anna?" Charles's voice. "Are you paying attention?"

"S-sorry," she stuttered. "I was woolgathering."

Charles sighed heavily. "I need you to be on your game, young lady. Without Nicole here, I'm appointing you as Judd's P.A. He's going to need the support of someone who knows Wilson Wines from the ground up. You're the only one I trust for that role."

"His P.A.?" Her heart gave an uncomfortable lurch. "But what about you?"

"I'm sure you can draw on one of the girls from marketing to help me when I need it. That redhead who covers for you when you're on holiday, she'll do. It's not as if I'm in here for full days, anyway…although I suppose that will have to change now Nicole's gone."

He suddenly slumped in his chair, his face gray. Anna rushed to his side.

"Are you all right? Do you need the doctor?"

Charles shook his head. "No, don't fuss, Anna. I'm not sick. Not physically, anyway. It just isn't right. I finally get Judd back and I lose Nicole."

Anna fought the urge to tell him she'd tried to warn him that what he was doing would drive a wedge between himself and his daughter. She found consoling words instead to replace the ones that hung bitterly on the tip of her tongue.

"You haven't lost her, she'll be back before we know it, I'm sure."

"In the meantime, you have us," Judd commented. "And speaking of which, I think you should head home and rest and leave the running of the office to Anna and me. We can call you if anything arises that we can't manage."

Anna felt a burst of cold panic at the thought of her and Judd alone together in the office, but still, she found herself agreeing with him. Anything to see to Charles's comfort. After the older man had been driven home by his new temporary P.A., Anna showed Judd into Nicole's office. Charles had stipulated that he should work from there, and while a little voice inside of her had objected vociferously, she accepted the practicality of it. If Judd was to assume Nicole's duties quickly, he needed information to be at his fingertips. Where better than in Nicole's office?

It was lunchtime when he came out and over to Anna's desk.

"I see Nicole had a trip planned to Nelson, leaving on Thursday. I thought Wilson Wines primarily imported from overseas markets."

"We do, but Nicole campaigned to introduce several wines from New Zealand to our catalogue as well, with a view to distributing only to select wine sellers and collectors. She felt it was a strong counter to Jackson Importers' ability to cut prices by dealing through the internet. This way we'd have top-quality wines but without the additional costs involved with importation."

Judd nodded. "Makes good sense. So this project is still in its infancy?"

"Yes, she's already visited a few North Island wineries. This week was to source specific wines from the top of the South Island."

"You'll need to change her tickets to my name and book a set for yourself, as well."

"Me?"

A small frown creased between his eyebrows. "Why not?"

"I don't usually do these trips. My role is more one of support here, at home."

"I need you with me."

"Surely you can—"

"Anna, you're coming with me. We're not departing until early evening on Thursday and will be returning to Auckland on Tuesday morning. The office can survive a few days without you."

"But Charles—"

"Has a new P.A. now. Or had you forgotten that?"

* * *

Judd eyed Anna carefully. He hadn't expected an opportunity to get her alone and to himself quite so quickly but he certainly wasn't going to waste it. Getting her out from under his father's roof and into his own bed had become a task he'd begun to relish. His sister's display of pique had fallen right into his hands. He'd thank her for it one of these days. Probably right about the time he offered his controlling interest in Wilson Wines over to Nate Hunter.

After the weekend's development, he'd shelved his original plans to hand over the company right away. Oh, he still intended to take Wilson Wines apart…but not quite yet. Charles was still reeling from Nicole's actions, and Judd wanted him feeling secure and invulnerable again when Judd struck. Besides, seducing Charles's mistress away from him would be a lot easier when she was forced to work right at his side.

For now, business was the least of his concerns. His sights were very firmly set on the woman in front of him. The woman whose scent, even now, tantalized him. Living under the same roof and not touching her—imagining her with his father—had been torture these past few days. He hadn't seen any overt displays of affection between them, but she'd certainly been hovering over Charles nonstop. Judd also hadn't forgotten her state of dishabille last Thursday evening when he'd caught her coming from the old man's rooms.

Each time he'd had an opportunity, he'd cut her from Charles's attention over the weekend, even going so far as to brush against her from time to time. He knew his touch unsettled her—the faint flush of color on her cheeks had been a dead giveaway—but she'd managed to gracefully extricate herself from each situation and create a distance between them that had left him frustrated both physically and mentally.

This trip to the South Island was a godsend. She would be

his willing lover before they returned, and stage one of his decimation of the things his father loved would have begun.

By the time Thursday morning rolled around Judd felt as if every cell in his body was taut with anticipation over what this trip would bring. He'd done some more research and had personally contacted each of the wineries they were to visit to explain that he was coming in his sister's stead. So far the reception had been promising, as had been the sample wines that Nicole had in her office that she'd received in advance of the trip. He could see why she'd chosen them. They had distinct appeal on many levels. His sister definitely had a strong talent for innovation and combined it with exemplary taste.

The business side of the trip aside, he was looking forward to the concentrated time alone with Anna Garrick. That she very clearly wasn't only made the prospect more appealing and the challenge even more enticing. He still well remembered her response to his kiss that first night at The Masters'. Remembered the feel of her body, her full breasts, the soft curves of her body against his, the taste of her. Damn if he wasn't getting hard just thinking about it.

He walked into the dining room at the house that already felt like home and saw Anna at the sideboard helping herself to cereal and milk.

"Good morning, all ready for the trip?" he asked.

She took her bowl over to the table and sat down before acknowledging his presence.

"Good morning," she said, her voice a little husky as if she'd not long been awake.

The fresh scent of her and her immaculately applied makeup gave lie to the thought that she'd tumbled straight from bed. Add to that the fact that she was dressed smartly in a cream blouse neatly tucked into a pair of taupe-colored trousers that she'd cinched at the waist with a wide black belt, suggested she'd been up for some time. The blouse was made of some sheer floaty fabric that clung to her in all the right places. Beneath it he caught a hint of a lacy camisole. He was going to have to exhibit some control, he decided, if he wasn't to walk around all morning in a state of constant arousal. But there was something so carnally alluring about her, he knew it would be easier said than done.

Anna pushed her cereal around in her bowl, clearly not finding the prospect of breakfast at all tempting. In the meantime, Judd helped himself to some fluffy scrambled eggs and a couple of strips of grilled bacon.

"Are you sure you really need me to come with you on this trip?" she blurted as he sat down and reached for the coffeepot on the table.

"I wouldn't have said so if it wasn't necessary."

She sighed, the action making her breasts rise and fall beneath the gossamer-fine fabric and making his fingers itch to touch it and what lay beneath.

"I really don't think I should be leaving Charles, what with Nicole gone, as well."

Judd felt his resolve harden. "He's an adult and quite capable of taking care of himself."

"But he'll be alone."

"In a house filled with staff? I don't think so. I've spoken with Mrs. Evans already. She'll keep a close eye on him."

"It won't be the same," Anna replied, a mutinous set to her mouth.

He'd just bet it wouldn't be the same. And if he had anything to do with it, it wouldn't be the same ever again. If Anna was going to pay a furtive visit to anyone's room, it would be to his from here on in.

"He'll cope. Mrs. Evans will be staying in and has all the necessary numbers if she needs assistance." He looked at her swirling her spoon in her now-soggy cereal. "Are you going to eat that?"

She looked down at her bowl, a flash of surprise on her features when she saw the mess in there.

"Um, no. I'm not hungry."

"Are you sure? There's no meal service on the flight."

"I'm aware of that. I'll be fine."

"You don't look fine."

She huffed another sigh. "Look, I don't like small aircraft, that's all. But I'll be okay."

"Fifty passengers isn't such a small aircraft. If you're that worried, I can hold your hand for the entire flight. Rest assured, I'll take good care of you, Anna," he said, giving her a look that intimated a whole lot more than hand-holding.

"I think I'll be able to manage without that. Besides, it's more likely that the prospect of being with you for the next few days is what makes me anxious."

She got up and placed her bowl and spoon on an empty tray at the end of the sideboard. Judd stood and blocked her path as she went to walk past him.

"Now, why would that be, I wonder?" He lifted one finger and traced the edge of her lower lip. "Could it be that you're *anxious* to repeat that kiss we shared in Adelaide?"

"N-no, of course not," she refuted.

"Really?" he said softly. "Do you ever think about it?"

She shook her head and he leaned in a little closer.

"I do." He let his hand drop. "And I look forward to the next time."

"There won't be a next time," she said adamantly, nudging past him and heading for the door.

He watched her leave with a small self-satisfied smile on his face. Oh, yes, these next few days would prove very interesting indeed.

Anna shot up the stairs to her bedroom and closed the door firmly behind her as if another barrier could make a difference to the way Judd Wilson made her feel. She rested a hand on her chest, feeling her rapid heartbeat beneath her palm.

He's just teasing me, she told herself. *Playing games like a cat with a mouse. I certainly don't want a repeat of that kiss.*

Liar! her alter ego whispered in her ear. She shook her head to rid herself of the word echoing in her mind and mentally rechecked her luggage for the trip away. She had everything she needed and then some. All of it nondescript and practical, with not a single low-cut neckline or suggestive hemline amongst it all.

Externally, at least, there'd be nothing about her to tempt Judd Wilson. She hadn't been unaware of his presence these past days. In fact, she could almost say she'd been hyperaware of him. She'd chosen the blandest combinations of clothing she possibly could every single day, and yet, on several occasions, she'd caught him looking at her as if he'd like to eat her all up.

The visual image of him doing just that forced a moan from her constricted throat. The flat of her hand drifted down to her breast, to where her nipple peaked against the fabric. She couldn't deny it. He had a near uncontrollable effect upon her.

Sex. It was just sex. He was a strong healthy male and he hit all her hot buttons. She really needed to get out more, she decided. Meet new people. Maybe when she got back she'd get a hold of one of the guys at work who was always teasing her about a date. Maybe then she would be able to work this aching tension out of her body and inure herself to Judd Wilson's overwhelming magnetism. She'd get onto it the minute they got back, she promised herself. The very second.

Eight

Anna was shattered by the time they made it back to their riverside hotel in Nelson on Thursday night. They'd arrived at Nelson airport just after two in the afternoon and had hopped into their rental car and driven straight out to the first of two vineyards and wineries that they'd visited today.

The visits, and subsequent talks, had gone well. Nicole's dream was being well and truly brought to reality. Anna fought back the pang that her friend wasn't the one actively seeing her idea come into fruition. Still, it couldn't be helped. She'd made it clear that she'd washed her hands of Wilson Wines, her father and, by association, Anna and Judd, as well. It still hurt that her best friend had severed all ties between them so instantaneously, but she had to respect Nicole's decision.

She rubbed wearily at her eyes, feeling as if she had no more control of her life right now than a leaf did, floating on the river outside. Warm fingers closed over her forearm.

"Are you okay?"

Judd. Always Judd. Always right there, in her face, in her space, in her mind. Somewhere along the course of this week she'd begun to depend on him—on his unwavering sense of command and his capable manner. Even Charles had begun to defer to him—something Anna had never believed she'd see in her lifetime. She had to get a grip on herself—to break the spell Judd was so easily waving about her. She opened her eyes and looked pointedly at where his hand made heated contact with the bare skin of her arm.

"You can let go of me. I'm not about to keel over," she said tartly.

"Of course you're not. Here, this is your room key. We have adjoining rooms. I thought we should eat in tonight and then go over the proposals we discussed with John and Peter today."

"And I suppose we *must* do this tonight?"

"It'll pay to iron out any potential kinks early, don't you agree?"

"Sure," she said, resignation in her voice. "I'd like to freshen up a bit before we eat."

"No problem. I'll order for both of us and have it delivered to my room. Just come through the connecting door when you're ready."

When she was ready. That was rich. *How about never,* she thought defiantly. But she knew she would go through to his room to dine with him. She owed it to Charles if no one else. Already rumors had begun to circulate this week about Jackson Importers approaching at least three of Wilson Wines' major European suppliers. They'd had exclusive contracts with those suppliers but they were all coming up for renewal. A fact that Nicole had known only too well. Was she behind this attempt to undermine her own father?

"Sounds good. Give me half an hour."

"There's no big rush. Take an hour if you need it."

"Thanks, I will." Another hour she didn't have to spend in his company was all good as far as she was concerned.

When she let herself into her room, she cast her eyes around, familiarizing herself with the layout. Basic but comfortable, were the first two things that came to mind, until she stepped into the bathroom and saw the spa bath installed against a white-tiled wall. A sound of anticipation mixed with pure pleasure escaped her and, as she ran the bath, she quickly divested herself of her travel-worn clothes.

She lost track of how long she'd soaked until she heard a muffled knocking from the connecting door. She dragged herself from the water and wrapped herself in a towel. A quick glance at the bedside clock confirmed she'd used up her one hour of grace.

"I'll be right there," she shouted at the closed door, and quickly dried herself off.

She unzipped her case and grabbed fresh underwear, the sheer shell-pink panties clinging a little to her skin as she shimmied into them. She hooked up her bra and then padded on bare feet back to the bathroom to apply some moisturizer and to brush out her hair. She wasn't going to the effort of reapplying her makeup, not when she hoped to be in bed—her own bed, and alone—very soon.

Back in the main room she extracted a lightweight, loose-fitting cotton sweater in taupe and a pair of black Capri pants, before shoving her bare feet into a pair of silver leather slides. A long silver chain with a large silver spinner on the end completed the ensemble. There, that should do it, she decided.

Another knock at the connecting door startled her. She reached out and pulled open the door. Her gaze flicked over him as he filled the frame, making her wish she'd waited a few seconds for him to move away before opening the door. He'd obviously had a shower and changed, too, and her nostrils twitched at the light scent of his cologne. His hair was still wet, making it look blacker than black, and his jaw looked freshly shaven. He'd changed into blue jeans and a black T-shirt that clung to his broad shoulders and chest as if it were made for him. Probably was, she thought cynically. He'd never looked anything less than tailor-made this whole time she'd known him.

"You look worth the wait," Judd said smoothly.

"What's for dinner?" she asked, ducking under his arm and moving into his room.

It was the mirror of hers, with the exception of a California king-size bed instead of the queen she had. She swallowed as she tore her eyes away from the expanse of linen, the bed already enticingly turned down for the night.

"I chose two entrées and a shared main from the menu that I thought would complement a couple of the wines we tried today. We can share the entrées or have just one each. Your choice."

The idea of sharing a dish with him, let alone two dishes, was a bit daunting, but Anna reminded herself she was here to work.

"We can share," she said with as much nonchalance as she could muster.

The autumn evening was still surprisingly warm, and the covered dishes on the trolley near the door to the balcony emitted a mouthwatering aroma. A table for two was set on the balcony overlooking the river, a squat white candle burning in a hurricane lamp providing illumination. Altogether it was a shamefully idyllic and romantic setting. She should have insisted on dining in the main restaurant, she thought, as she took her chair and Judd placed the two entrées in the middle of the table between them.

Anna busied herself filling their water glasses, while Judd poured them each a small measure of the pinot gris they'd brought back with them today.

"So, what shall we start with?" she asked, suddenly very hungry.

"Black Tiger Prawns on a bed of noodles with this wine, I think," Judd suggested, lifting the cover off the first plate.

By the time they'd enjoyed their way through the prawns, followed by a sampling of Green Lipped Mussels and then their shared main course of a trio of meats, Anna felt as if she'd eaten enough to feed an army.

"The new Syrah should be very popular, don't you think?" Judd commented as he leaned back in his chair and took another sip of the wine he'd just mentioned.

"Indeed. It's a variety that seems to be growing in popularity here. To get exclusive distribution on this label is going to be quite a coup. Charles will be pleased."

And there he was again, Judd thought. His father, still intruding.

"Why is his approval so important to you?" he asked.

"He's my boss," she answered simply, turning her face away to look at the lights from the marina sparkling on the now-inky dark water that ran alongside the hotel.

"He's more than that, though. Isn't he?"

She sighed. "Yes, he is. He's always been there for me, and for my mother while she was alive. Without him, I wouldn't be where I am today. I owe him a huge debt of gratitude."

He couldn't quite get a handle on it. It was clear by the tone of her voice, and her actions with his old man, that she loved him. But just where did that love lead?

"He's quite a guy," Judd commented, a little of his frustration creeping into his tone.

"The way you say that…" She shook her head. "You don't know him. Not really."

"And whose fault was that?" he said pointedly. "Look, let's not talk about my father, okay? Let's talk about something else."

She stifled a yawn. "I'm sorry, I think I need to turn in. I haven't been sleeping well lately, and we have an early start for the day tomorrow."

"Sure," he said.

She did look tired, he admitted to himself as he rose from the table and walked with her back to the connecting door. But even with the dark rings under her eyes she was intensely appealing. He'd enjoyed sharing dinner with her—her keen insights into the wines had been valuable, and her company had been surprisingly soothing while they ate. But his enjoyment of her companionship hadn't dampened his desire for the evening to end on a far more sensual note. His body tightened as he considered his plans for this time away together, and as she turned to say good-night, he reached out and caught a few strands of her hair between his fingers, twirling them over and over.

Her mouth parted, as if in protest, but the objection never came. He leaned a little closer.

"Don't you ever wonder?" he asked, pitching his voice low and watching her pupils almost consume the hazel irises of her eyes.

"Wonder what?" she asked, her voice that husky whisper that did crazy things to him and sent a heated jolt of need straight to his groin.

Her eyes had fixed on his lips as he spoke. He moved closer still, until there was no more than a hand width separating their faces.

"What it will be like when we kiss again."

"Who said we'll kiss again?"

"Oh, we will. Don't you want to know if what happened the first time will happen again? Whether we could be *that* good again?"

She blinked and drew in a breath, the word *no* beginning to form on her lips. The sound never made it, as he closed the short distance between them, caressing her lips with his—at first gently and then, when she didn't pull away, with more pressure. His fingers tunneled through her hair to cup the back of her head.

The sensation that shuddered through his body was intense. Even more potent than the last time. He stepped closer, aligning his body with hers and wrapping his free arm around her waist, drawing her against him—feeling the heat of her, the softness, and letting her know in no uncertain terms of the strength of his arousal for her. Slow seduction be damned. The contrast between their bodies incited him to want more, to want it all, to want it now.

His tongue traced the seam of her lips, and as she parted them, he stroked it across the tender inner membrane before tasting her deeper. She met his assault with a parry of her own, her hands now clutched in the fabric of his T-shirt, clinging to him, her hips pressed tight against his own. He flexed his pelvis, gently grinding his hardness against her mound. A moan vibrated from deep in her throat and he captured the sound with his mouth.

Her nipples were hardened points against his chest and he knew without a doubt that one kiss would never be enough. His need to possess her overwhelmed everything else—every need, every thought, other than one. He wanted Anna Garrick like he'd never wanted anything in his life before.

Anna fought to clear the fog of desire that clouded her mind but failed miserably. Hot, hungry need clawed through her as Judd kissed her deeply and she kissed him back just as hard. She knew she should pull back, call a stop to this before they went past the point of no return, but somewhere deep inside she acknowledged that they'd passed that point long ago. What would happen now was inevitable. Nothing—not even the vow she'd made to herself for so many years to never have an intimate relationship with her boss—could stop her from giving in. She wondered whether she would still be able to walk away with some pride, with her heart intact, but her feelings for Judd had crossed some unseen line. Even back in Adelaide, she'd been drawn to him in a way she'd never experienced before. She wanted to take this further—to know him better, to *know* him in every meaning of the word.

There was no reason left that was strong enough to convince her that she shouldn't reach out and take what he was offering. No reason at all. And in return she could give in to him. Anna loosened the fists of her hands and skimmed her palms over his muscled chest and down toward the waistband of his jeans. She yanked the cotton fabric of his shirt loose and shoved her hands underneath, desperate now to feel his skin against hers. But it wasn't enough. His skin burned beneath her touch, igniting her to want even more.

The taut coil of desire deep in her womb tightened even more, and between her thighs she felt herself grow swollen and wet with need. Judd loosened his grip on her, using both hands to push aside her sweater. They broke apart momentarily as he swept the garment up and off her body, exposing her to his gaze. He groaned and bent his head to her neck, nuzzling the tender skin behind her ear and leaving a heated trail of kisses along the way to the hollow of her throat.

One hand cupped her breast, his thumb flicking a distended nipple through the sheer lace of her bra. Her legs threatened to buckle beneath her as his mouth traced a beeline for the tightly beaded nub. He tugged the edge of her demi-cup bra down, exposing her to his hungry mouth and sending a sizzle of pure fire to her core. She clutched at his waist, anchoring herself to him, and arched her back, easing his access to her as he alternately laved and suckled her.

"You taste so good," he said against her sensitive skin. "But it's not enough."

"Not enough?" She could barely manage to get the words past her lips.

"No, I want to taste all of you."

Judd straightened and gently pulled her hands out from

under his T-shirt before he led her back into his room and to his bed. As she watched in silence, he stripped off his shirt and kicked off his shoes. She reached for him and unbuttoned the top buttons of his fly, her knuckles brushing against the unmistakably swollen ridge of his penis. He grabbed her hands with his.

"That's more than I can handle right now," he groaned, pressing one of her palms against his erection. "Can't you feel what you do to me?"

Words failed her. Her entire body was on fire, liquid molten heat that slowly consumed her inside and out. Judd skimmed his hands up to her shoulders and slid the straps of her bra down before reaching behind her and unsnapping the hooks. The garment fell away from her. He stared at her for so long she began to feel self-conscious, but then he lifted his gaze to hers, his eyes glittering.

"You are so beautiful," he said, reaching out one finger and tracing the pink areola that contracted even tighter under his gentle touch.

He unfastened her pants and pushed them down her legs, the black fabric swiftly followed by her panties. He knelt before her, helping her to step out of the wisp of fabric, then let his fingers glide up her legs, over her trembling thighs and pausing for a second to let his fingers brush the moisture that gathered at their apex.

"You feel so hot, so ready for me," he murmured before pressing his lips where his fingers had been.

His tongue darted against her most sensitive spot, teasing and tasting as if she were some decadent dessert to be slowly savored. Anna clutched his shoulders as he increased the pressure of his tongue, as his lips closed over that sweet bundle of nerve endings, as she was hit with a sudden sharp wave of pleasure that radiated from her core and out to her extremities in a crescendo that tore a cry of satisfaction from deep within her.

She could barely stand another moment. Judd rose swiftly to his feet and guided her back onto the bed. Against her overheated body the sheets were a welcome stretch of coolness, but that coolness was soon swamped by the heat of Judd's body as he rose over her.

He'd said she was beautiful but he was far more so. The symmetry of his body, the strength of his muscles, the golden tan of his skin and the heavy maleness of his arousal—each inch perfection in itself, let alone presented to her as whole.

He'd already grabbed a condom from somewhere and sheathed himself.

"I'm sorry," he grunted as he positioned himself between her thighs. "This is going to be hard and fast, but I promise to take longer next time." He eased his swollen length inside her, his face flushed with concentration. "And the next," he said, his voice strained as he thrust forward, "and the next."

Anna rocked her pelvis to meet his every move, her hands clutching his forearms as they braced at her sides, her legs wrapping around his hips. Her body responded to his fierce possession, a delicious tightening of her inner muscles heralding another orgasm. And then she was there, spasms of pleasure heightening in concentration until she thought she might break apart from the sheer strength of them. Judd lunged within her, his whole body shuddering as he, too, reached his pinnacle of completion.

When he collapsed against her, his breathing was ragged, his body still rocked intermittently by tiny tremors. It was several minutes before he withdrew and rolled to one side. He stroked away several strands of her hair that had settled over her face.

"I'll be right back," he murmured.

Anna nodded, too shattered to speak. A delicious lassitude consumed her body and she lay back on the sheets, barely daring to believe what had just happened between them. Judd came back from the bathroom and slid into the bed beside her then gathered her to him, whereupon he made good on his promise to take longer the next time. And the next.

Dawn was breaking when she awoke. She was sprawled across Judd's chest, her legs tangled in his as if she couldn't get close enough to him. The last time they'd made love she'd been poised above him, and in their aftermath she'd collapsed right where she lay. Their lovemaking had left her nearly incoherent. She'd never felt this close to another human being ever before.

In bed, Judd Wilson was a completely different man. Gone was the underlying tension that always kept Anna on edge in the office, wondering what was really going on in his keenly intelligent mind. No, in bed there had been nothing between them, quite literally. No past, no future—only the present.

Anna carefully loosed her legs from between his and levered herself onto the sheets beside him. Judd barely moved, lost in a sleep so deep his face relaxed into lines that made him look so much more approachable than he did on a day-to-day basis—less driven, less ruthless.

In the gray light filtering through the windows she looked her fill and wondered where they would go to from here. She couldn't be angry with herself for breaking her long-standing rule—clearly Judd was a man who could never be resisted for long. But now that they'd started this affair, she didn't know what came next. She didn't want the kind of relationship her mother had had with Charles, which, while it was a deep and loving friendship, had never given her mother the full security of marriage which Donna Garrick had quietly craved. Her mother's quiet acceptance of everything had made Anna angry with her for just *settling* for a half life.

Charles and Donna had been occasional lovers, a fact that was governed partially by his diabetes-related impotence and by the strictures of Donna being in his employ. There'd always been an imperceptible barrier between them. One that neither of them had fully crossed. Anna had always felt that her mother had compromised her own happiness for the sake of that vague relationship. Perhaps her need to provide a home and a quality education for her daughter had driven her, or perhaps, after her husband's death, she wasn't prepared to risk her heart again for a passionate love.

Anna had been five when her father had died unexpectedly, and her mother had been offered the position as Charles's housekeeper. Anna had grown up under Charles's roof lacking nothing materially. Deep inside, though, she knew that she wanted more—the emotional strength that came with being intrinsically linked with another soul being first and foremost on her list.

Judd was the kind of man she'd always believed she'd fall in love with one day. His looks aside, his intelligence and ability to provide made him an exceptionally attractive mate. But he was more than all that. This past week she'd seen so many of his strengths—his ability to calm Charles in the wake of Nicole's defection being a perfect example.

Could she have all she wanted with Judd? Did he feel the same way about love and marriage and building a life together forever? Did he feel the same way about her? She almost laughed in the early-morning gloom. God, she was pathetic. Here she was after one night of mind-blowing sex and already she was marching him down the aisle. She didn't even know for certain how compatible they were in other aspects of life. All she knew was that the moment she'd set eyes on him she'd reacted to him on an instinctive level she'd never experienced before. Bearing the brunt of his anger when he'd discovered her deception over her reasons for being at The Masters' had been painful to bear. But once they'd gotten to New Zealand, things had changed. She'd seen sides of him she hadn't suspected before. And then last night…well, last night had changed everything. Now she knew for certain that she wanted a future with him. But was that what he wanted, too?

Guilt drove a splinter into her thoughts. And what about his relationship with his sister? What about hers? Nicole already thought she'd gone over to the enemy by having represented Charles in Adelaide. If she knew that Anna was now considering getting seriously involved with Judd, she'd be even more angry—even more hurt. A lifetime of friendship shattered for a man she'd known for only a matter of weeks.

And what about Charles? How would he react to all of this? He'd seemed to encourage the two of them to spend time together, but would he approve of them having a real relationship?

Of course, all of that presupposed that a real relationship was what Judd wanted with her in the first place. Did she dare to even ask? So much was at stake—so much could be ruined if this went badly. Her job, her closeness to the people who meant the most to her, nearly everything she had, including the roof over her head in the house she'd lived in for nearly all her life, could all be lost.

She looked over again at Judd's sleeping form. Even now, the urge to touch him was irresistible. In spite of herself, she curled up closer at his side, feeling a little thrill of pleasure when his arms tightened around her.

For now, he wanted her and she couldn't deny that she wanted him. And away from her friends, from the gossips at the office, from Charles, he was too tempting to resist. Things would change when they got back to Auckland. If nothing else, she certainly wouldn't want to engage in anything inappropriate under Charles's roof. But for now…for now, she'd fall back asleep in Judd's arms. She'd worry about the consequences later.

Nine

Judd felt Anna's withdrawal from him grow incrementally larger as they got closer to home. It started at breakfast on the last morning of their trip, where she'd suggested eating in the restaurant rather than in their room as they had the past few days, and it had continued through their final appointments and for the duration of their plane trip to Auckland. Now, it was dark as Evans drove them up to the house and even though she was sitting right next to him, it felt like she was a million miles away.

After Evans had taken their bags inside the front foyer and gone to put the car back in the multicar garage, Judd turned to Anna.

"Will you stay with me tonight?"

"Judd…" She shook her head, not making eye contact.

"Why not?"

Suspicion roiled inside of him. Was it because they'd be under his father's roof? Or maybe it was because she'd be sleeping in Charles's bed tonight. Anger flared hard on the heels of his suspicions. She'd been his, all his, the past three nights. Those nights hadn't been anywhere near enough to sate the hunger he had for her and he damn sure wasn't sharing her—especially not with his father.

"It just wouldn't be right," she said, picking up her weekend bag and starting up the stairs.

"We could be discreet," he heard himself say. "Although you would have to try harder not to scream when I—"

"Don't. Just, please don't," she said, her voice shaking and warm color spreading across her cheeks.

"I only want to give you pleasure, Anna. Nothing more."

Her hazel eyes locked with his, and for a few seconds he thought he had her, but then she shook her head again and turned away up the staircase.

He watched her retreat from the bottom of the stairs, his whole body humming with frustration. Leaving his bag at the base of the stairs, he turned and went through to the salon, reaching for the brandy decanter and splashing a measure in one of the crystal tumblers he'd swept up off an engraved silver tray on the sideboard. He knocked back a generous mouthful of the spirit and relished the burn as it traversed its way down his throat.

She might have refused him tonight, he decided, but he hoped it would be the last time she did so. Anna Garrick had become an addiction he had no desire to shake. He finished the last of the brandy and headed for his room and his frustratingly empty bed.

The next morning Judd watched Anna under hooded lids as she summarized their trip to the South Island to Charles—leaving out what he felt to be the most important details, of course. For all her poise and aloof elegance, she was neither poised nor aloof in bed. No, in bed she was voracious and generous, two qualities he held in high esteem in a lover. After that first night they hadn't bothered with booking two rooms again, spending their days visiting various wineries and their nights exploring every inch of one another's bodies.

And what a body. Full in just the right places, and firm in others. A man could lose himself in her. And he had, over and over again. It had been difficult to keep his hands off her when they took their business meetings, especially when he'd seen the way other men looked at her—drawn to her beauty, her charm, her sharp mind tempered with such inherent sweetness. She was phenomenal in every respect, and it had been all he could do to keep from crowing that she was his.

Or rather, she *had* been his, until they'd returned to Charles.

Sleep had been a long time coming last night in his large empty bed. She'd well and truly gotten under his skin, he admitted. He wanted her now, even as she showed Charles a swiftly cobbled together PowerPoint presentation showing where they believed the company would make gains on the current market with their new trend of stocking domestically produced wines.

Judd shifted in his chair to ease the sudden tightness in his groin, his movement drawing Anna's attention. Her eyes flew to his face, a question in them—he merely smiled in response and narrowed his eyes just a little. She blushed, a totally delightful quality, and a dead giveaway as to her physical state. He let his eyes drop deliberately to where her nipples left the tiniest peaks through her bra and against the fabric of her blouse. He didn't mistake her sharp intake of breath, nor her very deliberate body language when she turned away from him and wrapped up the presentation.

"So, you see, Charles, all in all, Nicole was on the right track."

"Well, she's not now," he grumbled. "So you're both convinced that this is the right way to go?"

Judd rose from his chair. "New Zealand has long held a

strong position on the world stage for its superior-quality wines. Our clientele deserves to be offered the exclusivity of these labels. We'd be foolish not to. And, I would suspect, if we don't act soon, someone else will."

"Jackson Importers, you mean?" Charles asked sharply. "We can't have them upstage us. How soon before we can get these varieties into distribution?"

As Anna smoothly took over the logistics of the proposal, Judd sat back to watch her in action. Yes, she was the whole package, all right. Intelligent, beautiful and sexy as hell. And she was his; she just needed a little reminding of it.

Later, after Charles had left the office for the day, Judd called her back into his office.

"Close the door behind you," he instructed as she came in.

"Is there a problem?" she asked as she sealed off the outer office, leaving them cocooned together.

"Oh, yeah, there's a problem, all right."

"What is it? Is it an issue with the new wines?"

"No, come over here."

She did as he asked, a worried crease in her brow. The instant she was within reach, he drew her to him, one hand sliding up her back to cradle the back of her head. He lowered his lips to hers and took them in a kiss he'd been waiting for since yesterday. It had been only hours and yet he'd missed this physicality between them with an ache that had plagued him all last night and all day long.

She pulled away from him. "Stop. What if someone comes in?"

"I've already instructed that all our calls be held. No one will interrupt us, but if you're really worried…"

A few steps across the carpeted floor and the door was securely locked. Anna turned, her back to his desk, and faced him.

"What do you think you're doing?"

He smiled in response. "What I've been wanting to do since we got home."

He backed her up to his desk, boosting her up onto its surface, and, hitching her, oh, so sensible office skirt up to the top of her thighs, he stood between her legs.

"If you won't stay with me in my room, we'll just have to make do," he whispered as he bent his head to her neck and lavished the sensitive skin there with alternating nips of his teeth and licks of his tongue.

He felt the quiver of longing that rippled through her.

"But we're in the office, people will know," she protested, but he knew her heart wasn't in it.

Even now her hands were at his waistband, unfastening his belt and sliding his zipper down to gain access to his body. As her hands freed him from his boxer briefs he shuddered in response, relishing the silky softness of her fingers as they closed around his hardness and squeezed with just the right kind of pressure.

"No one will know but us," he groaned into her mouth as he reached between her legs and found her hot and wet already.

His fingers eased behind the fabric of her panties, sliding along her slick crease, back and forth, back and forth. She moaned in response and he kissed her again, flicking his tongue within her, mirroring his actions with his fingers. She rocked against him, trying desperately to force him to make contact with that part of her that he knew would send her flying over the edge, but this time he wanted to extend the torture just a little longer.

Somewhere along the line in the past few days she'd become necessary to him, and sleeping without her last night had been something he wasn't in a hurry to repeat. He wanted her to want him so much, to need him so much, that she wouldn't consider sleeping without him again.

He eased her back down on the desk and took his time

with his free hand flicking open the buttons of her blouse. One by one he worked his way down, his knuckles skimming the soft swells of her breasts as he lingered on those in particular.

"Please, Judd. Let's just do this."

"In good time," he answered, but even as he did so he privately acknowledged that he wouldn't be able to control his desire for her for much longer. Even now he ached to be inside her, his erection at an almost painful level.

She'd given up touching him, so mindless as she was now to his touch. He bent and blew a cool breath across the exposed skin of her breasts, noting with pleasure how the skin raised in tiny goose bumps, how her nipples pressed against the smooth cups of her bra. This one had a front clasp, he realized with a carnal smile, and he wasted no time in squeezing the clasp and letting it ping open. It was like peeling open a luscious, ripe and forbidden fruit.

There she was, on his desk, upon the papers he'd been working on before their meeting with Charles, her hair spread in disarray over his notations, her blouse fallen open together with her bra and her beautiful luminous skin exposed to his hungry gaze. Her nipples, the palest of pinks, were tight nubs of arousal.

He bent down to take one taut peak softly between his teeth, rolling the tip of his tongue against the hard bead of flesh. Beneath him, Anna moaned and squirmed, her pelvis rocking hard against his hand, still striving to make contact with that part of him that now drove him almost to madness. And this was madness. Taking her here, like this, on his desk. It was the ultimate foolishness, and the ultimate fantasy all rolled into one.

It was too much for him. She'd get her wish—he couldn't wait any longer. He reached into his pocket and pulled out a condom then pushed his trousers and briefs down. Sheathing himself took only a moment, but even as he did so she watched him with eyes glazed with such passion he almost lost it right there and then. He eased off her panties and let them drop to the floor and then spread her legs wide. He would never lose this image of her from his mind, he thought as he positioned himself at her slick entrance.

She groaned as he pushed inside her, a guttural sound that made his balls tighten and the head of his penis swell even tighter. He reached for her hands, linking his fingers through hers and bending her arms up so her hands were beside her head. She lifted her legs up to wrap around his hips and he thrust inside her again, watching her eyes cloud with the sensations that spiraled through her. She had caught her lower lip between her teeth and he felt her ripple against him as he increased his pace. Her body began to shake and a soft cry escaped her. He lowered his face to hers, taking her mouth and absorbing the sounds she made as she crested the peak of their passion, the spasms of her body wringing a climax from him that took all his strength not to shout with the sheer power of it.

He collapsed over her, his breathing hard and fast, the slick of perspiration making his business shirt cling to his back. Suddenly the incongruity of their situation struck him, and a chuckle bubbled up from deep inside.

"We must look a sight from the doorway, hmm?" he said, nuzzling her neck before nipping her skin ever so lightly.

"I can't believe we did that," she said, loosing her fingers from his and pushing firmly on his chest. "I won't be able to face anyone in the main office after that."

"You won't need to. Let's go home for the rest of the day."

"We can't, there's too much to do."

Judd allowed her to push him away and stepped away from her, allowing her to slide off the desk and begin to straighten her clothing. She bent to pick up her panties and wriggled back into them, then she grabbed a wad of tissues from the dispenser on his desk and put out her hand.

"Here, let me get rid of that," she said as he removed the condom.

"I wondered why Nicole kept tissues on her desk," he said.

Anna shook her head. "I doubt that's why she had them there."

He smiled in response. "You never know." He adjusted himself and pulled his briefs and trousers back up, tucking in his shirt and straightening his tie. "There, now no one will ever know but us."

"But they may well wonder," Anna said dubiously. "I always swore I'd never…"

"Never what?"

"Never leave myself open to gossip."

He frowned. "What makes you think anyone will gossip about us?"

Was she worried about it getting back to Charles? So let it, if that was the case. He'd even go so far as to start the rumor himself if it meant he had her wholeheartedly.

"Just the nature of people. It was tough at first, starting here while Mum was still alive. Everyone knew she'd worked for Charles before she left to get married and everyone had something to say about us living with him after my dad died."

"How did that come about, exactly?" Judd asked, hitching one hip against the desk they'd just made love upon. God, even the briefest memory of what they'd just done and it was enough to put his blood on a slow burn again.

"A whole string of things, really. Poor financial decisions on my parents' part, a bit of bad luck, as well. Dad was killed on the job. He was driving to a sales call when a tanker blew a tire and hit a bridge abutment. Dad couldn't stop in time and hit the wreckage. They said he died instantly. It was all so sudden. Mum went from being a happy, stay-at-home wife and mother to a single parent with no income, a stack of funeral bills and no prospects of the life-insurance payout until all the paperwork surrounding the accident was taken care of. Charles approached Mum to offer help and when he realized what a terrible position we were left in, he offered her work and a home for both of us. I was only five, and too young, and too sheltered, to remember most of it. All I knew was that I got to live in a big house and that I had a built-in playmate."

Judd began to put two and two together. "So you grew up with Nicole?"

"Pretty much like sisters, really. Charles even sent me to the same school as her. He did far more for my mother and me than was due. I owe him a lot."

"So, he and your mother. Were they…close?"

"Were they lovers do you mean?" she asked bluntly. "Only very occasionally, from what I understand. Once, after a particularly nasty bout of bullying at school, I confronted Mum about their relationship. She tried her hardest to be honest with me and said that theirs was more a relationship based on companionship. Perhaps she was a bit too honest, but she wanted me to understand. Apparently, one of the long-term side effects of Charles's diabetes was a constant struggle with impotence. It had affected him for years, probably since before you and your mother went to Australia. But you know, even despite their closeness, Mum was always still very much an employee. When I was younger I used to hate that she allowed herself to be taken advantage of that way—now I see it was a choice she made to keep us both secure."

"So you and he—"

"Charles and I what?"

"Were never lovers?"

A look of horror passed across Anna's face. "No! Never. How could you even think that? He's always been a father figure to me, nothing more, nothing less."

"So that night I saw you coming from his rooms, half undressed—"

"I'd been waiting to talk to him about Nicole. I fell

asleep—on his sofa, in his sitting room. And then when I woke up and realized how late it was, I was in a hurry to get back to my room and hop in the shower so I could get ready for dinner. I can't believe you'd have thought that of me." She crossed her way to the office door and pointedly unlocked it. "I'm going to the ladies' room to get rid of this, and then for the rest of the afternoon I'll be in my office if you need me."

Judd felt momentarily giddy from the swell of relief that coursed through him. She wasn't Charles's lover. Her devotion to the old man was merely like that of a daughter. Hard on the heels of that thought, he realized just how much he'd hurt her with his assumption, and discovered that he was genuinely sorry to have upset her so deeply. He needed to make amends.

"Anna?"

She hesitated. "Yes?"

"Look, I'm sorry. I jumped to the wrong conclusions. Let me make it up to you. Stay with me tonight and I'll show you just how much."

She shook her head emphatically. "No, whatever you might think of *me*, I won't disrespect Charles that way."

Without saying another word she swung open the door and stalked off. Judd watched her until she was out of his line of sight before crossing around to the other side of his desk and realigning his paperwork. She hadn't exactly embraced his apology, but at least she hadn't closed the door on them both completely, either. It was time to rethink his strategies with respect to his father and to Anna. One thing he remained certain of—he wanted Anna Garrick for himself—no matter the consequences.

Anna spent the rest of the day at work in a state of total turmoil. Was she destined to be her mother's daughter after all? Was this what it had been like for Donna with Charles? That all he had to do, when he wanted to, was beckon his finger and Donna had been his for the taking, just as Anna just had been with Judd? She'd told herself that their interludes during their trip had been a fluke, that once they got back to Auckland, it would be back to business as usual, but when he'd touched her in the office, she hadn't been able to resist.

Her body still thrummed with the aftereffects of her orgasm, making it difficult to concentrate. That, along with the disbelief and shock that she'd allowed herself to be coerced into making love with Judd in his office, and on his desk no less. She'd have a few bruises tomorrow, no doubt. Her own participation in the event had hardly been that of a submissive.

She'd never been incapable of refusing a man before. She'd been selective with her sexual partners—civilized. This thing with Judd was most definitely not civilized. It was earthy sensuality at its most basic level and it had been, oh, so very good. Even now she wanted him again—but at least this time rationality prevailed. Saying no to him had been driven by her respect for Charles. She smiled at herself. Ironic, it was her respect for the very man who'd made her lose a measure of respect for her mother that now governed her choices and decisions. A psychologist could no doubt have a field day with that.

But there it was. It was how she felt. Charles hadn't had to be a mentor for her in her youth, nor had he been obliged to continue to provide a home for her after Donna had died. Yet he'd been a rock for her. Now she owed it to him to be that rock for him, which—for her, at least—meant not sleeping with his son under his own roof.

It stung that Judd could have thought that she and Charles were having an affair. She shuddered. Nothing could have been further from her mind, or Charles's, she had no doubt. But what would have made him think that?

What, or who?

A niggle of doubt emerged from the back of her mind. Something just wasn't right and she couldn't figure out what or why. But there were so many other things on her mind just now that it was easy to dismiss it.

The next few days kept her very busy in the office. Following up with the wineries they'd visited and processing exclusivity contracts with them, making sure every *i* was dotted and every *t* crossed, was the kind of work she welcomed. Right up until four out of the six wineries they'd sent contracts to sent them back with a note saying they'd received another offer of distribution that they had decided to accept.

Four phone calls later and Anna was feeling sick to her stomach. Jackson Importers had apparently aggressively wooed away the business that she and Judd had thought was in the bag. She wasn't looking forward to sharing the news with Judd or Charles.

As expected, Charles was apoplectic.

"How dare she? I can't believe a daughter of mine would stoop so low as to steal business from her father."

"I hate to point this out," Judd said, "but it was her idea all along. By the looks of things, these people's loyalty sat with Nicole rather than with Wilson Wines. It's my fault for not anticipating this might happen."

"Your fault? Rubbish. She's doing this to spite me."

"Maybe," Judd agreed, "but maybe she just followed through with her new boss on an idea she felt had merit. Did you ever give her credit for coming up with this?"

Anna sat back in her chair, stunned into silence. What was this? Judd championing Nicole? Up until now they'd barely discussed Nicole at all. Anna had assumed that Judd felt the same animosity toward her that Charles did, and had been careful not to bring her up. But to hear him supporting her ideas and giving her props for following them through, that was something Anna had never anticipated from him.

"Of course not, it was her job. She did it competently."

"A little more than competently, I would say," Judd observed, a note of censure in his voice that Anna found herself in total agreement with.

Charles had often been strict with his daughter. He had sheltered her, yes—in that respect he'd taken his responsibilities as a father most seriously. But Anna had seen how being the older, single parent of a beautiful, headstrong daughter had left him feeling that he had to be firm, set high expectations and offer limited praise in order to keep her from running wild.

It probably hadn't helped that he had been so busy with business concerns. Anna knew that Nicole had devoted herself so completely to Wilson Wines in the hopes of winning her father's approval, but it had seemed to add even more tension to their relationship. Charles never grew comfortable straddling the line between boss and father, and had been rather too hard on Nicole in his attempts to avoid showing favoritism. Plus, his old-fashioned attitudes about women in the workplace had been a constant source of irritation between them.

The end result was that Charles had stifled Nicole's adventurous spirit to a point where Anna's friend had often complained to her that she felt her opinions meant nothing to him. Charles did love Nicole, but Anna had always felt as if he struggled with how to show it—and frequently made things worse by saying the wrong thing. In fact, as she'd grown older, it had occurred to her that he may even have actively fostered their friendship so that he could use her as something of a go-between with him and Nicole—someone who could understand both of them and carry messages back and forth without causing offense.

"Well, you'll just have to do it better, my boy. I know you can do it. Let's show Jackson Importers that we're made of sterner stuff. Forget about mounting this New Zealand–based initiative."

"And the wineries who have decided to contract with us, what about them?"

"We'll use them as a test on the market. Could be a flash in the pan—who knows. If it's worth developing further, we'll look into it when the figures start coming in. In the meantime, what about expanding our range of Californian wines?"

After their meeting, Anna went back to her office to create a list of potential contacts for Judd to follow up on based on Charles's directives. She was just checking her email when a message came in that she wasn't expecting to see. Nicole. The subject header was blank, giving her no insight into what the other woman wanted. Feeling as if a thousand eyes watched her, Anna opened the message, her eyes scanning the contents quickly. Her friend wanted to see her, was begging her, in fact. She said she'd meet Anna at a waterfront restaurant in Mission Bay at one o'clock. That was in about ten minutes' time. She could make it from their Parnell offices if she left right now.

Anna chewed her lip. She'd missed Nicole terribly, but the choice her friend had made to join Jackson Importers put them on opposite sides, yet how could she refuse her longtime best friend's request?

The accusations Nicole had flung at her before leaving that awful night had hurt—mostly because she knew she'd deserved them. Loyalty to Charles aside, it had always been her and Nicole. She should have found some way to have given her friend prior warning of the bombshell that was about to be dropped on her life. No doubt Charles would be dead set against her seeing Nicole, but bolstered by Judd's clear support of his sister earlier, Anna reached her decision and fired a response back—*I'll be there.*

Ten

Judd sat in his office and realized that the feeling he'd been carrying around with him for the past several days was happiness. Assuming control of Wilson Wines had turned out to be just the kind of challenge he needed. The pressure being put on them by Jackson Importers gave him an appetite to succeed where his father had failed. Strangely, though, handing Wilson Wines to Nate Hunter on a platter didn't hold quite the appeal he had thought it would anymore. He shook his head slightly. Where was that inner fire that had burned deep down inside all these years? Where was the urge to inflict upon his father a measure of the pain the older man had inflicted upon him? He must be going soft.

Of course, there was still the matter of the house. His mother had emailed him, asking when she could visit and put her redecorating schemes into action. He'd put her off for now, but he knew she wouldn't be held back for long. How Charles would handle being under the same roof as his ex-wife was another matter. Judd had noticed his father tiring in the past week. The half days he was spending in the office were taking a toll but, in typical Charles-like manner, the older man had waved aside Judd's concerns and had flat-out laughed at Judd's suggestion that his father cut back to perhaps only three, or maybe four, half days a week until he was feeling stronger. His father was nothing but stubborn—a trait, he acknowledged, he also shared.

He glanced over the report Anna had left on his desk earlier this morning, barely even seeing the words. Stubbornness didn't just run in the Wilson family. Anna Garrick had her fair share of it, as well. While it had given him no small amount of pleasure to know she wasn't his father's mistress, she still refused to sleep with him under his father's roof. She was nothing if not principled, but it was enough to drive a man to rent a hotel room.

Judd flicked back through the report again. Something didn't make sense. Ah, there it was, it was missing a page. It wasn't like Anna to make a mistake like this. Maybe frustration was eating her up inside, too. And maybe he could persuade her that a hotel room at lunchtime was a good idea.

With a smile on his face, he went through to Anna's office. He cursed softly under his breath—it looked like he'd just missed her. Through her office window he caught a glimpse of a flash of red as her car headed out the office car park and down toward The Strand. He'd have to find the page of the report in her computer himself.

He reached for her mouse and brought her flying-asteroid-ridden screen back to life. Uncharacteristically, she'd left her email account open. Judd went to minimize the window but his sister's name caught his eye. What on earth?

He double clicked on the email and read its contents before flicking to the sent-items folder and seeing what Anna had said in return. Without stopping to get the page he needed from the report, he went and grabbed his car keys before heading out the office. They'd suspected Nicole of following up on her earlier contacts in the Nelson wineries debacle, but what if it had been something else entirely? What if it had been Anna who'd fed his sister the information she'd needed to usurp Wilson Wines all along?

A part of him didn't want to believe it could be true. She was doggedly loyal to Charles—but she'd been vociferous in her support of Nicole, too. Wasn't that what she'd been trying to do the night he'd seen her leaving Charles's rooms? Attempting to defend his sister? A sister she was closer to than he probably ever would be, he acknowledged with an unexpected pang of regret. He had to see for himself what they were up to.

The drive to Mission Bay didn't take long and Judd luckily had no trouble finding a parking spot in the first car park area at the city end of the beach. As he strolled toward the old stone building that housed the restaurant mentioned in Nicole's email, he saw Anna's car also parked nearby. He could just wait here in the sunshine, he thought, and ask her when she returned to her car, but a piece of him wanted to watch the two women together.

He stepped inside the restaurant, his eyes taking a moment to adjust to the darker interior from the autumn sunshine outside. He spied Nicole and Anna immediately in the corner near the back of the restaurant and allowed the maître d' to guide him to a table not in their immediate line of sight but from where he could still observe the two women.

"I ordered for us already," Nicole said, as Anna settled in the chair opposite.

"Thank you, I think."

"Oh, Anna, don't look at me like that, please."

"Like what?"

"Like you don't know whether I'm going to hit you or hug you."

"Well, you weren't exactly happy with me the last time we talked to each other," Anna said with a weak smile.

Nicole smiled back, reaching across the table to squeeze her hand. Anna began to relax. There was the friend she'd known and loved since she was five years old. Somehow they'd sort everything out, it would all be okay. The waiter arrived with chicken Caesar salads for them both, and after he'd gone, Anna gave her friend a good hard look.

"How are you, really?" Anna asked.

Nicole was a little thinner than before, and her face was taut with tension.

"I'm doing okay. Things are…complicated right now."

"You're telling me. Why on earth did you go to work for Nate Hunter? Your father is beside himself."

"Pissed him off, huh?" Nicole said, with her characteristic cheek, before a look of regret shadowed her expressive eyes.

"That's one way of putting it."

"How is he? Someone told me they'd seen him the other day but that he wasn't looking so good. It made me worry about him and it's not like I can just pick up the phone and call him to ask how he is."

"He's doing okay. This whole upset has slowed him down a bit, but—and I'm sure you probably don't want to hear this—Judd is picking up the reins pretty capably."

"Figures. The golden child. Even though I was always there, and he wasn't, I could never measure up to him, you know." Nicole's mouth twisted into a bitter line.

"Your father loves you, Nicole."

"I know, but it's not the same. I could never fill the hole that Judd left, and now he's back."

Anna's heart twisted. She was sure that that wasn't the case. Charles loved both of his children—he'd just gotten in such a habit of being strict with Nicole that he didn't know how to show it. Still, she knew how much it had to hurt to see

Charles lavish the affection on Judd that Nicole had always craved for herself.

"So you won't be coming back to us anytime soon?"

Nicole gave her a haunted look and shook her head. "I…I can't."

"What do you mean, you can't? Of course you can. Your home is with us, your career was with us. Come back, please?"

"No, it's not that simple. Not anymore."

"Why? What is it?"

Nicole shook her head again. "I can't talk about it just now. Maybe later, who knows? I just wanted to see you again and to say sorry for the horrible things I said before. I was upset and I needed someone to blame. Unfortunately, you were it."

"So are we all good now?"

"Yeah, we are. I've missed you so much."

"I've missed you, too."

They finished the rest of their lunch while discussing anything and everything other than work, or men. For some reason Nicole was cagey about the questions Anna started to ask her about Nate Hunter, and Anna certainly wasn't prepared to talk about her feelings for Nicole's brother to her face. It was easier to skirt over those issues and just skim the basics. By the time she had to head back to work, Anna felt so much better for having been able to spend some time with Nicole.

"I'm glad you emailed me," Anna said, standing and giving her friend a hug as their lunch together drew to an end.

"I'm glad you're still talking to me. I don't deserve you, you know."

"Of course you do, and more," Anna replied. "I'll settle the bill, okay? Next time will be your turn."

"Are you sure?"

"That there'll be a next time? Of course there will."

"Not that, silly." Nicole laughed.

Anna felt a sense of relief that she'd finally brought a smile to her friend's face, a smile that, however briefly, dispelled the tension that had been there. She watched Nicole head out the restaurant before she went to the cashier to settle their account. To her surprise, it had already been paid.

"There must be some mistake," she said.

"No, there's no mistake," said an all too familiar voice from behind her. "I figured it was worth the price of lunch to find out what you were up to."

Judd caught her elbow in a firm hold and guided her out the door toward the car park.

"What are you doing here?" she asked, hating the panic in her voice.

"More to the point, what are you doing here?"

"Nicole asked to see me for lunch, that's all."

"All? Seems kind of interesting that the week we lose a considerable amount of business to Jackson Importers you should meet her for lunch. Are you sure you weren't discussing anything else, like the Californian wineries on our list, for example?"

"Of course not! I wouldn't dream of doing anything of the sort." Indignation fueled her to add, "I don't know where you managed to form this incredibly low opinion of me, and I really don't care, but don't keep bringing your insinuations to my face. They are, without exception, wrong."

"So why were you together?"

"We're friends. We've been friends for most of our lives. Did we need a reason?"

"I understood that your friendship was pretty much severed over me."

"Don't rate your effect on people so highly. As I said, we've known each other a very long time. It would take far more than someone like you to destroy that. Look, if you feel that strongly that you can't believe me, why don't you just fire me? In fact, forget that. I quit. I can't work for someone who doesn't even begin to know the meaning of the word *trust*."

Anna pulled her arm free of his hand and headed for her car. She was shaking with anger to think that he could even begin to imagine that she'd do anything to deliberately sabotage Wilson Wines. It would be like slitting her throat, both professionally and personally.

She heard his footfall behind her and she dug in her handbag for her car keys, desperate to get away from him. She wouldn't let him know how much his words today had hurt, just like she hadn't shown him how his belief that she and Charles had been lovers had also cut her.

"Anna, wait!" he called.

But she didn't want to wait. She wanted distance and she wanted it now, before he saw the sheen of tears that now glazed her eyes. Damn it, where were those keys? Long, warm fingers closed over her hand as she finally extracted her keys from the depths of her bag and her finger depressed the remote to unlock her car.

"Anna, stop. I'm sorry. I jumped to conclusions."

"You're pretty good at that, aren't you?" she said bitterly, blinking back the moisture that stung her eyes.

"What can I say, I have a suspicious mind." He smiled back at her, and despite herself she was charmed by his self-deprecating tone. And that was more than half the problem, she acknowledged. He could get under her defenses with no more than a smile.

"I need to get back to the office. Please let me go."

She stared pointedly at his hand, which still captured hers within its warmth.

"Not yet. I want to apologize to you properly. I've been an idiot and I've treated you very unfairly. In my defense I can only say that it started back in Adelaide."

"But surely you can understand why I didn't tell you the truth about why I was there right from the start? For all I knew, you would have just shipped me off the property—which is what you pretty much did anyway after you read the letter."

"I can understand now. And like I said, I am sorry for allowing myself to let that color my judgment about you."

"Fine, I accept your apology. Now let me go."

"Ah, Anna, in such a hurry to leave me?"

He stepped a little closer and Anna felt that all-too familiar thrum of awareness course through her veins. He was like a drug to her, and she was rapidly losing, becoming addicted. She'd let herself become dependent on his kisses, his touch, everything.

"Don't, please."

She dropped her handbag and put up her hand, but he didn't stop moving, not even when her hand became trapped between the wall of his chest and her breasts. He was so close she could see the silver striations that feathered his irises and lent his eyes their particular vivid blue hue. Her heart quickened as she watched his pupils dilate.

"Don't what?" he asked, his voice soft, enticing.

"Don't kiss me."

"Afraid of me, Anna?"

"No," she admitted. "I'm afraid of me."

"I'll keep you safe," he said.

His kiss was short and incredibly sweet. The seal of a promise that offered so very much—perhaps even a chance of a future together that was no longer threatened by the shadows of his family's past. She was trembling when he released her, her entire body screaming for more than just that brief embrace.

Judd bent to collect her bag and handed it to her, then opened her car door, holding it for her as she slid into the driver's seat.

"Will you be okay to get back to the office?"

"Sure," she said, willing her body back under her control.

"I'll see you there."

"Judd? How did you know where to find me?"

He gave a small frown before answering. "There was a page missing from the report you gave me. I went to your computer to reprint it and you'd left your email open."

So for all his apparent mistrust of her, he hadn't been actively snooping. And, he'd *listened* to her—really listened. The thought gave her another little thrill of hope. Anna nodded and pulled her door closed before starting the engine and backing out of the car space. Judd stood to one side, watching her leave. She gave him a small wave and drove out of the car park.

Judd went straight into Anna's office when he arrived back at Wilson Wines.

"About your resignation," he started, closing her office door behind him.

Anna looked up, surprise on her face. "My resignation?"

"Yeah, back at the restaurant. You quit, remember?"

"Ah, yes, so I did."

"Just for the record, I don't accept it."

"For the record," she repeated, a tiny smile on her face, before slowly nodding. "Okay. So we're all good now—I can get back to work?"

"No."

"No? What's wrong?"

"I miss you," he answered simply.

"Miss me? But we see each other every day," she protested.

"Is that enough for you? Really? Tell me, Anna, how are you sleeping at night, knowing I'm just down the hall from you—wanting you as much as you probably want me?"

He watched the muscles in her throat work as she swallowed.

"What? Lost for words?" He moved across the office and

sat in the chair opposite her desk. "Seems to me that we have a pretty good thing between us. Wouldn't you agree?"

"Physically, yes," she finally concurred, although he could see how reluctant she was to admit even that.

"Don't you think we should let that play out? Keep exploring it to its fullest potential?"

To his surprise, sadness seemed to cloud her eyes. Her voice, when she spoke, was flat. "No, I don't. Tell me, Judd, how do you define *potential?*"

Her words surprised him. "Define it? Are you kidding me? You mean you have this level of physical synchronicity with every man you sleep with?"

"And there we have it," Anna said, throwing her hands in the air. "Just how many men do you think I've slept with?"

"Does it matter?"

"No, it doesn't matter, but you continually imply I have loose morals. First you accuse me of sleeping with your father, then you jump to the ridiculous conclusion that I was sharing company information with Nicole." She shook her head emphatically. "There's no way I can even begin to contemplate any kind of relationship with you when you don't trust me at all—over anything!"

"You're right," he admitted, deciding to take another tack on this argument.

He had assumed the worst about her all the way. In the beginning that had partly been her own fault, but he was man enough to admit it had been far easier to remain guarded around her than it was to examine just how much he wanted her, or why. He'd hoped that, as with all his conquests, he'd enjoy the ride while it lasted. After all, he didn't plan to stay in New Zealand forever.

The moment he thought that, though, everything in his mind rebelled. For some reason this had stopped being a temporary fling. He'd gone at this whole exercise looking upon everything as being temporary—expendable even. But somewhere along the line things had changed, and that change started with Anna.

Her voice pulled his attention back. "Of course I'm right. So you'll agree that we should forget about there being any kind of relationship between us, except for at work."

"I can't do that, Anna."

"I beg your pardon?"

"I can't do that. What I can do, if you'll let me, is learn to trust you. To get to know you better and to show you that I'm worth you giving me that chance. Will you at least try with me?"

He watched as her emotions played across her face.

"You want me to try to let *you* trust *me?* You hurt me, Judd—both on a professional level and on a personal one. After we made love down in Nelson and here, in your office—" Her voice hitched and she paused and swallowed before continuing. "Did you honestly think I was so promiscuous as to go from one man's bed to another, and back again?"

"Since we're being honest, I have to admit that it made me furious to think that you could do that."

"But I'm not like that!" Her voice rose in obvious frustration.

"I know that, Anna. I'm learning all the time."

"Fine. Okay, I will try with you. But on one condition."

"What's that?" he asked, knowing the answer before she even verbalized it and hating that, in this at least, he could read her so well.

"I'm not sleeping with you. Not straightaway. We can get to know each other the way normal couples do."

"We've missed a few steps, that's true."

"And I want your word of honor that you won't try to persuade me otherwise. I'm helpless against you. There, I admit it. Show me that I can trust *you.* Don't use that knowledge against me."

Every particle in his body rebelled against the idea, but he found himself nodding in agreement.

"Agreed," he managed, even though his jaw felt tight and his throat barely allowed the single word past it. "A date tonight, then. That'd be a good start. I'll meet you downstairs in the lobby at the house at seven."

What the lady wanted, the lady was definitely going to get. And while it would be a living torment every second until she capitulated to him, he knew that very soon, she'd be his again. And once she was, no matter what his plans for Charles Wilson, he knew she'd stay by *his* side.

Eleven

Anna waited in the lobby at the house and paced the black-and-white-tiled entrance nervously. This was going to be their third date in the three days since last Thursday, when they'd agreed to take things slowly and learn to get to know one another. So far it had been an exercise in pure torture. Judd had been nothing but a complete gentleman. It was driving her crazy.

Today he'd apparently planned a picnic and told her to dress accordingly. Without any idea of what one wore to a picnic these days, she'd opted for a pair of flat navy leather shoes with a peep toe and clear-colored beads embroidered on top, and teamed them up with a pair of three-quarter-length jeans with the cuffs rolled up and a fine-knit pale pink sweater.

Charles came through the lobby.

"Heading out again?" he asked.

"A picnic today, apparently."

He chuckled. "Have to hand it to the boy. He's not only

picked up the business quickly but he hasn't wasted time with you, either. I knew sending you to get him would be a good idea."

A frisson of discomfort spread through her at his words. Had he meant all along for her and Judd to become close? She didn't like the sensation of being manipulated, not even by Charles, who had probably had the greater hand in guiding her life than anyone she knew—even herself. Before she could respond, Judd came down the stairs.

Dressed in jeans and a silver-gray long-sleeved turtleneck, he looked good enough to eat. Anna blinked and turned her head away. She shouldn't be thinking about him along those lines. He'd adhered to her dictates about their dating to the letter. It was contrary of her to wish now that he hadn't.

"All ready, that's good."

Judd flung her a smile that lent his eyes a wicked gleam. He was up to something, she just knew it. Every cell in her body responded to him as he drew closer and put an arm around her shoulders.

"We'll probably be out for most of the day. Will you be okay?" he asked his father.

"Sure, I'm fine. There's always someone around here if I need something." Charles waved his inquiry away.

Anna looked at the older man sharply. His color wasn't good today and there was an air of frailty about him that sent a ripple of concern through her.

"Are you feeling all right today?" she asked. "We can postpone our outing, it's no bother."

"Anna, I've said it before and I'll say it again. Stop your fussing. I'm big enough and old enough to look after myself. Now off you go and have a great day. Don't you worry about me."

"You heard the man," Judd said, steering her toward the front doors. "Besides," he reminded her when they were out of Charles's earshot, "the household staff has our cell numbers. I've already talked to them about calling me if he seems like he needs help."

"So you agree with me, then. He's not looking so good this week, is he?"

"I've noticed. At the beginning of the week I tried to talk to him about cutting his hours down, but he's nothing if not stubborn."

"A family trait, no doubt," Anna commented.

Judd's lips quirked in response. "No doubt," he agreed.

They went out the front doors of the house and down the stairs to the driveway. Anna looked around but there was no sign of a car.

"Are we walking? Maybe I should change my shoes."

"No, don't change a thing. You're perfect as you are. We need to go to the tennis courts."

"Tennis? Then I definitely need to change my shoes."

"No, we won't be playing tennis," Judd answered.

Totally puzzled, Anna walked alongside him. As she did, she became aware of the air-beating sound of rotors coming toward them. A helicopter? Sure enough, a sleek black chopper was coming toward them, stirring up the air and the early-falling leaves as it lowered onto the tennis courts at the end of the property.

Anna turned and looked at Judd. "You said we were going for a picnic."

"And we are. Just not locally."

He shepherded her to the helicopter and opened the rear door, handing her up into one of the seats and passing a headset to her before following her up and settling in next to her. Anna felt her stomach lurch as the chopper slowly lifted off and circled the property before heading out toward the harbor.

"Did I mention that I don't like small aircraft to you?" she asked, her knuckles white as she gripped the edges of her seat.

Judd's hand pried one of hers free from its hold. "I remember, but I was hoping that perhaps I could distract you on this trip."

He lifted her hand to his mouth and kissed her palm. The instant his lips touched her she felt the familiar tug of desire swell through her body. Oh, yes, he could distract her that way, all right. She hazarded a look out the window as Judd stroked the soft inner skin of her wrist, then dragged her eyes back to him again. His clear gaze met hers.

"Trust me, Anna. I won't let anything hurt you."

She nodded and swallowed, his voice soft and gentle as it filled her ears from within the cups of her headphones. He kept up a steady stream of soothing words, and she'd lost track of how long they'd been in the air when the helicopter began to descend and her stomach lurched again. Judd's fingers closed around hers reassuringly.

"You're doing great," he said. "Anyone would think you're an old hand at this."

"I doubt that, but thanks," she managed, feeling a surge of relief as the skids touched down on terra firma. Judd opened his door and hopped down before turning to help Anna out.

"Keep your head and arms down," he warned.

No problem, she thought as the wind whipped her hair around her face. She ducked down and let Judd lead her toward a glass-fronted building not far from where they'd landed. Behind them, the helicopter took off and wheeled away back over the water.

"He is coming back for us, right?" she asked.

Judd laughed, the sound curling around her heart and squeezing it tight. She felt a momentary panic. When did he start meaning so much to her?

"Of course, all in good time."

"Where are we?" Anna asked, looking around her. As far as she could tell, the dwelling ahead of them was the only one to be seen and there were no boats moored at the small bay in front of them.

"Near Kawau Island. I heard about this place and thought we'd enjoy the solitude. Come on, let's go and see what's on the menu."

Anna followed him up to the building and inside, where a spacious lounge/dining area flowed into a well-equipped kitchen. As Anna walked around to get the lay of the land, a small but luxurious bathroom with floor-length clear-glass windows facing back into native bush behind the building surprised her, while another room, a bedroom, saw her closing the door on it quickly. She didn't want to think about that. Not when they were just starting to get to know one another.

In the kitchen, Judd had removed a bottle of chilled champagne from the refrigerator as well as a platter of antipasto.

"Let's take this outside," he suggested. "Grab the glasses, will you?"

Anna reached for a pair of champagne flutes from a shelf over the kitchen sink and followed Judd out onto the wide deck that faced the bay.

"This is beautiful," she said, sitting down next to Judd on the simple wooden steps that led down off the deck and onto a well-kept lawn. "It's like a world within a world."

Judd reached up and smoothed a strand of hair from her cheeks. "It's a great place to get to know one another better, without everything else intruding."

He deftly dealt with the foil and the cage on the bottle before pouring them each a foaming glass of the golden sparkling liquid.

"Mmm, French," Anna commented, sighting the label and then taking a sip. "Oh, yes, there's nothing quite like it."

Judd didn't comment, and her eyes flew to his in the silence that stretched out between them. He was watching her, his gaze intent, the pupils dilated, his lips parted as if he'd been about to say something but the words had fled before they could be uttered. He blinked, breaking the spell that had locked them together all too briefly, and lifted his glass to his lips.

"I agree," he said, putting his glass down and reaching for a stuffed olive on the platter. "The French definitely have a knack for it."

They fell silent for a while, enjoying the wine, the food, the setting, but then Anna turned to Judd to ask, "Do you remember much of your time with your father, before you went to Australia?"

He sighed and for a moment she wondered if she'd trod on some very sensitive memories.

"I remember quite a bit. I was six when we left. I remember him always being larger than life. Always busy, always entertaining, always booming with noise. I couldn't wait for the moment he stepped in the door at the end of a day, and when he was away on business I'd mark every day off on the calendar until he returned. Despite the fact he was constantly busy with work and clients, he always made time for me."

"It must have been hard when you left."

"Hard?" He laughed but the sound held no joy to it. "I was devastated. My mother was angry and hurt, and no one in Australia had a good word to say about him. It was like my life had turned upside down overnight. I had quite a few issues with his abandonment of me—of both of us."

"No wonder you weren't keen to reestablish a relationship with him."

"No, I wasn't. Despite the fact that I know there are two sides to every story, I find it very hard to understand, or forgive, the way he just cut me from his life like that."

Judd's dark brows drew together, lending a fierce cast to his features.

"But he's reached out to you now. You're here, you're working with him. You must have forgiven him."

The expression on Judd's face cleared. "Yes, I am working with him now."

There was something in the tone of his voice that struck a chord of concern deep inside. It occurred to her that he hadn't agreed that he had forgiven his father. Before she could say anything more, he flashed a smile at her and rose to his feet, putting out a hand.

"Come on, let's go for a wander along the shoreline."

Anna put her hand in his and pushed her worries aside. She was probably being oversensitive, a state she was becoming used to around Judd Wilson.

When they returned from the beach, they went inside to gather together the rest of the lunch fixings that had been left in the fridge for them. Judd poured them each another glass of champagne outside on the deck, while Anna made up plates of slices of fresh-baked ciabatta together with ripe wedges of Camembert and slivers of prosciutto. She added a few slices of sun-dried tomato from the leftover antipasto to the open sandwich she'd put together on her plate and lifted it to her mouth to take a bite.

"Oh, my, that's good," she said after she'd chewed and swallowed the mouthful.

"It looks delicious," Judd agreed. "Mind if I have a taste?"

"Sure," she said, offering him her sandwich.

He ignored the offering in her hand, instead leaning over their dishes, and licked the lower edge of her bottom lip. She saw a tiny piece of cheese on the tip of his tongue before he swallowed it.

"Oh, yes, just how I like it. Ripe and soft. Warm and ready to eat."

A heated flush spread through her, a flush that made every nerve ending stand on end. It had been her call to keep the physical side of their discovery of one another out of the equation. A call he'd respected to a degree that had slowly begun to drive her crazy. Crazy for him.

"Would you like some more?" she managed to say, not taking her eyes from his.

"Sure," he answered.

She picked up a small wedge of the cheese between a thumb and forefinger and held it up to his mouth. His lips closed around the morsel, his tongue abrading her fingers as he did so and sending a shudder of longing straight to the pit of her belly. A familiar tingling started low down in her body and spread out to her extremities.

"More?" she asked.

Instead of answering, he reached out to cup one hand behind her head and gently drew her to him.

"More of you," he said simply before his mouth took hers.

His lips were gentle, coaxing, and she felt herself melt into him. She heard the clatter of dishes as he swept them to one side before hooking his arm around her waist and sliding her closer to him. Suddenly she couldn't be close enough. Her arms lifted and hooked around his neck, her breasts pressed up against his chest—and still she wasn't close enough.

She pulled her lips away.

"Um, Judd? About that condition I made? About us not…"

"Uh-huh," he said, nuzzling her neck.

"I was reacting under duress. I—"

"Anna?"

"Mmm?"

"Shut up and kiss me again."

So she did. Judd lifted her up and guided her to straddle his lap, shoving his hands up under her top and across her back. His hands were hot against her skin and she wanted to feel more of him. She reached for the hem of his sweater, pulling it up and exposing his belly and chest before grazing her nails across his muscled torso. Beneath her fingertips she felt the disks of his nipples grow firm and rigid and she gently pushed him back down onto the wooden deck. As she did so, Judd eased the turtleneck off, leaving his upper body completely bare to her touch.

She bent down and placed a kiss in the hollow at the base

of his throat before tracing her tongue across his collarbone. Every now and then she paused to nip at his skin. He felt so fine, tasted so good, she wanted to savor every second she had with him at her mercy. Her fingers traced the muscles that corded his rib cage, feeling his skin react under her feather-fine touch, and she smiled against his skin as she traced ever-decreasing circles with her tongue around his nipples.

Her hands worked their way lower, slowly unbuckling his belt and unbuttoning his jeans before easing inside the now-constricted fabric. She rubbed one hand along the length of his powerful erection, back and forth through the fabric of his briefs, her lips slowly following the path of her hands until her breath warmed his skin at his waistband. She tugged at his jeans and he lifted his hips slightly, allowing her to slide the fabric down to his thighs and tug down the elasticized band of his briefs, exposing the tip of his arousal to her gaze. A tiny bead of moisture gathered at the swollen dark tip of him and she bent her head, tasting it with the very tip of her tongue.

Oh, yes, he tasted so very good. She closed her lips around him, rasping her tongue around his tender flesh again and again before she drew him deeper into her mouth. Judd's fingers pushed through her hair, cupping her head and holding her against him. Not so firmly that she couldn't withdraw if she wanted to, but encouraging her to continue her assault on that most sensitive and responsive part of him.

Anna curled the fingers of one hand around the base of his shaft and moved them firmly up, then down again, all the time taking him deeper into her mouth while stroking her tongue along him with ever-increasing pressure. She felt him begin to shake beneath her and increased the speed of her movements, one hand still stroking him, the other clutching at the bunched fabric of his jeans. A groan tore from his throat as he began to come, and she took it all with a sense of power that vied with her own arousal to see him so undone beneath her ministrations. She might be helpless in the face of her desire for him, but he was equally so for her, she realized, and the knowledge gave her a sense of control and power she'd never known before.

Spent, Judd relaxed back on the deck, his fingers still tangled in her hair as she slowly released him, first with her hand, then with her mouth. She slid up his body, peppering the surface with tiny kisses all the way, swirling her tongue inside the indent of his belly button—the action making his penis twitch in response against her.

She rolled to his side, letting the fingers of one hand stroke softly over his belly and chest as his breathing slowly returned to normal.

"When you change your mind, you really change your mind, don't you?" he said.

"I like to do things thoroughly, or not at all," she replied in kind.

"Then you won't object if we go inside, where we can *thoroughly* explore the aspects available to us?"

In reply, Anna rose to her feet and held out a hand to Judd's supine form. He took her hand and levered himself up, straightening his briefs and yanking his jeans up to his hips, but leaving them undone. She had never seen anything so sexy before as the man standing in front of her. His hair was mussed, his eyes still glowing with the residual pleasure she'd given him. And his body—he was muscled but not heavily, strong but not overpowering. And he was looking at her like she was the only woman in the world. He was everything she'd ever dreamed of, and more. Judd lifted up the champagne bottle and their glasses, and together they walked back into the cottage.

He hadn't been kidding about being thorough. By the time the helicopter returned for them, it was dark and Anna had never felt more sated on every level. Together they'd made love, eaten, bathed, made love and eaten again. If she could ever repeat a day in her life over and again, it would be this one and it was with this thought that Anna acknowledged the truth of her feelings. She was in love with Judd Wilson.

Twelve

Judd woke to a Monday morning heralded by rain and gusting winds. The flip side of autumn had arrived, and with it Anna had capitulated. Last night she'd come to him, breaking what she had insisted was her hard-and-fast rule about respecting Charles and refusing to sleep with Judd under his father's roof. Strangely, he hadn't felt the smug satisfaction he'd expected when he'd felt her slip naked in between the sheets of his bed.

Something had changed during the day while they'd been alone together. Something that made her body curving around his, within the expanse of his bed, the most natural thing in the world. Something he didn't want to deal with. Later would be soon enough, he decided, as he rolled out of the covers and padded on bare feet across the thick carpet toward his en suite bathroom.

By the time he'd completed his shower, Anna had left his bed, and when he got downstairs to the breakfast room she was already there, looking her usual serene and unruffled self and talking to Charles. No one would have dreamed she was such a vixen in bed.

"Good morning," he said with a smile.

To his delight, she blushed. "Good morning to you, too."

"Sleep well?"

He couldn't resist provoking her. He, better than anyone, knew how well she had slept in those tiny snatches when they were both so exhausted they finally left one another well alone.

"Thank you, I did," she replied before lifting her morning coffee to her lips.

Lips that had done wild things to him yesterday. He slammed the door on his wayward thoughts. There was a time and a place for everything. For now he needed to concentrate on Wilson Wines. He felt like he'd reached a crossroads in relation to the business. While he'd come here with the express intent of undermining everything his father had worked for, and delivering his share of the business on a platter to his father's strongest competitor, there was a part of him now that hesitated.

Growing Wilson Wines in a new direction excited him, but did he really want to throw away the revenge he'd longed for ever since he'd accepted his father would never come to get him? It was a difficult decision, and one he would have to face soon.

As an added factor, his mother had started to email him regularly, asking for updates on the house and pestering him to allow her to visit. Right now, Cynthia was the last complication he needed. Her bitterness toward Charles had only grown over the years, and the prospect of seeing the two of them under one roof again was enough to make the milk in his cereal curdle.

He shot a look across the table at Charles. The older man looked gray and tired. Judd had no doubt that following through on his initial plans would see his father into an early

grave and that thought clenched tight in his chest. Somewhere along the line, he'd developed respect for Charles and
particularly for his business acumen. He'd held it together
through stock market crashes, recession and more. Wilson
Wines, while not reaching its fullest potential, was still doing
extremely well in what had been a difficult and competitive
market.

Judd still bore a grudge over the way Charles had handled
his personal life, and the way he had treated his wife and son,
but he felt a little more sympathy now. He'd seen how deeply
angry and hurt Charles could be at what he perceived as disloyalty from someone he loved. Even though he'd jumped to
conclusions and judged unfairly, the suspicion that Cynthia
had been cheating on him must have hit him hard.

Additionally, the challenges for Charles of running a
company—by himself, since the split with his business partner had happened around then, hadn't it?—and dealing with
a marriage that had been falling apart must have taken its toll
on his behavior. And according to Anna, Charles was already
struggling with diabetes-related health issues then, which
couldn't have helped. None of that justified his actions, but
taking everything into account did help to put them in perspective.

He looked again at Charles, watched as he picked up his
knife to butter a slice of toast and saw the way his hand
trembled, then looked away as a sharp spear of concern shot
through him. He didn't want his father's further deterioration
to be on his hands.

A loud clatter of cutlery on a plate, followed by Anna's
gasp of shock, dragged his attention back to Charles, who
now leaned to one side in his chair, his color even worse than
before, his eyes closed and his breathing laboring in his chest.

"Quick," he said to Anna, "call an ambulance."

Anna raced out the room and Judd shot to his father's
side, loosening his tie and the top button of his shirt before

lowering Charles to the floor. Charles's skin was cool and clammy to the touch, and Judd felt a surge of genuine fear pour through him.

Charles slipped in and out of consciousness, oblivious to Judd's voice as he repeatedly fired questions at him in an effort to keep his father awake. By the time the ambulance arrived, Judd was beginning to worry that the older man wouldn't make it.

As Anna gave the paramedics a rundown of Charles's health and medications, he began to understand just how fragile his father's life was.

"I'll go with him in the ambulance," Judd said as Charles was lifted onto a gurney and carted out toward the waiting vehicle.

Anna nodded and squeezed his hand. "I'll see you at the hospital. I'll just need to make a few calls first. Let people know we won't be in to the office."

"Thanks."

Judd followed the medics out to the ambulance and was directed into a passenger seat in the front of the vehicle. The ride to Auckland City Hospital was short, although for Judd it felt as if it took hours. Craning his head to see in the back, he watched as the ambulance officer attended to his father and took stats, which he then radioed ahead to the hospital emergency room. Seeing Charles so helpless made the seriousness of his father's state really hit home.

At the hospital there was a blur of activity, and Judd was forced to wait as a medical team took over his father's assessment and treatment. Finally Anna arrived, her face pale and concerned but lightening a little when she saw him. The instant they made eye contact, Judd began to feel some of the tension within him unwind just a notch and he took Anna into his arms, relishing the feel of her and soaking up the comfort her embrace provided.

"How's he doing?" Anna said as she pulled away.

"They're still doing tests."

A sudden flurry of activity at the emergency room door dragged his attention in that direction and he saw his sister striding through the door.

"Where is he? I want to see him."

Anna interceded before he could speak.

"He's with the doctors. They're still assessing him."

"What happened?" Nicole demanded, turning to Judd, her eyes snapping fire.

"He collapsed at breakfast," Judd replied.

"I thought your being here was supposed to make him feel better, not worse," Nicole fired back before promptly bursting into tears.

Judd bit back the response that flew to his tongue, that perhaps if his sister hadn't left the way she did, Charles wouldn't have been pushing himself so hard with work when he should have been taking things easier. But he could see Nicole was fighting her own demons.

A nurse came toward them. "Mr. Wilson, you can see your father now."

Judd reached for Anna, who shook her head. "No, take Nicole. She needs to be with him more than I do."

With a shrug, Judd turned to Nicole. "Are you coming?"

"Of course I'm coming. He's *my* father."

Together they followed the nurse. Charles was conscious but still looked terribly ill. Lines ran into his arms and monitors were beeping around him.

"What's she doing here?" he rasped, staring at Nicole with a mixture of surprise and anger.

Judd felt his sister stiffen at his side.

"I came to see if you were all right, but obviously you're just fine. You won't be needing me here," she said with a quiet dignity that didn't quite mask the hurt in her eyes.

Judd watched her walk back the way she'd come. Anna

went to intercept her but was brushed away as Nicole kept walking straight toward the exit.

"Was that really necessary?" Judd asked his father, going to stand next to his bed.

"She betrayed us. She made the decision to leave us—that means that this isn't her place any longer, here with us. You'd do well to remember that, my boy." The strain of forcing the words he'd had to say took its toll, and Charles's eyes slid closed again.

A bitter taste flooded Judd's mouth. Betrayed, yes, like his father had betrayed the love and trust of his only son by sending him away—banishing him with his mother to another country. Judd couldn't believe that only an hour ago, he'd been halfway convinced he should forgive his father's actions. The man didn't deserve Judd's compassion, or his forgiveness. Look at how he'd just treated his daughter—banishing her with the same ease he'd banished Judd and his mother so long ago. The concern he'd felt for his father diminished as it was replaced by the old familiar anger, and with it, his resolve to continue on his original course hardened.

Anna straightened up the last of the paperwork she'd been collating and put it in her briefcase, ready to bring home and discuss with Judd this evening. She and Judd took turns at the hospital during the allocated visiting times—today was his turn while she covered at the office.

Charles had slipped into a coma after his admission and things had been touch-and-go over the past five days. If he recovered, it was clear that dialysis would be a regular part of his life from here on in. There was no word yet on when he would be allowed back home, but Anna had already made inquiries with private nursing bureaus to ensure he had the care he would need when, God willing, that eventually happened.

While Judd went through the motions of visiting with his father, Anna was certain there was a new distance now between son and father. Something had happened on the day Charles was admitted to hospital, which had created an intangible wall between them. Judd wouldn't be drawn on the subject and Nicole had also retreated back behind her curtain of silence. Well, there was nothing for it but to be there if they needed her, Anna had decided and, as far as Judd was concerned, being where she was needed meant that she was in his bed at night and by his side during the day.

Rain swiped at her windscreen as she drove home. It was already dark and she was bone weary as she pulled her car into the multicar garage at the back of the house. What she needed most right now was a long, relaxing soak in the bath, followed by dinner and maybe a good movie. She wondered if Judd would be up for that, too. A bath together would be just the distraction they both deserved after the past working week. She already could feel herself relaxing by increments as she imagined it.

Anna felt the difference in the house the moment she set foot inside. It wasn't anything she could immediately put her finger on, but something had changed and it was more than the fact that the hall flowers were arranged on the left-hand side of the hall table, rather than the middle where they normally stood.

She made her way to the front of the house and the main stairs but her feet arrested on the tiled surface of the lobby as a vaguely familiar voice greeted her from halfway up the stairs.

"I should have known you'd be living here," Cynthia drawled with an expression of distaste on her elegant features.

"Cynthia? I didn't know you were coming," Anna managed through lips that felt stiff with shock.

"I'm sure Judd doesn't find it necessary to tell you *everything,* my dear," Cynthia replied as she continued down the stairs and came to a halt one step up from the bottom—a position that continued to force Anna to look up at her.

"I trust Mrs. Evans has made you comfortable."

"Mrs. Evans? Oh, yes, that housekeeper. She'll have to go when I'm back here permanently, you know. No idea of etiquette whatsoever."

"What do you mean, when you're here permanently?"

"When my ex-husband dies, of course. I came as soon as I heard he was ill. So sad for you all, but only to be expected."

"Charles is improving every day. I don't know where you got the idea that he's dying," Anna replied staunchly. "And I'm not that certain he would like you under his roof."

"I think you're forgetting a vitally important point," Cynthia said with a smile that was as cold as the expression in her eyes.

"And what would that be?" Anna asked, feeling the hairs on the back of her neck rise in response to the woman's attitude.

"That this is Judd's house now and, very soon, he'll be giving it to me."

With that, Cynthia swept past Anna in the direction of the salon. All thoughts of a relaxing bath now banished from her mind, Anna went upstairs to her room to change and try and clear her head. Of course the house was now Judd's. How could she have forgotten that? Had he planned to install his mother back in here all along? And what of Charles? What would happen to him when he was well enough to come out of the hospital?

She rushed through a shower and changed into a more comfortable pair of wide-legged black trousers and a long-sleeved tunic top, also in black but chased with silver threads that broke the starkness of the garment. Once she was dressed and had reapplied her makeup, she felt better able to cope with the perfectly coiffed woman who was downstairs. During her shower she'd all but talked herself into believing that Cynthia was sadly mistaken and that Judd transferring the property into her name was a possibility so remote it was laughable.

But a tightening low down in her gut told her it was entirely possible. The doubts that she'd had for the past few days surged up to remind her of what Judd had told her about his mother's obsession with Masters' Rise.

Anna drew in a deep breath and tried to summon the courage she knew she'd need to face Cynthia downstairs. No, it was no good. No amount of breathing would make her feel right about this. She'd just have to haul on her big-girl panties and get it over with. She descended the stairs with a knot in her stomach the size of a boulder, and headed for the salon. Inside, Cynthia sat upon one of the love seats, a glass of wine in her hand and a disapproving look upon her face.

"I'll need to do quite a bit of upgrading," she commented. "Charles has really let this place slide."

Anna felt her back stiffen in response. Not only had Charles done everything *but* let the place slide, Anna's mother had enjoyed a free hand in redecorating and refurbishing as and when required.

"It's a home," Anna answered carefully. "Charles felt it was important that we be comfortable."

"Well, you've certainly been comfortable here, haven't you? I imagine it was quite the come up in ranks from where you and your mother used to live. Tell me, how is dear Donna these days?"

"My mother passed away several years ago," Anna responded uncomfortably. She'd bet Cynthia never called Donna Garrick "dear" anything to her face the whole time she'd known her.

"I am sorry to hear that." Cynthia took a sip of her wine before continuing, "And yet, you're still here. Why is that?"

"Charles said it was to be my home for as long as I wanted."

"But it's no longer his place to offer you that roof over your head." Cynthia shook her head, an expression of sympathy on her face that looked as false as the tone of her voice. "I'd suggest you begin looking elsewhere for your accommodation, although I doubt you'll be as lucky as to find anyone as…*accommodating* as Charles."

"I really don't think it's quite your place to suggest where I should be living," Anna snapped back, suddenly angry where before she'd only felt apprehension. "Judd wouldn't dream of putting me out from under his roof."

"Ah, so the kitten has claws. How charming." Cynthia laughed—the sound grating along Anna's last nerve. "Although you may not feel quite so inclined to leap to Judd's defense when you understand what Judd's plan was all along. Ask yourself, with everything he has in Adelaide, why else would he have come back if not for some well-aimed revenge? It's not as if Charles was ever a father to him.

"You look shocked. Poor dear, I suppose Judd has taken you to his bed and now you've gone and fallen in love with him." Cynthia shook her head and tsked softly. "He's only using you, you know. Despite everything, Judd's a lot like Charles. He won't marry you. Do you really think you're worthy of a place like this when your mother never was? Like father like son, like mother like daughter. My son will ask you to leave soon enough. Wouldn't you rather save face and go before that happens?"

Anna reeled under the onslaught of Cynthia's words. "Judd wouldn't do that," she said woodenly.

Or would he? Her fingers curled in her palms, her nails biting into the skin—the pain an offset to the pain that now squeezed her heart tight. She really didn't know Judd Wilson beyond what he'd presented to her. She knew he was determined and had an edge of ruthlessness lingering beneath the surface at all times. Could Cynthia's words be the truth? She didn't want to believe it. She loved him. He wasn't that kind of man.

Anna felt an arctic chill shiver through her body. Despite her instinct to protest Cynthia's words, they held all too much of a ring of truth about them. The older woman had given voice to Anna's greatest fear—that she would never have the wholehearted love of the man she loved in return.

Thirteen

Judd was exhausted as he got out of his car and climbed the front steps into the house. Funny how it had so rapidly begun to feel like home, he realized, when before it had always been nothing more than something to be acquired and used. Perhaps it was the thought of the woman waiting inside for him. He knew Anna had already left the office and would be waiting for his report on Charles's condition.

He felt like a hypocrite attending the old man at the hospital, but today hadn't been a good one for his father, with his health deteriorating further. Even unconscious, Charles didn't make a good patient. In fact, Judd suspected the word "patient" was totally lacking in his vocabulary. Still, he'd seemed more settled when Judd had left him.

It had been a tough day all around, really. He'd battled with his decision to go ahead and test the waters with Nate Hunter but, in the face of Charles's treatment of Nicole at the hospital, eventually he'd decided to go ahead. He'd spent the better part of the morning trying to set up a meeting with

Hunter, but the man was as elusive as quicksilver. Judd hadn't wanted to leave a message with Nate's staff—all too aware that Nicole could easily intercept it and somehow block him reaching the other man altogether. Maybe tomorrow would see success.

Judd considered the paperwork inside his briefcase. He hadn't dared to leave it in the office in case Anna saw it before he'd completed his plans. Everything had to be lined up just so for all this to work. She wouldn't be happy, and he hoped their burgeoning relationship would weather the fallout once it all went ahead. Her place was with him now; surely she'd see he had no other choice.

He waited for the sense of satisfaction that usually infused him when he thought of his plans coming to fruition, but instead he felt oddly flat. Must just be tired, he rationalized. Between nights with Anna, demanding days in the office and even more demanding time at the hospital, he was definitely not operating at his peak.

As he entered the front lobby he could hear women's voices from the salon. He dropped his briefcase near a hall table and walked through, gritting his teeth as he tried to force a welcoming smile onto his face. The last thing he felt up to right now was company, but appearances had to be maintained.

He could barely believe his eyes as he pushed open the salon door.

"Mother?"

Cynthia rose from her seat and put out her arms to her son. Automatically, Judd crossed the room and allowed his mother to embrace him.

"My boy, I've missed you."

"Why are you here?"

Cynthia pouted. "What? Didn't you miss me, too?"

"Of course," Judd said, brushing her words aside.

She was the last person he wanted to deal with right now.

His plans for Wilson Wines needed to be carefully executed and he didn't need the distraction of worrying if his mother was about to preempt his weeks of carefully layered construction—or *de*construction as the case would be.

He cast a look in Anna's direction. She was pale and sitting with her spine rigid. Her hazel eyes were clouded with an emotion he couldn't quite put his finger on. His protective instincts rose to the surface—surprising him with their intensity. Anna had been fine when he'd spoken to her at the office before he'd headed off to the hospital, which meant that whatever had upset her had happened between then and now. That only left one person who was likely to be the cause, which begged the question, what had Cynthia done to upset Anna?

"Everything okay at the office?" he asked.

"Of course," Anna replied. "I have some papers in my case for you when you have a moment."

"Surely you two can leave work alone for one evening. I've just arrived and I want to hear everything about what you've been up to while you've been gone," Cynthia interjected.

"Let me leave you two to it," Anna said, rising coolly from her seat. "I have plenty to attend to while you catch up."

"You don't need to go," Judd said, wondering why Anna seemed so keen to create some distance between them.

"Let her," his mother said, her long fingers tightening around his forearm. "It'll be lovely to be just the two of us over dinner, don't you think?"

He didn't think anything of the kind. Something was terribly wrong and he had no idea what it was.

"I'll speak to you later, then. If you're sure you won't join us?"

A crooked smile twisted Anna's lips. "Oh, I'm sure. You two enjoy catching up. I'll leave the papers in your room."

He watched with narrowed eyes as Anna left the room, closing the salon door with silent precision. Something was very wrong and the minute she'd gone he felt the exhaustion of earlier tug at him again.

"I wish you'd told me you were coming to visit," Judd said to his mother as they assumed their seats.

"I was hoping to surprise you."

Judd felt a flare of anger burst inside. Surprise him? She had to be kidding. When everything hung so carefully in the balance it was the last thing he needed.

"You certainly succeeded at that," he said ruefully. "How long are you planning to stay?"

"A week, maybe," Cynthia replied. "Longer, if necessary."

"Longer?" The word slipped out before he could prevent it. He was more tired than he thought.

"What's the matter, Judd? You know what we planned."

"Yes, and I also know you were supposed to wait until I told you to come over."

"But I heard that your father was gravely ill—not from you, I might add."

"He's ill, Mother, not dead."

"Well, either way," Cynthia said airily, her hands fluttering in the air, "if you want him to be aware of your revenge, then you're running out of time. You've got to get to work on taking it all over and doing with it what you want to—which is to give the house to me, right?"

That was what they'd planned, but Judd felt himself reluctant to commit to agreeing with her. The whole time he'd grown up at The Masters' he'd always felt as though he didn't fully belong. Strangely enough, he felt as if he fitted here.

He redirected his mother's conversation to the family back at The Masters' as they went through to dinner, but all the while he was acutely conscious of Anna's empty chair at the table. When he was finished with his meal he excused himself, citing business he urgently needed to attend to, and he went back to the lobby to retrieve his briefcase.

He was surprised to see a stack of suitcases by the front

door. They hadn't been there when he'd arrived home, and they couldn't be his mother's. She would have complained long and hard if the airline had lost her luggage, however temporarily. A sound on the staircase behind him made him turn to see Anna, an overnight bag in one hand and her handbag slung over one shoulder.

"What's this?" he demanded, his hand flung out toward the cases at his feet.

Outside, he heard a car pull up on the driveway and give a toot.

"My stuff. I'm moving out. That'll be Mr. Evans with my car." She stepped past him to open the front door and hefted one of her cases onto the front porch. "Thanks for bringing my car around. I hope we can fit everything in," she said to the handyman as he came up the stairs to get her cases.

"What do you mean, you're moving out?"

"Just that." She turned to Evans and gestured to the rest of her things in the lobby. "All of these, too, please."

"Hold on a minute. Where are you going and, more important, why?"

Anna shook her head. "I think you know why. Tell me, did you really come back to wreak revenge on your father? Did you mean to give this house to your mother all along?"

He stood in silence. A silence that damned him in her eyes. Eyes that were now hazed with pain and a sorrow that went so deep he wanted to do anything and everything to make it go away.

Her voice was hoarse when she spoke. "You always thought the worst of me, but it never occurred to me to think you were capable of something like this. I didn't want to believe you could be so calculating, but it seems I was terribly wrong. I really don't know you at all, do I?"

Evans had collected the last of her bags and was now waiting by her car. Anna started to head out the door. Judd wanted to call out to her, to physically restrain her from leaving, but he knew he had no right. He *had* meant to give his mother this house all along and he had meant so much more harm to Charles, as well. Right now, though, none of that seemed important anymore as the woman he suddenly realized had come to mean so much to him walked out the door.

A slow burn of anger started deep inside of him. He had never lost control of a situation ever before, and right now everything he'd worked hard for these past weeks, his whole lifetime, in fact, started to crumble. He rubbed at his eyes, unable to dislodge the picture of the misery on Anna's face no matter how hard he tried.

"It's for the best, Judd." His mother's voice came from behind him and he whirled around to face her.

"For the best? What makes you say that?"

"She had ideas above her station and she'd have eventually dragged you down to her level. You know that, don't you? After all, look at what her mother did for Charles. Nothing. She was a convenient mistress and a passable housekeeper. No doubt Anna's been riding on her mother's abilities to sneak her way into Charles's wealth through his bed, too." Cynthia stepped closer, placing one hand on his arm and closing her fingers around it in a hold that surprised him with its strength. "Trust me, Judd. You're better off without her."

He stared at his mother's fingers and their clawlike grip, the physical manifestation of her hold on him the perfect analogy for how she'd tried to direct him all his life. As her words ran through his mind—words that he knew, in this case, to be totally untrue—he wondered what else his mother had told him that had been twisted and distorted away from the truth to suit her own manipulations.

"Did you tell her?"

"About the house? Of course I did. She needed to know, Judd. She doesn't belong here any more than her mother ever did."

"She was an *invited* guest under this roof."

His mother's face paled beneath expertly applied cosmetics. "I don't like your implication, Judd."

"Like it or not, it's still my name on the deed to this property."

"A mere technicality. You know what this place means to me."

"More than anything or anyone else, yes."

Weariness swamped him with the awareness that Cynthia's obsession with this property was outside normal perceptions. Clearly she felt it was owed to her for all she'd lost when she was younger, and for all she'd endured during her marriage to Charles and her subsequent banishment back home to Australia. It was unhealthy and Judd was annoyed with himself that he'd never seen it before now.

Cynthia was Cynthia. She'd never pretended to be anything else but what she'd presented to the world. Subterfuge had never been her style, ever, which was why he'd always assumed that she'd never been anything but honest with him. Only now did he realize that while she didn't lie, per se, her accounts on matters that affected her deeply were twisted by her bitterness into something that only vaguely resembled the truth. Accepting that, and the fact that as an adult he should have seen it sooner, filled him with a fury at himself that he could barely contain.

She'd always be his mother, and he'd always love her as such, but right now he didn't like the person she was very much at all. He needed some distance between them before his anger bubbled over and he said something he might regret.

All his instincts urged him to follow Anna, but with that he was forced to admit he had no idea where to go to look for her. Frustration rose within him anew. Even if he did know where to find her, he doubted she was in the mood to listen to him. He pulled himself free of his mother's clasp, the movement as metaphorical as it was literal.

"Look, it's late and I have work to get through. I'll see you in the morning and we can discuss your return to The Masters'."

"My return? But I've only just arr—"

"We'll talk in the morning," he said firmly, and grabbing his briefcase he went upstairs.

Anna didn't know how much longer she could take this. Working with Judd and feeling about him the way she did, yet knowing just how ruthless he really was, was making her feel sick inside. She had hardly slept over the weekend. The cheap motel she'd discovered on Friday night was hardly in a secluded area and the constant traffic noise and the racket from a nearby bar and club had ensured her nights were punctuated by the kinds of sounds that had dragged her from her restless sleep with a start more than once.

When she'd left the house on Friday she'd been too distraught to think carefully about where she was headed. In the end, to avoid creating an accident, she'd pulled into the motel thinking that it would be for only a night before she found an apartment in the city. But the weekend had passed in a blur of visits to the hospital, timing them to avoid Judd, and spending the rest of her time wallowing in a blend of self-pity and self-disgust that she could have been so foolish as to lose her heart to a man as cold and unforgiving as Judd Wilson.

After a lifetime of promising herself she deserved so much more than her mother had settled for, she'd just gone and found herself falling into the same pattern. Falling in love with a man with whom she would never be an equal—a man who would never offer her more than a job and his bed to sleep in.

She wished she could turn her feelings off as easily as Judd had appeared to do. He'd come into the office this Monday morning with nothing but a professional attitude and a driving work ethic. She should be grateful for that, at least, she thought as she brought his mail in to him.

He was on the phone and she made to put the opened correspondence on the desk in front of him and walk away, but when she did, he reached out and clasped her hand in his, preventing her from walking away. The instant he touched her she flinched, and saw the corresponding frown that crept between his brows as she did so. Anna gave an experimental tug but he continued to hold her firm.

The touch of his fingers on her skin was torture. How many times had those same fingers traversed the length of her body and wrought pleasure from her such as she had never known before? She bit back the sound that threatened to rise in her chest at the memory. The memory of the passion and the betrayal.

Finally, Judd finished his call and relinquished his hold on her.

"Get your bag, we're going to the hospital," he said in a voice that brooked no argument.

"Is Charles all right?" she asked, fear clawing at her throat at the serious expression on Judd's face.

"He's come out of the coma and he's asking for us. Both of us."

The journey to the hospital seemed to take forever, or maybe it just seemed that way because she was bound in this small space inside Judd's car. She was intensely aware of him, from the grip of his hands on the steering wheel to the set of his jaw. And his scent—the scent that insidiously reminded her of dark nights when all she knew was the feel and smell of him, and the sensation of her own pleasure, as he made love to her all through those nights.

She let out a sigh of relief as they pulled into the hospital parking lot and strived to keep her distance from Judd as they walked together to the elevator bank that would take them to the intensive-care unit.

"Only one at a time and only for five minutes," the nurse instructed.

"You go first," Judd said to Anna. "I know how important he is to you, how worried you've been."

She silently examined his words, searching for a hidden meaning behind them, but there was nothing about his expression that suggested his words meant anything other than what was said. She nodded her acquiescence and went into the room where Charles was hooked up to all manner of equipment. He opened his eyes as she entered, a shaky smile on his lips.

"Oh, Charles," she said, sinking onto the visitor's chair beside his bed, tears filling her eyes, "we've been so worried about you."

"Ah, Anna, still fussing?"

He reached for her and she gave him her hand, surprised at the strength she felt in his fingers as he squeezed tight.

"Of course I'm still fussing. I wouldn't be me if I didn't, right?"

He sighed and smiled a little wider. "That's my girl. How are things between you and my boy? Before this little incident I was beginning to hope there was something special growing between you."

Anna didn't want to talk about her and Judd, not now. "Hardly a little incident, Charles. You have to take better care of yourself. In fact, when you go home I've arranged for nursing care for you until you're back on your feet."

Her voice trailed away as she realized what she'd just said. If Cynthia Wilson had her way, Charles wouldn't be returning to the home he knew and loved. In fact, if what she'd said last Friday night held any truth to it, Charles had nowhere to call home at all. The news would shatter his chances at recovery. Somehow she had to persuade Judd to allow his father to live out his years under the roof that had been his home for over thirty years. She felt sick at the prospect but fought to keep her fears from her face. As ill as Charles was, he'd always been pretty astute. He'd know something was wrong if she didn't control herself.

"Pshaw!" he scoffed. "Nurses. I've only been awake a few hours and I've already had my fill of them. But you're not answering my question. You and Judd. What's happening there?"

"We're working well together," Anna hedged.

"Working well together." He said the words as if they tasted like something nasty. "Sounds like you've had a lovers' spat, hmm? You know, I hope you two can work out whatever it is that's keeping you apart. I know you haven't exactly had the best of role models for long-term commitment—Lord only knows I didn't treat your mother as well as I ought to have. She stood by me, you know. She held me together and loved me even when I didn't deserve it. I owed her more than companionship, but I wasn't capable of offering her more."

"Mum was happy, Charles, really." Tears pricked at Anna's eyes.

"Ah, always the mediator. You deserve more than I gave her, Anna. It's your due. Remember that."

Out the corner of her eye she saw the nurse gesture to her. "Look, my five minutes is up and I don't want to use up Judd's time with you, too. We can talk about this later."

Much later, like never, she hoped as she leaned forward to give him a chaste kiss on his cheek.

"Seemed like a very quick five minutes to me," Charles grumbled.

"I'll be back tomorrow, okay?"

"Tonight. Come back tonight."

"If I can," she promised. "Now do as you're told while you're here. Promise me?"

He merely grunted. As she passed Judd in the doorway

she took care not to brush against him, a fact that wasn't totally lost on Judd, judging by the expression on his face.

"I'll wait for you downstairs," she said, desperate for some
air.

"Sit, sit." Charles gestured to the chair beside his bed.

Judd did as he was told. His relief at seeing Charles alert
again was palpable, but even he couldn't answer himself as
to why. Was it because he wanted his father to be fully aware
of the payback he had coming to him, or was it something
else?

"What, nothing to say?" Charles asked with a bark of
laughter.

"I'm glad to see you're feeling better," Judd said stiffly.

Charles snorted. "I'll accept that, it's probably all I deserve. There's one thing about facing your own mortality.
It makes you want to clear away the messes you've made of
your life—and believe me, I've made a few."

"It's how we deal with the messes that's most important,"
Judd replied, fighting to keep his voice neutral. Did his father
plan to apologize? Did he think that saying "sorry" would
make everything okay?

"That's why I needed to speak to you now. You need to
know the truth about your mother and me."

"I think I know enough," Judd said, stonewalling.

"No, you don't know the half of it. I will admit it was my
fault our marriage failed. I knew what I was getting into by
marrying someone so much younger than me, I knew she deserved more than an older man could offer." Charles sighed
and lapsed into silence.

Judd shifted uncomfortably on his chair, waiting for the
older man to finish what he wanted to say. He didn't have to
wait too long.

"I won't beat around the bush, my boy. I wasn't man
enough for her. Now don't go getting all embarrassed. I know

kids don't want to hear about their parents' sex lives." He made a self-conscious grimace. "I promise to keep it PG. Do you know much about diabetes?"

"Not a huge amount, no."

"Mine went undiagnosed for many years—part of the reason I'm here now. But one of the issues I suffer with the disease is impotence. I was thirty-five when I married your mother and I was already beginning to have problems. She was only nineteen when I met her and such a beauty. I wanted to offer her the moon and the stars. I was prepared to give her anything just to keep her. But when I started having problems in the bedroom I was ashamed. I didn't want to talk to anyone about it—not her, not my best friend, not my doctor, no one. I just threw myself into work. By the time Nicole came along we were barely sleeping together anymore.

"I just kept on working, kept on providing for Cynthia. She had the house, she had you and your sister. I just went on, hoping against hope it would be enough to keep her. She wasn't happy, but I didn't know what I could do to change that anymore. Your mother and my best friend always did get on, and Thomas seemed to be hell-bent on cheering Cynthia up. I got jealous. Started to suspect them of having an affair, of both of them cheating on me.

"One day I came home from work early. Thomas had already left the office and I found him in your mother's room, holding her, as if they were about to make love. I accused them of all sorts of things. I didn't listen when they tried to explain. Turns out she was desperately unhappy and he was consoling her, but I didn't see it that way at the time. I lost a helluva lot that day. My wife, my best friend, my son."

"You didn't have to send us away," Judd said bitterly. "She wasn't unfaithful to you, was she?"

"No," Charles acknowledged, his voice so soft Judd had to lean forward to hear him clearly. "She wasn't. But she let me believe she had been. She told me you were Thomas's child.

That she and Thomas had been having an affair for years and how much he satisfied her. She knew exactly how to hit me where it would hurt the most.

"You know the rest. I could barely see, I was so angry. I told her she could go and take you with her. I never wanted to see either of you again. When Thomas heard what I'd done, he tried to reason with me, to get me to believe the truth, but Cynthia's lies were already rotting my heart and my mind. I wouldn't listen and we never spoke again.

"He died just over a year ago. He'd arranged for his lawyers to pass on a letter to me, should he predecease me. A letter where he told me what an idiot I'd been and how he'd never touched Cynthia, ever. I knew that if he was telling the truth I'd wasted twenty-five years on a hatred I'd had no right to feel. I had to know the truth, but it took a warning from my doctors about my health before I actually found the courage to reach out to you—to admit I was wrong. It wasn't an easy thing."

Judd didn't know what to say. Everything his father told him made sense. Instinctively he knew, even though he didn't want to believe it was the truth, that Cynthia was quite capable of being so spiteful as to spin out a lie of such enormous proportions. But why had she allowed it to go on for so long? Why had she been prepared to walk away from her marriage? And had she never considered, ever, what it had meant to him to be rejected by his father—for his sister to grow up without a mother?

"Judd." Charles shifted and reached a hand toward him. Judd took it, intensely aware of the papery texture of his father's hand and remembering a time when it was strong and warm as it guided him the first time he'd ridden his bike without training wheels. "I want you to know I'm sorry, son. So very sorry for everything I put you through. I was an inflexible, prideful fool. I can't get back what I threw away, but I hope that now you know the truth you can find it in your heart to forgive me and that maybe we can start anew from here."

Judd felt unexpected moisture prick at his eyes. Every wish he'd ever had was here before him. His father was reaching out, wanting to make amends for the past. Charles had talked about his own bitterness being a waste of the last twenty-five years, but what of Judd's own? Channeling his own anger against his father for so long had been just as destructive as his father's toward Cynthia and Thomas Jackson.

"Is that why you offered me the controlling share in the company as well as the house? To make it up to me? Did you really think that would be enough?"

Charles nodded. "I hoped so. I knew you were already successfully running The Masters'. I had to sweeten the bait to bring you home—where you belong. I thought that once you were here that we could start to build a bridge between the past and now. To learn to be father and son again."

He'd come so close to throwing it all away. To destroying everything his father had worked so hard to build.

"Thank you for telling me. It's a lot to take in after all this time. I've been very angry at you for most of my life."

"I deserved that. Are you still angry?"

"Yes, but it's different now—there's more regret than anger. Frustration, too. I just wish things could have been different."

"They can be. We can make it so."

"Yes," Judd said, squeezing his father's hand gently. "Yes, Dad. We can."

By the time Judd joined Anna downstairs she felt as if she had herself back under control, externally at least. He'd been with his father for quite a while longer than she'd expected.

"What did you think?" she asked as they walked back to the car.

"He's a tough old bird. I reckon he'll be around for a few more years yet."

"Did the nurse say anything to you about when he could go home? Supposing he has a home to go to, of course."

Darn, she could probably have handled that better, she thought. But it was too late now. The words hung between them like an invisible challenge.

"What makes you think he doesn't?"

She looked at him in disbelief. "You're kidding me, right? Cynthia and Charles under one roof? She'll never allow it."

"What she will and won't allow isn't an issue," Judd said firmly as they reached the car.

"She seems to believe it is."

"Well, there's a lot that people believe at the moment. Not all of it is true," he said.

His vagueness pushed Anna to speak again. "Are you saying that Cynthia lied to me on Friday night? That it wasn't your intention to turf Charles out and install your mother back where she so supremely believes she belongs?"

"I'm not admitting or denying anything. Charles will have a home to go to—that's all you need to worry about for now."

Anna lapsed into silence, frustrated by Judd's stonewalling tactics. They were nearing their office block before she spoke again.

"I'm going to look for another job. I can't work with you. Not now. Not knowing what you're really like."

"That's your choice, but do you really think the timing is right to leave just now? Without Charles and Nicole, you're pretty much it for historical knowledge and continuity around the place. Anyone would think you want to see Wilson Wines collapse into dust."

"That's not fair. You can't expect me to keep working with you, not now that we—"

"Not now that we what, Anna?"

"Nothing."

"And your resignation?"

"I will wait until Charles is better. That's all I'm promising for now."

The thought of leaving Wilson Wines, the only job she'd ever known, terrified her. But she couldn't continue there, working for Judd, seeing him every day. Wanting him every minute.

Fourteen

Judd's head was reeling. The last thing he needed to deal with right now was Anna walking out on him. If anything, he needed her back home where she belonged as well, but he knew he had some hard work to do in that department before she'd even consider it.

What occupied his mind first and foremost now was something else. Something that challenged every belief he'd grown up with. Logically he'd always known there were two sides to every story, but he'd never dreamed his father's side of things could be so different to what he'd always been told. He'd wanted to refute the words that had poured from his father's mouth, but the man was virtually on his deathbed. Charles had no reason to lie and even with what Judd had always held to be the truth, there was a ring of honesty to what his father had said that demanded he give his old man full justice.

He couldn't concentrate on his work in the office and surprised Anna by telling her he was leaving for the day.

"Call me at the house if you need me."

"I won't," she said bluntly.

He could only give an ironic smile in response. Tough to do when what he really wanted was to lean across her desk and kiss her so thoroughly she would forget what day of the week it was. He'd save that for another time, though. Right now, he had more pressing business to attend to.

Fifteen minutes later, as he pulled into the driveway, he stopped and stared at the massive stone structure that dominated the property. He shook his head. It was only a building—yet it was so coveted, and at what cost? He eased his foot off the brake and slowly drove up the driveway. A van was parked near the front door and he pulled up alongside it, frowning as he read the lettering on the side. Decorators? He shook his head as he got out of the car and let himself in through the front door.

He could hear Cynthia in the salon and the softer murmur of another woman's voice answering her. When he opened the salon door, both women looked up, his mother's face wreathing in a smile of welcome.

"Judd, you're home early! What a lovely surprise. Here, you can tell me what you think of these." Spread before her were a stack of open books of decorating samples and she picked up a selection from the top, handing them toward him. "I think these will be perfect in here, don't you?"

"No, I don't," he said grimly before turning to the other woman. "I'm sorry, but it seems my mother has wasted your time. We won't be needing any decorating advice at the moment. Let me see you out."

The other woman looked shocked, but to her credit she hastily gathered her samples in her arms, shooting worried glances between Judd and his mother as she did so.

Cynthia sat in mutinous silence, her dark brows drawn in a straight line—a harbinger of her temper. She would never argue with him in front of a stranger but he had no doubt that her blood pressure was rising to monumental proportions right now. If there was one thing his mother hated, it was being thwarted in her goals.

Let her be angry, he thought. It was nothing compared to how he was feeling right now. By the time he'd shown the decorator out and returned to the salon, his body was rigid with tension.

"How could you do that to me, and in front of a total stranger?" She rose to her feet and demanded the instant he'd closed the door behind him.

"You're getting ahead of yourself," he said calmly. Strangely enough, in the face of her fury, he began to feel himself settle down by degrees. "The house is still mine."

"Don't you dare tell me after all this time you're changing your mind. This house is mine by right, it always has been. I just bet it's that upstart, Anna Garrick. Has she been poisoning your mind all morning? That type will always try, you know. They cloud your judgment with sexual favors and then they try to pull your strings for the rest of your life."

"Is that what you tried to do with Charles?" he asked pointedly.

Slap! In all his life his mother had never struck him, but it appeared he'd crossed a line with her today. Judd tested his stinging jaw and locked his gaze with hers.

"Now that's out of the way, perhaps you could answer my question."

"How dare you!"

"No, Mother, how dare you lie to me all these years. What kind of mother lies about her son's paternity and deliberately keeps a boy from his father?"

"Whatever I did, I did for you, Judd. *I love you.*"

"Inasmuch as you're capable of loving anyone more than you love yourself, and this house."

"You don't understand."

"Oh, I think I do. I understand you were young and foolish when you met Charles and that you saw in him a chance to relive the former Masters glory that you had pined for all your life." He shook his head. "Why did you lie to him, Mother? Why did you let him drive us away? Was it really worth hurting him so badly?"

"We'd grown apart. After I had Nicole it was as if he lost all interest in me as a woman. At first he said he was having to work longer hours and didn't want to disturb me, but then it became another excuse, and then another until we weren't even sharing a room anymore."

Judd knew his mother better than probably anyone else, and he knew that, for Cynthia, losing Charles's attentions would have been a dreadful blow to her self-esteem. For a woman who appeared so strong, she was more fragile than others knew. She measured herself by the success around her. If the physical side of her marriage was failing, then *she* was a failure.

"Why did you lie to him about Thomas Jackson?"

"You know about Thomas?"

"Only Charles's side. Now I want to hear yours. The truth this time."

His mother began to pace the room, every now and then stopping to finger one ornament or another.

"You don't know what it was like. Charles was such a dashing man when he came to visit us at The Masters' that time. And he was clearly smitten with me. The age gap didn't seem ridiculous to me—he was such a charismatic and *vital* man. He promised me everything I'd ever wanted. He promised me this." She flung her arms out wide before wrapping them tight around her middle. "He made me feel as if his entire world revolved around me. But then, he started pulling away.

"I didn't know what to do or where to turn. I had no other family here. He was my everything, and suddenly he didn't want me anymore. I just wanted to make him jealous. To make him want *me* again. So, I turned to someone else for attention, to show him that if he didn't want me, another man would."

"But his best friend? What were you thinking?"

"I wasn't thinking, that much is quite obvious. Thomas could see there was a growing rift between Charles and me. He loved us both and wanted to do whatever he could to help us over our rough patch, as he called it. I, shamefully, took advantage of his friendship and used it against him. I just wanted to hurt Charles any way I could at that point. I didn't realize then just how much I would end up hurting everyone else. When Charles threatened to send me back to Australia alone, I overreacted. I couldn't lose you and Nicole as well as my home and my marriage. I lied to him about Thomas being my lover and I led Charles to believe it was Thomas who was your father."

Cynthia sighed deeply and sank into a nearby chair. A glance at her face told of the toll her honesty had taken on her after all these years of perpetuating a lie.

Judd chose his words carefully. "They never spoke again, did you know that? Charles refused to see or speak to Thomas for the rest of his life, despite his best friend's repeated entreaties. You destroyed their friendship as thoroughly as if you really had slept with Thomas Jackson. It was only when Thomas died recently that Charles began to wonder if Thomas had really been telling the truth all along."

She nodded and wiped an errant tear from one eye. Judd wasn't moved by her unexpected emotional display. He wasn't even convinced it was genuine until she looked up and met the censure in his eyes. For the first time she showed every one of her fifty-one years and then some.

"I've been such a fool. I was so angry and so bitter it was easier to perpetuate the lie than it was to tell the truth. Besides, once Charles had it in his head that you weren't his, he couldn't wait to see the back of us. I hit him where it hurt the hardest, and he got me right back."

"You could have told him the truth at any time."

"I couldn't. I wanted him to hurt, to know what it was like to be rejected."

"He never rejected you, Mother."

"Really?" She shook her head at him. "Then what do you call him removing himself from my bed, my whole life, the way he did? If that's not rejection, then what is it?"

She stood opposite him, so proud and defiant and yet still hurting inside after all these years.

"Charles is diabetic. At that stage his illness was undiagnosed and untreated. He had no idea that's why he'd become impotent until years after, but he was too proud to seek help for the problem."

She drew in a shaky breath. "You mean it wasn't me all along?"

Cynthia's voice broke as genuine tears began to fall down her cheeks. Despite her focus still being so self-oriented, Judd felt his earlier anger toward his mother defuse entirely. He could begin to understand how her need for payback had molded her ambitious nature into one of harshness—even cruelty. She hadn't been solely responsible for what had happened; both his parents had their crosses to bear, but maybe now they could begin to heal some of the hurt they'd caused. It was going to be a monumental task. So many years and words lay like an echoing chasm between them all. He'd had enough of it. It was time for change—for all of them. Charles, Cynthia, Anna and himself.

He took a step toward his mother and drew her into his arms. Forgiveness had to start with a first step; he only hoped that he could begin to make things right before it was too late.

Judd and his mother talked for hours. When she was finally spent, he saw her to her bedroom with a light meal on a tray and went to his own room to change. She'd agreed to go back to Adelaide in the morning. She would definitely be back, but at a time when emotions weren't so fraught and when Charles was better. Who knew, perhaps between the two of them, his parents could finally lay old ghosts to rest and find some peace between them.

What a freaking day it had been. Exhaustion pulled at every part of his body. Whoever said that the truth will set you free never once mentioned the high emotional toll that could take. Today's revelations had taught him a very important lesson. Life was too short to let go of what mattered to you, especially of what you loved. He didn't want to live the rest of his life plagued by bitterness and regret over relationships he'd allowed to fall apart, as his parents had. He grabbed his cell phone from on top of his briefcase on the bed and punched in Anna's number.

She didn't pick up. No problem, he decided as he descended the stairs and headed for his car. He could ring her and ring her until she eventually gave up and answered. He knew she wouldn't turn off her phone altogether because she was one of the emergency contacts for the hospital.

"What?" she demanded as he called for the ninth time.

"Where are you? We need to talk."

"We have nothing to say."

"Yes, Anna, we do. We have everything to say to each other. I won't give up, you know. I will call you and call you until you give in."

"Look, I'm tired. Can't this wait until tomorrow at the office?"

"I need to see you now. Please? It's important."

He heard her sigh before she answered, "Fine, then."

She rattled off an address that he rapidly keyed into the GPS of the late-model Mercedes he'd bought so Evans would be free to drive Charles whenever he needed him.

"I'll be there in half an hour," he said, checking the ETA on the screen.

"Don't rush on my account," she answered before severing their connection.

By the time he pulled into the budget motel at the address Anna had given him, he felt a knot of anticipation grow tight in his gut. He parked beside her Lexus, which was outside one of the motel units that formed an L-shape just back from the road. Her door opened as he got out of his car.

"Why here?" he asked as he walked the short distance to her door.

"Clean, cheap and close to the motorway. Is that all you wanted?"

She didn't so much as budge from the doorway, nor did she seem to be in a hurry to invite him inside.

"No, that's not all I wanted."

"Then please say what you wanted to say and leave."

Anna's grip on the edge of the door made her fingers ache but she had to hold on to something, anything. If she didn't, she was afraid she might reach out to Judd, to touch him, and then she'd be lost. As much as he'd hurt her, she couldn't deny her body's response to him.

"I'm not doing this outside on the forecourt of some tacky motel, Anna. Let me in."

He spoke quietly but she had no doubt that he meant every word he said.

"If it means I'll be rid of you sooner, then, sure, come on in," she said with false bravado.

She pushed the door open wide and held her breath as he stepped over the lintel and into the compact unit she'd inhabited for the past three nights.

"Can we sit down, please?" Judd asked.

She gestured to the saggy two-seater sofa and settled herself on one of the scarred wooden chairs from the small dinette. His rangy body filled the sofa, making her all too aware of his presence in the shabby room.

"Well?" she prompted, really wanting to get this over with as soon as possible.

"I had an ulterior motive when I came to New Zealand. For years my father had spurned my mother and me, and for years I'd dreamed of what I would do if I had the opportunity to pay him back for all the heartache he'd caused when he sent us away." He paused and rubbed his jawline with a thumb and forefinger of one hand. "I should have known as I grew older that nothing is as straightforward as it seems."

"Nothing ever really is," Anna agreed, wondering where he was leading with this.

She knew he had an ulterior motive for coming to New Zealand, a motive that included turning his own flesh and blood out of his home and installing a woman whose vitriol had flayed strips off Anna's soul. Well, for all Cynthia's subtle viciousness, she'd opened Anna's eyes to the man Judd really was. She should thank her for it one day, she thought with self-deprecating irony.

"No, you're right. Nothing ever really is. My plans were originally twofold. One, to give my mother back the home she deserved, the other to ruin Wilson Wines by selling my shares to its biggest competitor."

Anna gasped. "You can't be serious! It will break Charles's heart. How could you even think of doing such a thing? How could you be so calculating?"

"Calculating? Do you have any idea of what it was like to grow up knowing your father *hated* you so much he sent you away forever? I was six years old!"

Anna recoiled as he abruptly rose to his feet and paced the small room, pushing a hand through his hair. On seeing her face, he sat back down on the sofa.

"Anna, relax. I've already begun to question what I'd planned to do with the business. Aside from the fact that I'd been bored with my work in Adelaide for some time, working at Wilson Wines has provided me with new challenges within the industry that make me very excited for the future of the company—not to mention valuable insights into how hard Charles has worked to keep the business running all these years. If nothing else, I learned to respect him for that.

"Look, I don't expect anyone to think that my plans were honorable—revenge very rarely is. But I've both learned and been forced to face some home truths about my parents and myself that have turned everything upside down."

"I don't see what any of this has to do with me. Why are you telling me?" Anna clenched her fingers together in her lap.

"Because you were part of that revenge."

Fifteen

A bitter taste flooded her mouth. She'd heard as much from Cynthia, but hearing the words directly from lips that she'd kissed in deepest passion, lips that had caressed her entire body and brought her ultimate pleasure, made her stomach lurch. She shot up from her seat.

"I think I've heard enough. I'd like you to go."

Judd stood and reached for her, his fingers closing around her upper arms and gently encouraging her back down on her chair.

"No, you haven't heard nearly enough, and I won't leave until you know it all."

"I don't want to hear it, Judd. You hurt me so much it pains me to see you at work every day. I can't keep putting myself through this. I don't deserve to be made to feel this way."

"No, you don't, and that's why I'm going to make it up to you. Look, when I met you I was instantly attracted to you. That attraction was definitely mutual, as we both established on your first night at The Masters'. But it wasn't until the next morning when my mother told me that she'd figured out who you were that I made a decision to use that attraction against you.

"You see, I had no reason to believe that you weren't there as Charles's puppet. You were so loyal to him, so defensive. It made me wonder just how deep the relationship between the two of you went. I assumed, wrongly I know, that the two of you were lovers, and to add to my revenge plans I wanted to win you off him. To show him that he didn't deserve to be loved the way you obviously loved him."

A tiny sound of pain emerged from Anna's mouth. She'd known that Judd had thought she was Charles's lover, but to hear him put in words what he'd been thinking hit her like a physical blow. She wrapped her hands around her stomach and hunched over as if by doing so she could protect herself from what he insisted on saying.

"Anna, I'm so sorry I treated you like that, and I hope that you'll be able to forgive me. I based my need for vengeance on a life that was as orchestrated as what I'd planned to do to my father. Granted, he's no angel, but he didn't deserve what I had planned to do."

A difficult silence fell between them, a silence punctuated by nothing more than the overloud hum of the old refrigerator and the ticking of the cheap plastic wall clock. Finally, Anna summoned up the courage to ask him the one question that now burned inside her.

"So what changed your mind?"

"You."

He looked up and his eyes burned a hole straight to her heart. Anna swallowed against the fear that formed a lump in her throat.

"You'll forgive me if I say I find that hard to believe."

He gave a humorless laugh. "I don't blame you, but it's true. In everything around me, you are the only thing that's good. You're the only one who remained true to the people you love. I learned today that the truth I'd always believed growing up was nothing but a lie fabricated by one person's need for attention and another's pride standing in the way of giving it."

"What do you mean?" Anna asked, suddenly confused.

A stricken look of pain settled on Judd's face. "My mother lied to me for most of my life. Forcing the truth from her today was one of the hardest things I've had to endure."

"But how did you know she'd lied to you?"

"Charles told me his side of their story today at the hospital. It was the bare-bones version, given how weak he is and how much time we were allowed together, but it made me stop seeing him as the villain in the piece and start to see him as he is. Faults as well as strengths. I knew he had accused my mother of having an affair. She told me that much when I was about fifteen. What she didn't say was that she'd deliberately led him to believe it, then told him I wasn't his son." He shook his head. "And to think I was prepared to crush him without knowing all of that.

"I can't believe I almost threw everything away. Everything—everyone—I'd ever wanted in my life were mine all along, if only I'd had the courage to fight for them. Learning the truth was a real eye-opener for me."

"What you were going to do was despicable. What you did, to me, was despicable."

"I know, and I'm more sorry for that than you'll ever know. It seems betrayal runs in the family. My mother lied to Charles about my paternity in retaliation for what she saw as his indifference to her. She had no idea that what she perceived as his coolness toward her masked a bigger problem."

Anna caught on quickly. "His diabetes. My mother said he'd probably had it for years before he was diagnosed."

"Yes, he was too proud and too embarrassed to seek help, and so frightened that he would lose his beautiful young wife because of it that he poured himself into work so he could at least keep her in the lifestyle he'd always promised her.

"I learned some awful truths about my family today, Anna. Not least of which were the truths about myself. Truths I'm so bitterly ashamed of. I want to make it up to you, if you'll allow me. Everyone deserves a second chance, right? A chance to put things back the way they should have been all along?"

"I don't know if I can do that, Judd. All my life I watched my mother be treated as an afterthought, appreciated to an extent but never really given the love she craved. She deserved more than that—so much more—and so do I. From an early age I told myself that I would only be with someone who loved me completely and put our relationship first.

"When I realized what you thought of me, why you had sex with me," she said bluntly, because no matter how engaged her feelings it could only have been sex, not lovemaking, "I felt second-rate. Your revenge came first, not me. I don't know if I can forgive you that. I really don't."

Judd reached across the short distance between them and took her hands in his, his thumbs stroking across the tops of hers.

"I love you, Anna. I never thought I'd want to trust another person the way I want to trust you. With my mother's lies about my father poisoning the way I saw love, I never wanted to go through what I thought was the greatest weakness in the world. Allowing yourself to become vulnerable to another person, to hand to them the means to hurt you so much, alters the entire course of your life. But I want to be that vulnerable to you. I trust you. I know you. You are loyal and loving and everything I was never taught to be. I would do anything for you, and I swear that from now on I will always put you first. Please, let me show you that I love you."

Anna lifted her head and met his intense and pleading gaze. Her heart wanted to say yes to him, but her head cautioned her to take care. She'd suffered so much these past weeks. Yes, she'd experienced the highest of highs in her life, but along with those came the lows to which she never wanted to descend again.

She took a deep breath. "So, if I asked you to show me you love me by leaving me now, by never talking to me again, by never making another attempt to see me, you'd do it?"

She saw the pain that speared across his features, the light in his eyes dim as he saw all hope of their reconciliation being dashed against his mistakes of the past. Judd let her go and stood up.

"Yes," he said. "I will do that for you."

His hands were trembling and it shocked Anna to her core that his emotions affected him so deeply. Judd Wilson, the ice man, vulnerable to her.

Before he could reach the door of the unit, she flew to her feet.

"Judd! Stop!"

She ran toward him, throwing herself against his back and flinging her arms around him as if she could physically stop him from leaving her.

"Don't go, please don't go. I love you, Judd. Don't ever walk away from me again, please?"

He turned in her arms, wrapping his own around her and holding her close. As she looked up at his face she saw tears tracking down his cheeks. She lifted shaking hands to wipe the moisture away.

"Oh, Judd, don't."

She drew his head down to hers, sealing his mouth with her lips and putting her heart into her kiss, telling him how much he meant to her with actions rather than words.

"God, don't do that to me again. I couldn't survive it another time," he groaned against her mouth.

Suddenly she understood just what it had cost Judd to walk away from her like that. He'd been a confused little boy when his father had cast him off like a forgotten and unwanted piece of his life. By his own admission he hadn't learned to love or to trust easily, and he'd given her his heart, laid all his truths on the line for her. Her happiness came first with him, she knew that now.

"I won't. I won't ever send you away from me and I won't ever leave you again, I promise."

She kissed him again before taking his hands and leading him to the bedroom. It was small, it was basic, but it was all she needed as the stage to show him how very important he was to her.

He didn't move so much as a muscle as she undressed. His eyes, however, tracked her movements as avidly as a child watching the presents under the tree at Christmas. When she was naked, she reached for his sweater and pulled it over his head before reaching for his belt and the button fly of his jeans. Goose bumps raised on her skin as she looked her fill of this beautiful man who'd laid his heart on the line for her, but they had nothing to do with a chill in the air.

She stepped into him, at first wrapping her arms around his waist and feeling the heat of him seep into her—skin to skin, head to toe. Then she turned her face into him and traced a line of gentle kisses across his chest before taking his hand again and leading him to the bed. She yanked down the covers, exposing the crisp white cotton sheets, and pushed him onto the mattress with a smile that spoke of all the things she wanted to do with him.

Judd's pupils dilated, consuming the blue of his irises, as she straddled his legs and began to gently stroke his body with a feather-light touch that made his skin jump and heat beneath the soft pads.

"I love you, Judd Wilson," she whispered against his skin as she lowered her mouth to repeat the trail her fingers had taken, and punctuated each word with a press of her lips.

"I love you, too, Anna Garrick. I want to marry you. I want to do this right. Will you be my wife?"

"Judd, you don't need to marry me. I know how you feel about your parents' marriage. I don't need a formal union to know you love me."

Judd reached for her and rolled with her, tucking her body beneath him. He cradled her head between his hands.

"I mean it, Anna, I want to do right by you. I want to spend the rest of my life with you, make babies with you and raise those babies to be wonderful people. People who know their parents are right there behind them, through everything."

"Are you sure, Judd? We can do all that without marrying."

"I know, but I *want* to marry you. I want the world to hear my pledge to you and to know that you will be mine for all time."

Anna lay beneath him, feeling the warmth of him, the strength of him, the passion within him, and she knew she wanted it, too. She raised a hand to trace the lines of his beautiful face, letting her fingers settle on his lips as she reached her decision.

"Yes," she answered tremulously. "Yes, I'd be proud to be your wife."

"Thank you." He rested his forehead on hers and closed his eyes. Anna could feel the tension easing from his body. "I will make sure there is not a day that goes by that you regret it."

"I'll hold you to that," she said with a soft smile.

And then words were redundant as they showed one another the reaches of the physical manifestation of their love. Anna cradled him with her body, her legs parting to allow him to nestle at the core of her. She felt the blunt tip of him nudge at her opening, felt him slide inside. She tightened around him, welcoming his possession. Judd raised himself slightly, his eyes locked with hers as he began to move, at first slowly and then with increasing rhythm, never once losing focus.

Pleasure began to build inside of her but it was different than before. This time they were so much more connected— mind, body and spirit. And when she began to shake with the intensity of her orgasm, she felt him tremble also until with a raw cry he spilled himself within her. Making love had never felt so right or so perfect. A tear slid from the corner of her eye as emotion overwhelmed her.

He was her man, her love, her forever. And she was his.

* * * * *

A FORBIDDEN AFFAIR

BY
YVONNE LINDSAY

One

Nicole's hands shook uncontrollably as she tried to fit her key into the ignition. Damn, she dropped it again. She swiped the key ring up off the floor of her classic Benz, and gave up driving as a bad joke. If she couldn't even get the key in the ignition, how on earth did she expect to drive?

She got out of the car, slammed the door hard and swiped her cell phone from her bag. Thank goodness she'd had the presence of mind to grab the designer leather pouch from the hall table after her grand exit from the family dinner to end all family dinners.

Her high heels clipped a staccato beat as she marched down the well-lit driveway of her family home to the street, calling a taxi service as she went. Fine tremors shook her body as she waited for the car to arrive. The chill air of the autumn night made her glad she hadn't had a chance to change out of her tailored wool suit when she'd arrived home from work earlier.

Her father had requested that she dress up for dinner in honor of a special announcement he'd planned to make, but by the time she'd gotten home, there just hadn't been enough time. She hadn't thought her father would mind that she'd chosen to put in the extra time at the office instead of rushing home to get ready. After all, if anyone should understand her drive to devote her time and energy to Wilson Wines then surely it would be Charles Wilson, founder and CEO. Her father had invested most of his life into the business he had built, and she'd always intended to follow in his footsteps.

Until tonight.

Another rush of anger infused her. How dare her father belittle her like that, and in front of a virtual stranger, as well? Who cared if that stranger was her long-lost brother, Judd. Two and a half decades after their parents' bitter divorce had split their family in half, what right did he have to come back and lay claim to the responsibilities that were supposed to be *hers?* She clenched her jaw tight and bit back the scream of frustration that threatened to claw its way out of her throat. She couldn't lose it now. Not when she had just discovered that she was the only person she had left to rely on.

Even her best friend, colleague and life-long confidante, Anna, had shown her true colors when she'd arrived home in New Zealand from Adelaide, Australia, late last week with Judd in tow. Sure, she'd tried to convince Nicole that she'd only been following Charles's orders to find Judd and bring about a reconciliation, but Nicole knew where Anna's loyalties lay, and they certainly weren't with her. If they were,

Anna wouldn't have kept the truth from her about what Charles planned to use as Judd's incentive.

A painful twist in her chest reminded her to draw in a breath but despite the fact she obeyed her body's demand to refill her lungs, the pain of betrayal by her best friend—the woman she loved like a sister—still lingered. How *could* Anna have known what was going to happen and not given her prior warning?

In her bag, her phone began to chirp insistently. Thinking it might be the taxi company calling back to confirm her details, she lifted it to her ear and answered it.

"Nicole, where are you? Are you okay?"

Anna. Who else? It certainly wouldn't be her father calling to see if she was all right.

"I'm fine," Nicole answered, her voice clipped.

"You're not fine, you're upset. I can hear it in your voice. Look, I'm sorry about tonight—"

"Just tonight, Anna? What about your trip to Adelaide? What about bringing my brother home for the first time in twenty-five years, so he could take everything that was ever mine away from me?" Even Anna's gasp of pain at Nicole's accusations didn't stop Nicole's tirade or do anything to lessen the hurt of betrayal that rocketed through her veins right now. "I thought we were friends, sisters by *choice,* remember?"

"I couldn't tell you what Charles had planned, Nicole. Please believe me. Your dad swore me to secrecy and I owe him so very much. Without his support of me and my mum…you know what he was like…even when she was dying—"

"His support, huh?" Nicole shut her eyes tight and squeezed back the fresh round of tears that fought to escape. "What about your support of me?"

"You always have that, Nic, you know that."

"Really? Then why didn't you give me a heads-up? Why didn't you tell me that he was going to bribe Judd to stay by giving him my home as well as the business?"

"Only half the business," Anna's voice came quietly over the line.

"A controlling share, Anna. That's the whole business as far as I'm concerned."

The shock of her father's announcement had been bad enough. Worse was the way he'd justified the decision to give everything to Judd instead of her. *Just you wait,* he had said, *you'll find some young man who'll sweep you off your feet and before I know it you will be married and raising a family. Wilson Wines will just be a hobby for you.* Years of hard work, of dedication and commitment to the business and to further her father's plans and dreams dismissed as just a *phase,* a passing fad. The thought of it made her blood boil.

"Dad made it quite clear where I stand in all this, and by aligning yourself with him, you've made it quite clear where you stand, too."

Nicole paced back and forth on the pavement at the end of the driveway, filled with a nervous energy that desperately needed an outlet. Anna's voice remained steady in her ear; the sound of her friend's voice was usually a calming influence but tonight it was anything but.

"He put me in an impossible position, Nic. I begged him to talk to you about this, to at least tell you that Judd would be coming home."

"Obviously you didn't beg hard enough. Or, here's something to consider, maybe you could have just told me, anyway. You could have picked up a phone or fired me an email in warning. It's not that hard to do. You had to know what this would mean to me, how much it would hurt me. And still you did nothing?"

"I'm so sorry, Nic. If I could do it over I'd do it differently, you have to know that."

"I don't know anything anymore, Anna. That's the trouble. Everything I've worked for, everything I've lived for, has just been handed to a man I don't even know. I don't even know if I have a roof over my head now that Dad's given the deed of the family house to Judd. How would that make *you* feel? Have you asked yourself that?"

A sweep of lights coming down the road heralded the taxi she'd summoned, and not a moment too soon. She had enough dander up right now to march back on up the driveway and give her father a piece of her mind all over again—for whatever good it would do.

"Look," she continued, "I've got to go. I need some space right now to think things over."

"Nicole, come back. Let's talk this out face-to-face."

"No," Nicole answered as the cab pulled up alongside the curb. "I'm done talking. Please don't call me again."

She disconnected the call and switched off her phone for good measure before throwing it into the bottom of her bag.

"Viaduct Basin," she instructed as she got into the taxi and settled in the darkened interior with her equally dark thoughts.

Hopefully the vibrant atmosphere at the array of bars and clubs in downtown Auckland would provide her with the distraction she needed. Nicole repaired her tear-stained makeup as well as she could with the limited cosmetics in her bag. It annoyed the heck out of her that anger, for her, usually resulted in tears, as well. It was an awkward combination that plagued her on the rare occasions she actually lost her temper, and it made it hard for her to be taken seriously.

She willed her hand to be steady as she applied a rich red lip gloss and gave herself a final check in her compact mirror.

Satisfied she'd done her best with her makeup, she sat back against the soft upholstery of the luxury taxi and tried to ignore the echo of her father's words, the faintly smug paternal tone that seemed to say that she'd soon get over her temper tantrum and realize he was right all along.

"Over my dead body," she muttered.

"Pardon, miss, what was that you said?" the neatly suited taxi driver asked over his shoulder.

"Nothing, sorry, just talking to myself."

She shook her head and blinked hard at the fresh tears that pricked in her eyes. In doing what her father had done he'd permanently damaged his relationship with her, fractured the trust between her and Anna, and virtually destroyed any chance of her and Judd building a sibling bond together. She had no family she could rely on anymore—not her father, her brother, her sister and certainly not her mother. Nicole had not seen or heard from her mother since Cynthia Masters-Wilson had taken Judd back to her native Australia when he was six and Nicole only one year old.

Nicole had long since convinced herself she'd never wanted to know her mother growing up. Her father had been everything and everyone she'd ever needed. But even as a child, she'd always been able to tell that she wasn't enough to make up for the wife and son that her father still missed. It had driven Nicole to work harder, to be a top student and to learn everything she could about the family business, in the hopes of winning her father's approval, making him proud. Goodness only knew running Wilson Wines was all she'd ever wanted to do from the moment she'd understood just what held the balance of her father's attention every day.

Now that Judd was back, it was as if she didn't exist anymore. As if she never had.

Nicole reached up to remove the hair tie that had held her hair in its no-nonsense, businesslike ponytail all day, and shoved her fingers through her hair to tousle it out into party mode. She would not let her father's actions beat her. Once she'd worked this upset out of her system she'd figure out a way to fix things. Until then, she was going to enjoy herself.

She alighted from the taxi and paid the driver then undid the top button of her suit jacket, exposing a glimpse of the gold-and-black satin-and-lace bra she wore beneath it. There, she thought defiantly, from business woman to party girl in one easy step. Squaring her shoulders, Nicole headed into the first bar on the strip. Oblivion had never looked better.

Nate leaned against the bar and watched the pulsing throng of bodies on the dance floor with disinterest. He'd only agreed to come along tonight for Raoul's sake. Hosting the guy's stag party was small recompense for the work Raoul had done holding Jackson Importers together after Nate's father's sudden death last year. Knowing the running of the business was in Raoul's very capable hands until Nate could return to New Zealand to pick up the reins had been a massive relief. Extricating himself from Jackson Importers' European office and appointing a replacement there had taken time, and he owed the guy big for stepping up to the plate.

His philanthropy didn't assuage his boredom, however, and Nate was on the verge of saying his good-byes and making his way home when she caught his eye. The woman moved on the dance floor with a sensuous grace that sent a spiraling swell of primal male interest through his body. She was dressed as if she'd come from the office, although he'd never seen any of his staff look that good in a suit. Her jacket was unbuttoned just enough to give a tantalizing view of creamy feminine swells of flesh supported by sexy black satin and gold lace, and while her skirt wasn't exactly short, her long legs and spiky heels certainly made it look that way.

He felt a familiar twinge in his groin. All of a sudden, heading out to his home on the ocean side of the Waitakere Ranges wasn't his top priority anymore—at least not immediately and, hopefully, not alone.

Nate cut through the throng of seething bodies to get nearer. There was something familiar about her but he couldn't place it immediately. Her long dark hair swung around her face as she moved to the beat of the music and he imagined it swinging in other areas, gliding over his body. Oh, yes, definitely gliding over his body—or even spread across the starkness of his Egyptian cotton sheets while he glided across hers. He clenched and unclenched his jaw as every cell in his body responded to the visual image.

He let the beat of the music infuse him and eased in beside her. "Hi, can I join in?" he asked with a smile.

"Sure," she replied, before flicking her hair from her face and exposing dark eyes a man could lose himself in, and a delectably red-painted mouth that was made for pure sin.

They danced awhile, their bodies moving in synchronicity—close, but not touching. The air between them was incendiary. Would they move in such unison alone together, too?

Another dancer jostled past, knocking her against his chest. His hands whipped up to steady her and she looked up into his eyes with a smile that started slowly before spreading wide.

"My hero," she said, with a wicked gleam in her dark eyes.

He found his mouth curving in response. "I can be whatever you want me to be," he said, bending his head slightly and putting his mouth to the shell of her ear.

She quivered in his arms. "Anything?"

"Anything."

"Thank you," she said, so softly he almost couldn't hear her over the noise around them. "I could do with a dose of *anything* right now."

She draped her arms over his shoulders, the fingers of one hand playing with his hair where it sat at the nape of his neck. Her touch did crazy things to him. Things that made him want to do nothing more than take her out of here and transport her to his home, his bed.

Nate wasn't into one-night stands. Aside from the fact his mother had drilled respect for women into him from an early age, he'd never been that kind of guy. Nate liked to plan, to calculate all the angles—spontaneity wasn't really his strong suit, especially in his private life. He knew how important it was to be cautious, to keep people at a distance until you were sure of their motives. But there was something about the girl in his arms that made him want to take a chance.

He looked down into her face and recognition began to dawn. Suddenly he knew why she'd seemed familiar. She was Nicole Wilson—none other than Charles Wilson's daughter, and the second in command at Wilson Wines. Her picture had been in the dossier of information he'd asked Raoul to gather on the competition's business—and most especially on the man who had once been his father, Thomas's, closest and oldest friend. Charles Wilson, who had—after an angry row, rife with false accusations—subsequently become Thomas's bitterest rival.

Once, when he'd been a turbulent teen, Nate had promised his father he'd seek revenge for what Charles Wilson had done. Thomas, ever the peacemaker, had told him he was to do no such thing while Thomas still drew breath. Sadly now, his father was dead—not so sadly, all bets, in relation to Charles Wilson, were off.

Nate wasn't normally one to deliver on the sins of the father, but tonight's potential now took on a whole other edge. He'd been biding his time with Charles Wilson. Accumulating information, and planning his strategy carefully. But even if it hadn't been part of his plans, he wasn't about to ignore the opportunity that had just dropped into his arms.

A waft of Nicole's fragrance drifted off her heated body and teased his nose. The scent was rich and spicy, very much, he suspected, like the woman he held— their bodies moving in unison, undulating to the beat of the music that thrummed around them.

Nate didn't hide the arousal he felt for her. What was the point? If this didn't work out, then there'd be no foul. His plans would carry on regardless. But if it did, if she was responding to him the same way he reacted to her, his plans for revenge against Charles Wilson would take a very interesting turn indeed.

Nicole knew she'd had too much to drink tonight, and she knew full well that she should call another taxi to take her home. After all, it was only Thursday and she still had work tomorrow. At least, she thought she still had work tomorrow.

Thinking about work made her head hurt and the idea of returning to the house tonight just tied her stomach in knots and reminded her again of her father's low opinion of her. Earlier, she'd blocked out that reminder with a shot, and then another, egged on by a group of acquaintances she'd barely seen since she'd graduated from university and whom she could hardly call friends. Still, their lively and undemanding company tonight had been just what she sought. No questions, no answers. Just being lost in the moment. And right at this moment she was feeling very lost indeed. Lost in the undeniable attraction between two healthy young people in their prime.

Very little separated her and her dance partner and as her lower body brushed against him again, a classic Mae West line ran through her alcohol-clouded mind. She couldn't stifle the giggle that bubbled up from inside.

"Care to share the joke?"

She pressed her lips together and shook her head. There was no way she was sharing that little snippet.

"Then you have to pay a forfeit—you know that, don't you?"

"A forfeit?" she asked, her lips spreading into a

smile once more. "Surely you can't punish a girl for being happy?"

"I wasn't thinking of a punishment," he said.

She should be laughing at the line he'd just uttered, she told herself, yet, for some reason, a wicked coil of lust tightened inside her.

"Oh?" she managed through lips that she suddenly felt the urge to moisten with the tip of her tongue. "What were you thinking of?"

"This," he said.

She didn't have time to think, or room to move had she even wanted to dodge him, as he lowered his lips to hers. Lips that were unexpectedly cool and firm. Lips that sampled, tasted and teased her own.

The tight sensation inside her spread, tingling through her body like a slow-building charge of electricity, sensitizing her hidden places, draining her mind of any awareness of her surroundings. All she could think of, all she *wanted* to think of, was the touch of his mouth on hers. Of the delicious pressure of his body as his hands on her hips gathered her closer.

They continued to move to the music—her pelvis rolling against his, her awareness of his arousal becoming a hunger for more than the illicit touch of bodies through clothing. A moan built deep in her throat, a moan she fought to keep inside as he lifted his mouth from hers.

She swallowed and opened her eyes. In this light it was difficult to tell what color his eyes were, but they were definitely unusual and their hooded stare captured her and held her mesmerized. Didn't certain beasts of prey do the same? Was she about to be devoured? The thought didn't upset her as much as it should. God, she had to pull herself together.

"So, that's a forfeit, huh?" she asked, her voice thick with desire.

"It's just one of many."

"Intriguing."

Intriguing wasn't the word. His kiss had totally fried her synapses. It was all she could do to prevent herself from dragging his face down to hers again and repeating the experience. Once more with feeling, she thought, although she certainly hadn't been devoid of feeling while he'd been kissing her. For that moment in time she'd forgotten everything. Who she was, why she was here, what she had left to look forward to.

She'd liked that. She'd liked it a whole lot. She wanted to do it again.

"Hey, Nic!"

One of her acquaintances, Amy, appeared at her side and her dance partner released her. She instantly rued the loss of contact.

Her friend shouted to be heard over the music. "We're off to another club, you coming?"

Nicole's usual prudence screamed "safety in numbers" at the back of her mind, but tonight she wasn't in the mood to be prudent at all.

"No, I'm fine. I'll get a taxi home later."

"Okay. Hey, it was cool catching up again. Let's not leave it so long next time."

And then Amy was gone with the crowd she'd been hanging with.

"Are you sure you didn't want to go with your friends?" her dance partner asked.

"No, I'm fine. I'm a big girl, I can look after myself," Nicole answered.

"I'm pleased to hear it. I'm Nate, by the way."

"Nicole," she answered shortly, happy to keep their

introductions brief as she threw herself back into the thrum and energy of the DJ's latest sound selection.

She was distracted by the flash of someone's camera, no doubt someone's shenanigans would be broadcast on some social networking site tomorrow, but before long her focus was solely on the man in front of her. Boy, but he could move. Some guys just looked as if they were trying too hard on the dance floor but for him, movement came very naturally. And he was so good to look at, too.

His hair was dark, but not as dark as her near-black tresses, and his face was both masculine and had a re-fined elegance at the same time. And those lips—she was very keen for a repeat of what they had to offer.

"Do I pass muster?" he asked, one corner of his mouth twisting upward.

She smiled in response. "You'll do."

He laughed and the sound went straight to her toes, making them curl in delight. Was there anything about him that wasn't gorgeous?

The crowd around them had begun to thin and Nicole started to become aware that eventually this night would have to end. At about that point she'd be feeling the pain of dancing in high heels for sev-eral hours, along with the aftereffects of too much to drink. She hated that reality had to intrude again, es-pecially when she was having such a good time. Nate said something, but over the frenetic pulse of the music she didn't quite make it out.

"What was that you said?" Nicole asked, leaning closer.

Mmm, he even smelled great—like a cool ocean breeze.

"I said, would you like a drink?"

She'd probably had quite enough for one night but an imp of mischief prompted her to nod her head.

"Here? Or we could head back to my place if you'd rather."

She felt a frisson of excitement. Was he suggesting what she thought he was suggesting? She'd never done this before—gone back to some random guy's house for a drink, at least not without a posse of friends with her. But for some reason she felt as if she could trust Nate, and then there was that amazing energy between them. She deserved to find out if those sparks were real, didn't she? Wouldn't it be some solace for the night she'd put up with?

"Your place is fine."

Actually, anywhere but home was fine.

"Great." He smiled, the action sending a sizzle of anticipation thrilling through her veins.

Sore feet and the prospect of a hangover were the furthest things from her mind as Nate took her hand and led her toward the exit. And if thoughts of "danger" or "risk" occurred to her, she brushed them aside. Tonight was a night for taking chances.

And besides, what was the worst that could happen?

Two

Nate caught Raoul's eye as he led Nicole away, giving his friend a nod. He briefly saw Raoul's answering wink before the expression on the other man's face changed to one of shocked recognition. Nate fought back the smug smile that pulled at his lips.

In all the years he'd spent imagining how he would bring Charles Wilson to his knees, he'd never once imagined this scenario. But then, he'd never imagined taking Charles Wilson's daughter in his arms and feeling such a searing sense of attraction, either. With such a ripe opportunity before him, he'd be a fool not to make the most of it—in every way possible. Still, he had to be careful. It wouldn't do to put the cart before the horse. He could just as easily be calling a taxi to take Nicole home after their drink, but something inside him told him that was very unlikely.

He reached in his pocket and pressed the remote to

the low-slung silver Maserati that waited for them at the curb.

"Very pretty car," Nicole commented as he held open the passenger door for her and she folded her delicious long legs into the passenger bay.

"I like to travel in style," he answered with a smile.

"I like that in a man," she answered, her lips curving in response.

He just bet she did. She'd never wanted for anything and every part of her life had been to the highest standard. It stood to reason that Nicole Wilson's demands of her men would be high. It was a gauntlet he relished picking up.

Unlike Nicole, Nate knew what it was like to struggle—his father had been a living example of the concept for most of Nate's childhood. After Charles Wilson had kicked him out of the business they'd built together, it had taken years for Thomas to reestablish his credibility and build a company of his own. Nate had watched as his father poured his everything into his fledgling business in an attempt to provide something, anything, to the woman he'd accidentally gotten pregnant and the son their liaison had borne. And while Thomas had done his best to shield his only child, the experience had left its mark, resulting in two rules that Nate had lived his life by ever since. Rule one: be very careful who you trust.

Rule two: all's fair in love and war.

Nate slid into the driver's seat and started the car, maneuvering it smoothly toward Hobson Street and the entrance to the North Western motorway.

"You're a Westie?" Nicole asked.

"After a fashion," he answered. "I have a couple of

places. Karekare is where I call home. You still want that drink at my place?"

His challenge hung between them in the dark interior of the car. He shot her a glance and saw her press her lips together and swallow before answering.

"I'm all good. I haven't been out to Karekare in ages."

"It's still pretty much the same. Wild and beautiful."

"Like you?" she asked, her eyes gleaming as she shot him a glance.

"I was thinking more along the lines of you."

She laughed, the sound filling the cabin of his car and making his gut tighten in anticipation.

"Oh, you're good. You know all the right things to say to salve a wounded soul."

"Wounded?" he probed.

"Just family stuff. Too complicated and too boring to bring up now," she hedged.

Was all no longer well in the Wilson household? Nate wondered. He'd made it his business to know what happened within Wilson Wines and he'd heard of the return of the prodigal son. Had Judd Wilson's arrival served to uplift the mantel of golden child off Nicole's shoulders?

"We have a long drive," Nate pointed out as they entered the motorway and his car picked up speed. "I'm willing to listen if you want to talk about it."

"Just the usual," she said with an attempt at flippancy. An attempt that failed judging by the tone of her voice.

"Sounds serious," he commented, keeping his eyes looking forward out the windscreen.

She sighed, the sound coming from somewhere deep

down inside her. "I had a fight with my dad. At the risk of sounding clichéd, he doesn't understand me."

"Isn't that a parental prerogative?"

She laughed, a short, sharp sound in total contrast to the last time she'd done so. "I suppose so. I just feel so used, you know? I have spent my whole life trying to measure up, to be the best daughter, the best workmate, the best—well, everything. And he thinks I should settle down and have *babies!* As if. You know, I think he values a paper clip on his desk more highly than he does me. I've spent the past five years helping him to keep our family business thriving and he tells me it's a nice *hobby* for me."

"I suppose this argument is what led you to the club tonight?"

"Too right it is. I couldn't stay under his roof another second. Oh, no, wait. It's not *his* roof anymore, nor mine. He's gone and given it all to my dear long-lost brother." She expelled an angry huff of air. "I'm sorry, I'm always letting my mouth run away with me. I shouldn't have said that. Just pretend you didn't hear that last bit, okay? I think we should change the subject. Talking about my family is just going to spoil my mood."

"Whatever the lady wants, the lady gets," Nate replied smoothly, even though his curiosity burned to know more about the Wilson family home situation.

"Now that's more like it." Nicole laughed in response. "A girl could get used to that attitude."

"What, you mean that isn't always the case?"

Nicole swiveled slightly in her seat and stared at him. "You say that as if you think you know me."

"You misunderstand me," he said smoothly. "I just

would have thought that a woman like you would have no trouble getting what she wanted."

She gave an inelegant snort, then change the subject. "Tell me about your home. Are you overlooking the beach?"

He nodded. Partly in concession to her change of subject and partly in answer to her question. "I'm on a slight rise looking out onto Union Bay."

"I've always loved the West Coast. The black sand beaches, the crazy surf. There's something so, I dunno, untamed, unpredictable about it all."

"You surf?"

She shook her head. "No, always been too chicken."

Somehow she didn't strike him as the type of woman to be afraid of anything, and he said as much.

"Some boundaries I just never pushed. I grew up as an only child with a parent who could be pretty strict. Sometimes my dad took overprotectiveness a little far."

"Only child? You mentioned a brother?"

"He lived with our mother up until recently. And how on earth did we get back on that awful topic again?"

She pushed a hand through her tangled long hair, exposing the sweep of her high cheekbones and the determined set of her jaw. His fingers itched to trace the fine bone structure, to taste the smooth skin that stretched over it. Nate tightened his grip once more, dragging his eyes back to the road and his mind back to the goal at hand. Yes, he wanted her. And yes, he had every intention of having her. But he couldn't let himself lose control. He had to keep the endgame in mind.

"What about you?" she asked, turning in her seat to look at him. "What's your family like?"

"Both my parents are gone. My mother while I was

in university, my dad more recently. I never had any brothers or sisters."

"So you're all alone? Lucky you." She gasped as if she realized the potentially pain-filled minefield she'd just trodden into. "I'm sorry, that was insensitive."

"No, it's okay. I miss them but I still count myself lucky to have had them both in my life. And my dad was a great role model. He worked his heart out, literally, to provide for us, and I got to repay that once I graduated and started working in the family firm."

Nate deliberately kept things vague. He wouldn't, for a moment, begin to elaborate on exactly why his father's health took such a beating as he strived to build a new business from the ground up. Or who was responsible for that.

"So, surfing?" he asked, very deliberately changing the subject as he took the exit he needed that would eventually lead them out toward the beach.

"What about it?"

"Want to try it over the weekend?"

"This weekend?"

"Sure, why not stay. I have spare boards, spare wetsuits."

"Spare clothes, underwear?" She gestured to her voluminous bag on the car floor. "It might be a big bag but it's hardly *Doctor Who's* TARDIS, you know."

Nate laughed. Her sharp wit was refreshing and appealing at the same time.

"Let's play it by ear then, hmm? Trust me?"

"Sure. If I didn't think I could trust you, I wouldn't be here."

He reached across and took her hand, caressing the soft skin of her inner wrist with his thumb.

"Good."

He let go and placed his fingers firmly back on the steering wheel. From the corner of his eye he saw that she stroked her wrist with the fingertips of her other hand. He allowed himself a small smile of satisfaction. This night was going perfectly.

So why *did* she trust him, she wondered as she lapsed into silence and looked idly out the passenger window. It's not as if she knew him. She'd acted purely on instinct, a fact that—despite her earlier assertion about being a chicken—had gotten her in trouble many a time before.

She gave herself a mental shake. She deserved this night. She had it coming to her after the crap she'd put up with at dinner on top of everything else this week. And everything in her body told her that this was the man to take all her problems away—at least for the night.

Her skin still tingled where he'd touched her, the sensation a delicious buzz of promise hovering just beneath the surface. Did he expect to make love to her tonight? Just the thought of it sent a thrill of longing through her body, making her womb clench tight on a swell of need that all but knocked the air from her lungs. She'd never had this intense a reaction to anyone before. Just sneaking a glance at his hands on the steering wheel, at the way his long fingers curled around the leather, made her want those fingers on her, in her. She pressed her thighs together and felt the swollen heated flesh at her core respond. Just thinking about him touching her was nearly enough to make her go off. What would it be like when he did?

She cleared her throat against the sudden anticipatory lump that lodged there.

"Everything okay?" Nate asked.

"Sure. It's quite a drive from the city to your place. Do you work in town?"

"Yeah. I keep an apartment there for the nights I'm too tired to make it back out to Karekare, or if I have an early run to the airport or early meetings. I sleep better with the sounds of the sea and the rainforest around me, though."

"Sounds idyllic."

"You'll see soon enough for yourself."

She fell silent as they entered Scenic Drive, letting her body sway with the roll of the car as they wound on the narrow ribbon of road higher into the ranges, before winding back down again on the other side. She must have dozed off a little because the next thing she knew the Maserati was driving up a steep incline and pulling into a well-lit garage. A glance at her watch said it was almost 2:00 a.m. The drive had taken nearly an hour. She was miles from anyone she knew, miles from home. She should find the fact daunting—she didn't. In fact, she welcomed it. Knew that with her choice to come home with Nate that she'd thrown her cares to the wind.

"Home sweet home," Nate said, coming around to her side of the car and opening the door for her.

Nicole accepted his hand as he helped her out the car, her senses purring at his touch. To her surprise he didn't let go, instead leading her to a doorway which, when opened, revealed a short set of stairs leading down into a massive open-plan living/dining and kitchen area.

The furnishings were comfortable but spoke plainly of their price in the elegantly simple designs and top-quality fabrics. A large, open fireplace, bordered with

gray slate, occupied space on one wall. Even the art-
works on the walls and small sculptures on the occasional shelving were beautiful and no doubt expensive.
What he surrounded himself with said a lot about him
and, so far, she liked it.

"Still feel like that drink?" Nate asked, lifting her
hand to his lips and pressing a kiss against her knuckles.

"Sure, what are we having?"

"There's champagne in the fridge, or we could have
a liqueur."

"A liqueur, I think."

Something potent and heady, just like him, she
thought privately. Nate let her hand go and moved
toward a built-in sideboard on the other side of the
room. She gravitated toward the wall of glass that faced
the inky darkness outside. Beyond the floor-to-ceiling
windows she could hear the sound of waves rolling
heavily into shore.

In the reflection of the glass she saw Nate come to
stand behind her, one arm coming around to offer her
a small glass of golden liquid.

"A toast, I think," he said, his breath warm in her
hair and making her scalp prickle in awareness.

"To what in particular?" Nicole asked, accepting her
glass and raising it toward Nate's pale facsimile mirrored before her.

"To wounded souls, and the healing of them."

She nodded and raised her glass to her lips, her taste
buds reacting instantly to the smooth, sweet tang of
aged malt whiskey. She allowed the liquid to stay on
her tongue for a moment before swallowing.

"Now that is pretty fine," she said, turning to face Nate.
Her breath caught in her chest as she saw the look

in his eyes. Eyes that were only a shade darker than the deep gold fluid in their glasses.

"Only the best," he answered before closing the distance between their faces.

Nicole felt her heart race in her chest. If this kiss was to be anything like the one at the club she couldn't wait to experience it. Her lips parted expectantly, her gaze focused solely on the shape of his mouth, on the sheen left there by the liqueur. Her eyelids slid closed as she felt the warmth of him, as his lips took hers, as his tongue swept gently across the soft fullness of her lower lip.

He made a sound of appreciation. "Now that's what I call the best."

His lips pressed against hers once more and she curved into his body as one arm slid around her back and drew her closer to him. He was already aroused, a fact that triggered an insistent throb in her veins— a throb that went deeper into her center. She pressed her hips against him, feeling his length, his hardness. Feeling her body respond with heat and moisture and need.

She could taste the liqueur on his lips, on his tongue—its fusion of flavors intrinsically blended with his own. When he withdrew she felt herself move with him, toward him. Drawn as if by some magnetic force.

Nate put his liqueur glass on a shelf nearby before also taking hers and doing the same again. He then lifted his hands to her hair, pushing his fingers through the long mass until his fingertips massaged the back of her scalp, gently tilting her face to his once more. This time his kiss held a stronger taste of hunger, a promise of things to come.

Nicole tugged his shirt free of his waistband and

shoved her hands underneath, her nails gently scoring his back as she traced the line of his spine, up, then down. Logic tickled at the back of her mind a final time, telling her she shouldn't be here, shouldn't be doing this, but need and desire overcame logic with the same inexorable surge and release of the waves that echoed on the darkened shore outside.

He wanted her. She wanted him. It was basic and primal and it was all she needed for now. That, and a whole lot of satisfaction.

Nate's hand shifted to the buttons on her jacket, swiftly loosening them from their button holes and pushing aside the fabric, exposing her to him. His hands were broad and warm as they swept around the curve of her waist before skimming her rib cage and moving up toward her bra.

He released her lips, bending his head lower, along her jaw line, down the sensitive cord of her neck and across her collarbone. She felt her breasts grow heavy. Her nipples beading tight, almost painfully so, behind her expensive lace-covered satin bra. When the tip of his tongue swept across one creamy swell she shuddered in response, the sensation of the point of his tongue electric as it traced a fine line across the curve of one breast. He awarded the same attention to her other breast, this time sending a sharp spear straight to her core.

His tongue followed the edge of her bra before dipping in the valley between. Her breath came in quick pants, her heart continuing to race in her chest. She felt his hand at her back, felt the freedom of the clasp of her bra being released, the weight of her breasts falling free as he slid her jacket off her shoulders and pushed her bra straps down to follow. With scant regard for the designer labels of both garments, Nate let them drop to the polished timber floor.

Nicole was beyond caring as his mouth captured one extended nipple, pulling it gently between his teeth, laving it with the heat of his tongue. Her legs began to tremble and she clung to him, near mindless with the pleasure his touch brought her. When his hands went to the waistband of her skirt she barely noticed, and then, with a slither of silk lining, her skirt joined her bra and jacket on the floor at her feet.

Dressed only in a scanty pair of black-and-gold panties and her high-heeled, black patent pumps she should have felt vulnerable, but as Nate pulled away, his eyes caressing every inch of her, she felt powerful. Needed. Wanted.

"Tell me what you want," he demanded, his voice a low demand that vibrated across the space between them.

"I want you to touch me," she replied softly.

"Show me where."

She lifted her hands to her bare breasts, her fingers cupping their smooth fullness, lifting them slightly before her fingertips abraded the distended tips, sending another shudder through her.

"Here," she said, her voice thicker now.

"And?"

One hand crept down, over her flat belly, and to the top band of her panties.

"Here." Her voice trembled as she felt the heat that pooled between her legs, felt the moisture that awaited his touch, his possession.

"Show me what you like," he said, his hand sliding over hers.

"This," she replied, letting their hands push beneath the scrap of fabric.

She led his fingers toward her opening, dipping them in her wetness before sliding them back up toward the budded bundle of nerves that screamed for his touch. She circled the sensitive spot first with her fingers then with his, increasing the pressure then slowing things down before repeating the cycle once more.

"Keep touching yourself," he commanded, even as he slid his fingers out from beneath her hand, dipping them lower until they played within the soft folds of her flesh.

He hooked his other arm around her, supporting her weight as he stepped in a little closer. She felt the fabric of his trousers against her bare legs—a fleeting awareness only before all concentration went when he stroked one finger inside her body, then another. Her muscles clenched against him as his fingertips glided in and out, caressing with careful and deliberate pressure against her inner walls.

Sensation swirled throughout her body, drenching her with heat and pleasure. The combination of both their touches filled her with an overpowering awareness of him, his strength, his power over her. She'd never felt anything this deep, this intense. Had never been this reckless.

Nate bent slightly, capturing one nipple with his mouth, drawing the sensitive bud into his heat, his wetness, and suckling hard. As he did so, she felt the pressure of his fingers inside her increase and with that subtle change, her body splintered apart on a wave of satisfaction so intense, so immeasurable, that her legs buckled beneath her and tiny pin pricks of light danced behind her eyelids.

Her whole body shook with the intensity of her orgasm as ripple after ripple of pleasure coursed through her. She felt Nate withdraw from inside her, even as her inner muscles continued to pull and tighten against him, heightening the sensations and sending her into another short, sharp paroxysm of bliss. He slid one hand behind her knees and, with his other arm still supporting her back, he swept her into his arms and strode across the open plan area toward a darkened room.

His bedroom, her shattered senses finally recognized as he placed her on the bedcovers. In the fractured blend of moon and starlight that shone through the massive picture window, she watched as he stripped away his clothing. Exposing every inch of his silver-gilded male beauty to her gaze. He reached for her feet, removing the shoes she only just now realized she still wore, then his hands slid up the length of her legs. When he reached her panties he slowly removed them from her before lowering himself to the bed and gently kneeing her legs apart, settling between them.

He leaned across her and ripped open a bedside cabinet drawer and removed a box of condoms. Extracting a packet he made short work of ripping away the wrapper and rolling the protection over his jutting erection. Her hands fluttered to the breadth of his shoulders, his skin burning beneath her touch. Despite his clear and evident arousal, his movements were smooth, controlled and deliberate as he positioned himself at her entrance and looked up to meet her eyes, even now giving her the chance to change her mind, to decide for herself what she wanted. In response, she instinctively tilted her pelvis to welcome his invasion.

Nate lowered his face to hers, his lips a heated seal against her own, his tongue gently probing her mouth even as he eased his length within her. She felt her body stretch to accommodate his size, felt an unmistakable quiver deep inside. Nicole lifted her hands to his head, her fingers lacing through his hair as she held him to her and kissed him back with all she had left in her.

Her body swept to aching life as he began to move, his thrusts powerful and deep, so deep it felt as if he touched her very soul before she plunged into the abyss of sensual gratification once more. In answer, his body stiffened, buried to the hilt, and a nearly stifled cry of release broke from him as he gave over to his own climax, shuddering as her body clenched rhythmically around him. His lips found hers again as he settled his weight on top of her, and she welcomed him. It was real, he was real. His heart thudded in his chest and hers beat a rapid tattoo in answer.

What they'd done together was something unsurpassed in her experience and finally, as she drifted to sleep, the cares and worries of her life wafted away into oblivion.

Three

As Nate woke, he slowly became aware that he'd fallen asleep not just on top of Nicole, but still inside her, as well. He silently castigated himself for his inconsiderate behavior as he carefully supported his weight without waking her.

He ignored the unfamiliar urge to settle closer to her rather than pulling away. After all, certain precautions had to be observed, he reminded himself. He reached between them, feeling for the edge of his condom and cursing when he couldn't find it. He pulled farther away from her, his body instantly lamenting the lack of contact with her lush warmth. The condom was still inside her. In a moment of panic he wondered if she was on the Pill but that fear was quickly assuaged. A woman like Nicole wasn't the type to leave things to chance. It was highly unlikely that pregnancy was something either of them needed to worry about just now.

No, now was a time to concentrate on pleasure. They'd had sex once and he couldn't wait to repeat the experience.

He eased his hand between her splayed legs and found the condom, removing it carefully before disposing of it in his bathroom. As he eased his body back onto the bed beside her he safeguarded them once more by rolling on another sheath and gathered her to him. She curled instinctively against his body, her softness pressing against the hard muscled planes of his chest, her inner heat already beckoning to him.

Her eyes flickered open, a slow smile spreading across her face. He cupped one cheek in his hand. It was one thing to know from Raoul's report that Nicole Wilson was an attractive woman with an incredibly sharp business mind, but it was quite another to discover that she was also a warm and generous lover. The knowledge skewed his vision of how this would ultimately play out.

Sending Nicole back to her father was no longer an option. With a little luck, her anger against her father and her brother just might be deep enough and strong enough to make her willingly defect to Jackson Importers...and to Nate's bed. With Nicole at his side he could take Jackson Importers to the ultimate heights of success, while ensuring his nights were equally, if not more, satisfying.

Of course, there was always the possibility that loyalty to her family would win out. Nate would be a fool not to plan for that contingency. If that happened, he'd have to be more...creative in the methods he used to keep Nicole. He didn't want to hurt her—Charles was his only target—but if upsetting her a little was the price to get his revenge *and* keep Nicole in the bargain, then that was a price he was willing to pay.

Sooner or later, she'd thank him for it. He'd already known her father hadn't utilized her intelligence to his best advantage. But Nate would. And she'd know she was appreciated while he did it. Every glorious inch of her.

"You're so beautiful," he said, meaning every syllable.

"It's dark," she replied, a teasing note in her voice. "Everyone is beautiful in the dark. You can't see their bad side."

"You don't have a bad side," he said, leaning forward to kiss her.

"Everyone has a bad side, Nate. We just don't always show it."

There was a painful truth in her words. A truth he knew related directly to him and his intentions but he didn't want to think about that right now. More pressing matters were most definitely at hand.

"Sometimes it's better not to see, then, isn't it?" he asked before leaning across the short distance between them and kissing her.

Their lips touched in a burst of heat and desire, his every nerve striving to attain the heights of fulfillment he knew he would reach in her arms. This time the fire inside him burned steadily, not threatening to overwhelm him as it had before, but his hunger for her had not lessened despite the change in his appetite. This was to be savored, slowly, completely.

Time faded into obscurity and nothing mattered right now except the giving and receiving of pleasure. Each touch destined to bring a sigh or a moan from its recipient, each kiss a seal of the promise of what was yet to come. And when she positioned herself over his body and lowered herself over his straining flesh he gave himself over totally to her demands.

Their peak was no less intense than that first time together, and this time, when Nicole fell into his arms lost in the aftermath and falling rapidly into sleep, he made certain the same accident with the condom didn't occur a second time.

The next time he woke, sunlight was filtering through the native bush outside and into his bedroom window. He reached across the bed. Empty. Where was his quarry now, he wondered as he swung his legs over the side of the bed and stood, stretching as he did so.

"Nice view," a voice said from behind him.

He turned slowly, a smile on his face. A smile that widened when he saw that Nicole had found the camcorder he kept for filming some of the more wild surfing antics on the beach.

"Do you have a license to drive that thing?" he asked.

"I'm the kind of girl who likes to learn as she goes along," Nicole answered in response.

She was wearing just the shirt he'd worn last night, the fine cotton covering her body but leaving her long legs exposed to his hungry gaze.

"So you're more of the hands-on kind?" he said, feeling his body stir and his blood pump just a little faster.

"Oh, yes, definitely hands-on," she said, her voice a little rough around the edges.

"I've always thought practical experience to be vastly underrated, haven't you?" He was fully hard now. Every cell in his body attuned to her, to the camcorder she held, to the idea that now blossomed in his mind.

"Definitely underrated. And the value of visual aids, too."

Oh, God, he thought. She had just read his mind. "I have a tripod for that thing, you know."

She laughed, a deep throaty chuckle that made him clench his hands at his sides to stop himself from reaching for her.

"More than one, I'd say," she said, dropping the lens of the camera down, then slowly back up again to his face.

She was wicked. He liked that in a woman. He liked that a whole lot. "I'll go get the other one," he said with a slow wink.

Before she could say another word he brushed past her, dropping a kiss on the curve of her lips as he went by. "Why don't you get yourself comfortable on the bed? I'll be back in just a minute."

It took less than a minute before he was back in the bedroom and setting up the stand diagonal to the bed. She passed him the camera, her cheeks flushed with color, her eyes bright with anticipation. Beneath the fabric of his shirt he could see the sway of her breasts as she moved on the bed, not to mention the sharp peaks of her nipples that told of her excitement. She passed the camera to him and he carefully positioned it on its mount, ensuring the whole bed was square in the frame.

"You're sure about this?" he asked.

"Oh, very sure. And later, when we review it, we can see where we can improve."

He didn't think it was possible to get any harder but at that moment he did. It was one thing to know they were videoing themselves, another to know she wanted to watch it later.

"Where do you suggest we begin?" he asked, fighting to keep a lid on the carnal urge to simply have at her, to let her have at him and to hell with finesse.

"I think I need to get to know you better, don't you?" She patted the edge of the bed beside her. "Why don't you sit down?"

He sat and watched her as she slid off the tumbled linens and knelt between his legs on the rug beside the bed, placing her hands on the outside edges of his thighs, scratching lightly with her fingernails.

"It seems to me," she continued, "that last night was all about me. So this time, it's going to be all about you."

A fine tremor ran through his body and he watched as her hands stroked up his thighs and down again, each time working a little closer to the inside.

"Do you like that?" she asked.

He was beyond words and merely nodded.

"How about this?"

His mind nearly exploded as she bent her head and flicked the tip of her tongue over the aching head of his arousal. His penis jumped in response to her touch, a bead of moisture appearing only to be licked away just as quickly. Nicole's hair brushed against his inner thighs, obscuring her face. He reached down and pushed her hair aside, holding it against the back of her head with each fisted hand. He wanted to see this, all of it. And, just in case, he wanted the camera to see it, too.

Nicole felt an unaccustomed sense of possession as she lightly stroked her tongue along the length of

Nate's erection, painstakingly following the line of each vein from tip to base and back again. Heat rolled off him in waves as she did so and she felt him tremble as he fought to maintain control. But that control shattered the instant she took him fully in her mouth. He groaned, a guttural sound that came from deep in his belly, and she knew the exact moment he was going to climax. She increased the pressure of her mouth, her tongue, increased the rhythm of her movements until he spent himself. She slowed her pace, taking the last drop of his essence as he groaned again, his hands falling to his sides and his body falling back onto the bed behind him.

She pushed herself up onto the bed and lay propped on one elbow alongside him, letting her fingers trail up and down across his belly and chest as he caught his breath once more. His recovery said a whole lot about his fitness and stamina, she thought as he reached one arm up to her and dragged her down to kiss him. Already he was stirring again, and the knowledge gave her a wonderful feeling. It was all because of her.

"Mmm," she said, her lips bare centimeters from his. "Must be time for breakfast."

"Not yet," he said. "I think we should work up a bit more of an appetite first. And I think you should take that shirt off, too."

He deftly flicked open each button and slid one hand inside, cupping one breast and flicking his thumb across its hardened crest.

"I'm very hungry already," she purred. "I may take some convincing."

"You want convincing? I can be convincing," he said, pushing the shirt off her shoulders and then pressing her onto the bed.

What followed was an education in how someone could deliver a lifetime of hedonistic delight in very short order. Nate applied himself to her with assiduous intent, showing her just how artful he could be with the merest accessories—the tip of a tongue, a feather of breath, the stroke of a fingertip.

She was on the verge of begging, no, screaming for release when he finally sheathed himself with a condom and took them both over the edge of sanity and into a realm where only blithe elation resided.

The camera caught it all.

Their morning set the tone for the next three days. From time to time they would rise, bathe or eat—once taking a long stroll along the beach, Nicole wearing ill-fitting borrowed clothes—before the draw of their fascination with one another would take them back to bed again. By Monday morning Nicole was spent. Physically and emotionally, happy just to curl up against the hard male body beside her and revel in the intimacies they'd shared. Last night Nate had burned a DVD of their video and they'd viewed it while attempting to eat a civilized meal in the main room of the house.

The clothing they'd only recently donned—him in a pair of jeans and T-shirt, her in a sweatshirt of his with the sleeves rolled up and its length skimming the back of her thighs—had soon hit the floor. Their food cooling on their plates as the on-screen activity had incited a new hunger for one another all over again.

Nate still slept beside her and she watched his chest rise and fall on each breath. She was amazed at how natural it felt to be with him, especially considering how little they actually knew about one another. She'd heard the girls at work talk and giggle over their occasional one-night stands—guys they never expected, or in some cases even wanted, to see again—but she'd never believed she'd indulge in something quite so illicit herself. She felt as if the past few days had been a vacation, not just from work and responsibility, but from herself—her own fears and anxieties. On Friday she hadn't even given a care to the fact she had probably still been expected at the office, nor that over the course of the whole weekend she hadn't so much as told anyone where she was, nor checked her cell phone for messages.

It wasn't as if they cared, anyway, a little voice said from deep down inside. Her father didn't believe she had a valid contribution to make to the company, her best friend had turned on her and her brother? Well, he didn't even know her, nor she him. So what difference would it make if she walked away from all of them for good?

A whole lot of difference, she realized. She'd been angry on Thursday night. Really angry. And she'd acted completely out of character. Deep down she knew her family, including Anna, loved her and had to be worried about her having been out of touch for so long.

This person in the bed with a stranger, that wasn't her. Sure, it had been a great time, but all good things had to come to an end sometime, didn't they? Nothing this good ever lasted for long.

A wave of guilt for her behavior swamped her, driving her from the bed and into the bathroom where she gave in to the sudden well of tears in her eyes. She'd behaved irrationally. Stupidly. She had no idea of who she was really with. Everything that had anchored her these past twenty-six years lay on the other side of town—with her family, in her home. So what if her father had signed the property over to Judd? Her brother wasn't about to summarily eject her from the only home she'd ever known, surely. Judd was as much a victim of her father's shenanigans as she. So was Anna, who was far too grateful for all that Charles had done for her and her mother to ever tell him no.

And as for her father… It would be difficult for her to forgive or forget his words on Thursday night. But she couldn't forget twenty-six years of him sheltering and protecting her, either. For better or for worse, he was still her father. They'd just have to find a way to reach an accord. She was willing to take the first step, and come back home.

Nicole dashed her face with water and dried it before quietly letting herself out of the master bathroom and padding quietly across the bedroom floor. As she closed the door behind her she let go the breath she hadn't realized she'd been holding. She gave herself a mental shake. For goodness sake, she was an adult. Her decisions were her own, her choices were her own. The weekend had been great, just what she'd needed, there was no need to sneak around like a thief in the night.

She squared her shoulders and made her way to the laundry room where she'd hand washed and hung her underwear to dry during the course of the weekend. Her suit was on a hanger and had been brushed and steamed to get the creases out after being summarily left on the living room floor for several hours after Thursday night. She slid into her underwear and put on her suit. It felt strange to be dressed so formally after a weekend where clothing had been minimal.

She picked up her bag from in the living room and brushed out her hair before heading back to the bedroom to retrieve her shoes. She'd have to call a cab to get herself into work, she thought as she twisted her hair up into a knot and secured it with a clip she'd found in the bottom of her bag.

Nate was awake when she pushed open the door.

"Going somewhere?" he asked, his eyes unreadable as he watched her slide her feet into her shoes.

"Yeah, time to get back to reality." She sighed. "This weekend has been great. Better than great, thanks."

"That's it?"

"What—" she laughed nervously "—you want more?"

"I always want more, especially of what we've had."

"I never said I didn't want to see you again."

"But you implied it."

Nicole shot him a nervous glance. Was he going to get all weird on her now?

"Look, I need to get home and then head into work."

"No."

She shot him another look, this time the curl of fear in her stomach unfurled to bigger proportions.

"What do you mean, no?"

"What I mean is, you're coming to work with me."

Nate pushed aside the bed sheets and rose to his feet, calmly picking up the jeans he'd discarded last night and sliding them on. Nicole struggled to avert her gaze from the fine arrow of hair that angled down from his belly button to behind the waistband of his pants. She'd followed that path, and more, several times this weekend. A hot flush of color rushed to her cheeks. She couldn't let herself get distracted by sexual attraction. What on earth did he mean when he said she'd be working with him? She didn't even know what he did for a living. And he didn't know anything about her… did he?

"You've got it wrong, I have a job. A job I love, with a family I—"

"Don't tell me you love them, Nicole. Not after what they've done to you."

Instantly she rued the way she'd mouthed off in the car when he'd brought her here, and the truths she'd shared over a bottle of red wine as they'd curled naked beneath a blanket on the couch in front of a burning fire, late on Saturday night.

"They're still family. At the very least I need to clear the air with them."

"Oh, I think that's a bit more than they deserve. Besides, the air will clear soon enough."

Nicole crossed her arms across her stomach. "What on earth are you talking about?"

"When they learn who you've just spent this past weekend with, I very much doubt they'll be welcoming you home with open arms. I'm pretty much persona non grata with your father."

Nate's lips lifted in a half smile, as if he was laughing at a private joke.

"You're speaking in riddles. Why should they care who I spent the weekend with?" she snapped.

Nate came to stand in front of her. "Because I'm Nate Hunter—Nate Hunter Jackson."

Nicole's mind reeled on his words. Nate Hunter? *The* Nate Hunter? The reclusive billionaire who was the new head of Jackson Importers, her family firm's arch nemesis? Her father had never had a kind word to say about Thomas Jackson, or his staff.

Hang on a minute. Nicole replayed his words in her mind. Had he said Nate Hunter *Jackson?*

"I see you've made the connection," Nate said coolly. "And, yes, I am Thomas Jackson's son. Sweet, isn't it? All that time your father accused my dad of screwing around with your mother, he was actually with mine."

Nicole looked at him in horror as his words slowly sank in, leaving her mind reeling. She hadn't just been sleeping with a stranger over the entire weekend—she'd literally been sleeping with the enemy!

Four

Nate watched the shock and dismay play across Nicole's features as understanding clouded her beautiful brown eyes.

"So you knew who I was all along? This weekend has all been about you getting some twisted revenge on my family?" she asked. Her voice shook, betraying just how much his words had upset her.

It might have started that way, Nate admitted to himself, but now he'd been with Nicole so intimately he knew that for the better part of their time together, revenge had been the last thing on his mind. At least, revenge on *her*. Her father, of course, was another matter entirely.

"Did you hunt me out?" she demanded, her voice stronger now.

"Our meeting was by chance," he said smoothly. "A happy chance from my point of view." He stepped forward and reached one finger to her cheekbone, tracing the smooth feminine contour to the corner of her lips. "And I don't regret a second of it, Nicole."

She jerked her head away. "Of course you don't," she said angrily. "Well, your little game is over now. I'm heading back into the city to my family and my job."

"I don't think so," Nate responded smoothly, crossing his arms in front of him.

"You can't possibly be serious about me working for you."

"I'm serious, all right."

"No." Nicole took a step back from him, putting one hand out as if she could physically prevent his words from holding any truth. "There's no way in this lifetime that I'd do such a thing, even if my father didn't want me at Wilson Wines. It would destroy every last vestige of our relationship together. He may not understand me as well as I'd hoped for, but he's still my father. I won't do that to him. I just won't."

Why couldn't she have stayed angry at her family? That would have made this so much easier, Nate thought to himself. Was there any way he could stoke that anger again?

"You *are* talking about the man who said that Wilson Wines was a nice hobby for you, aren't you?"

She shook her head, more in frustration, he imagined, than to negate what he'd just said. Nate pursued his advantage in the face of her silence.

"And you're talking about the man who, without a word of discussion with you—his right hand at Wilson Wines—gave away a controlling interest in his business to someone who is essentially a complete and utter stranger to both of you."

"Stop," she moaned, wrapping her arms about herself and holding them tight. "I know that's what he's done, you don't need to repeat it. He's my father. No matter what, he'll always be my dad. I'll always be loyal to him."

"Really? Why? He's even given away your family home, Nicole. Again, without any prior warning to you, nor any assurance for you that you will have a roof over your head anymore. Haven't you asked yourself yet what kind of man would do that to his daughter?"

Nate was angry, furiously angry. Not at Nicole, who seemed determined to forgive her father anything, but at the man who was at the root of all Nate's unhappiness. The man whose brutal rejection of his best friend had crushed Thomas Jackson's spirit and had forced him into dire financial straits. And the man who had withheld his encouragement and support from his daughter for so long that she'd forgive any insult for the chance to earn his approval.

He pressed on as she stood there silent and pale.

"You deserve more, Nicole. You deserve so much more. You're a strong, intelligent and incredibly capable woman. You should work somewhere where you're valued and appreciated. Think about the team we'll make. We'll be the best the business has ever seen."

She raised tear-washed eyes to his face and he fought to ignore the spear of regret that penetrated somewhere in the region of his chest. He knew his words hurt her but he couldn't afford to be soft, not now. If she didn't give in soon, he'd have to hurt her a lot more. He didn't want to, but he would, if it came to that. All was fair in love and war. And this was war.

"Nicole, your loyalty to Charles Wilson is commendable, but sadly misplaced. Work with me. Help me grow Jackson Importers to its fullest potential. Be a part of something special."

She swallowed before speaking. "And what's in it for you? You can't expect me to believe you're doing this out of the goodness of your heart."

He laughed, a short humorless sound that hung in the air between them for only a second or two. "No, I'm not doing it out of the goodness of my heart. I'm a businessman. I play to win, at all times and," he hesitated a moment for effect, "at all costs."

She shook her head again. "I won't work for you and I'm leaving right now. You're not the man I thought you were, Nate. I can't do what you're asking of me."

"Nicole, I'm not asking."

"I still have some say in this, don't I?" she demanded, turning and heading for the front door.

"Sure, you still have a say," he said, his words halting her in her tracks. "But so do I, and there's still a card left for me to play."

"I wasn't aware this was a game," she said coolly.

"Not a game at all," Nate said, smiling, even though his voice held no warmth anymore. "But all the same, I *will* win." He gestured toward the video camera still on the tripod in the corner of the room. "Ask yourself this, how would your father feel if he saw our amateur movie? What would hurt him more? Seeing you work for me, or knowing that you'd spent this past weekend in my bed?"

"Th—that's not fair," Nicole stammered, struggling to keep her balance. It felt as if the floor had been knocked out from under her. "I didn't know who you were then."

"I never said I play fair, Nicole. Your father already

hates the Jackson name. Already believes your mother slept with my father—it's what tore Charles and Thomas's friendship apart, what divided your family and what destroyed mine. I'll be sure to include a note with the DVD, explaining my parentage. How do you think he'd feel about seeing his daughter intimately engaged with Thomas Jackson's son?"

"You wouldn't!" Nicole uttered the words even though her throat felt as if it had constricted with shock and fear.

"Oh, believe me. I very much would. I want you, Nicole. I want you in my boardroom, in my office, in the field as well as here—in my home and in my bed."

Her skin tautened as his words fell upon her ears. Her nipples hardening even as a rush of warmth spread through her lower belly and her inner muscles clenched involuntarily in reaction to his words. Stop it, she told herself. He wasn't simply talking about sex. He was talking about her betraying her father. About her walking away from the company she'd hoped all her life that she would eventually take over. The job that was so much more than a job. It had been her way of life— her dream. It had been everything to her father and, ergo, everything to her, as well.

What Nate was suggesting was appalling. If she quit her job at Wilson Wines to work for Nate, her father would never understand, never forgive her. But could she take the risk that Nate would follow through on his threat and send her father a copy of their illicit week-end? Even as the thought presented itself in her mind, she knew without a shadow of a doubt that Nate would do exactly what he said. Men like him didn't always play fair or clean—and they rarely bluffed. It would

hurt her father if she worked for Nate but it would probably kill him if he saw that video.

"You're a bastard," she said quietly.

"Oh, yes, no question about that," Nate answered, a
thread of bitterness in his voice that she hadn't heard
before.

She racked her memory. Her father had rarely
spoken about the man who had been his best friend
from school, but when he did it had been in scathing
terms. Thomas Jackson had never married. Never even
publicly acknowledged he had a son. Was Nate even
telling the truth about his relationship with the man?

She was hit with a sudden wave of hopelessness. Did
any of her conjecture even matter when right now Nate
held all the cards very firmly in those dexterous hands
of his? Hands that had done wickedly delicious things
to her over the past seventy-two hours. She clamped
down on the thought before it took her over again. She
had to forget the man she thought she'd grown to know
a little these past few days. Had to remember, instead,
the hardheaded businessman who had so mercilessly
embarked on their time together knowing full well who
she was and what being with him would mean to her
family.

Her family. They were what had gotten her into this
mess. Them and her blasted impulsiveness. She could
see the lines of disappointment carved into her father's
face even now.

"So, Nicole, what's it to be?"

Nate stood opposite her, his hands loosely on his
lean jean-clad hips, his chest still bare, his shoulders
still showing evidence of their passion where she'd
clutched him tightly—her nails imbedding in his skin,
lost in the throes of yet more pleasure. Even now, with

his intentions out in the open, she still had to fight her desire for him. What did that say about her? She didn't even want to begin to examine that question.

She couldn't do it. She couldn't let her father see her wanton behavior, especially with the man who epitomized everything her father had fought against in the past twenty-five years. She had no other choice. She had to do as he said.

"You win."

"There, that wasn't too difficult, was it?"

She flung a fulminating look at him. "You have no idea."

She was damned if she did as he'd demanded, and she was damned if she didn't. At least this way she could protect her father from seeing the full extent of her own stupid behavior. Her face burned with shame as she remembered that she had been the one to pull out the camcorder in the first place. Furious and embarrassed, she pushed the thought away.

Nate Hunter Jackson might have won this round but he wouldn't win them all, she silently vowed. One way or another, she'd get her own back on him.

"This doesn't have to be a bad thing. At least with me you won't be taken for granted, Nicole," he said.

She ignored him. Being taken for granted was the least of her immediate worries. "I need to go home and get my things, and pick up my car," she said with as much control as she could muster.

"That won't be necessary."

She gestured to the suit she'd put back on this morning. Despite her attentions to it, the garment still looked a little the worse for wear and in need of a professional dry clean.

"Sorry to disappoint you, but I need my clothes. I can't wear this forever."

"Personally, I kind of like the idea of you not wearing it."

"Personally, I don't care what you like," she retaliated. She may have been forced into agreeing to his terms but she'd take a long walk off a short pier before she'd take her clothes off again at his behest. "I need my things—my car, my cell phone charger, everything. And I'll need to tell my father and brother that I won't be working for them anymore."

"I'll arrange for your car to be collected. As to your clothes, we can take care of that on the way into work. And, as to your father and brother, I'll take care of letting them know. There's no way to break it to them gently, and being blunt would be a miserable experience for you, but will be quite a lot of fun for me. Now, give me five minutes to shower and change. We can have breakfast in the city before we shop."

He turned and headed for the bathroom.

"I'm not hungry," she said to his retreating back.

Nate stopped and turned around, his hands already at the button fly of his jeans and exposing his lower abdomen to her gaze. "Not hungry? That's a shame. I'll have to have enough appetite for the both of us, then, won't I?"

Nicole dragged her eyes from the half open fly of his jeans and up to his face. His eyes burned with a heat that sent an answering response coursing through her body.

"Yes, you will," she said through teeth clenched so tight her jaw ached. She forced herself to relax the tiniest bit before continuing. "Because I have absolutely no appetite at all."

There, she thought, take that. She spun on one high heel and stomped through to the massive picture window facing the sea in the living room. Even there she was destined for disappointment, she thought. Instead of the rough roiling ocean she'd come to expect from the wild west coast beach ahead of her, there was nothing but a clear-blue autumn sky, rolling deep green water and foaming white crests of waves caressing the sparkling black sand shoreline. It was a complete contrast to the storm of emotion that tossed around inside her.

She was going to work for the son of her father's biggest business rival. He'd never forgive her this. Not in a million years. She shouldn't care, she told herself. He was the one who had summarily dismissed all her years of hard work for Wilson Wines and along with that dismissal had put aside her business and marketing degrees, not to mention the years of after-school and school holiday work experience she'd doggedly labored through so she could understand his business from the ground up. He'd never realized how important the business was to her because he'd never grasped how important *he* was to her.

Somewhere along the line, and from a very early age, Nicole had understood that her father's business was his everything. It was what he poured his heart and soul into every waking hour of every day. She'd thought that if she did exactly what he did, she'd earn his respect. And still he thought it was no more than a dalliance for her. Something to fill in her time before the more important matters of marriage and making babies filled her life.

Her hands tightened into fists, her perfectly manicured nails biting into the skin of her palms, as all her latent frustration built deep inside her. Getting angry at her father all over again would make it easier to walk away from Wilson Wines...but deep down, she knew the anger wouldn't last. She loved her father, and she knew that he loved her, even if they'd both fallen short on finding a way to connect. But even now, she refused to believe that it was too late. She closed her eyes to the perfection of the view outside and forced herself to draw in a steadying breath, and then another. Somehow she'd work her way through this. Somehow she'd work her way back to her family again.

"You ready?"

Nate's voice came from behind her. She opened her eyes and turned around. In a tailored charcoal-gray suit, with a crisp white shirt and flame-colored silk tie, he was a world away from the sensual creature who'd filled her weekend with sybaritic delight. A world away, but no less appealing. She ruthlessly pushed aside the admission.

"I was waiting for you, remember?" she said, scathingly.

He smiled, the action making something inside her tug hard. She silently cursed him for having this effect on her.

"Let's go, then."

The drive into the city was interminable. Nicole checked her cell phone for about the sixteenth time since they'd started out on the road. She hadn't had her phone on all weekend but even now the thing was down to only one bar of battery left. One bar and no blasted reception. Just as they crested a hill, she saw she finally had a signal and, with that, her phone began to vibrate in her hand as one message after the other poured in. By the time it settled down she saw she had six missed calls, an equal number of voice messages and more texts than she cared to count. Before she could do anything about them, though, her phone died—all the beeping and vibrating having drained the last of its charge.

"Argh!" she growled in frustration.

"Problem?" Nate asked, infuriatingly calm.

"My phone just died."

"No problem, I'll get you a new one. It'll be better that way—start over fresh."

"I like this one," she said doggedly. "It already has everything I need in it."

"It has what you needed for your old life—not for your new one. You've got a whole new list of people you'll be working with, communicating with. Besides, that was probably a company-subsidized phone—and you're not with that company anymore."

To her surprise, Nate took one hand off the steering wheel and reached across to take the phone from her hand.

"Needs updating, too," he said, giving the technology a cursory glance. "The one I get you will have better programming—and better access, too. I can't have you out of range whenever you're at the house."

"There's noth— Wait! What the hell are you doing?"

His driver's window rolled down smoothly and he lobbed the phone out onto the road where, to her horror, it was promptly run over by a truck coming in the opposite direction.

"How dare you? That was mine."

"I told you, I'll get you a new one. That one's no good anymore, anyway."

"No thanks to you."

She fought back the tears that suddenly came into

her eyes. This was a complete nightmare. Did he have to control everything? Maybe it would have been better to bite the bullet, after all, and suffer the consequences of her father seeing the DVD. Even as she thought it, Nicole pushed the thought from her mind. Her father's health had been declining in recent years. He'd ignored his diabetes for too long and the damage it had wrought on his system was beginning to tell on him, making him look much older than his sixty-six years. She didn't even want to imagine the impact a major shock to his system would have on his health.

No, she was in this for the long haul. No matter what it took, no matter the toll on her.

"The replacement had better be top of the line," she said, putting as much steel into her voice as she could.

"Of course. Nothing but the best for you, I promise."

"That's quite a promise. Do you really think you can meet it?"

Nate flicked a glance in her direction before returning his gaze to the traffic ahead.

"I'm a man of my word."

"That remains to be seen," she muttered, focusing her attention out the passenger window.

The way he'd said it, it held more threat than promise, and for some reason that, more than anything, chilled her to the bone.

Nate watched as Nicole was taken through to the fitting room of the third designer store they'd been to so far this morning. She'd insisted on getting a new wardrobe before eating, which now left him starving—but not for any food. He was hungry for her. For the feel of the texture of her skin beneath his touch, for the taste of her on his lips, for all the little sighs and moans she made while they explored one another's bodies with intimate precision.

Part of him wanted to say to hell with work—and clothes—and just head back to the house for another day in bed. Only two things stopped him.

The first was the office. Jackson Importers was his father's legacy in so many ways, and when Nate had taken up the mantle as CEO, he'd promised himself that he would invest every energy, every effort, into making the company the absolute best it could be. He didn't balk at long hours or working weekends, and even when he'd been stuck at home with a stomach bug, he'd still checked in through email all day long. Calling in sick on Friday had undoubtedly raised a few eyebrows. If he missed work on Monday, too, his staff would probably send an ambulance out to his house.

The second reason was Nicole, herself. Yes, he wanted her badly—both in bed and out of it. She was more than he'd ever dreamed of. He already knew she had a very smart mind—the dossier Raoul had prepared on the Wilson family had been thorough. If Nate could have found a way to headhunt Nicole Wilson for Jackson Importers after his father's death, he probably wouldn't have even needed to come home from Europe to take over the business. Her misplaced loyalty to her father was well documented, however, and he hadn't even bothered trying to steal her away.

That loyalty was the problem he was dealing with now. He supposed it had been too much to hope that her frustration with her family would lead her to welcome the chance to enact a little revenge along with him.

But her dedication to her father wouldn't be an obstacle forever, he rationalized. Sooner or later, she'd have to realize that Nate treated her better, and appreciated her more, than her father ever could. When she accepted that—and when she realized that the passion between them was impossible to ignore or deny—she'd turn her loyalty to him. She didn't know it yet, but he would be the best thing that had ever happened in her life. He just had to be patient until she came to terms with that—and watch her closely.

Yes, watch her *very* closely, because if the glares she kept giving him were any indication, any hand he reached out to touch her would come back to him bleeding. She was furious with him for forcing her into this position—and a smart, capable woman with a grudge was a dangerous creature, indeed.

So he'd have to be on his guard. Nothing new there—he was always on his guard. And he knew, far better than his father ever had, to be very careful before giving a Wilson his trust.

"Miss Wilson is finished now, Mr. Hunter," the store manager said, coming through with an armful of clothing and a smile that told of the sizeable commission she'd no doubt be earning today.

"So soon?"

"She has very specific tastes and was quick to decide on what she needed."

Nate gave the delivery address of his inner-city apartment for the clothing and handed over his platinum card, then looked back toward the changing rooms. Nicole was walking toward him in a new outfit, one that made his breath still in his lungs and all the blood in his body race to a very specific part of his anatomy. The ruby-red dress, while probably perfectly acceptable office wear on anyone else, skimmed every curve of her graceful figure. The scooped neckline of-

fering a tantalizing hint of the swell of her full breasts.
The three-quarter-length sleeves exposing her slender
forearms. Forearms that led to delicate wrists and elegant hands. Hands that had gripped him and teased
him and delivered all kinds of pleasure.

"All done now?" he asked as she drew alongside
him.

"I just need some underwear and sleepwear."

"Sure. Do you want to eat first or keep shopping?"

"Still got that appetite?" she said, with a hint of an
acerbic humor.

He looked her up and down very deliberately before
meeting the unspoken challenge in her dark-eyed stare.
"Always."

His reward came in the sudden flush of color that
suffused her cheeks.

"We'd better get some food, then," she said sharply,
breaking eye contact and giving her attention to the
store manager—thanking the other woman for her assistance.

They stopped at a café in Vulcan Lane where he
consumed Eggs Benedict while she played with a
mixed berry muffin on her plate. While lingering over
his coffee, Nate picked up the complimentary newspaper the café provided. He flicked through the pages,
emitting a long slow whistle when he reached the society page.

"Looks like I might not have to make that call to
your father's office, after all," he said, folding back the
page and showing it to Nicole.

Five

They danced together, right there in black and white. Caught in time forever. Their intense absorption in one another as clear as day on their faces. Opposite him, Nicole paled and drew in a sharp breath.

"Did you orchestrate this?" she demanded.

Nate laughed. "I'm flattered you think I have that much power but, no, I didn't."

She looked at him as if she didn't believe a word that came from his mouth.

"Obviously you want to hurt my dad, but why go to all this trouble with me over something that happened so long ago? Our fathers fell out. Their friendship broke up. It happens."

Nate looked at her over the rim of his coffee cup. Did she really think it was that simple?

"Your father accused mine of something he didn't do. He wouldn't listen to reason nor would he ever accept he was wrong. He broke my father's heart, broke the man inside him, destroyed his honor. And thanks to your father's actions, my father had to work himself to the bone just to make ends meet as he got Jackson Importers off the ground, ruining his health and making him die before his time. My father deserved better than that and so did my mother."

"And will hurting mine bring them back? Will it make it all better again?"

"No, but it will give me the utmost satisfaction when Charles Wilson is finally forced to admit he was wrong."

Nicole shook her head. "You're the one who is wrong, Nate. Let this go. Let *me* go."

Let her go? Before her father had learned his lesson? Before Nicole had accepted how good they could be together? Oh, no.

"Not going to happen." He picked up his cup and drained the last of his coffee. "If you're finished playing with your food, we should get the last of your shopping done before heading into the office."

They walked together up Queen Street toward Auckland's oldest department store. It amused Nate that Nicole maintained a clear foot of distance between them at all times. Not easy to do in the throng of business people, shoppers and tourists who congested the footpaths. When they reached the department store, Nicole lingered awhile at the cosmetics counters on the ground floor leaving Nate to hand his card over again as she purchased skin care, fragrance and cosmetics.

"You don't need to do this," she objected, her own credit card in her hand already.

"Humor me," he said, taking her card and examining it. "This in your name or under your father?"

"It's all mine, paid for by my very own wages. Is that okay?" She snatched it back from him and pushed it back into her wallet before gathering up her bags from the shop girl and heading toward women's wear upstairs.

"I'll get you another one."

"This one is perfectly fine."

No it wasn't, he thought. Anything that led back to Charles Wilson in any way was, in his book, tainted—and her previous earnings definitely led back to Charles Wilson. Nate had every intention of paying her a generous salary, and until that began, he intended to take care of things. Take care of *her*. Nothing but the best for her—he'd promised her that, and he'd meant it.

Upstairs in the lingerie department he was again relegated to a chair while Nicole browsed rack after frothy rack of underwear. When she'd finally made her selection and gone through to the changing rooms he got up from his chair and paced the floor. As he did so, his eye latched onto a stunning ensemble on a floor mannequin. The ivory lace-and-chiffon nightgown and matching peignoir was both innocence and pure sin in one simple package.

Attracting the eye of the sales clerk he gestured to the ensemble.

"Include one of these in Miss Wilson's size with her purchases, thank you. And, please, keep it as a surprise."

He flashed the woman a wink and a smile and the blushing clerk hastened to fulfill his request before Nicole returned from the changing rooms. Already he could imagine peeling the diaphanous garment from Nicole's lithe body, but not before he'd tormented both her, and himself, with touching her through its silken texture first.

It would be torment enough for him waiting for her to come back to his bed. But the waiting would pay off sooner or later. It would all pay off in the end.

It was well past lunchtime before they made it into Nate's offices in a high-rise overlooking Auckland's Waitemata Harbor. He settled his hand on the small of her back as they exited the elevator and directed her toward a set of glass doors emblazoned in gold leaf with "Jackson Importers" and its stylized logo of a bunch of grapes.

He reached forward and opened the door, holding it for Nicole as she walked through and into the reception area. His receptionist looked up and smiled. He introduced Nicole immediately.

"April, this is Miss Wilson, she'll be working with us from now on. I'd like you to call all the staff into the boardroom to meet her in about fifteen minutes."

"Surely that won't be necessary," Nicole protested. "I can just—"

"I want everyone to know who you are and why you're here," he said in a voice that brooked no argument. "Tomorrow I'll introduce you to the staff at our warehouse and distribution center."

She pressed her lips together, clearly biting back whatever it was that she wanted to say. He guided her down the corridor and pushed open the door that led into the boardroom. Seeing her there, in his offices, in that stunning dress, his self-control cracked. The instant the door closed behind him, he couldn't stop himself from sweeping her into his arms, drawing her against his body and lowering his head to capture her mouth. The second their lips touched he felt electrified, the charge of energy he got from her sizzling a slow burn all the way to the pit of his stomach.

"I needed that," he groaned against her lips when he'd sated his need, however temporarily.

"Well, I didn't. I'd appreciate it if you kept your hands, and all your other body parts, to yourself," Nicole answered, moving out of his reach and smoothing her dress in a gesture that spoke more of nervousness than any real desire to stay out of reach.

Well, he couldn't say he hadn't expected that. But still… "You can't deny you enjoyed it," Nate said, observing the brightness of her eyes, the rapid rise and fall of her chest.

"How I might respond to you physically is one thing. Whether I actually want to, is another. Don't touch me again."

"Ever?" he asked, narrowing his eyes.

"Ever," she adamantly replied.

"So you're telling me that if I did this," he touched a fingertip to the slight swell of her breasts visible above the neckline of her dress, "that you don't *want* more?"

Nicole fought to control the wave of need that trembled through her body. She couldn't show him any weakness, not for a minute. Men like Nate Jackson capitalized on weakness and she could not afford for him to get any more leverage on her than he already had.

"There's a name for what you're doing," she managed to finally say. "I believe it's called harassment."

To her surprise, Nate laughed. Genuine pleasure at her words making his eyes lighten and shine.

"You're priceless," he said through his good humor.

"Harassment. Would you have said it was harassment at about 3:00 a.m. this morning, when I—"

Nicole was saved from the torture of hearing him repeat what they'd been doing in the small hours of this morning, and saved, thank God, from giving him an answer when the door behind them opened.

"Ah, Raoul, please meet our newest addition to the team, Nicole Wilson. Nicole, this is Raoul Benoit. Don't be fooled by his name, he's just as much a Kiwi as you or I."

Raoul inclined his head in acknowledgement of Nate's introduction and gave Nicole a shy smile.

"Miss Wilson, it's a pleasure to meet you, and even more of a pleasure to have you on our team."

"I…" What on earth could she say? She couldn't exactly tell Raoul she was here under duress. That she'd virtually been kidnapped and forced to come here. "Thank you."

Raoul looked at Nate and she didn't miss the question in Raoul's eyes as he did so. The expression of supreme satisfaction on Nate's face told her everything she needed to know. Raoul Benoit knew exactly who she was and exactly what Nate was up to. It made her feel alienated, as if she was completely alone in this horrible situation.

Nate's voice broke into her thoughts. "I've asked April to get the staff in here to meet Nicole. I think it's a good idea to let everyone know she's going to be with us from now on."

His words made her feel like nothing more than a trophy, but before she could utter a word of protest, the door opened again. A steady stream of people came into the boardroom, sitting where they could and standing, lining the wall, when all the seats were taken. She was surprised Jackson Importers carried such a large staff in their Auckland offices, and Nate had spoken of a warehouse and distribution staff, as well. It rammed home the reality of what he'd coerced her into doing—working with the thriving and very competitive enemy. The next quarter hour passed in a blur.

By the time Nate showed Nicole to his office, her head was spinning and she was beginning to regret not having eaten that berry muffin at breakfast.

"And this is where you'll be working," he said as he closed the office door behind them.

Nicole looked around the sumptuously appointed office, at the amazing view of the harbor beyond and then back at him.

"This is your office. I can't work here."

He shrugged. "I'm prepared to share my space with you. All my space, Nicole. Together we're going to head up the most successful wine importation business in the country. Why would I want you anywhere else but at my side?"

That all sounded very impressive—but what did it really mean? "Is that a fancy way of saying that you want to keep an eye on me?"

He smirked. "I'll always enjoy having my eyes—or anything else—on you." Nicole huffed in frustration, and Nate continued, "If you're asking if I'll be watching your work, then the answer is yes. I know that right now, you don't want to be here and you're angry with me for forcing your hand. I think that'll change. I think that once you understand the opportunities for you here, you'll see that this is where you belong. When that day comes, you can have any office you want. Until then, you'll understand if I prefer to keep you where I can see you. After all, I'll certainly enjoy the view."

"What about privacy for phone calls and things like that?"

"Worried I might overhear your conversations?"

"Do you plan to follow me to the bathroom, as well?" she demanded, her temper finally fraying. Since his very unwelcome revelation this morning, he'd been controlling everything about her except for how she drew breath—and even that was under deliberation. Every time he brushed past her she got a tightness in her chest that was all his fault.

"Do you need me to?"

"I don't *need* you for anything," she said mutinously.

"Like your father doesn't need you?"

He knew exactly how to cut to precisely where it hurt. Nicole turned from him and tossed her handbag onto his desk.

"Well, if this is where I'm supposed to be, I'd better get to work, then, hadn't I?"

He smiled and gestured to the laptop and cell phone on the desk that he'd arranged to have delivered while waiting outside her dressing rooms. "They're all yours, have at it."

"Mine. Already?"

"I told you I'd take care of you, Nicole. I meant every word I said."

She swallowed against the lump that suddenly filled her throat. He said it like he meant it. As if she was something—no, some*one*—important to him. She didn't want to believe it. Couldn't believe it. They'd had a weekend of great sex. Okay, it was off the scale great sex. But that was all. There couldn't be anything more between them, especially not now he'd made his intentions toward her father explicitly clear.

"Where do you want me to start?" she asked, crossing behind the desk and opening the laptop, determined to keep this on a professional level even if it was likely to destroy her.

"How about you spend some time on coming to grips with our new internet-only business? It's taken off far quicker than we anticipated and reaches beyond our existing New Zealand market and allows us to trade overseas, as well. It cuts overheads considerably as, in many cases, we've been able to coordinate shipping direct between the vineyard and the buyer, thus cutting freight and storage costs to a minimum."

Nicole felt the thrill of excitement at learning a new business model ripple through her. For years, she'd been urging her father to consider an online ordering system rather than solely relying on hands-on distribution. True, hand selling often gave wine-store customers a chance to try something new that they might not have considered before, but to hope that would continue to buoy the market forever was professional suicide. The world changed at an incredibly fast pace. The wine distribution industry no less so.

Another thought occurred to her. Nate's approach to supervision had thrown a spanner in her initial plans to use her access to sabotage some of Jackson Importers' business, but there was still a chance to come out ahead here. Deep down she knew this situation couldn't last. Eventually she'd find a way to return to Wilson Wines, and Nate was giving her the perfect opportunity to learn as much as she could of their successful business practices and think about how Wilson Wines could implement them, or use them to create something even better.

Remaining focused on business was easier said than done as Nate pulled up a chair next to hers and brushed against her as he keyed in the URL that would take her computer onto the Jackson Importers portal.

"You'll need your own password. I'll get IT onto that immediately. While I go and sort that out, why don't you cruise around the website and make a list of questions you want to ask me?"

She merely nodded as he stood again, sucking in a deep breath of relief when he left the office. She'd thought her anger and resentment toward him would allow her to cope better with his close presence here in the office. The opposite couldn't have been more true. She'd found her eyes riveted on his long fingers as they'd flown over the keyboard of her new laptop, and had been forced to quell the memory of what those fingers had felt like as they'd flown over her body.

Nicole leaned back in the high-backed, leather office chair and swung around to face the view out over the Waitemata Harbour. Even on a workday the water was scattered with yachts making the most of the autumn sunshine and the strong breeze. How she wished she could emulate their freedom. But freedom was something that would remain in limited supply for her until she could work a way out of this mess. Somehow, someway, she'd find a way to get her own back on Nate Jackson, and, like his father before him, he'd be sorry he'd ever tangled with a Wilson.

Six

Nate spent the rest of the afternoon with Nicole, discussing the wines they imported and the systems that Jackson Importers had in place both in New Zealand and overseas for distribution to their worldwide network of buyers. By the time the sun was dipping below the Waitakere Ranges in the distance, they were both looking pretty exhausted.

"I think it's best if we stay in town tonight, at my apartment," Nate said as he stood and stretched out the kinks he'd gathered in his back from sitting at his desk so long.

"Whatever you say," Nicole muttered.

"Would you rather head out to Karekare? We'll have to swing by the apartment and collect your new things first."

"I'd rather go home—to my home—but since that's

not going to happen, I don't really care one way or the other where I sleep tonight."

Her dark brown eyes met his in a silent challenge—as if she was daring him to contradict her. Nate knew full well when to pick his battles and she'd be disappointed if she thought he was going to rise to her bait this time around.

"Good then, it's settled. The apartment it is."

A flush rose in her cheeks. Annoyance, perhaps? Irritated or not, she gathered her bag and followed him out the office. She remained silent until they reached the undercover parking below the apartment complex.

"Is that my car?"

While she'd been interested and had plied him with questions about Jackson Importers all afternoon, this was the first sign of genuine animation he'd seen in her face since the weekend.

"Sure is. I have two spaces here. It makes sense for you to have your own wheels easily available, but we'll probably commute together most of the time."

She hastened out of the Maserati and he watched as she checked over her vehicle, examining every panel.

"It's a Roadster, right?" he asked.

"Yeah," she replied, finally satisfied the vehicle had come to no harm. "A '58 300 SL, to be precise. Good to see your people didn't do any damage."

"I only use the best," he replied.

Nicole eyed him over the soft top of her car. What would he do, she wondered, if she just jumped in, started it up and gunned it out of here? The instant the thought blossomed in her mind she knew she'd never carry it through. Not when he held such damning evidence over her and especially not now that the photo of the two of them last Thursday night had probably been brought to her father's attention.

"I'm pleased to hear it," she finally managed.

"Come on up to the apartment. You must be starving by now."

Now that he mentioned it, she was pretty hungry. She'd only had a nibble of the muffin at breakfast and had refused to stop and eat lunch.

"Sure, it's not like there's anything else to do," she said with a touch of defiance.

For some reason he gave her a look that she could only describe as approving. What? She'd subtly insulted him and he beamed back at her? The man was a conundrum, all right. A very powerful and sexy conundrum with an inordinate amount of control over her life right now. She may not like it, but she would just have to get used to it, she told herself. Even so, she didn't have to make him positively happy about the situation.

The trip in the elevator was smooth and swift and the doors opened to a corridor lined with expensive artwork. Her heels sank into the thick carpet as they walked to the end of the corridor where Nate swiped a key card and then pushed open one of two massive double doors and gestured her inside. Her breath caught in her throat as she took in the vista in front of her. She'd thought the view from his office was stunning, but this was something else. She could see over North Head and Mt. Victoria, out to Rangitoto Island and beyond.

"You certainly like your sea views," she said, dropping her bag on one of the wide and comfortable-looking leather sofas that faced out to the balcony.

"I do."

His answer was short and succinct and came from

right behind her. Suddenly she was aware of him. Painfully aware. Every nerve in her body attuned to the knowledge that right now very little space separated them. After that one kiss in the boardroom, he'd kept his distance. She hadn't realized up until now just how much she'd craved his touch. But she wouldn't give in. Couldn't. She had some pride left.

Before he could do anything, she stepped away, creating a void between them as she turned and faced him. A void that left her body silently screaming but which she refused to acknowledge, because that would only have her fall very firmly exactly where he so obviously wanted her, again. She might not be able to control much else in her world right now, but she could have some mastery over herself—however hard fought for.

"Where is my bedroom?" she asked.

"The master suite is right through there," he said, pointing down a wide hallway.

"No, not your bedroom," she said pointedly, "mine. I agreed to work for you. I never said anything about anything else."

"Anything else being?"

"You know exactly what I mean."

"Oh, you mean this?"

Nate traced the neckline of her dress with the knuckle of his forefinger, smiling approvingly when her skin reacted with a scatter of goose bumps. Nicole didn't move, she could barely breathe. One touch from him was about enough to send her up in flames. Already her entire body was invested in that tiny point of contact. She steeled herself for more, knowing she daren't so much as betray another measure of reaction.

"Are you going to force me, Nate?" she asked, her

voice deadly calm and at total odds with the swirl of desire that fought for dominance.

"Force you? No, I don't think so."

"Believe me, I don't want you."

"You don't want me—or you don't *want* to want me?"

She held her ground, refusing to answer, still not moving so much as a muscle. Eventually Nate let his hand drop.

"There's a guest bedroom and en suite second on the right. I'll move your things in there."

"Thank you."

Nicole allowed herself to breathe again. It was a small victory but an important one. She felt as if she'd conquered Everest.

It was Thursday evening, a week since they'd met, yet it felt as if it had been a lifetime. Nicole shut down her laptop and grabbed the overseas market reports she planned on using as her bedtime reading tonight. Sleep had been elusive these past few days. Knowing Nate was only meters down the hall from where she slept each night was unnerving. *It was your own choice,* she reminded herself sternly.

She'd been surprised to find Nate appeared unperturbed by her insistence on separate rooms, and it made her wonder whether she was alone in believing their lovemaking had been way outside the usual realm of experience. Maybe he was like that with all his women. She was surprised at the bitter taste that formed in the back of her mouth at the thought. How many other women lay in their bed each night reliving, caress by caress, the exquisite beauty of his touch against their skin, the possession of his body as it filled theirs?

She closed her eyes as a surge of need billowed through her body. It was just sex, for goodness' sake, she reminded herself as she shook her head slightly and opened her eyes. She could live without it. *Liar,* an insidious voice in the back of her mind whispered.

The office door swung open and the object of her thoughts filled the doorway. Her eyes roamed his body, taking in every aspect of his perfection from the hand-tooled leather of his Italian shoes to the sharp line of his tailored suit jacket. Slowly she raised her eyes to meet his, cursing the flush she knew colored her cheeks.

"I'm glad I caught you," Nate said, dispensing with any social pleasantries.

He was like that, she'd noticed. Charming as all get out when necessary, but straight to the point when it wasn't. Clearly she fell into the "not necessary to be charmed" pile now, Nicole thought with an internal grimace. *Or maybe,* that little inner voice whispered again, *he's just as frustrated as you are and this is how he shows it.*

"What's up?" Nicole answered, forcing a nonchalance into her voice she was far from feeling.

"Your brother and Anna Garrick headed down to the Marlborough region today."

"Judd and Anna? Why?"

"I was hoping you'd be in the position to answer that. We all know it's one of New Zealand's major wine producing areas but Wilson Wines has only ever sold imported product for distribution before."

"Oh, no!" Nicole lifted a hand to her mouth.

"You know why they're there?"

She shook her head. "I can't be certain. Dad pretty

much dismissed my study as being a waste of time and energy."

"Study?" Nate's expression became intent, every muscle in his body drawn tight.

"With the rising cost of international freight and the fluctuation of the New Zealand dollar, I thought it would be a good time to explore the internal distribution of a solid range of New Zealand wines. Wines not already being sold through major liquor retailers and supermarkets. The kinds of wines people might find in upmarket restaurants, bars and hotels. But make those wines a bit more accessible to the average consumer," she explained.

"Makes sense." Nate nodded. "Why did your father dismiss the study? Was it not feasible?"

Nicole laughed. "You think my father explained his decision to me? You don't know him as well as you think. No, he just told me we weren't pursuing it any further and not to waste any more of my time on it. So I didn't. Judd or Anna must have found my reports and somehow persuaded him the idea had merit."

"They've gone down to solicit new suppliers?"

"I'd say so."

Nicole fought to hide the hot rush of anger she felt toward her father for his about-face on her recommendations.

"You must have put a lot of work into this. It pisses you off, doesn't it, that your brother is getting to see through what you started?"

"That's a polite way of putting it," Nicole said. She was angry and hugely disappointed that she hadn't had the opportunity to see it all through. "I'd already approached several wineries whose management teams were very keen to come on board."

"Then I'd suggest you stop wasting time," Nate said, a half smile on his face.

"Time?" She felt like an idiot. What on earth was he talking about.

"Yeah, get down there and win back your business. Show me you can go at this with everything you've got."

Nicole looked at him in amazement. Carte blanche to progress her idea? Just like that? What if it failed? There were already so many wonderful and inexpensive New Zealand wines on the market, could it support more? Would there be a demand for the more exclusive vintages? And what about the upmarket imported wines they already sold? Would they be eating into their current business instead of growing new opportunities?

Her market analysis and research had borne out a definite niche of demand. Maybe she'd been too quick to let her father quash her idea. Maybe she just should have fought harder for what she believed in, what she knew to have great potential. Excitement began to bubble through her veins.

"Right, I'll get right on it," she said, reaching into her handbag for one of the backup memory sticks she always carried with her and powering her computer back up. She'd show Nate, all right. Success or fail, she'd show him, and maybe—just maybe—somewhere along the line she'd get to show her father her true worth to him, after all.

"Need any help?" Nate offered.

"No, I think I'll be okay. I'll start making calls first thing tomorrow and plan to head down on Sunday. I'd rather not bump into Judd and Anna while I'm down there so if I can work out who they're likely to be seeing first, and when, I can follow along behind and make an offer the wineries can't refuse."

"I like the way you think. I take it you have those reports on your drive?"

She nodded, automatically pulling up the files even as he spoke.

Inside, however, she alternated between disbelief that Nate believed in her ideas and the sheer joy of being told to implement them. She hesitated before sending the print command, waiting for him to reveal the catch or to shut her down, but, to her surprise, it didn't come.

"If you print me off a set we can go over them together. I'll order some dinner up for us while you do that."

Nicole nodded again, forcing her focus on the screen in front of her as Nate left the room. He was really going ahead with this. She'd reprinted her list of contacts and her feasibility study by the time Nate returned to the office.

"I've asked a few others to stay back in case you need them," he said as he grabbed a chair and pulled it next to her.

"Really?" she said, trying to control the sudden acceleration in her heart rate as his large body filled the space next to hers.

"We're a team here, Nicole. I wouldn't expect any of my staff to do this all alone. Besides, when it comes to you making an offer your clients can't refuse, I think it would be best if that offer came from a brainstorming session among us all so that it is completely unbeatable."

Nicole murmured her assent and concentrated on her computer screen as unexpected tears sprang to her eyes. A team. Even though she was here under duress, Nate still trusted her with all the resources of his company, backing her play and giving her room to develop her plan collaboratively, with all the help she needed. It was quite a change from Wilson Wines, where an idea of hers would have had to be fully formulated, presented and approved by her father before any backup was given.

It was a system that had probably worked well when the company first began, and it had been so crucial to have a clear chain of command to keep the business stable and the employees on track. But even when the company had grown past that stage, the management style had never changed. At Wilson Wines she'd had to fight for change tooth and nail, losing more often than not to her father's dictatorial management style. When she had her emotions in check she asked Nate a question.

"Has Jackson Importers always done everything by committee?"

She aimed to keep her tone light, teasing even, but she knew she'd come off as sounding critical when Nate shot her a dark glance.

"For the very important stuff, yes. When we succeed, and we do tend to do that a whole lot, we succeed together. When everyone has a hand in it, everyone works harder and feels far more satisfaction on an individual level. Why, don't you think that's important?"

"No, no, it's not that. I've just…not really come across that before."

"Well, you have only ever worked at Wilson Wines, right? Even on your school holidays? You never took any other kind of after-school job, did you?"

She was surprised he knew that information. He

seemed to know a terrible lot about her. Just how much? she wondered, feeling a little as if she was under a microscope—pinned, as she was, by his intent gaze.

"No, I didn't. All I ever wanted was to work with my father."

Nate's expression softened and, if she wasn't mistaken, his eyes gleamed now with something more akin to compassion.

"I know what you mean. From when I was very young and I knew that Dad was working all the hours that God sent so he could provide for me and my mother, I knew that I wanted to help him. I couldn't qualify soon enough. If he'd have let me, I'd have started with Jackson Importers straight from school, but he insisted that I complete university first, and that I take jobs and internships with other companies while I was a student, so I could be sure Jackson Importers was where I wanted to be. At the time, I was upset that he thought I didn't know what I wanted, but now I can appreciate the experience I gained. It helped me have more insight than I would've had if I'd only ever worked here."

"And then you went overseas?"

"Yeah, first of all for a bit of a holiday—again, at his insistence—then, while I was there I just saw so many opportunities for our company if they had a man on the ground right there in the heart of our major European suppliers."

"Your father just let you do that without any experience in the company? You must have been so young."

Nate shrugged. "What can I say? He liked my proposal and he felt we had nothing to lose by it. I worked my butt off on my own for the first few years and then, over time and as we continued to grow, we built up our staff."

Nicole fought back the pang of envy that struck her fair and square in the chest. What would it be like, she wondered, to be able to just pitch an idea and then have a free hand in following it through? Suddenly it occurred to her that that was exactly what Nate had done for her here and now. He'd heard her out, he was now examining her report and making notations on a pad of paper on the desk in front of him, and he'd assembled a team to support her in it.

Her mind reeled with confusion. He was forcing her to stay here—blackmailing her. Why, then, was he basically handing her the chance to see her idea through—an idea that her father had rejected—without any question?

There was a knock at the office door and it opened. Raoul stood there, his tie loosened at his throat and his shirtsleeves rolled up as if he meant business.

"Dinner has been delivered. We're setting up in the boardroom. You guys ready to join us?"

"We'll be through in a minute," Nate said. Once Raoul had gone, Nate stood and gathered up his notes and Nicole's papers. "Are you all set?"

"Sure," she said. "Just one thing."

"What's that?"

"Why are you doing this?"

"This?" he asked, holding her report up in one hand.

"Yeah. Why? It could just as easily fail and cost you a whole lot of money."

Nate shrugged, an eloquent movement of his broad shoulders beneath the fine wool of his suit. "I trust you, and I know you're onto a winner here. I can see it already in the work you've done to date. Why waste it? Besides, I can't wait to imagine the look on your father's face when we win."

"You think we will?"

"Don't doubt yourself or our team, Nicole. We're invincible when we put our minds to it." Nate crossed the room and held the door open. "Shall we?"

She nodded decisively and picked up her handbag and laptop and followed him through to the boardroom. Invincible. It should scare her that he was so supremely confident, but for some reason it gave her strength, instead. Strength and a belief that she could do this.

Hard on the heels of that thought she realized how much she was enjoying working with Nate. Too much, in fact. As an employer, he was the antithesis of Charles Wilson. She didn't have too much time to dwell on her thoughts, though, because once they entered the boardroom they were full-on. Nate invited her to explain her concept to the group in summarized format and then gave them his overview of her report. Over a selection of Chinese takeout they brainstormed ideas back and forth until Nicole barely recognized the idea as her own anymore. Even so, there was one thing she knew for certain. She was really excited about the direction this was taking and the fact that she'd been integral in instigating it.

By the time she and Nate went back to his apartment she was shattered, and yet incredibly buoyed up at the same time. They had a solid plan in place and she had all the ammunition she needed for when she went to win over any business that Judd and Anna might already have secured.

As she went to turn in for the night she paused in the hallway leading to the bedrooms.

"Nate?"

Nate was almost at his door and he stopped the instant she called to him. "Yeah?"

"Thank you for today."

He walked back up the hallway toward her. She couldn't read his expression in the dim lighting but as he drew nearer, she could see the half smile on his face.

"You're thanking me?" he asked.

She nodded. "For believing in me."

He shook his head slightly. "You're worth it, Nicole. I don't know why your father kept you under a bushel the way he did but, with your mind, the whole world should be at your feet. I'm just letting you use what is your own natural talent."

"I—I appreciate it," she answered, unused to receiving such direct praise. "I hate to admit this, but I really enjoyed this evening."

"Hey, there will be many more of those," Nate said.

"Well, like I said, thanks."

She hovered outside her door, her mind still humming with all the excitement of seeing her brainchild grow and expand into a working business plan. A plan she'd be implementing the moment her feet touched Marlborough soil.

It only seemed natural to brush her lips against Nate's cheeks and then, when that wasn't enough, to kiss him on the lips. He remained still for a moment but then his arms were around her and his mouth was hungry against hers. Her heart rate accelerated as she accepted the inevitable. They were going to make love. A part of her was glad of it, glad she no longer had to fight her instinctive and constant response to Nate's presence. But deep inside she knew she was, in part, surrendering to him. Giving a piece of herself that she'd held back. A piece she knew she'd be lucky to get back whole, ever again.

Seven

Nate backed Nicole against her bedroom door and relished the taste of her as they consumed one another with their kiss. He'd known it would only be a matter of time before Nicole capitulated to him again. With a passion as incendiary as theirs, it was bound to happen. Knowing that hadn't made the waiting any easier, but having that advantage over her—making her stay with him—had tempered his desire just enough to take the edge off. Just enough so that he could wait patiently and let her come to him as he'd planned. And now, at last, everything was falling into place.

It had been exhilarating seeing her in action today. There was nothing sexier than a woman with confidence and intelligence, and Nicole had both in spades. That she was perfectly assembled with features that could make even an angel weep was a welcome bonus, in his mind.

But now it was most definitely time to stop thinking and start doing. Doing and feeling. He reached behind Nicole and eased her bedroom door open, walking her slowly inside before closing the door behind them. Cocooning them in darkness only vaguely punctuated by the lights across the harbor that were visible through her bedroom window. He continued to guide her backward into the darkened room. At the edge of the bed he stopped, reaching for the zipper at the back of her dress and easing it down carefully before working the fabric away from her delectable body. For a split second he wished he'd taken the time to turn on a light, so he could feast his eyes upon her as he planned to feast with his mouth very shortly. But compulsion overcame his need to see what he was doing to her, to see her reaction to it. Instead, he would rely on his other senses.

His body craved urgency, but he held on to enough reason to know that he wanted to take his time, to stretch this out for as long as humanly possible. To give and to receive over and over again until neither of them could stand another second of the torment.

Nicole made a little humming sound in the back of her throat as he bent his head and traced a fine line from the edge of her jaw and down the cord of her neck with his tongue. Her hands gripped his shoulders as he moved lower, following the very top of the swell of her breasts inside the expensive lingerie he knew she wore. Lingerie he had paid for. Lingerie he'd tortured himself with all this week by picturing—wondering whether she was wearing the sapphire-blue ensemble, or the ruby red. Or maybe it was one of the other myriad feminine provocations he'd seen delicately wrapped in tissue before being placed in the store's shopping bag and handed over to her.

Here and now, in the darkness, he knew color didn't matter. All that mattered was sensation and, oh, God, she felt amazing in his arms, beneath his lips. He reached behind her, unsnapping the clasps of her bra.

He dispensed with the garment in an easy movement and reached with both his hands to cup the fullness of her breasts, testing their weight and lifting them slightly so he could bury his face in their softness before laving at the crease he'd created between them. He stroked the pads of his thumbs over her nipples, delighting in the straining peaks and the knowledge that his touch was making them harder, making her want him more.

Her hands let go their grip on his shoulders and moved to the collar of his shirt, unknotting his tie and sliding it free before her fingers were at his buttons, unsteady yet determined in their mission. He bit back a growl as her nails scraped across his chest, across his own sensitive nubs. Her hands shifted to the buckle of his belt and then, mercifully, eased down his zipper and pushed his trousers to pool at his feet. His erection strained at the restriction of his boxer briefs, strained for her silken touch, but instead, she scraped her nails softly along his length and he almost lost all control.

Nate eased her back onto the bed before bending to swiftly kick off his shoes and peel off his socks so he could step out of his trousers. He slid his briefs away, allowing his swollen flesh to spring free, and joined Nicole on the bed. Waves of heat rolled off her body, heat that intensified as his fingers roamed inside the fabric of her panties—sought, and found, the slick core of her. He played his fingers across her cleft, reveling in the heat and wetness of her body, knowing it was like this in readiness for him and him alone. She gasped when he brushed the tip of one finger across her clitoris, her gasp turning into a moan as he increased the pressure ever so slightly before easing it off again.

She pressed up into his hand, the movement making him smile. She'd been so controlled all week and now here she was. Her movements uninhibited. He gently slid her free of her underwear and then tugged it away from her body completely before settling himself between her legs. He felt her thighs tremble as he ran his palms across their silky smoothness. Tremble and then tighten as he lowered his mouth to her damp heat. He rolled his tongue across the bead of flesh hidden at her apex. Over and over until her body was so tense he knew she was seconds away from completion.

Completion he would give her. He closed his mouth around that special place and sucked hard, the action sending her over the edge.

Nate waited until the spasms that rocked her body eased off, then rose over her, reaching for the bedside cabinet where, as a good host, he knew there was a stock of condoms. He eased open the drawer and reached inside.

"They're not there," Nicole said from beneath him.

"They're not? Then—"

"I cut them up and threw them out. I didn't want to be tempted."

He'd have laughed if he wasn't so hard he was on the point of agony. Instead, he pressed a kiss to her lips.

"Don't move," he said, "I'll be straight back."

He covered the distance between their bedrooms in record time, then came back with a handful of condoms that he dumped into the still-open drawer, with the exception of the one that he ripped open and swiftly used to sheath himself.

"This time when you come," he continued, as he reached for the beside lamp and switched it on, "I want to see you."

She made a sound as if to protest but the noise cut off as he eased his length inside her. He gritted his teeth together, clenching his jaw tight as he fought to restrain the urge to take her hard and fast. To bring them both to a crashing climax within the shortest time possible. Instead, he moved slowly, painstakingly. She met his rhythm and he smiled down at her as she tried to hasten him in his movements.

"It'll be better this way," he said. "Trust me."

He knew it had been worth the wait as he felt her inner muscles begin to quiver and tighten around him. Nicole's eyes were glazed, her lips parted on a panting breath and her cheeks flushed. A fine dew of perspiration gathered at her temples. His own climax was only seconds away, and in the instant her body began to ripple around him he let go, letting her body wring his satisfaction from him. Giving himself over to the pulse that spent itself all the way from the soles of his feet.

Nicole lay beneath him, waiting for her heartbeat to return to normal, if such a thing were possible. It seemed that from the moment she'd laid eyes on Nate Jackson, she'd been in a constant state of hyperawareness. Colors were brighter, scents stronger and pleasure so much more intense than she'd ever known. She had no idea where this was all going to lead. She only knew, deep down inside, that she would probably never feel this much again with another man. The thought terrified her, because she knew this couldn't last.

She'd never been enough for anyone before. That's

why she hadn't been able to make her mother love her, or to make her father proud. And now she had Nate, who made her feel as if she could do anything...but she knew better than to rely on that. Because she wasn't enough for him, either—not on her own. He was only with her now to enact revenge on her father—once that was complete, she'd go back to being not enough.

Nate shifted above her, pulling from her body before rolling away. Despite the sternly chiding voice in her head telling her not to get too comfortable or too attached, she still made a sound of protest as his warmth left her—right before she froze at his next words.

"Let me get rid of this, we don't want another near miss like last weekend."

Every last vestige of afterglow fled her body as her blood ran cold. "What do you mean 'near miss?'"

"Didn't I mention it? We went to sleep like this that first night. The condom came off. But you're on the Pill, right?"

She wasn't. But that wasn't the issue. He should have told her straightaway so she could have gone to a pharmacy and gotten the morning-after pill. Being with Nate was bad enough but how on earth would she explain a baby to her father?

"Nicole? You *are* on the Pill, aren't you?"

"No, I'm not," she told him, a panicked flutter beginning in her chest. "Why didn't you tell me? What if—"

"I'll deal with it," he said firmly.

He'd deal with it? What about her? Didn't her thoughts or feelings on the matter count at all? And just how would he deal with it? Would he insist on a termination, or would he use a pregnancy as another tool to hurt her father? It occurred to Nicole that while

Nate had given her all the freedom in the world when it came to the workplace, he gave none in her personal space whatsoever. When Nate came back into the bed she had already rolled onto her side and was feigning sleep. She had a lot on her mind—and she knew she wouldn't be able to think if he was touching her.

By the time Wednesday morning rolled around Nicole had everything in the bag. Four out of the six wineries Judd and Anna had visited had jumped ship to Jackson Importers, due in part to the relationship she had already built with them during her feasibility study. And along with them she'd also picked up at least three additional contacts, who were excited about the prospect of widening their distribution.

Her days had been full-on. Judd had done a very good job of selling Wilson Wines to the contacts she'd had on her list, but she'd done a better one and it felt good to be on top. As she awaited her luggage at the baggage carousel at Auckland's domestic airport, she allowed herself a smile of satisfaction.

"Well, if you don't look like the cat that got the cream, hmm?"

Her pulse leaped in her veins as Nate's voice surrounded her in its velvet softness. She turned and faced him, willing her heart rate back under control. Willing her body to calm and cool down just a notch so he wouldn't know just how much she'd ached for him each night she'd been away.

"It went well," she said smoothly. "I didn't expect you to be here to pick me up. I could have taken a taxi."

"I wanted to see you," he said simply.

He bent and kissed her on the lips, a hard press of skin against skin and then he was gone again. She fought the urge to press her fingers to her lips, to hold him there for just a moment longer. Nate constantly surprised her. On the one hand he could be so overbearing and yet, on the other…

"Oh, there's my bag," she cried, seeing the distinctive iridescent red case coming through on the carousel.

She'd been delighted with the set of luggage when Nate had had it delivered to the apartment before her departure, even if it was a little brighter than anything she'd owned before. Still, it was distinctive and cheerful.

Nate moved to collect her bag, appearing nonplussed about carrying such a feminine item as he placed one hand at the small of Nicole's back and guided her out to the parking building.

"Are we heading straight into the office?" she asked as he directed the car up George Bolt Memorial Drive and toward the motorway interchange.

"No."

"Oh, I thought—"

"I told them we wouldn't be in until after midday."

Nicole was surprised. She'd thought he would have wanted her to debrief the team and keep the ball rolling. Losing momentum with this could be disastrous, as Judd and Anna would shortly find out, to their cost.

Judd and Anna—that was a combination she'd never considered before. And yet the representatives from the wineries had told her that her brother and her best friend had worked quite well together, and had, moreover, seemed…close.

She sighed. There was a time when she would have been the first to know if there was a new man in Anna's life. The two of them had shared everything, and there had never been any secrets between them, until now. They'd been friends from childhood, her father's new housekeeper bringing an inbuilt playmate when she'd taken on the role.

They'd even attended the same private schools, with Charles picking up the tab for Anna's fees so his daughter would never be without her best friend. Thinking about it, she could see why Anna was so fiercely devoted to her father. Charles Wilson had given her the world on a platter. A world her mother couldn't have provided alone on a housekeeper's salary. If Anna hadn't done what Charles had asked of her, it would be like saying she didn't appreciate everything the old man had done for her over the years, and Nicole knew without a shadow of doubt that he would have held his own loyalty to Anna over her head in some subtle way.

She desperately wanted to reach out to Anna again. To mend the breach that had been caused by the conflict of loyalties. To rebuild their friendship if they still had that chance.

And while she longed to talk to Anna about Judd, and the rumors she had heard about the two of them, she also wished for a chance to talk to someone about her relationship with Nate. Nicole snuck a glance over at the man beside her and had to resist the urge to squirm in her seat. Just looking at him drove her crazy—she needed a good dose of Anna's gentle practicality to get her thoughts and feelings in order.

Nicole knew she *wanted* Nate—that was impossible to deny. Yet she still resented what he was doing to her, the leverage he held over her head. And underneath it all, she worried about what would happen next. How long would she spend as a pawn between her father and her lover, and how would it all end?

Nate was surprisingly quiet as they journeyed into the city and he handled the car with very deliberate movements, staying at the upper limit of the speed restrictions. By the time they pulled into the covered car parking at the apartment building she could feel tension rippling off him in waves. What on earth was wrong?

He stayed silent as they traveled in the elevator to his floor but the instant they were inside the apartment, she got her answer.

Nate pulled her into his arms and kissed her, really kissed her this time. Hot, wet and hungry. Her body bloomed with heat, moisture gathering at her center in rapid-fire time. Barely breaking contact with one another, they shed their clothing in a heap on the tiled entrance floor and Nate lifted her onto the marble-topped hall table. She gasped at the cold surface against her bare buttocks, but the marble didn't feel cold for long. She was on fire for him, resenting the time it took him to sheath himself with a condom. And then, thankfully, he was sliding inside her, stretching her with his hard length and driving her to the point of distraction as his hips began to pump.

Her orgasm took her completely by surprise. One moment she was accepting him into her body, the next she was flying on a trajectory that led to starbursts of pleasure radiating throughout her body. She clutched at Nate's shoulders, her heels digging into his buttocks as wave after wave consumed her, barely hearing his cry of satisfaction as his own climax slammed through his body.

It took several minutes for her to come back to reality, to realize just what they'd done and where. Nate rested his forehead against hers.

"I told you I wanted to see you."

Nicole laughed. "Well, you're definitely seeing all of me now. I was beginning to think something was wrong. You were so quiet in the car."

"I wanted to concentrate on getting here as quickly as possible. Believe me, the airport hotels were looking mighty good there at one stage."

He withdrew from her and caught her mouth with another deep kiss. This time with the sharp edge of passion assuaged, and with a tenderness she hadn't sensed in him before. It confused her, but then he was constantly doing that. In some respects he seemed to want to dictate every part of her life, yet in others he let her have her head. She could never predict how he'd react. She wanted to push back at him, verbally and physically sometimes, just to get a bit of space and control back in her life, and then he'd go and literally sweep her off her feet and do something like this. Something that transcended reason and gave her an insight into just how she affected him on a personal level. Or did it? Was she still reading him wrong—seeing what she wanted to see? There was no way to know for sure. She doubted she'd ever have him figured out completely.

Nate lifted her from the tabletop, allowing her body to glide against his as her feet found her footing. She shuddered anew at the skin-against-skin contact. There was nothing she wanted more right now than to prolong the physical link they had between them. In that, at least, they were in perfect harmony.

In their earlier eagerness they hadn't noticed the enameled brass vase had toppled off the surface of the table—its fall to the floor leaving a sizable chip in one of the tiles. Nicole bent to lift the vase back into its place.

"That's a shame," she said, gesturing to the floor. "Will you be able to get it repaired?"

"I won't bother. I like the reminder of how it got there," Nate said with a smile that sent tingles through her body all over again. "Come on, let's go take a shower."

It was well after midday by the time they made it into the office and Nicole was feeling the effects of making her 6:45 a.m. flight and the vigorous lovemaking she and Nate had indulged in before going into work. She made it through her debrief without making any mistakes or leaving any glaring holes in her rundown of who had come on board with them and why, and what she had negotiated in their individual contracts.

The meeting was just tying up when she overheard Raoul mention her father's name to Nate.

"…he wasn't looking all that good. Are you sure you want to keep this up?" Raoul said in a voice that was meant for Nate's ears only.

Nate flicked her a glance before turning his back to her and saying something to Raoul that saw the other man glance her way also before giving Nate a slight nod. Raoul gathered his papers and left the room, signaling the exodus for the rest of the staff. Nicole waited until everyone else had left the boardroom before fronting up to Nate.

"What's wrong with my father?" she demanded.

"Nothing more than the usual," Nate responded flatly.

"So what were you and Raoul talking about?"

"Look, he just mentioned he saw your father at a function over the weekend and that he looked more tired than usual. He hasn't been well, has he?"

Nicole shook her head. No, he hadn't been well. And her leaving Wilson Wines and working for Jackson Importers would be exacerbating that. Responsibility struck her fair and square in her chest as she realized the further ramifications of the business she'd just secured and what it would mean to her father on a personal level. She'd been so focused on beating Judd to the finish line, on winning the business away from *him*, that she'd lost sight of her father's stake in all this. Wilson Wines had been holding on to its market share by the skin of its teeth in recent years. She knew that better than anyone. And yet, with her usual impulsiveness, she'd just made matters worse for them. In particular, worse for her father's already weakened health.

"Nicole, it's not your fault he's not well." Nate's voice broke through her fugue of guilt.

She raised her eyes to meet his. "No, but my being here won't be doing him any good, either, will it? Did you know about his health problems all along? Was that a part of your plan, to take a sick man and make him sicker?"

"What, you think I want your father dead?"

"An eye for an eye, a life for a life. Isn't that what revenge is all about?"

"Nicole, you misjudge me if you think I'm capable of something like that. I'm angry at your father, yes, I'm very angry for what he did to mine. I'm furious that he's never admitted, ever, that he made a mistake in treating his best friend the way he did. But it's not his state of health that I want to change—it's his state of mind. Your father needs to stop thinking of himself as the one on top who is always right, and who can never be questioned. Don't tell me you haven't realized that about him, or that his autocratic ways haven't hurt you, too. *That's* the revenge I want—for him to realize that the world doesn't run on his terms. That he's made mistakes, and people have suffered as a result. Then he can finally start to take responsibility for the damage that he's done."

"Can't you leave it in the past?" Nicole pleaded. "Yes, he made mistakes, but he's paid for them, too. For twenty-five years, he didn't even know if Judd was truly his son!"

"You think that's enough to make up for what he did?" Nate sneered. "He *destroyed* my father. Do you know what that means? He sucked every last bit of joy out of him, every last bit of pride. With his accusations he tainted my father for life. Dad lost more than a friend and a business partner over your father's twisted blame. He lost the respect of his peers, as well, not to mention his income. The roll-on effect to my mother and myself was huge. Don't ever underestimate that. Life became very hard for us all. While you were still in that gothic monstrosity you call home, eating hot meals every night and wearing your designer labels, my mother and I were reduced to being reliant on food parcels and hand-me-downs."

Nate's words rained down on her like hail from a black cloud and, through it, all she could hear was the hurt in his voice. The pain of a boy whose father had changed and withdrawn from him. A boy who'd spent his whole life driven by the dispute between two men.

"But do you see what you're doing to him now?" she asked softly, all her earlier anger and defensiveness having fled. "You're the one in the position of power this time," she reminded him, "and how much damage are *you* doing by refusing to forgive?"

"Look, we're never going to see eye to eye on this and I'm not prepared to discuss it any further."

"Well, that's a lovely cop-out," she pushed back, not ready to let things go just yet. She deserved answers. "You think you were the only one affected? I lost my mother and my brother over the whole situation. Isn't it enough for you, now, that my brother is back? That my father knows that *he* is Judd's father and your father isn't?"

Nate shook his head. "It's not as simple as that."

"Yes, Nate. It is," Nicole insisted. "Judd's DNA testing proved he is Dad's natural-born son. The argument between our fathers was just that. Between *them*. Why let that keep affecting us now?"

"Because he's never apologized. Charles Wilson has never admitted he was wrong," he said stubbornly.

"And if he did, would that make it all go away? Would that change the fact that you and your mother suffered while your father found his financial feet again?"

"You don't understand."

"No, you're right," she said sadly. "I'll never understand. Too many people were hurt back then, Nate. Don't carry on the feud. It's just not worth it."

"I'm not letting you go back to him, Nicole."

"I don't think you can stop me."

"Aren't you forgetting something?"

"No, Nate, I'm not forgetting that you can still hold that DVD over me. I'd just hope that you'd be man enough not to."

Eight

They went back to Karekare that night, their journey completed in silence, and once at the house Nicole said she was turning in early. She woke in the early hours of the morning to find the bed still empty beside her, a faint flicker of light coming from the main room down the hall. She got up from the bed and pulled on the peignoir that matched her ivory chiffon nightgown. The floor was cold against her bare feet, yet she made no sound as she padded along the polished wooden floor.

The room was in darkness, the only light coming from the massive LCD television screen mounted on the wall. Nate was sitting on the couch opposite the TV, a glass of red wine on the coffee table in front of him. Even though the sound was off on the television, he hadn't heard her enter the room, his attention fixed on the screen.

Nicole hazarded a look and instantly wished she'd

stayed in bed. There, in all their glory, were the two of them—making love. At the time she'd thought it would be a bit of fun. After all, she'd been the one to instigate it. Again, her rashness getting her into a situation she'd have done better to avoid. She closed her eyes for a moment, but behind her lids she could still see the images of their bodies entwined. Of the expression on her face as Nate did things to her she'd never allowed any other man to do. Of how she'd trusted him and loved every second of it, never for a moment thinking there could possibly be any consequences.

Opening her eyes, she turned and left the room before Nate could sense or hear her there. In the bedroom she yanked off her peignoir and threw herself back into the bed, closing her eyes tight once more— but not tight enough to stop the flow of tears that came from beneath them.

Nate sat alone in the dark, staring at the screen in front of him, at the evidence of the incredible connection he had with the flesh and blood, passionate woman sleeping in his bed down the hall.

He'd threatened her now twice with the DVD. The first time he'd meant it. The second? Well, he'd thought he'd meant it. Until now. Until he'd started to watch it again and had realized that he could never use this against her.

He still wanted his revenge against Charles Wilson. But he wouldn't—couldn't—hurt Nicole to achieve it. Her words today had struck deep inside him. Logically he knew she was right, but emotionally he was still that determined little boy who'd wanted to make his father's eyes smile again.

Nate had always understood his parents' relationship

was an anomaly amongst his friends' parents' bonds.
Deborah Hunter and Thomas Jackson had never married. Never even lived together. Yet they were united
as one on the upbringing of their son. He'd asked his
mother once, when he was still small, why his daddy
didn't live with them, and his mother had had such a
sad expression in her eyes when she'd told him that
Thomas simply wasn't like other daddies. Nate had
never wanted to see that sorrow on his mother's face
again, had never pushed for more answers.

It wasn't until he was older that he'd realized what
it was that made his father different, and it was something that had made him even more determined to
teach Charles Wilson a lesson. Thomas Jackson was
gay. His sexual orientation had been misunderstood
and even feared by others when he was a young man—
if it had been public knowledge then he would have
been touched by a stigma that might have seen him
lose friends, not to mention business.

Nate himself was the result of a last-ditch attempt
on his father's part to disprove the truth about himself.
Thomas had explained it to Nate during his last visit
to Europe before he'd died. How he'd met Deborah
Hunter and, desperate to deny his own sexuality, had
embarked upon an affair with her. It was a short-lived
fling, but it had resulted in Nate's conception—a fact
that had bound both Thomas and Deborah together
as close friends for the rest of their lives. Nate didn't
doubt that his mother had loved Thomas deeply, nor
that he loved her in return. Just not in the way his
mother needed.

The knowledge had explained a lot to Nate. Had answered so many questions he'd had but had never put
into words. Nate knew his father could never have had

the affair with Cynthia Masters-Wilson that Charles had accused Thomas of. It was something Charles Wilson should have known from the start—*would* have known, if he'd truly been a good friend to Thomas. But the man was known for his up-front, old-fashioned and often righteous attitude. In itself that was probably the reason why Thomas never confided his homosexuality to him. He had been afraid that he would lose Charles's friendship—and he had, even if it wasn't in the manner he'd anticipated. But Charles should have trusted Thomas, and the loss of that trust had decimated his father.

Yes, Nicole had been right when she'd said he couldn't change the past. But the little boy inside him still suffered. Charles Wilson had to pay. Nicole, on the other hand, had already paid more than enough, having to walk away from her home, her friends and her family.

Nate reached for the remote and snapped off the television. No, he wouldn't use the DVD against Nicole. The content of it was theirs, and theirs alone. But if he told her he had no intention of using it against her anymore, how could he ensure she would stay? Now that he had her, he didn't want to let her go.

Sure, knowing she was a pivotal member of the Wilson Wines hierarchy, he'd wanted to use her to hurt their business—and if her recent trip was any indication, he'd succeed quite well in that goal. And he'd relished the thought of staking his own claim on someone who Charles Wilson took for granted would always be there. But keeping Nicole with him was no longer just about pulling her away from her father. Now he just *wanted* her, for reasons that had nothing to do with anyone but him and her.

It was more than desire, he admitted, although that was in itself an itch he found he couldn't scratch hard enough, or often enough with her. No, he wanted Nicole in a way he didn't fully understand, and could never describe. A way that had nothing to do with his plans.

And the truth of that scared him.

She was still alone when she woke in the morning but through the bathroom door she could hear the shower running. She lay between the tangled sheets that were the evidence of her restless night and wondered what Nate had been thinking while he'd watched the DVD last night. Was he imagining her father's anger and disgust? Would he send it with a letter accompanying it, explaining that he, Nate, was Thomas Jackson's son? A son Thomas Jackson had raised while Charles had sent his own away in a fit of pride and anger?

The very thought of her father opening such a letter, or even beginning to watch the DVD, made her feel physically ill and she dashed from the bedroom to the guest facilities, heaving over the toilet bowl until her stomach ached with the effort. She flushed the toilet and leaned both hands against the basin, willing her body back under control. With a shaking hand she turned on the faucet, letting the cold water splash over her hands and wrists before rinsing out her mouth and vigorously scrubbing at her face.

She felt like death warmed over. In fact, when she thought about it, she hadn't felt physically fit in days. Was this all the toll of the days she'd spent in Nelson and Blenheim and the emotional demands of living and working with Nate every day, or was there something else she should be worried about? She didn't want to think about the night Nate had said his condom had come off inside her as they'd slept. She didn't want to believe that she could have been vulnerable to falling pregnant for even an instant.

Pregnant? Her stomach clenched on the very thought and she stared at herself in the mirror, noting the dark shadows under her eyes, the lankness of her hair, the pallor of her skin. It had to be the stress, it just had to be. She was worried about her father and under immense strain with Nate.

Nicole wondered again about Charles. It worried her to think that his health had worsened, and she wished she could get a fuller report. Short of visiting him, though, where she had no doubt she would be told in no uncertain terms of how unwelcome she was, she had only one other option. She had to ask Anna. Her friend would know the truth about Charles's health. She'd email Anna today when they got into the office, arrange to meet for lunch if the other woman was willing. And then maybe, just maybe, Nicole would begin to get her life back on track again.

Sharing an office with Nate hadn't bothered her before but today it most definitely did. She had to wait until almost lunchtime, when he headed out for a meeting, before she could compose the email she wanted to send to Anna. By now Wilson Wines would know that she'd wrested their new business from them. Would Anna even respond to her email? There was only one way to find out. She typed in the short missive and hit Send before she could change her mind.

She waited, drumming her fingers on the desk to see if Anna would respond. Maybe she was away from her desk, or maybe she was just ignoring the request to meet at Mission Bay for lunch. She couldn't stand it. She powered her computer down and grabbed her handbag. She'd wait at the restaurant. If Anna showed up, she showed up. If she didn't, well, then Nicole would just find out about her father some other way.

Nicole couldn't get over the relief that swamped her body as Anna made her way through the tables to where she was sitting at the back of the restaurant. Even so, the relief was tempered with a generous dose of apprehension as Anna sat in the chair opposite.

"I ordered for us already," Nicole said, hoping that Anna wouldn't mind she'd gone ahead and done so.

"Thank you, I think."

Dread clutched her heart. Was there to be no reconciliation between them, after all? If the look on Anna's face was anything to go by, twenty-odd years of friendship was about to go down the tubes.

"Oh, Anna, don't look at me like that, please."

"Like what?" her friend said, giving nothing away.

"Like you don't know whether I'm going to hit you or hug you."

Anna smiled, but it was a pale facsimile of her usual warmth. "Well, you weren't exactly happy with me the last time we talked to each other."

No, she hadn't been. She'd been feeling betrayed at the worst level possible, and she'd felt angry and trapped. A situation which she'd only made worse by yelling at her oldest friend, and running off. Nicole forced a smile to her lips and reached across the table to squeeze Anna's hand, the tension in her body easing just a little when the other woman didn't pull away. The waiter arrived at that moment with their Caesar salads and she let Anna's hand go. Once they were alone again, Anna asked her how she was doing. How she was really doing.

Nicole ached to tell her the truth, to tell her she'd gotten herself into an awful situation and that she couldn't see her way out of it, but she held it all inside, instead skating across the reality her life had become. But, she reminded herself, meeting with Anna today hadn't been about her. It was to find out how Charles was doing. She wasn't surprised when Anna told her he was less than impressed with her working for Nate. And, of course, Charles still had no idea that Nate was Thomas's son.

She asked about Charles's health, and was partially relieved when Anna told her he was okay. Anna wouldn't lie about something as important as that. What did hurt, though, was hearing about how easily Judd had picked up her side of things at Wilson Wines. She'd never been able to measure up to him, even though he'd grown up in another country. Always, she felt as if she'd been found lacking, and when Anna began to beg her to come back to Wilson Wines, to come home, she felt as if her heart would fracture into a million tiny pieces.

"I...I can't," she said, shaking her head, wishing the opposite was true.

"What do you mean, you can't? Of course you can. Your home is with us, your career was with us. Come back, please?"

If only it was that simple. Even if she told Anna about the blackmail, how could she admit the deeper truth—that she actually liked working for Jackson Importers? That she felt more valued and appreciated there than she had in her father's own company.

Nicole was ashamed of herself for even thinking it. She skirted around the issue and focused instead on the much-needed apology she had to deliver to the woman who had been her best friend for as long as she could remember. To her relief, Anna accepted the apology with her natural grace and they turned their discussion to anything and everything other than work, or men. How she felt about Nate was too raw and complicated for her to share with Anna just yet. She didn't even fully understand it herself, and until she did, talking about him was off limits. By the time their lunch was over, it almost felt as if everything was back to normal. As normal as it could be without them both returning to work in the same office.

"I'm so glad you emailed me," Anna said, standing and giving her an enveloping hug.

"I'm glad you're still talking to me. I don't deserve you, you know."

"Of course you do, and more," Anna replied. "I'll settle the bill, okay? Next time will be your turn."

"Are you sure?" Nicole had issued the invitation, lunch should have been on her.

"That there'll be a next time? Of course there will."

"Not that, silly." Nicole laughed, happy, on one level, that they were back to their usual banter.

But her joy was short-lived. Being with Anna had just reminded her of all she'd walked away from. All she'd thrown away with her reckless behavior. And now she had another problem to consider—that her impetuosity had possibly gotten her pregnant. That sense of fear and nausea she'd experienced this morning swirled around inside her again. Before Anna could notice she wasn't feeling well, or say another word that might see Nicole blurt out the whole ugly truth of what she'd gotten herself into, she gave her friend a farewell hug and left the restaurant.

The sunshine outside did little to dispel the coldness that dwelled deep inside her. Seeing Anna was an all-too-painful reminder of all Nicole was missing— her father, despite his recent behavior to her, her best friend. Even the opportunity to somehow carve a new relationship with the brother she'd never had a chance to know, and work with him to help stabilize and protect the family company. Instead, she was working against them all—and enjoying it. Shame swamped her. Somehow she had to make things right for what she'd done. Anna hadn't mentioned how the Nelson and Blenheim wineries business loss had been taken in the office, but Nicole knew it must have hurt. She had to find a way to make that up to them.

It was during the short drive back to the city that Nicole's mind began to work overtime. There was most definitely a way she could continue working with Nate and yet remain loyal to her father and Wilson Wines. It would be tricky, but hey, no one had made her sign a confidentiality agreement. She could feed information to Anna on Nate's current development plans. Not enough that it would immediately point a finger at her when it came to light—and it most definitely would come to light, she had no doubt about that at all—but hopefully enough to give Wilson Wines an edge against Jackson Importers. After all, in very many cases they were competing for the same business, anyway. It would only be natural to assume they'd continue to cross swords in the marketplace.

Satisfied she'd finally found a workable answer to her situation, Nicole continued to the office, steadfastly ignoring the conflicted sensation that what she was about to do would hurt the very people who'd welcomed her into Jackson Imports with open arms. She swallowed against the lump that formed in her throat. If she could make this work, Charles would have to see her in a different light. Would have to value her worth to him. Wouldn't he?

Nate came from the 7:00 a.m. Monday morning meeting with his head of IT undecided about whether he was furious with Nicole or filled with admiration for her audacity. Over the weekend, while he'd thought she was sulking in her room, she'd been emailing information to Anna Garrick at Wilson Wines. Information he could well do without them knowing. At least, thanks to the tracking software he'd had installed on her laptop right from the beginning, his team had been able to find out exactly what information she'd passed on. Between the software and the team he had tracking her laptop activity, keeping an eye on Nicole had been an expensive investment, but well worth it if it made him aware that this was the tack she was taking.

But why was she doing it? She'd seemed satisfied with her success with the Marlborough district wineries. Then they'd had that blasted discussion, which had turned them back into silent ships that passed in the office, and in the night. Even at the Karekare house, she'd moved into another bedroom. He couldn't understand it. She was just as strongly attracted to him as he was to her. He knew it to his very bones. Knew it in every accidental touch from the ache it created deep within him and in the clouded look of suppressed need he saw in Nicole's eyes immediately afterward.

And it wasn't just physical. He was making every effort to satisfy all of her needs—including her need to feel valued and appreciated for her work. He was giving her every opportunity to excel at what she did best and yet it still wasn't enough. What more could he possibly give her? And why was everything he'd already given her not enough to make her happy? Was it truly that necessary to her to please her father, to the point where she'd throw away everything else he'd given her for the chance to make Charles Wilson proud?

He could cope with the collateral damage this time, but what she was doing had to stop. For his sake, for the company's sake, and for *her* sake, too. If there was one thing Nate knew, it was that Charles Wilson was a stubborn bastard who never forgave. Not his best friend, or his daughter. Nicole couldn't buy her way back into her daddy's heart with Jackson Importers secrets—she could only sabotage her own chances of succeeding with them. And he wasn't about to let her do that.

He pushed open the door to his office and felt a jolt of satisfaction when she jumped in response to his presence.

"I thought you were in a meeting," she said, swiftly covering her discomfiture.

Rain battered at the office window behind her as autumn's weather finally did an about-face and delivered on its usual wet and windy promise. The weather suited his mood.

"I was," he replied, his voice short as he chose his next words very carefully. "A very interesting meeting, in fact. It seems someone from our office has been feeding information about our latest initiatives to Wilson Wines. I don't suppose you'd know who that was, would you?"

To his satisfaction, she paled visibly under the onslaught of his words.

"How...?"

"How I know isn't relevant. But it's going to stop right here and right now, Nicole."

"You can't stop me," she said defiantly, rising from her chair and lifting her chin. "If you're going to make me work here and I'm privy to certain information, you can't prevent me from sharing it. I haven't signed any confidentiality agreement."

"No? I would have thought that the DVD was enough of a substitute, wouldn't you?"

She wavered where she stood and he fought to control the urge to comfort her. To take her in his arms and assure her he would never dream of using the DVD against her anymore. But he had to stop her in her tracks. Had to keep her where she belonged, where she could be appreciated and valued—*with him.*

"Remember, Nicole. I can just as easily give you access to bad information as I can to good. Ask yourself this—how would you feel if what you were so merrily passing onto your friend at Wilson Wines was enough to turn very strongly to their *dis*advantage? What if it was the straw that broke their financial back?"

She sat back down in her seat, her face drawn into harsh lines of worry. "Have you?"

"Not this time, but don't be so sure I won't in the future. Now, let this be the first and last time you do this, or I will take punitive action, Nicole. Don't think I won't."

"I—"

She was interrupted in her response by the chirp of

her cell phone. He watched as she glanced at the screen and, if it were possible, paled even further.

"Your friend, I assume?" he sneered.

In response, Nicole snatched the phone up and dismissed the call, only to have it start ringing again a few seconds later.

"You'd better take it," Nate growled, "and while you're at it, tell Ms. Garrick that they can expect to have to do their own research and development in the future."

He turned and stalked out the office.

Nicole watched the door close behind him before answering the call. In the face of what she'd just been through with him she really didn't think her day could have gotten any worse, until she'd seen her home phone number come up on her screen. Try as she might, she couldn't fight back the feeling of dread that suffused her.

"Hello?"

"Nic, it's Anna. Charles collapsed this morning at breakfast. Judd's gone with him in the ambulance. You should meet us at Auckland City Hospital's emergency department as soon as you can. It doesn't look good."

"But you said he was doing okay," Nicole protested, at a complete loss for anything else to say.

"He has obviously been feeling worse than he let on. Look, I must get going. I'll see you at the hospital."

Anna severed the connection before Nicole could say another word. Shaking, Nicole grabbed her handbag and headed straight for the elevator bank. She slammed her hand against the call button several times waiting for the car to arrive at her floor.

Finally the elevator doors slid open and she dashed inside, punching the ground floor button as she did so.

The doors began to slide closed but suddenly an arm appeared between them, forcing them to bounce open again.

"Going somewhere?" Nate asked, entering the car and standing close beside her.

"It's my dad, he's collapsed. I need to see him. Please don't try and stop me."

Nate's expression changed rapidly. "How are you planning to get there?"

"I don't know, taxi, something!" A note of sheer panic pitched her voice high.

"I'll drive you."

"You don't n—"

"I said, I'll drive you. You're in no state to be left on your own." He reached forward and pressed the button for the level below ground.

"Thank you," she said shakily, watching as the car slid inexorably down to the basement parking floor.

She couldn't have said later on how long it took to get to Auckland City Hospital. The journey should only have taken about ten minutes but, as with everything since she'd received Anna's call, it seemed to take forever. The second Nate rolled his car to a halt outside the emergency department she shot out the door and headed inside, not even waiting to see if he followed her or not. Ahead of her she could see her brother and Anna. She strode across the floor, her high heels clicking on the polished surface.

"Where is he? I want to see him."

"He's with the doctors," Anna said quietly. "They're still assessing him."

"What happened?" Nicole demanded, turning to Judd, more than ready to lay blame for their father's current condition firmly at his feet. Life had been simple before he arrived. Not necessarily always happy but certainly less complicated.

"He collapsed at breakfast," Judd replied.

"I thought your being here was supposed to make him feel better, not worse," Nicole fired back before promptly bursting into tears.

God, what was it with her these days? So overemotional. She needed to hold it together, especially if she wanted them to let her in to see her father.

A nurse came toward them, "Mr. Wilson, you can see your father now."

Nicole didn't notice that Judd had reached for Anna until she heard her friend say, "No, take Nicole. She needs to be with him more than I do."

What was with that between the two of them? Were they a couple?

"Are you coming?" Judd asked with thinly veiled impatience.

Her tears dried instantly. How dare he act and speak to her as if she didn't belong. It wasn't her fault her father was in there, possibly fighting for his life. "Of course I'm coming. He's *my* father."

Nicole was horrified when she saw her father. Lines ran into his arms and monitors were beeping around him. He looked so ill, so frail. So very old. Guilt assailed her anew.

"What's she doing here?" he rasped, turning his head away from her.

But not before she saw the anger and rejection in his eyes. Nicole stiffened and halted in her tracks. The words of love and care that were on the tip of her tongue drying on her tongue like a bitter pill she'd been unable to swallow. She reached down deep and found what dignity she had left.

"I came to see if you were all right, but obviously you're just fine. You won't be needing me here."

She turned and pushed past Judd, desperate now to get out of the cubicle. Desperate to get anywhere where her father wasn't. He hated her. That much was all too clear. As far as he was concerned, she'd burned her bridges when she'd walked out on him and straight into Nate Hunter Jackson's arms. He'd never stopped to listen before, why should he start now? Well, two could play at that game, she decided, ignoring Anna who was still waiting outside, and kept her gaze fixed on the exit ahead of her.

Nate waited outside in the chilled morning air.

"How is he?" he asked, stepping forward as she came out through the main doors.

"He's about as much a bastard as he ever was. Take me home, please. I can't face going back to the office today."

Nate gave her a searching look before nodding. He wrapped one arm across her shoulders and gathered her to him.

"Sure, whatever you need."

The Maserati ate up the miles that led them back to the beach house and the instant they were inside she turned into his arms, wrenching away her clothing and then his, and pouring her energy into setting his soul on fire for her all over again.

She dragged him to the bedroom and pushed him onto the bed, sheathed him with a condom and then straddled his body. There was no finesse, no whispers of passion. Her movements were hard and fast and before he gave himself over to her frenetic love-making, he made her a silent promise. Charles Wilson would never hurt her again.

Nine

Nate watched Nicole as she slept beside him. She'd been like a madwoman exorcising a demon. As if she was desperate to fill all the loss and pain inside her with something else. While he didn't regret that whatever had happened at the hospital had driven her back into his bed, he hated that she was hurting so much inside. Throughout the day she hadn't said a word about her father's condition or whatever it was that he'd said or done that had upset her so deeply. Even as they'd walked along the beach during a break in the bad weather, wrapped up tight against the bracing wind that streamed across the sand, she'd adroitly steered their conversation away from work and anything associated with her family.

Throughout their talks he'd begun to get a clearer picture of what her life had been like growing up. It hadn't all been a bed of roses, as he'd assumed. For a start she'd only had her father, and while he'd lavished his extensive resources upon her and given her every childhood heart's desire, including a live-in friend in the shape of Anna Garrick, he hadn't been able to atone for the fact that her mother had essentially abandoned her. Mostly, he hadn't tried.

After the collapse of his marriage and his family life, Charles had dedicated himself to his work. When he'd spent time with Nicole, it had mostly been in the role of stern authoritarian, making sure she did her homework, got good grades, behaved well in school. She'd worked hard to excel, hoping to win his approval, but his praise was sparse and hard to gain. And when she fell short of his expectations, well…

Little wonder that right now, Nicole felt as if she'd been cast adrift by both her parents. He knew she was in pain but he didn't know how to make it any better. He also knew that he was responsible for some of the scars she bore right now, and the knowledge carved at his chest with relentless precision.

He could make this all go away. He could destroy the DVD and release her. Even as he thought of it, everything within him protested. She murmured in her sleep as he gathered her against his chest. No, there was one thing these past few days had taught him and that was he never wanted to let her go. Ever.

Charles Wilson didn't deserve her. In contrast, Nate would do everything in his power to make sure Nicole wanted for nothing while she was under his roof. Surely someday, that would be enough.

Nicole poured her energy into two things for the rest of the week, work and Nate. By Friday evening she was shattered. Lack of sleep and the concentration her

work demanded as she finalized every last contract for
the Marlborough wineries had culminated in a thump-
ing headache by the time she and Nate drove back to
the apartment. She wished they were heading out to
Karekare. The sounds of the waves and the birds in
the bush that surrounded the house were just the kind
of tranquility she craved right now. They would drive
out there late Saturday evening, though, and she was
looking forward to the time-out. Perhaps she'd even
take Nate up on that earlier offer to learn to surf, she
thought, as they waited for yet another change of lights
before they could get closer to their final destination.

Her cell phone chirped in her bag and she ignored
it. She should have turned the damn thing off before
they'd left the office. After all, any calls she got tended
only to relate to work—or Anna, who had been giving
her unwanted updates on her father's medical condition.

Things were looking pretty bad for Charles Wilson
but Nicole refused to let herself think about that. Refused, point-blank, to acknowledge that the one biggest influence on her entire life could soon be gone if
things didn't improve. He hadn't wanted her there at
the hospital. He'd made it abundantly, and painfully
clear on Monday morning.

Was she so unlovable? Her chest tightened on the
thought. Her mother abandoned her, her father now
hated her. Even Nate only wanted her because of what
it would do to her father and her brother. Nicole had
never felt more adrift in her entire life. The pounding
in her head sharpened and she must have made a sound
of discomfort because Nate reached across to take one
of her hands in his.

"Are you okay? You're looking really pale."

"Just this darn headache. I can't shake it."

He shot her a look of concern, his hand lifting from hers and touching her cheek and forehead before returning to the steering wheel.

"I don't think you have a fever, but do you think you should see a doctor? You haven't been looking well all week."

"Look, it's been a stressful week, you know that. I'll be fine. I just need a couple of painkillers and then about a month's worth of sleep."

"Well, I can't promise a month but I have no objection if you want to stay in bed all weekend."

She gave him a weak smile. No, she had no doubt he'd be happy to spend that whole time in bed with her, too. It was about the only time she could dismiss everything else and just concentrate on the moment, on how he could play her body like a finely tuned instrument. But right now, forget-the-rest-of-the-world sex was the last thing she felt like.

"Hey, I can change my plans for tonight. I don't feel so good about leaving you alone if you're not well."

"No, no," she protested. "Raoul's wedding rehearsal is important. You must go."

"If you're sure?"

"Of course I'm sure," she told him. Right now the only thing she craved was maybe a warm bath, those painkillers she'd mentioned a moment ago and then sleep.

In the apartment, Nate went straight through to the master bedroom to get ready for the wedding rehearsal and subsequent dinner that was being hosted in one of Auckland's premier hotels. Raoul had extended both a dinner and wedding invitation to Nicole, as well, but she'd refused, saying she'd feel like a gate-crasher. The wedding was tomorrow at midday, and she'd planned to go into the office in an effort to get ahead for next week.

Half an hour later she was on her own. She roamed through to the master bathroom and ran a deep bath, treating the water with lavender-and-rose-scented bath salts. Already she could feel the tension in her head begin to ease. She took a couple of headache tablets just before she undressed and lowered herself into the soothing water.

In the living room, she heard her phone begin to chirp again. She sighed, and gave herself a mental reminder to check the thing before turning it off. There was no need to rush to check it right away. If Nate needed her, and couldn't get through, he would ring the apartment, and who else would need to reach her right away? She closed her eyes and leaned her head back against the edge, letting the water and the pain relief weave their magic.

The water was cooling by the time she dragged herself out and dried her body before wrapping in a luxuriously thick bathrobe. There was no point in putting on a nightgown. Nate would only remove it the minute he got home, she thought with an anticipatory smile. Besides, her headache was completely gone now and she was ravenous. Maybe she'd watch a movie on cable while she had something to eat, she thought, abandoning her earlier idea of having an early night. And then, by the time Nate got home, maybe she could meet him at the door, dressed in nothing but a smile. The idea began to sound better and better.

First, though, she had to check her phone. Two missed calls, both from the same caller, and one voice mail. Nicole immediately identified her old home number and her blood ran cold. Had Charles's condition deteriorated again?

She punched the numbers to listen to the voice mail, and was surprised when the well-modulated tones of an unfamiliar woman's voice sounded through the speaker.

"This is Cynthia Masters-Wilson and I'm calling for Nicole Wilson. I'd like to meet with you for lunch tomorrow, one o'clock if you're free." She mentioned the name of an inner-city restaurant before continuing, "I think it's time we got to know one another, don't you?"

The call disconnected but Nicole still stood there, staring at her phone. Her mother? After all this time? She sank to the sofa as her legs weakened. Why now?

All her life she'd told herself she never wanted to meet the woman who had so callously abandoned her one-year-old daughter, never to look back, never to contact her or attempt to see her ever again. While she was growing up she'd told herself it didn't matter. She had her father, she had Anna and Anna's mother who was more Charles's companion than housekeeper in the massive gothic mansion Nicole had grown up in. Yes, it had always been easy to dismiss Cynthia Masters-Wilson as entirely unnecessary in her life.

But what did she have now? Nothing. Absolutely nothing. All week she'd been frantically trying to fill the emptiness inside her—working hard and playing twice as much so. If she was completely honest with herself, neither activity had managed to assuage the hollow feeling her father's rejection had left her with.

Reason told her to be cautious, though. This was the first ever, active contact her mother had made in twenty-five long years. As far as Nicole was aware, the woman had never spared her a second thought.

But what if she wanted to make amends? What if her reasons for leaving Nicole motherless for all those years were justified, her remorse for her absence in her daughter's life genuine? Surely she had to have a reason for finally getting in touch with Nicole after all this time.

Curiosity won out over caution as Nicole made up her mind. She would meet with Cynthia—she couldn't ever imagine calling her Mum, or Mother—and she would be seeking a few answers of her own.

Butterflies battled in her stomach as she entered the restaurant located in the historic Auckland Ferry building. She'd chosen to walk the short distance from the Viaduct, but with each step she'd come to dread her decision to attend. What on earth could they possibly have to talk about? And if her mother wanted to offer an olive branch, maybe even try to establish some form of mother-daughter relationship, why do it in such a public place? Surely a private meeting would be more appropriate for a mother and daughter reuniting for the first time in a quarter century.

"You must be Miss Wilson," said the immaculately attired maître d' as she hovered in the entrance, in two minds about turning around and walking back to the apartment. "Your mother is already seated. Please, follow me."

Too late now, she realized. The restaurant hummed with activity and most of the tables were occupied. The sun shined through the windows that looked out over the water, casting a solitary figure seated at a table there in silhouette.

Nicole swallowed back the lump that formed in her throat and focused on placing one foot in front of the other. She smiled at the maître d' as he held out her chair, not wanting to immediately make eye contact with the woman who had summoned her there. She kept her eyes downcast, fiddling with her bag before setting it on the floor beside her chair. Then, with a steadying breath, she raised her eyes.

It was as if she was looking at herself in another twenty-five years. Same eyes, same hairline, although Cynthia's hair now bore wings of gray, and while her features mirrored Nicole's own, there were lines around her mouth. Regret? Bitterness? Would she ever know the truth about that?

"Well, my dear, this is going to be interesting, isn't it?" Cynthia said with a tight smile.

Of all the things she'd imagined her mother first saying to her, that was most definitely not on the list. Nicole bristled.

"Why now?"

"What? No, hello Mother, pleased to finally meet you?" Cynthia gave another of those artificial smiles. "I don't blame you for being angry, my dear, but you have to realize that I'm as much a victim of your father as you and your brother."

A victim? Somehow Nicole thought that was stretching the truth. Her brother had already been proven to be Charles's natural-born son. Why would he have thought otherwise? Charles had believed his wife had an affair with Thomas Jackson. She couldn't imagine Nate's father having been the one to put that idea in her father's head, which only left one other person in that particular triangle.

"Ah, I see you don't believe me." Cynthia sighed. "I feared as much. Come, let's order, and hopefully we can talk."

Even though she didn't feel in the least like eating, Nicole placed her order with the waiter who'd materialized at Cynthia's request. Once they were each settled with a glass of wine, Cynthia began again.

"You're quite the beauty, aren't you? I'm so sorry that I didn't get to see you grow up. It was the hardest thing I've ever done in my life, walking away from you, leaving you with your father. But I knew he loved you, would protect you. Judd deserved the same, with me."

"How could you leave me like that?" Nicole blurted out the question. Goodness only knew she'd waited all her life for the answer.

To her surprise, Cynthia's eyes swam with tears. "Oh, my darling girl. Do you really think I wanted to leave you? Your father wouldn't let me near you. Once he'd come to his ridiculous conclusions about Thomas and me he wouldn't even let me *see* you. He had Judd and me out of the country before I could so much as blink."

She sounded genuine enough, and the grief on her mother's face certainly appeared real. Nicole found herself wanting to believe her, but an inner caution still held her back. Without being able to talk to her father, or her brother about this, she had no way of knowing if her mother was telling the truth. The waiter interrupted them with their lunch order and Nicole picked up her fork, playing with the mushrooms in her salad while her mother daintily tasted a sliver of scallop that had come with her dish.

"You could have written," Nicole said, still not willing to give an inch.

"I did. I wrote to you so many times over the years, but all the letters came back. I can only assume that your father had given the staff orders to return any mail addressed from me."

It was the sort of thing her father would have done, Nicole conceded, but there were still means around such a thing. After all, twenty-five years was a very long time. Nicole was an adult now—approachable in ways that were outside of her father's control. To never have been successful was a bit of a stretch of the imagination. Cynthia could obviously sense her skepticism and waved her hand in the air between them.

"That's all in the past now. We can't change that. But surely we can get to know one another now? Tell me about where you're living. Judd tells me you moved out a few weeks ago. I have to say I was very sorry to hear that you two haven't had a chance to get to know one another. I'm staying at the house now. I was hoping we could all be together again, the way it should be."

"Judd didn't tell you why I left?"

Cynthia gave her a sharp look before shaking her head and placing her fork down on her plate. She took a sip of the mineral water in her glass before speaking.

"He did mention something, but I'd prefer to hear it from you."

Nicole gave an inelegant snort. She'd just bet Judd would prefer their mother hear it from her. No doubt he'd already fed Cynthia a sanitized version of what had happened that night.

"My father and I had a disagreement about his plans for Judd. I felt it better that I be away from them both for a while."

"So where are you staying?"

"I'm living with Nate Hunter." She didn't want to let on about Nate's relationship to Thomas Jackson. As far as she was aware, no one at Wilson Wines knew him by his father's surname. Even at the office he was known as Mr. Hunter. "He's the current head of Jackson Importers. I'm working with him, too."

She watched her mother pale beneath her carefully applied makeup, her pallor making the lines around her mouth stand out even more.

"Would Jackson Importers be connected to Thomas Jackson at all?"

"It was his company before he passed away," Nicole confirmed cautiously.

Cynthia's brow furrowed for a moment. "Hunter? Would Nate's mother have been Deborah Hunter?"

Nicole stiffened. Had Cynthia made the connection? "That might have been his mother's name, yes."

"So, it was true. There were rumors that Thomas and Deborah were an item, but nothing was ever substantiated. Charles, of course, pooh-poohed the notion. He said if Thomas was having an affair he'd be the first to know about it." She made a sound that almost approximated a laugh. "As if he paid attention to anything but Wilson Wines. Anyway, I heard that she had a son out of wedlock, but since she didn't move in the same circles as I did when I lived here, I never really gave her another thought."

Nicole didn't know what to say. It hadn't been her secret to divulge and yet Cynthia had put two and two together so simply. If that was the case, why then had her father never reached the same conclusion?

Cynthia suddenly reached across the table, her slender fingers wrapping around Nicole's wrist and gripping tight.

"My dear, you have to get out of there. No one associated with Thomas Jackson can possibly be trusted. Who do you think lied to your father about me, ruining our marriage? Think of the damage that man's lies have done to our family. You have to realize, there's a lot of bitterness between those men. If you're with Thomas's son there can only be one good reason behind it—he's trying to get at your father."

Her words rang too true, as Nicole knew to her cost. Hearing it from her mother's lips only made her situation worse. She knew full well what had been on Nate's mind when he'd taken her back to his home that first night. She had no reason to believe his vendetta against her father had altered in any way. She was still his greatest weapon, even if through her own distress at her father's treatment of her she'd recently become a more willing one.

"Nicole, tell me, is Nate Hunter holding something over you? Is he forcing you to be with him?"

Her mother's astuteness shocked her and she bit back. "Is it too hard to believe that I might actually want to be with him for no reason other than that he treats me well and appreciates me?" Even as she said the words she was sure her mother would see them for the lie they were.

Cynthia shook her head gently, a look of pity on her face. "You love him, don't you?"

"No!" The single word of protest fell from Nicole's lips even as she questioned the truth of her rapid denial. Did she love him? How could she? She was his lover, his captive, his colleague. His tool for vengeance against her father. How she felt about him was far too complicated to examine in front of her mother. Instead, she settled for a middle ground, saying, "Our relationship—it's convenient for us both."

"Well, I certainly hope that's true, because I'm sure, if he's anything like his father, he has an agenda and that would probably be having some kind of revenge against Charles for when he kicked Thomas to the curb."

"Can we change the subject, please? I'd rather not talk about my relationship with Nate, if you don't mind. Besides, I thought you wanted to get to know me."

"You're so right. I'm sorry." Cynthia smiled, one that almost reached her eyes this time, and skillfully shifted their conversation onto other matters.

By the time Nicole walked back to the apartment she was in a quandary. When they hadn't been talking about Nate, or her father, Cynthia had been excellent company. She'd talked a great deal about her family home—The Masters, a vineyard and accommodation on the outskirts of Adelaide—and Nicole's cousins who lived there. Cousins! She had an extended family. One she'd never had the chance to know. And Judd had enjoyed the benefit of that, as well, on top of her father's total attention, her home and the job she'd loved. While she, even now, had absolutely nothing.

Ten

Nate knew something was up the instant he let himself into the apartment. Nicole was nursing a frosty glass of white wine in one hand, her gaze fixed on the twinkling lights of the Viaduct Basin below, her body language shrieking a touch-me-not scream. Every part of her was tense, a far cry from the languorous woman he'd left in their bed this morning before heading out to Raoul's wedding.

He knew she saw his reflection in the massive window in front of her, yet she didn't so much as acknowledge his presence. A flare of concern lit deep inside him.

"What happened? Is it your father?" Surely he would have heard if Charles had passed away. That kind of information would still have filtered through to the guests from Jackson Importers who were at the wedding.

"No." she huffed a short sigh. "My mother, actually."

"Your mother? I thought she lived in Australia."

"Apparently not. Apparently she's moving back to my old family home. Seems like everyone has a place there—but me."

Despite her attempt at nonchalance, he could hear the pain in her voice.

"Did she contact you?"

"We did lunch together. Such a normal thing for a mother and daughter to do, don't you think? Except we're not a normal mother and daughter, are we?"

He was shocked when she turned to face him, her eyes awash with tears. Instinctively he reached for her, enveloping her in his arms and ruing the fact that he hadn't been here for her when she so clearly needed the support. His father had never said as much in words, but Nate had always suspected Cynthia of being behind the lies that had torn apart Thomas and Charles's friendship. Her poison had tainted the lives of so many people, and now she was here, poisoning Nicole, as well.

"You know," Nicole said, her voice muffled against his chest, "as soon as I was old enough to realize that I didn't have a mother, I wanted answers. Even after I convinced myself I didn't need her in my life. I still wanted to know why I didn't have unconditional love from her the same way all my friends had from their mothers. She wants us to get to know each other. Now. After twenty-five years. Can you believe that?"

Nate remained silent, knowing she wasn't looking for an answer. At least not from him.

"And underneath it all, I don't think I can believe it. I don't know that I can believe *her*. And in spite of that,

I still *want* to believe her, because what girl doesn't want to think that her mother loves her?"

Nate set her away from him a little, so he could see her face. "I don't think you should trust her motives, Nicole."

Nicole laughed. A sharp brittle sound that was nothing like the usual humor in her he'd come to know. "Funny. She said exactly the same thing about you."

He stiffened. "She did? Why?"

"Oh, she had you pegged from the start. Said you were probably just like your father. And she knew your mother apparently. Not well, of course." Nicole lowered her voice. "We didn't move in the same circles, you know," she said, in a parody of her mother's tone.

A chill went through him. "I mean it, Nicole. The way she's come here, after all this time and while your father is so ill—something's not right. She could have reached out to you any time in the past. I don't think you should have anything to do with her."

Nicole pulled free from his arms. "Well, that's my judgment call, isn't it?"

Nate knew he'd overstepped the mark with his last comment but he couldn't take it back now. He'd been speaking his mind and he knew he was right. Cynthia Masters-Wilson was not a woman to be trusted. And he didn't want to see Nicole hurt ever again. But he didn't want this to turn into a fight.

"Yes, it is," he finally agreed with Nicole. "Do you still want to head out to the beach?"

Nicole shrugged and took a long sip of her wine. "Whatever."

"I think we should go, it'll do us good to get out of the city."

"Sure," she agreed, but without any enthusiasm.

He watched as she finished her wine and took her glass through to the kitchen. She rinsed it and put it in the dishwasher and then went through to the bedroom they were sharing again. Her actions were wooden, automatic, as if she'd retreated somewhere in her mind. To a place he knew he couldn't reach. The knowledge chilled him to the bone.

Being at Raoul's wedding today had struck something home to him. It had been a happy, relaxed affair, full of people Nate liked and valued—and yet he'd spent the whole time counting down the minutes until he could leave, wanting to come home to Nicole. Being with her had long since stopped being about having his revenge on her father. What was past, was very definitely past. What he wanted now—Nicole—was very much in the present—and he wanted her to stay that way.

Nicole sat quietly in the car, mulling over her meeting with her mother. It certainly hadn't been the reunion she'd always imagined. Cynthia was a piece of work, all right. Coming back into her life after all this time and then thinking she could tell Nicole what to do. It seemed that all around her everyone was telling her what to do these days. And she was letting them. Everything in her life had become topsy-turvy. Even her period was late and she was never late.

Cold fingers of fear squeezed around her heart. Could she be pregnant? *Oh, please, no,* she thought fervently. *Please just let it be stress.* She wasn't ready for this on so many levels it wasn't even funny. She and Nate hardly had the kind of relationship that could sustain a nurturing environment for a child. Not to mention, she had no idea how to be a mother. She'd always been so professionally focused, so determined to excel in her work at Wilson Wines that she'd never given much thought to building a home and family. Even if she wanted such a thing, she didn't know if she could pull it off. And she couldn't bear the thought of proving her father's prophecy about becoming a mother and downsizing her responsibilities in the workplace.

Suddenly it was all the more important that she know, one way or another. With everything else in her life spiraling out of control, surely fate couldn't be so cruel as to throw her a curveball like that, as well?

"Could we stop at the shops in Titirangi on the way?" she asked. "There are a few things I forgot."

"Sure," Nate said.

When they got to the township he pulled in off the road.

"Do you want me to come with you?" he asked, shutting down the engine.

"Oh, no. I'll be fine. I won't be long," she said, getting out the car as hastily as she could. "Really, I'll only be a minute or two."

Please don't come, she chanted in the back of her mind. *Please don't come.* Thankfully, he stayed in the car and she walked briskly toward the bank of shops near where he'd parked. Where to go now? she wondered. If she went into the nearby pharmacy he'd probably see her and he'd no doubt ask her what she'd been in there for. He kept a full stock of over-the-counter medicinal products at both his homes so she couldn't say she'd needed any painkillers or anything like that. And if she said she was after sanitary products, and she didn't need them, that would just open up a whole new can of worms.

Think! she exhorted herself. The grocery store.

Sure, it was smallish, certainly not on the scale of a full supermarket, but surely they'd carry pregnancy tests, as well. She ducked inside the store and scanned the aisles, praying she'd find what she needed. Finally, there it was. She grabbed a test kit and made her way to the counter. On the way she also pulled some moisturizer and a lip balm off the shelf to add to her purchase. The kit, she'd ferret away in her bag. The other items would be camouflage in case Nate asked what she'd bought.

She was back at the car in under five minutes.

"Get everything you needed?" Nate asked her as she buckled her seatbelt.

"Yes, thanks. I'd just run out of a couple of things."

He gave her a studied look, one that made the hairs on the back of her neck prickle. She'd never been an effective liar. Never had to be. She felt as if the test kit in her bag was emitting some kind of beacon. As if any second now, Nate would be giving her the third degree.

"Right, we'll be on the way, then."

She sagged back into her seat with relief. She was overreacting. He had no reason to suspect her of anything, although he had to realize that she should perhaps have had a period by now. She counted back. It was just over three weeks since she'd met him. Only three weeks and they'd been through so very much. She felt as if she'd lived through a lifetime with him. Even so, it gave her a window of at least another week before he might start to ask questions. Questions to which she hoped to have the answer very soon.

The rest of the journey to the house seemed to take forever, even though it was only just over twenty minutes. Nate kept her attention occupied by talking about Raoul's wedding and the people who had been there, often drawing a quiet laugh from her as he mimicked some of Raoul's older and more eccentric family members. She detected a note in his voice, though, that she identified with.

Neither of them had grown up with a large family group supporting them. No uncles, aunts, curmudgeonly great-anythings. No cousins to play or fight with. Just a tight unit of parent and child.

"Some people are lucky, aren't they?" she said, as Nate's voice trailed off as they neared the driveway to the house.

"Lucky?"

"To have the richness of all those people in their family lives."

"I don't know whether Raoul thought it was particularly lucky when his great-uncle got up to make a toast to absent friends. Fifteen minutes he went on."

She laughed again. She should have gone to the wedding rather than have lunch with her mother. By the sounds of it she would have been in a much happier frame of mind right now if she had.

"Still, it would have been nice, growing up..." Her voice faded on the thought.

Nate's hand came across and grasped hers, squeezing tight. "Yeah, I know what you mean."

They were both silent as they went inside the house. Nicole made her way immediately to the bathroom, locking the door behind her and carefully removed the test kit from her bag. Her hand trembled just a little as she opened the box and withdrew the instructions. It seemed straightforward enough. She extracted the test stick and followed the instructions to the letter.

If she'd thought the trip in the car had taken forever, this felt as if she was aging threefold with every second. She counted silently in her head, refusing to look at the stick until she'd counted over the time the instructions said. She could hear Nate in the bedroom. She needed to get this over with before he decided to check on her.

Nicole forced herself to look at the stick. Stripe in one window…the other window clear. A negative result! A rush of exhilaration coursed through her. She shoved the test back into its packaging, and scrunched the whole thing up as small as she could make it before shoving it into the waste bin in the bathroom, and throwing some crumpled tissues on top of it. That would have to do until she could empty the waste bin into a trash bag later on.

She flushed the toilet and then washed her hands at the basin. Her hands were still shaking with the aftermath of the adrenaline surge she'd felt at the confirmation. She was relieved, immensely relieved, but hard on the heels of that sense of relief came a vastly contradictory spear of loss. Would it have been so very bad to have Nate's child? While they didn't have a normal relationship, maybe something good could have come from all of this. Something that could have healed the rift that had been driven between Thomas Jackson and her father all those years ago.

Babies brought with them their own very special brand of implicit trust and love. At least if she had a child, wouldn't she then have its unreserved love? A love that didn't come with tags and conditions. A love she could return wholeheartedly.

Nicole looked at herself in the mirror over the bathroom vanity and shook her head at her fanciful thoughts. She had worked damn hard to establish her career and she wasn't about to walk away from that now. Not even for some pipe dream of a perfect family life. A dream that would probably go horribly wrong if she ever tried it in reality, just like her long-anticipated meeting with her mother.

No, things were definitely better this way. She had no time or space in her life for a baby, not when everything was so horribly complicated—not now, maybe not ever.

Nate had begun to hate Sunday afternoons. In the past it had never been an issue. He loved his time here at the beach house, even more so since he'd been spending it with Nicole. But for some reason the coming week filled him with foreboding. Something was off with Nicole, too. She'd been different all weekend. He'd tried to put it down to her dealing with her feelings about the meeting she'd had with her mother, but he sensed there was far more to it than that.

Even when he'd reached for her in bed last night, he couldn't help feeling as if she was just going through the motions. He knew she'd climaxed, that wasn't the problem. No, what worried him was the mental distance she'd maintained from him. With the roller coaster they'd been through in these past few weeks, the only time the veils they'd held between them had fallen away was when they'd been intimate.

Now, they didn't even have that.

It worried him. Something had happened to change her and he had no idea what it was or how he could fix it. Talking to her elicited no more than a polite response and when he tried to probe deeper, she just shut him down by changing the subject. Short of holding her down and refusing to let her up until she admitted the truth about what bothered her, he had no idea of what to do next. What he did know was that he was losing her, and that was unacceptable.

He went through to the garage to double bag the trash sack to avoid any leakage, and put it in the trunk of his car. It was easier to transfer his waste to the massive trash bin at the apartment building in town than to leave it on the appointed day at the rubbish collection area here. Sometimes being remote from the city had its drawbacks but this was one he could live with.

Nate was picking up the bag and easing it into the second one when a tear suddenly appeared in the plastic and garbage spilled onto the garage floor. Cursing under his breath he scooped up the offending articles and pushed them back into the bag. As he did so, he noticed a small cardboard box that had been twisted up. The lettering on the box was not completely obscured, though, and he saw enough to pique his interest.

He separated it from the rest of the trash and unraveled the packaging. A pregnancy test? There was only one person here who could be responsible for this. He fished the used pregnancy test out of the package, but frustratingly, it was probably too long since it had been used to still show the result. But the fact that she'd taken a pregnancy test at all was enough to have his heart racing.

Every cell in his body demanded he march right up to her and insist she tell him the result of the test, but he forced himself to remain exactly where he was until he could recover some semblance of calm.

Nicole, pregnant? The very thought sent a wave of longing and warmth through his body. He couldn't think of anything he'd like better than watching her ripen with his child. Of sharing each special milestone along the way until they could hold their newborn son or daughter in their arms. Of having a family of his own, a family that included Nicole at its very center.

His heart pounded in his chest at the thought. A family, together, forever. It was everything he'd ever wanted and yet denied himself because he'd been unable to trust, unable to let anyone close enough to have the chance to hurt him since he'd been so twisted by the pain his father had undergone. And now he had the opportunity to put all that bitterness behind him. To forge forward with something new and right and special.

No wonder Nicole had been distant all weekend. She was probably worrying about how to break the news to him, about how he'd take it. He would have to take extra pains to reassure her he would take care of her and the baby, and that she had nothing to worry about, ever, while he had it in his power to take care of her.

Nate forced himself to put the pregnancy test box back in the trash bag and tied off the sack. A few minutes later, as he washed his hands, he thought about what he would say. There was no easy way to approach this. How did you tell the woman you had blackmailed into being with you that you wanted her to spend the rest of her life with you?

Back inside the house, he looked for Nicole. Through the windows he could see her out on the beach, her clothing buffeted by the wind. She was just standing there. Alone. Contemplating the life she carried within her, perhaps? How could he reassure her that everything was going to be okay? That she could trust him?

He reached a decision. He'd just come straight out and tell her. He'd learned a long time ago that occasionally you had to take risks—especially when something was as important as this.

Without taking another moment to think, he pushed open the massive sliding door and headed down the stairs that led to the beach. Nicole must have sensed him coming because she shifted her gaze from the seagulls wheeling on the air currents and turned to face him.

"Nicole, we need to talk."

"We do? What about?" she asked, her long hair whipping around her face in the stiff breeze.

Nate shoved his hands in his jeans pockets. "I know what's bothering you and I want you to know it'll all be okay. I'll take care of you. Once we're married, you won't have a single worry in the world, I promise."

"Married?"

"Of course. There's nothing stopping us. We know we're totally compatible. You can even keep working if you want to, I won't stand in your way. I know how important your career is to you."

To his surprise Nicole just laughed.

Nate frowned, somewhat less than pleased with her reaction. "What? What did I say?"

"Why on earth would I marry you?"

"Of course you'll marry me. We owe it to our baby to provide a united front. You, of all people, know as well as I do what it's like to grow up with two parents who aren't together. Our situation is not ideal, but we can make it work. I know we can. I swore an oath to myself that, no matter what, when I had children I'd be married to their mother, and that's what's going to happen now."

"What makes you think I'm pregnant?" Nicole asked him, taking a step back.

"You've been different these past couple of days and now I know why. I saw the box, Nicole. I know you've taken the test."

Nicole stared at him in horror. He'd found the test? What had he done? Trawled through the rubbish bins? Was he so determined to control every facet of her life? No, she pushed the idea aside. If she was being totally honest with herself, deep down she knew he wasn't like that.

"So, what? You think that if I'm pregnant that we must get married? That's being very old-fashioned of you, don't you think?"

She watched as his face changed, becoming harder, more determined.

"Old-fashioned or not, Nicole, my baby will not grow up illegitimate."

"Of course it won't," she flung back at him.

How dare he be so dictatorial? Didn't her thoughts or feelings factor into this equation at all? Just because he said something was a certain way, didn't mean it had to be so. Even if she was pregnant, marriage to a man who patently didn't love her would be the very last thing on her mind.

The fact that she was totally peripheral to his entire proposal was borne out by his assertion that his baby—*his,* not *theirs*—would not grow up illegitimate. Did he give her any consideration as an individual at all? There was no way she was marrying Nate Jackson. Absolutely no way.

"Good, then it's settled. We'll get married. It doesn't have to be anything big. I'm sure we can sort something out within the next few weeks."

"You can't treat me like some possession to be ordered about. I'm a human being. I've already had quite enough of that kind of treatment from my own father and I certainly won't put up with it from you." She drew up short as a new thought had occurred to her. "My father…is that what this is about? Do you want to get married to rub it in his face? Is this the next part of your revenge?"

"No!" His protest was immediate, and almost seemed instinctive, but how could she believe him? He'd been following his plan of payback right from the start. How was she to know this wasn't his next step?

"Really?" she drawled.

"Look, I know this wasn't the most romantic of proposals—"

"Romantic?" She laughed again, a harsh sound that came from a place deep inside her. A place that hurt with an ache that throbbed through her entire body. "Sort out what you like, Nate, but I'm not marrying you. There were two possible outcomes when I took that test. One, that I was pregnant, the other, that I wasn't. I'm not pregnant, and I'm not marrying you, so you can shove your proposal right back where it came from."

She pushed past him and strode on up the beach toward the house. She thought he couldn't hurt her any more than he already had done. She'd thought that perhaps they'd found a workable solution to their situation. She did enjoy her work at Jackson Importers. She had a freedom there that she didn't have at Wilson Wines and she loved the opportunity to spread her wings and to brainstorm her ideas with others who were on the same wavelength. And she couldn't argue that she and Nate were exquisitely compatible in the bedroom. It had been about the only thing that had kept her sane these past weeks. Knowing that she could seek, and find, oblivion in his arms at night.

But right now she was so angry she could barely see the steps in front of her. She went inside the house, sliding the glass door closed so hard the panes inside it wobbled. Through the window she saw Nate standing on the beach, his hands still in his pockets as he faced the house.

Childishly, she wanted nothing more right now than to flip him the bird, but she wouldn't lower herself to that level. Instead, she turned away from the glass and tried to bring her roiling emotions under control.

Damn him. Damn him for asking her to marry him that way. For asking her to marry him at all! She didn't want to marry, she just wanted to be able to do her job. A job was something she could measure herself by. It had no feelings and only relied on her showing up every single day and giving her very best. A job wouldn't hurt her when the going got rough.

And yet, she couldn't help wondering how she would have felt if the situation had been different. If she had been pregnant, after all—if Nate's proposal had come from a different angle where he'd expressed a desire to have a family with her, even expressed affection or maybe even love for her—would she have been so quick to turn down Nate's suggestion? Nicole knew in her heart her response would have been "yes." She felt the same way he did about raising a child in a unified relationship. In a stable and loving environment. It had been a dream of hers from when she was a little girl. She and Anna had played families, both of them pretending their respective man-about-the-house was at work while they cared for their doll-babies with infinite maternal care.

No, she had to be honest with herself. No matter her feelings for Nate—feelings she couldn't quite put into words—with no mention of love spoken between them, they would only have been setting themselves up for failure. It took a committed parent to raise a child and parents who were not committed to one another, and yet still lived under the same roof, only created a divisive and, in the long term, unhappy home.

And that, sadly, left her right back where she'd started. A pawn in a game where she held none of the moveable pieces. Waiting for the inevitable checkmate when Nate reached his goal against Wilson Wines.

She wanted out of this horrible situation. She wanted out, right now. But how?

Eleven

Nate lay in the bed listening to Nicole breathe, her back as firmly presented to him as it had been when they went to bed. She had barely spoken more than a handful of words to him since the beach and he could hardly blame her. He'd been careless and stupid—thinking only of himself and what he wanted.

He'd used her shamelessly for weeks and expected her to simply roll over and agree to his demand without a single consideration for what it meant to her.

One thing he'd learned from this was that his feelings for her went far deeper than those of revenge. Far deeper than he'd ever wanted to acknowledge. Understanding had struck when she'd accused him of proposing as part of his revenge. That's when he'd realized that her father hadn't even crossed his mind when he'd found the pregnancy test. All he'd thought of was Nicole, and the child they might be having together.

He knew, now, that everything that mattered in his life was tied to the woman who lay in the darkness beside him—beside him yet not touching him and not allowing him to touch her. The woman who'd rejected him most emphatically on the sandy shore outside.

Nate wasn't the type of person who took no for an answer, yet in this he had to. He had no other choice. He'd messed things up between them, well and truly, and he could see no clear way to fix them.

He still had her here in his life, would continue to do so while he could hold the DVD over her. But what did that prove? Nothing. It only proved that, given the choice, she wouldn't be with him and that truth was the most painful of all.

He knew now that he loved her. He didn't want to imagine a life without her. These past weeks had been an eye opener for him. From the start he'd been attracted to her, but that attraction had very rapidly gone far deeper than merely a face-to-face—or skin-to-skin—appreciation of one another. He hadn't wanted to admit it to himself but her rejection had forced him to be honest.

Nate didn't just want to marry her to provide for her and their unborn child—the child that had existed only in his imagination. He wanted the whole shebang. He wanted to love Nicole and spend the rest of his life loving her. And being loved by her in return. He wanted to marry her, for *her*.

Problem solving had always come naturally to him. It was one of the things that made him good at his job—being able to see solutions before anyone else even fully understood the problem. Yet in this he was helpless.

How on earth could he convince her that his intentions toward her came from his heart? He'd tried to lay it on the line on the beach, but he'd gone about it in entirely the wrong way. Had told her, rather than asking her, how things were going to be. With each syllable he'd destroyed every last chance of creating the reality he had really wanted all along.

This was his mess. And for the first time in his life he didn't have a plan for dealing with it.

He pushed back the bedcovers and rose, leaving the room on a silent tread. Streaks of moonlight lit the rest of the house, cold and gray, just like the future that stretched ahead of him without Nicole willingly by his side. It was no better than he deserved for the way he'd treated her, but he didn't want to accept that. Couldn't accept that this was all over. Somehow he would find a solution. It was what he did. And this time, his very happiness depended on it.

They'd remained civil to one another, at least that was something she could be grateful for, Nicole thought as she studied the distribution reports that had been sent for her perusal. Civility was one thing, but how on earth would they continue to live together? Already she could feel the strain between them. She'd had no appetite for anything all day and she knew that food would not ease the hollow that echoed inside her.

Nate had told her to bring her own car into work today as he would be working late entertaining overseas clients. She hadn't suggested she assist him as she was only too grateful for the excuse to put a little distance between them. Leaving the office was a relief.

At the apartment, she'd barely had time to put her laptop case down when the phone began to ring. She let the answering machine pick up but hastened to lift the receiver when her mother's voice could be heard through the speaker.

"Hello?"

"Nicole, darling, I was hoping to catch you at home. How was the rest of your weekend?"

"It was fine. We went out to the beach house."

"I see. Have you thought any more about what I said to you about the Jacksons? I really don't think it's a good idea for you to spend any more time under that man's roof. Seriously, my dear, nothing good will come of it. Surely you can see that."

Another person telling her what to do. Nicole fought back the sigh that built in her chest.

"I'm an adult, Cynthia, and I'm long used to making my own decisions."

"I know, but allow me a mother's care in this instance. I know I wasn't there for you growing up, but trust me when I say I do know better in this case."

"Was there anything else you rang me for?" Nicole asked, struggling with a desire to hang up before she was bossed around again.

"Yes, well, there is, actually."

Was it Nicole's imagination or did her mother sound a little upset? She waited, saying nothing, until Cynthia continued.

"Things haven't really worked out here the way I'd thought they would and I've decided to go back to Adelaide for now. I'd really love it if you could come with me. I'm leaving in the morning and I'll leave a ticket for you at the check-in desk."

"I really don't think—" Nicole started, only to be shut down by Cynthia's voice talking over her.

"No, please, don't make a decision right this minute. Take the evening to think it over. We really haven't had a chance to get to know one another, have we? After all, one lunch together does not a relationship make." She laughed at that, the sound ringing false to Nicole's ears. "At The Masters' we could just spend some time learning to understand one another a little better and you would have the chance to meet up with some of your cousins—get to know your extended family. After all, you're a Masters by blood, and you have every right to be there with me. It's your heritage, too."

Nicole felt a throbbing pain start behind one eye. Did Cynthia instinctively know all of Nicole's hot buttons? But to leave, now, just like that? With her father still direly ill in the hospital and with Nate still holding the DVD over her head?

"Okay, I'll think about it," she conceded.

"You will? Oh, that's marvelous." She gave Nicole the flight time and details. "I'll expect to see you in the departure lounge, then. I can't wait."

Cynthia hung up before Nicole could say another word and Nicole replaced the handset of the phone on its station, a sensation of numbness enveloping her body.

Her life was in tatters. Could her mother's offer be the new beginning she really, desperately, needed? Could she just walk away and say to hell with the consequences of what would happen when Nate gave her father the DVD? She had no doubt he would do it. If she'd learned anything about Nate in this time, it was just how far he was prepared to go to get what he wanted. He wouldn't rest until he'd pulled her family down from its pedestal. She'd already done her part—he didn't need her anymore. When you got right down to it, she was as disposable to him as she was to her father.

Was she prepared to let him hurt her father like that without even trying to interfere? Was she ready to end their affair, once and for all? Could she really, in all honesty, walk away?

Nate woke to an empty bed. Nicole had been sound asleep when he'd come in last night, a little the worse for wear after a few drinks with his hard-drinking clients. His head gave him a solid reminder that drinking on an empty stomach was not conducive to clear brain function the next day. He felt across the bed. Her side was stone cold. A glance at the bedside clock confirmed it was much later than they usually rose. Obviously she'd left him to it and gone into the office already.

He dragged himself from the bed and through to the kitchen where he downed the better part of the liter of orange juice that was in the fridge, then grabbed a banana from the fruit bowl. It was all he had time for. He'd have to make up for it later in the day.

Showering and dressing took more effort than he wanted to admit and, concerned he may still be over the safe driving limit, he caught a taxi to the office. Nicole had her car there so they could travel home together at the end of the day.

"Is Miss Wilson not with you this morning?" April asked as he entered the office.

Nate felt the first pang of warning. "Isn't she already in the office?"

"No, she left a note for me saying she wouldn't be in. I thought she would be arriving with you."

Nate felt his blood run cold in his veins. She'd been into the office already?

"Let me know if she calls, will you?" he directed as

he strode through to his office and rang the concierge of the apartment building.

Five minutes later he had confirmation that her car had left the parking garage a little after five this morning. Another call confirmed she'd swiped in at the office block parking floor shortly after, but that she'd left again within ten minutes. Which begged the question. Where the hell was she now?

He punched the redial on his office phone for the seventh time this morning, only to get the same automated message—that her phone was either switched off or outside of the calling area. He thought about his own cell phone, which had been damnably silent all morning, and reached into his pocket.

Sometime during the night he'd turned it off while he was out and hadn't turned it back on again. He must have been more intoxicated than he'd realized. Nate thumbed the on button and waited for the phone to power up. The instant it had connected to its service provider the screen flashed up—one missed call, one message. Cursing himself for all kinds of idiocy, he hit the numbers required to play the message. Nicole's shaking voice filled his ears.

"I can't stay with you anymore, Nate. It's slowly killing me inside. Do what you like with the DVD. I don't care anymore. I just know that if I don't get some distance, from you, from everyone, I'm going to go insane. All my life I've tried to be everything for everyone. I even had to do it with you, but I can't do it anymore, not now, not ever again. It's all too much. I need to take care of *me* and to learn to put myself first for a change. In fact, I need to find out who I really am, and what I want. I'm sick to death of being told.

My mother has asked me to go with her to Adelaide. Please don't bother trying to contact me again."

She'd left the message at about six o'clock this morning and it sounded as if she was crying toward the end, as if she was teetering on the edge of a breakdown. Nate felt every muscle in his body clench as the urge to protect her fired through him. He had to find her, needed to find her. As vulnerable as she was right now, she needed a champion. Someone to watch over her while she got her act back together. Someone like him. Certainly not someone like Cynthia Masters-Wilson.

Nate remembered the GPS device in her phone, the one that could track where she was at any given time. He called through to his IT guy, Max, who promised to get on it and let him know within the next few minutes where her phone was. In the meantime, Nate hit the search function on his desktop computer and keyed in Auckland International Airport's departures. Hopefully he wouldn't be too late to stop her from leaving on the flight for Adelaide.

Hope died a swift and sudden death when he saw the only direct flight to Adelaide that morning had departed at eight o'clock. The time she left the apartment, the time she'd left the message for him—it all fit with her being on that flight out of the country. The flight with her mother.

Anger and frustration vied for dominance as he weighed up the idea of booking the next available plane to Australia and making his way to Adelaide to get Nicole back. He wouldn't put it past Nicole to refuse to see him, though, nor her mother to prevent him from making any contact with her. Even if he could track her now it wouldn't be much use to him.

His phone rang on his desk and he swept the receiver up.

"Nate, the tracker shows this address for the phone. Are you sure she's not hiding in your office somewhere?"

Nate bit back the growl of frustration at his computer geek's humor. He reached across and opened a drawer where Nicole had often put her things during the day. There, in all its totally specced-up splendor, lay her cell phone. A sticky note on the screen said, *I won't be needing this anymore,* in Nicole's handwriting. Nate slowly slid the drawer closed and thanked Max for the information, then hung up the phone and, propping his elbows on the desk, rested his head in his hands.

The headache he'd woken with was nothing compared to how he felt now. He closed his eyes for a moment and thought hard about what he should do next. Flying to Adelaide was a definite option, but before he did that he needed some ammunition behind him and what better ammunition than her brother's support?

Nate went to grab his keys, then cursed anew as he remembered he'd left his car at the apartment. Not to worry, there was a taxi rank near the office block. The fare to Parnell and Wilson Wines would be a short one but he'd make it worth the driver's while.

"I want to see Judd Wilson," he demanded as he walked past the reception desk at Wilson Wines about fifteen minutes later.

"Mr. Wilson isn't taking appointments today," the girl behind the desk stated very primly, her expression changing to one of outrage as Nate totally ignored her and started to climb the stairs that led to the management offices of the two-storied building. "Wait, you can't go up there!"

"Just watch me," he said, ascending the stairs two at a time.

At the top of the stairs he caught sight of a woman he recognized as Anna Garrick. Raoul's reporting had been spot-on as usual. The woman was attractive, not unlike Nicole in coloring, but her hair was a little lighter and she was a bit shorter, too.

"Mr. Hunter?" she asked, a startled expression on her face before she pushed it back under a professional facade.

"Where is Wilson? I need to see him."

"Mr. Wilson is still in hospital and visitors are restricted to immediate family only."

"No," he huffed in frustration, "not Charles Wilson, I want to see Judd Wilson, right now."

"Well, then," she said, now appearing completely unruffled. "If you would like to take a seat I'll check if he can see you."

"I'm not waiting. Just show me where he is. This is important."

"Is that so?" Another male voice sounded across the carpeted foyer. "Don't worry, Anna, I'll see him in my office."

Nate couldn't help but intercept the look that passed between the two of them. Questioning his presence, for sure, but there was something more between them. Something that made him feel very much on the outside.

"Where's Nicole?" he demanded, not taking time for introductions or finesse.

"Why don't you come into my office and we'll talk, hmm?"

Judd Wilson gave him a cool blue stare, one that reminded him that he was on their turf right now and in no position to be making demands. With ill-concealed frustration he moved into the room Judd had gestured him into and seated himself in a chair opposite a large mahogany desk. If Jackson Importers was everything that was modern and current, Wilson Wines was the opposite. There was a sense of longevity about the fixtures and fittings, even about the building itself. As if they'd been here awhile and they would be here for quite a while still to come.

The sensation that filled him now was not unlike envy. This should have been part of his father's business, too, part of his legacy. But he didn't have time to dwell on old bitterness and recriminations. Right now he had one priority. Nicole, and her whereabouts.

"Now, how about you tell me what it is you want?" Judd said from the other side of the desk, his gaze still unfriendly.

"Nicole's gone. I need to find out where she went so I can get her back."

"My sister is a big girl now, Hunter. I think if she cannot be reached by you, then perhaps she simply doesn't want to be."

"She's not herself at the moment. She's been under immense pressure and I don't think she's capable of making a rational decision right now. Please, you must help me," Nate implored, shoving pride to one side for the sake of the woman he loved and cared for more than anyone else in the world.

"Must? I don't think so. Not under the circumstances. She left us to be with you. Now she's left you, too. What makes you think we'd do anything to help you get her back?"

"I think she's gone to Adelaide with your mother."

Judd leaned back in his chair, the lift of one brow his only expression of surprise at the news.

"No, she wouldn't have done that," Anna Garrick's voice came from the door.

"Why not?" Nate asked, confused. Nicole had made the point quite clear in her voice message that her mother had invited her to leave New Zealand with her.

"Because she couldn't, that's why. Her passport is still here in the office safe."

Nate felt all the fight drain out of him. Now he had no idea where Nicole could be. Searching for her would be like looking for a needle in a haystack. He had no rights to find out where she was. She'd left on her own accord, severing all ties with him.

"Thank you," he said brokenly, getting up from his seat and making for the door.

"Hunter, can I ask why you're so desperate to find her?" Judd asked from behind the desk.

"Because I love her, and I've done the most stupid thing in my life by letting her go."

Twelve

The look of shock on Judd's and Anna's faces had been little compensation for the empty days, and nights that stretched ahead. By Friday night Nate was a mess—his concentration shot to pieces, his temper frayed. He'd never been this helpless in his life. Well, at least not since his father's fallout with Charles Wilson, when his whole world had turned upside down.

It didn't help that everything around him reminded him of Nicole. From the lotions and perfume on his bathroom vanity, to the items of clothing that were mixed in with his laundry. Even in the office there was the constant reminder of her phone in his drawer, her laptop neatly sitting on the top of the desk.

Every day since she'd left he'd asked himself where she could be. He'd toyed with reporting her missing to the police, but he was quite certain he'd have been laughed out of the station. After all, she was an adult.

They'd had a fight. The separation that had come next was a natural progression. Except it felt unnatural in every way, shape and form.

Someone had to know where she was. She was a gregarious creature, one who got along with people. A pack animal rather than a loner. He wracked his brains to think of who she could have been in touch with. Only one name came to mind.

Anna Garrick. She'd said very little when he'd been at their office on Tuesday morning. Mind you, he'd been an over-reactive idiot—making demands and being belligerent. Hardly the way to garner respect or assistance. It was possible, too, that Nicole may not have even been in touch with her at that stage, but who was to say she hadn't been in touch since?

The time between making his decision to speak with Anna and arriving at the Wilson home became a blur. As he directed his car up the driveway he couldn't help but admire the enormous replica gothic mansion that loomed at the top. It had taken a hell of lot of hard work to build all of this and then to hold on to it, he knew, and he found himself experiencing a begrudging respect for the man who had held it all together.

He went to the door and lifted the old-fashioned knocker, letting it fall against the brass plate behind it.

A neatly suited man answered the door.

"I'd like to see Ms. Garrick, please," Nate said, after he gave his name.

"One moment please, sir. If you'll just take a seat in the salon, I'll see if she's free."

Nate didn't know if Anna was playing games with him or if she was simply genuinely busy, but he didn't like having to cool his heels for a good twenty minutes before she came into the salon to greet him. He had to remind himself more than once that he needed to keep his impatience in check if he was to find out if she knew where Nicole was.

When she finally deigned to see him she was composed and solicitous, probably more so than he deserved after the last time he'd seen her. She offered him a drink, obviously comfortable in her role as hostess. Nate declined her offer, too filled with nervous energy to do anything but pace the confines of the room. She composed herself on an elegantly covered antique two-seater sofa and eyed him carefully.

"What can I do for you, Mr. Hunter?"

"Nate, please call me Nate."

"Nate, then. What is it that you want?"

He swallowed and chose his words carefully. "Have you heard from Nicole?"

"If I had, do you really think she'd want me to tell you?"

He sighed. "I take it you have, then. Is she—"

"She's fine, but she doesn't want to see you or anyone else right now."

Nate lifted his eyes to Anna's, searching her calm hazel gaze for any sign that she was worried about her friend.

"I need to see her," he said, the words blunt and filled with an edge of pain he couldn't hide.

Anna shook her head. "Isn't it enough to know she's okay?"

"What do you think?" he asked her, letting every raw pain of loss show in his eyes. "I love her, Anna. I have to tell her I'm sorry, and I need to see if she'll give me another chance."

"I would be betraying her trust if I told you where she was. I've already done that once, recently, and I have to tell you that I'm not prepared to do that again. It nearly destroyed our friendship."

"Don't you think I know that? I'm begging you here."

"I can't. She needs to know she can trust me."

Nate felt as if a giant ball of lead had settled in his gut. Anna had been his only hope. "I want her to know she can trust me, too," he said brokenly as he rose to his feet and headed out the room. At the doorway he turned, "Thank you for seeing me. If you talk to her soon, please tell her…ah, hell, don't worry, it wouldn't make a difference, anyway."

The pity in Anna Garrick's eyes cut him straight to his heart. Nicole was lucky to have a friend like her, he told himself as he forced his feet toward the front door and headed down the stairs toward his car.

The heavy tread of rapid footsteps followed him down the stairs.

"Hunter, wait up."

It was Judd Wilson. Nate turned to face him.

"Yeah," he said, without even the will to fake a politeness he certainly didn't feel.

"I know where she is."

Nate felt something leap in his chest. "And you'll tell me?"

"Anna will kill me for this, but someone needs to cut you a break," the other man said. "Anyone can see you're hurting. The two of you need to work this out one way or another. You both deserve that much." He gave Nate an address about a two-hour drive north of Auckland. "Don't make me regret this, Hunter. If you hurt her again, you'll be answering to me."

Nate proffered his hand, and felt an overwhelming

sense of relief when Judd took it. Their shake was brisk and brief. "I owe you," he said solemnly.

"Yes, you do," Judd replied just as gravely. "We can talk about that later."

Nate gave him a nod of assent and headed for his car. He needed to swing by the apartment before driving up to see her. There was something he needed to collect. It was late, but maybe Nicole would still be awake by the time he made it to where she was staying. And if she wasn't, well, then he'd just wait until she was.

Nicole brushed the sand off her feet with an old towel she'd been keeping on the edge of the deck for just that purpose. Late-night walks along the sandy shoreline of Langs Beach had become a habit as she tried to do what she could to exhaust herself into sleep every night.

Since making the decision to leave Nate, and risk the consequences, she'd hardly slept a wink. So far Nate hadn't sent the DVD to her father, she knew that much. Anna had been keeping her up to date on her father's progress and it looked as if he'd turned a corner health-wise. Of course, that could all change if he viewed the thing. And while that preyed on her mind, when she was honest with herself, she knew she wasn't sleeping mostly because she missed Nate. Missed his strength, his solid presence beside her at night.

She sighed as she made her way across the deck, her feet frozen in the frigid night air. She could have worn shoes, probably should have, but she loved the feel of the squeaky white sand beneath her feet and, at this time of night, she could enjoy the sensation completely on her own with only the stars above her for company.

The aged French doors groaned as she opened them to let herself inside the rather decrepit holiday home she'd rented. After she'd left her laptop and the phone Nate had given her at the office, she'd just driven north—stopping only long enough to pay for the toll charge on the Northern Motorway and to pick up a cheap prepaid cell phone from a gas station on the way.

She didn't know what had drawn her to the area, aside from the fact it was near the sea and it was nothing like the west coast beach that Nate's house overlooked. Of course, if her goal had been to avoid reminders of Nate, then she'd failed. She hadn't been able to stop thinking about the man since she'd gotten here.

Nicole secured the door and went through to the kitchen to put on the kettle. Maybe a cup of chamomile tea would make the difference tonight and help her to sleep. She stiffened as she heard the sound of a car's tires rolling along the gravel driveway that led to the house. No one knew she was here but Anna, and she wouldn't have come without calling Nicole first.

The walls of the cottage were thin and she could hear a heavy measured tread come toward the house. A tread that seemed to hesitate on the wooden steps that led to the front door before she heard a solid one-two-three knock on the peeling painted surface.

Her heart hammering in her chest, she moved closer to the front door.

"Nicole, it's me, Nate."

How had he found her? More to the point, now that he had, what was she going to do?

"Nicole, please. I'm not here to hurt you or to argue with you. I just want to talk."

She hesitated a moment before reaching a trembling

hand to the lock at the door and swinging the door open. Shock hit her when she saw him illuminated beneath the bare bulb that lit the front porch. As much as she tried to harden her heart against him, she couldn't help but be concerned at his appearance. He looked as if he hadn't slept or eaten properly in days. Probably much as she looked herself. Except when she looked at him all she wanted to do was comfort him.

She fought against the urge to hold her arms out to him, to offer him respite from the demons that had obviously ridden him this week. Demons that might be similar to those she'd been wrestling with herself—unsuccessfully, too, if her instinctive reaction to him was any indicator. She took a deep breath and forced her hands to stay at her sides.

"You'd better come in," she said stiffly, standing aside and gesturing toward the open-plan living room/kitchen.

The place was basic. One bedroom, one bathroom and everything else all there for anyone to see. The property's saving graces had been its proximity to the beach and a modern lock-up garage where she'd stowed the Mercedes.

"Can I get you a warm drink?"

She didn't want to offer him any alcohol before sending him back on his way again, especially not looking the way he did right now. The last thing she wanted to be responsible for was him having an accident.

"No, thanks," he said, his voice ragged. "How are you, really?"

She poured boiling water over the tea bag in her cup and then took it over to one of the chairs in the lounge. Nate sat down on the sofa opposite.

"I'm okay. Look, I don't know why you're here but you won't change my mind. I meant what I said in my message."

Nate reached inside his jacket pocket and took out a flat case. A case she recognized with dread. He tried to hand it over to her and when she didn't take it—she couldn't risk touching him—he placed it on the scarred coffee table between them. She could see her refusal to take the case had surprised him, perhaps even hurt him.

She looked at the case, lying there, inert on the tabletop. So seemingly nondescript, yet so potentially damaging at the same time.

"It's yours," he said.

"What? A copy?"

"The only copy," he said, lifting his face so his eyes met hers. "I couldn't send it to your father—I couldn't do that to you, Nicole. I want you to know that. I could never hurt you like that. I know I threatened to, more than once. But even if I hadn't fallen in love with you I couldn't have abused your trust of me that way."

A fist clenched tight around her heart. Had she heard him right? Or was this just another ploy to get her back where he wanted her?

"You seemed pretty determined. Why should I believe you've changed your mind now?"

The voice that came from her mouth didn't sound like her at all. It was harsh, unforgiving.

He hung his head. "I don't deserve for you to believe me but I hope that you can find your way clear to understand where I'm coming from." He lifted his head again, his eyes filled with anguish. "I know I've been a total monster. I should have told you from the beginning who I was. I should have left you in the bar that night. But I couldn't. Even then I was compelled to be with you. I wanted you and I had to have you."

Nicole gripped her mug tight, mindless to the heat that stung her fingers. Just hearing him say the words about wanting her had her body beginning to light up in response. The old familiar coil of desire tightening deep inside her, craving his touch. Craving him.

"And once you had me, you used me," she said bitterly.

"I'm sorry. I know it sounds trite and empty and worthless, but please believe me. I am so sorry I treated you that way. If I had the chance again I would do everything differently."

And so would she, Nicole thought. For a start she wouldn't have left the house that night. Wouldn't have stormed away and wouldn't have lost herself in the one man who could hurt her more than any other. The man she'd fallen painfully in love with. Her heart beat faster in her chest as she acknowledged the painful truth for what it was. Hopeless. She couldn't trust him. He was a master at manipulation, he'd borne a grudge against her father for most of his life. How could she even begin to believe his words were anything more than another tool to control her?

"Is that everything?" she asked coolly. She held her body so rigid that she was afraid she'd shatter into a million pieces if he so much as reached across the table and touched her.

"No, it's not everything. I could spend the rest of my life telling you how much I regret treating you so badly and it would never be long enough. I love you, Nicole. I'm ashamed that I had to lose you to admit it to myself, but there you have it. On the beach that day I asked you to marry me. I'd fooled myself into thinking it was for the baby's sake, and hurt you by asking you for all the wrong reasons when I should have just asked you for you. Will you give me another chance? Let me make it up to you. Let me love you the way you deserve to be loved."

Nicole shook her head. It was a slight movement but Nate saw it and recognized it for what it was. He tried one more time.

"Please, don't make your mind up right now. Give it a few more days. Come back to the city, come back to me. Let's try again and this time I promise I'll get it right."

"No," she said, feeling as if her heart would break with verbalizing that one syllable. "I can't, Nate. I can't trust you not to hurt me like that again. Me or my family. I just can't." And she couldn't trust herself, either. She loved him too much. If she went back, if she let herself be with him again, she'd find herself falling back into his plans, for better or for worse. And she wasn't going to do that again.

Nate looked at her for a full minute, her words hanging in the air between them like an impenetrable shield. Then, slowly he nodded and rose from the sofa. She didn't move as he crossed the room and moved down the short hall toward the front door. It wasn't until she heard the snick of the lock as the door reseated in its frame behind him, that the shudders began to rack her body and the sobs rose from deep within.

He was gone. She'd sent him away. It was what she wanted, wasn't it?

Nate walked to his car wrapped in a blanket of numbness. She'd refused him. It was his worst-case scenario come to living, breathing, painful, life. He settled behind the wheel of the Maserati, and switched the wipers on only to turn them off again as they scraped across the dry windscreen. It was only then he realized the moisture he felt on his face had not been from any rain outside, but from his own tears.

He started the car and eased it up the driveway, away from the house, away from Nicole, swiping at his cheeks and eyes as he did so. He felt as if he was leaving his soul behind, as if he was just a shell now. An empty shell. She'd completed him and he hadn't even had the good sense to know it or appreciate it until it was too late.

At the top of the driveway he looked back, hoping against hope that she might be silhouetted in the doorway, that she might beckon to him to come back. If she did, then together they could find a way to work past the damage he'd wrought. Instead, he saw the outside light extinguish, and with it his last remaining hope.

He blinked hard. He'd lost her. He'd abused her trust, he'd threatened her family. He had gotten exactly what he deserved.

Nate turned the car onto the winding road that would eventually lead him back to State Highway One, back to Auckland. Back to a life lived alone with his grand, empty plans for revenge.

His eyes burned in their sockets by the time he crossed the Auckland Harbor Bridge and turned off toward the Viaduct Basin. Weariness dragged at his body as he let himself into the apartment, a place that felt empty without Nicole inside. As exhausted as he was, sleep was the last thing on his mind. Somehow he had to find a way to convince Nicole she could trust him and that his love for her was real. There had to be a way, there just had to be, because he couldn't imagine the rest of his life without her by his side.

It simply wasn't an option.

Thirteen

Nate straightened from his car outside the Wilson family home. He hadn't slept all night and was running on pure adrenaline right now. He hammered at the front door and stood back in the portico waiting for someone to respond.

It took a while but eventually the door swung open to reveal Judd Wilson dressed in pajama bottoms and a robe. His hair was rumpled, as if he'd run his fingers through it in an attempt to tidy it before answering the door.

"Good grief, man, have you any idea what time it is?" he grumbled at Nate.

"Look, I know it's early but I had to talk to you. This is too important to wait."

"You'd better come in, then." Judd gave him a hard look. "Have you seen yourself this morning?"

Nate grimaced in response. He knew he looked

about as rough as he felt. He hadn't shaved or combed his hair and he was still in the clothing he'd worn last night.

"Judd? Who is it?" Anna's voice came from the top of the staircase.

"It's Nate Hunter."

"And Nicole? Is she all right?"

Anna came down the stairs, a dressing gown wrapped about her and tied with a sash at her waist.

"Nicole was fine when I left her," Nate ground out. "She doesn't want a bar of me but I'm hoping that we can change that, together."

Judd and Anna exchanged a look before Judd spoke. "You need to fight your own battles, Hunter. My sister is responsible for her own choices."

"I know, but I have a proposal I think you might find worth listening to. Something that will benefit you and Wilson Wines, and that just might show Nicole how much I care."

"Sounds like something best done on a full stomach with a decent cup of coffee inside you," Anna said. "Judd?"

"Sure, come through to the kitchen," Judd agreed.

"We gave our house staff the weekend off, so I hope you don't mind if things are a little more basic than we can usually offer," Anna said as she pushed open the swing doors that led into the spacious modernized kitchen.

"Food is the least of my worries," Nate said, lowering himself into one of the kitchen chairs and pulling a sheaf of papers from his coat pocket. "Please don't go to any bother on my account."

As Anna began to make coffee, Nate started to outline his plan. Judd remained silent through most of it, only stopping Nate every now and then to ask him to clarify one point or another. By the time Anna slid plates of French toast and bacon in front of them both, and topped up their coffees, he was wrapping up.

"So, to sum it all up, I suggest that we amalgamate Jackson Importers and Wilson Wines and go forward as one powerful entity for the future, rather than two companies, which are absorbed in competing with one another. It's how it was meant to be all along, it's up to us to make it that way again."

"Why?" Judd asked. "I mean, the idea is definitely worth exploring, but why now?"

"Because I don't see why we should continue to be victims of our fathers' falling out."

"Your fathers?" Anna asked. "You're—?"

"Yes, I'm Thomas Jackson's son."

Judd leaned back in his chair and gave Nate a hard look. "You're certain you want to do this?"

"I've never been more certain of anything in my life," Nate said emphatically.

"You realize I can't do anything without discussing this with my father and with Nicole."

"I understand that. If possible, I'd like to be there when you talk to your father. I think it's time that the past be firmly put to bed. That all the bitterness be dissolved once and for all. It's hurt too many people for too long. It has to stop."

Nicole missed Nate with an ache that went painfully deep. Nights were fractured with dreams of him, days were filled with trying to forget him. But try as she might, she failed miserably. If only they could have met under normal circumstances, without the stupid feud between their families. If only she could trust that he loved her for herself and not out of some twisted sense of revenge. A person didn't let go of that much animosity easily.

She'd thought that getting away from him, getting away from the city would help. But it hadn't helped a bit. If anything it had only served to magnify her feelings for him. Without anything else to distract her, he was all she could think about. Especially after he told her he loved her—and she'd had to send him away.

Maybe she should get a dog, she pondered as she sat on the deck outside the cottage in the watery sunshine and watched a local resident throwing a stick for his dog on the beach. Even as she considered it she knew it couldn't replace the hole in her heart loving Nate had left. Loving him? How could she love him? He'd virtually kidnapped her, had held her against her will, had forced her to work with him instead of where she rightfully belonged. She made a mental note to look up Stockholm syndrome as soon as she could access a computer. She had to find some reason for this irrational attachment to the man.

But was it so irrational? Their attraction that night at the bar had been mutual and instant. Fierce. At least it had been on her side. His? Well, the jury was still out on that one. He'd been following an agenda, hadn't he?

Seeing him last night was tough. Had their circumstances been any different, had he not been so bent on revenge for what her father had done, she'd have dragged him to the tiny bedroom and laid him bare upon the covers of the double bed and taken her time in punishing him slowly for his behavior.

Her body flushed with heat at the thought. Heat that was rapidly diminished by the cool breeze coming in off the ocean. Exercise, she needed exercise. Anything to wear her out and distract her from her thoughts. She grabbed her puffy jacket from inside the cottage and pulled on a pair of sneakers before heading north up the beach. The wind had risen by the time she reached the end and started to walk back, bringing with it the scent of rain.

By the time she got to the cottage the rain was driving across the sand. She hastened inside, taking her jacket off in the tiny bathroom and hanging it over the shower rail to dry. Making her way to the kitchen, she put on the kettle for a warming cup of tea, as she did so she noticed her phone flashing that she had a message.

Not just one message. Several. And several missed calls, as well. All of them from Anna. What could be so important on a Saturday morning? she wondered. She knew it wasn't her father. He was making steady progress at the hospital and they were even talking about him coming home soon. Dialysis would be a major part of his future but at least he had a future. The messages were all the same—Anna asking Nicole to call her back right away. Her friend sounded excited, but not upset, Nicole noted. She poured her cup of tea and took the cup and her phone over to the sofa where Nate had sat last night, the stuffing so worn that the imprint of his body was still there.

Before she could stop herself, Nicole reached a hand to where he'd been sitting, as if she could somehow sense the man in the impression he'd left behind. A particularly strong gust of wind drove against the beachside windows of the house, making her jump and shaking her from her reverie. She had a call to make. She didn't need to be thinking about Nate. Not now, not ever.

Anna answered the phone on the first ring. "Nic, Judd needs to speak to you. Hold on and I'll put him on."

Judd's warm deep voice filled her ear. "How's it going?"

"It's okay. The weather's rubbish but aside from that I'm doing all right." Ironic, she thought, one of the few conversations she should have with her brother and it should be about the weather.

"Glad to hear it. Look, I'll cut to the chase. I have some important Wilson Wines business to discuss with you but I don't want to do it over the phone. Can you come into the office on Monday? I'd really rather do this face-to-face."

Monday? She could do that. It wasn't as if she had any other pressing social engagements on her calendar, she thought cynically.

"Sure, what time?"

"Let's say eleven. That should give you plenty of time to get down here, shouldn't it?"

"I'll be there."

Judd wasted no further time on any pleasantries, severing the call almost immediately after her confirmation. Well, it wasn't as if they had a normal brother-sister relationship. They hadn't ever had the chance. She wondered what it was he wanted to discuss. Hopefully it would have something to do with her coming back to Wilson Wines and reassuming her position there. Then, maybe, she could undo some of the damage she'd done with her work for Jackson Importers.

Monday morning rolled around slowly and Nicole was on the road earlier than she needed be. After another night plagued with dreams of Nate, she couldn't wait to have something else to distract her. The traffic heading into Auckland was that and then some.

Pulling into her usual car park at Wilson Wines felt strange, but that was nothing to what it felt like walking back into the building. Everything was still exactly the same. She didn't know why she'd expected it to have changed in any way, except that she had been through so much since the last time she'd been here that she felt that time should have marked its passage here somehow.

Their receptionist told her to go on upstairs and that Judd was waiting for her. Anna met her at the top of the stairs and gave her a quick hug.

"Do you know what this is about?" Nicole asked.

"It's better you hear it from Judd," she said with a smile. "He's waiting in your dad's old office."

"Old office? So he's not coming back?"

"It's unlikely. Even though he's a lot better he's not up to the day-to-day demands of business anymore."

Nicole was shocked. Her father had always been invincible. A powerhouse. They'd butted heads over his unwillingness to accept her ideas for advancement but, that said, she couldn't imagine the company without her father at the helm.

"Is that what Judd wants to talk to me about?"

"Go and see him," was all Anna would say.

Squaring her shoulders, Nicole walked toward her father's office. Judd's office, now, she supposed. He got up from behind the desk when she knocked and pushed open the door.

"I'm glad you could come," he said, first holding out his hand and then drawing her into his arms for a swift embrace. "We haven't exactly been able to get off to a good start, have we?"

"No," Nicole said, a nervous smile on her face. Considering she'd pretty much been pouting like a spoiled brat when he'd arrived, followed a few days later by her storming out of the house, his comment was a mastery of understatement.

"Hopefully we can amend that, if you're willing?"

"Sure. Who knows, we might even like each other."

Judd flashed her a smile and in it she could see a hint of their father's humor. It made her instantly feel more comfortable with him. It was a comfort she clung to as he started to talk about what he'd asked her in to discuss.

"You mean this was Nate's idea? That he *wants* to amalgamate the businesses?"

She got up from her seat and walked over to the window that looked out over the city. Nate? Merge Jackson Importers with Wilson Wines? What ever happened to his passion for revenge? By his own admission it had driven him since he was a child. Why stop now? They both knew that the deal was to Wilson Wines's advantage. The company was in a weakened managerial position with Judd inexperienced with the firm and her father incapable of reassuming his role. If Jackson Importers wanted to put them out of business, now was the time. Why was Nate throwing them a lifeline, instead?

"It was his idea, and after discussing it with him and going over the figures, I'm inclined to accept. It makes sense. Not only that, but it closes a door that's been open too long. It gives both our families a chance to heal."

Nicole shook her head. She couldn't believe it. "Are

you sure he doesn't have some ulterior motive behind this?"

"We stand to gain far more than he does at the moment. I'm sure you're even more aware of that than he is. You've worked with him. You know how strong they are in the marketplace, here and overseas. He's done that. With him running the whole company, they're poised to grow even stronger. Of course, Wilson Wines brings a respected name and established reputation to the table—but unless we modernize and expand, our company will grow weaker while his grows stronger. This is just what we need to get back on track."

She sat back down in her seat. Could Nate have been telling the truth when he came to see her on Friday night? Was he really letting all that resentment and hostility toward her family go, just like that? Was this a chance to finally mend the gaping rifts in her family life and allow her to feel whole again?

Was this the chance for her and Nate, after all?

"And you want an opinion from me today? Really, I need some time to think about this," she said.

"Look, I know it's a lot to take in. Goodness only knows Anna and I have made the most of having the past couple of days to begin to get used to the idea. But it's not just my decision to make. It affects you, as well."

Nicole felt the old acrimony rise in her throat again. "No, it doesn't. You have the controlling share in Wilson Wines. Dad holds the balance. It's your decision, Judd, whether you want that or not."

Judd lifted an envelope from the top of the desk and handed it to her. "Here, maybe what's inside will help you make up your mind."

She took the envelope. "What is it?"

He laughed. "Nothing that'll hurt you, Nicole. Seriously, just open it."

She slid a nail under the flap and ripped the envelope open. Inside was a single sheet of paper. A company share transfer, to be exact. Her eyes widened as she read the terms of the transfer. Judd was giving her everything their father had given him. Not half, not less than half. All of it. If she signed this paper she would have the controlling share and the decision as to how Wilson Wines would go forward.

"Have you lost your mind?" she asked.

"No, if anything I've found it. I learned the hard way that a life bent on revenge is no life at all. I think that Nate has recently discovered much the same thing. I nearly lost Anna over my need to make our father pay for abandoning me and our mother. For denying me my birthright until it suited him to get Anna to bring me back. I don't want to lose out on anything else. Neither does Nate.

"We've all been hurt, Nicole. But we deserve to be happy—*really* happy. I know I'm doing the right thing in giving this to you and I know you'll do the right thing in return."

"And are you happy now, Judd?"

"With Anna, yes. I'm going to marry her, Nicole. I know you two are close and I want you to know I'm going to look after her."

Nicole sat back in her chair and looked at him, and smiled again. Her first genuine smile since she'd arrived today. Maybe her first genuine smile in a long, long time. "You'd better, or you'll answer to me."

"Noted," he said with a nod. "Now, how about you take the next day or so to think about things? Anna has a folder ready for you to take with you so you can analyze Nate's proposal in depth."

Nicole sat in her car in the car park still shocked by the news Judd had given her today, especially his intention to marry her best friend. When pressed, Anna had admitted her love for Judd in return, but said they weren't going to make a public announcement until Charles was home and settled again. They'd already sought his blessing, which had been rapidly forthcoming, apparently. Which left Nicole exactly where?

She had plenty to think about, she realized as she started the car and backed out of the car space. It wasn't until she'd headed for the motorway interchange that would lead her back up north that she made a sudden decision to turn around and drive back the way she'd come.

The Auckland City Hospital car park was pretty empty given the time of day, and it didn't take her long to find a space. In no time she was in an elevator, heading for her father's ward. She only hoped that he'd agree to see her. If, as Judd had said, they all deserved happiness, then it was time for some truths between her and her father, especially the truth about her more recent behavior. Only with everything out in the open could the wounds—both old and more recent—finally heal.

She fought to hide her shock when she saw him lying against his pillows, his eyes closed. The ravages of illness had made him lose a great deal of weight and his skin held an unhealthy pallor. She could have lost him. Would have never had the chance to make amends. And all for what?

"Dad?" she said tentatively as she closed the door to the private room behind her.

His eyes shot open and Nicole was relieved to see they were full of their usual fiery intelligence.

"You came back."

His tone of voice gave nothing away but she caught the telltale tremor around his mouth. And was that a hint of moisture in his eyes?

"Oh, Dad. Of course I came back. I miss you."

"Ah, my little girl. Come here," he said, his voice shaking as he parted the side of the bed and opened his arms.

Nicole shifted to his side and let herself be enveloped by his hug, mindful of the monitors and tubes he was still attached to. But all that was peripheral to the fact that she was here, that he hadn't sent her away again.

"I've missed you, too. I've had plenty of time to think, lately, and I know I owe you an apology. Several apologies, actually."

"No, Dad, it's okay," she protested. "I've always acted first, thought second. I should have stayed. We'd have worked it out."

"No, it's not okay. I never gave you a fair shot, did I? I was so angry with you for defecting to the enemy after Judd came home that the sight of you in the emergency department just made me see red. But I was wrong. When all is said and done, family comes first. I should never have pushed you away in the first place. I should have included you when I decided to approach Judd about coming back home. It was wrong of me to make those decisions, decisions that affected you, without any consultation as a family."

"It's okay, Dad, I understand. It hurt me, but I do

understand. You never got the chance to raise Judd the way you wanted to. All of that was stolen from you."

"Stolen with a single lie," he said sadly. "Did you know that? Your mother told me Judd wasn't my son. To my shame I believed her and when she named my best friend as Judd's father, I stupidly believed that, too. So many years lost, so much time wasted."

"But you can make up for that now," she urged, shocked at the way his body trembled and happier than ever that she had chosen not to run away from her problems to Australia with Cynthia. She did want to meet her family at some point—get to know her cousins and uncles and aunts, but cementing things with her family here took priority.

"For what time I have left," Charles replied. "You know, Nicole, pride is a terrible thing. Because of pride I lost my wife, my son, my best friend and my health. If I had my time over again, I'd do so much differently. Maybe then I could have been the husband Cynthia needed. I've made some bad decisions in my life, not least of which with you.

"I know you think I was holding you back at Wilson Wines and, yes, I suppose I was. But I could just see so much of myself in you. You were so driven, so determined to grow the business to the exception of everything else in your life. I've always wanted the best for you but when I saw you going down the same road that I went, I had to do something to hold you back. You deserve more than just a business. You deserve a life enriched with a husband and children and steadiness at home—not all your energy driven into work and serving the mighty dollar as I have done."

"But I love my work at Wilson Wines, Dad. I've missed it."

"I thought limiting your requirements at work would push you to invest more of your time and energy into relationships. I shouldn't have made that decision for you. I'll wager you had more freedom with that Nate Hunter than you had with me. Don't bother denying it. He saw a good thing and he took advantage of it."

"Dad, there's something you should know about him."

"Beyond the fact he's a fearsome business opponent? Can't help but admire him for that, if nothing else."

She didn't know how to phrase this carefully, so she just came out with it. "He's Thomas's son."

Her father closed his eyes briefly before giving a deep sigh. "That explains a lot," he said quietly. "Another life harmed. Clearly I owe him an apology, too. It can't have been easy for him growing up. Are the two of you an item?"

Nicole shook her head. "We were. But I ended it. He wanted me for all the wrong reasons."

"And what are those?" Charles urged.

"Revenge against you, for one thing," she admitted. It sounded so pathetic when she put it into words to the man it had been directed against. But that's pretty much what it all came down to in the end, wasn't it?

Charles chuckled. "A chip off the old block, hmm? Well, I can't say I blame him. He had just cause."

Nicole could barely believe her ears. All his life her father had spoken in derogatory terms about Thomas Jackson and now he laughed about Nate's vendetta?

"Aren't you angry?"

"Not anymore," he said with a deep sigh. "There's a lot to be said for facing your mortality. It makes you see things differently."

"Judd gave me his controlling share of the company," she blurted.

"Did he? Well, that was his choice to make. I should never have created such a divisive position between you two but it was so important to me to bring Judd home, and I really did want to force you to create some balance in your life."

By the time she left the hospital it was growing late. Despite a few dark looks from the nursing staff, she'd been allowed to stay at her father's side all afternoon and they'd talked to one another as they'd never talked before. As she clipped her seatbelt across her chest she recognized that the feeling inside her now was one of happiness and acceptance of her position in her father's heart. She held all the cards now. She was no longer a pawn, she was the player.

Which left her only one last thing to do.

Fourteen

Her headlights picked out the possum ahead of her on the winding curve of road. Thankfully she avoided it without incident and could focus her attention to the confrontation she had ahead. Nate hadn't been at the office when she'd called, nor had he been at the apartment when she'd stopped in there. Which only left the beach house.

How appropriate that this would end where it had begun.

She cruised through the bends in the dark ribbon of tarseal slowly, more familiar with being a passenger on the journey than the driver. It was an interesting analogy for her life. Despite her efforts to get ahead and to be noticed in her life, she'd always allowed herself to be acted upon rather than to take charge and be fully responsible for her own behavior.

The idea that she was free of her previous constraints, constraints she'd allowed even into adulthood, was intensely liberating. Even so, she felt as if hummingbirds danced in her stomach as she neared the driveway to Nate's house. She pulled up outside the garage door and walked around to the main entrance, pressing the door bell several times in quick succession.

The door opened.

"Nicole!"

Nate looked stunned to see her, but she felt his eyes roam her as if he were touching her. Her traitorous body responded in kind. She dropped her eyes from his, hoping he hadn't seen her reaction reflected in her gaze.

"We need to talk," she said brusquely. "May I come in?"

He stood aside and gestured for her to take a seat in the living room. "Can I get you anything?" he offered.

"This isn't a social visit," she said firmly. It was important to her that she set the parameters right from the start. "I need to know something."

"Ask me. I'll tell you whatever I can."

"Are you still playing some game with my family with your proposal to join the companies together?"

He looked surprised. "You know about that already?"

"Judd called me down from Langs Beach to discuss it. He's given me a written report, which I haven't read yet. I needed to talk to you first so I can decide whether to read it, or whether to use it to light a fire, instead."

He gave a disparaging laugh. "It's not a game—it's anything but."

"So this is really what you want?"

He looked her square in the eye and she could see

the truth burning there in those sherry-brown depths.
"Yes."

"And you're not doing this to somehow undermine
my family or to hurt them?"

"No, I'm not."

She took a deep breath. "Or to hurt me?"

"Never to hurt you, Nicole. That was *never* my intention. I wanted to give you every opportunity to succeed all along."

"Why are you doing this, then?"

Nate sighed and leaned forward, resting his elbows
on his thighs and clasping his capable hands in front
of him. His gaze was fixed on her face, as if he was
willing her to believe him.

"I made the suggestion for three very good reasons.
The first is that it makes sound business sense. If we
stop competing with one another we'll be in a stronger position when it comes to securing new business—
one less player in the market should give us an edge on
pricing. It's all in the report, when you read it you'll
see what I'm talking about."

Nicole nodded. "Okay, so that's one reason. What
about the others?"

"It was time to stop the feud. It's hurt too many
people for too long. One of us had to make the first
move. I decided it was time for me to let go of my
grudge. Sure, I had a tough upbringing, a lot of kids
did. I still had more advantages than most. Even while
my mother and I were living hand to mouth my father
was ensuring that I still had the best education that he
could provide for me. And having to struggle a little
made me tough, it made me determined. It made me
the man I am today. Flawed, sure, but I know what's

right, and letting go of the anger, letting go of the pain—it all had to happen so we can move forward.

"Pride can be a killer. I didn't want it to destroy every last thing I held dear."

Nicole nodded. Hadn't her father spoken along the same lines? She said as much to Nate.

He nodded gently. "You know, I want to see him if he's agreeable. We have a lot to talk about."

"I think he'd like that. I told him today about you. I was sure he was going to tell me that he'd be quite happy to carry on the competition between Wilson Wines and Jackson Importers indefinitely, but this latest illness has changed him, too. It's altered his perspective on things."

She paused for a moment, reflecting on the things her father had said, then reminded herself she was here for a reason. "What's the third reason?" Nicole pushed.

"The third reason? You already know that one."

She looked at him, puzzled. She already knew? When she said nothing, Nate continued.

"I love you."

"That's it?" She felt her skepticism rise.

"Yeah, that's it," he said with a deprecating chuckle. "Although I never quite expected to get that response."

"That's not what I mean—" she started to protest, but he cut her off.

"Nicole, I knew that after what I'd put you through, for you to believe that I love you would take an action on my part to prove it, beyond any shadow of a doubt. And I was already working at a disadvantage, because of the mistakes I'd made in our relationship. When I asked you to marry me on the beach out here, when I thought you were carrying my baby, I was prepared to do whatever I could to protect you and provide for you and our child, but I know I went about it all wrong. You have to understand. I grew up illegitimate. Sure, I know that wasn't the worst thing that could happen to me and I certainly wasn't the only kid in class from a single-parent family—but I wanted more for my child than I had."

He got up and began to pace the room, shoving his hands through his hair and sending it into disarray before pushing them deep into the pockets of his trousers. Nicole could see the outlines of his fists through the fine wool of his pants, could sense the tension in every line of his body.

"Go on," she urged softly. "Tell me the rest."

He stood where he was, staring out the window toward the dark shoreline, to where the moon and stars lit the foam of the waves that curled and raced inexorably onto the sand.

"I wanted to ensure that my child never wanted for anything the way I wanted, but at the same time I wanted him or her to know they were loved. You see, even though we struggled, even though I had to put up with the bullying at school because I was different—because my mother was seen shopping at the local thrift store or because one of the boys' mothers delivered our food parcels while doing her bit for the community—through all that I always knew I was loved. Always. I will never be an absentee father to my children. I will be a part of their lives and I will be there when they need me."

Nate turned and faced Nicole again. "That's the way I love, Nicole. With everything I am. It's the way I love you. I asked you to marry me without even fully understanding just how much a man could love a woman, but I learned that, and more, when you left me. You're everything to me and I knew that I had to prove that to you, even if it meant letting go of everything I'd always believed while I was growing up.

"That's it. I love you. Pure and simple."

Nicole sat there, stunned. What he'd just told her was anything but pure and simple. It showed the depths of the man before her. The man she'd rejected and who hadn't given up.

This wasn't the same person who'd calculatedly brought her back here on that fateful night just over a month ago, a man who was prepared to blackmail her over an illicit weekend of wild pleasure just to hurt her father. He'd changed. The old Nate would never have dreamed of combining their two businesses together to form one perfectly strong whole.

This was a man who loved her. Truly loved her. And she'd changed, too, into someone who wasn't afraid to love him back. She pushed herself to her feet and moved to stand in front of him.

"I believe you," she whispered, her voice shaking with the depth of her own love for him. A love she could finally acknowledge to both herself and to Nate. She raised one hand and cupped his cheek. "I love you, too."

The sound he made was part human and part something else. He turned his face into her hand, pressing his lips against her palm.

"It's more than I deserve," he said brokenly.

"We deserve each other. We're neither of us perfect, but together, maybe we can cancel out the bad and be nothing but good. Love me, Nate. Love me forever."

"You can count on it."

He pulled his hands from his pockets and swooped her up into his arms, carrying her to the bedroom where they'd already created so many special memories. This time they undressed one another slowly, painstakingly—taking their time to kiss and caress every part of each other as they bared skin. As if it was their first time—a voyage of discovery.

When neither of them could wait any longer, Nate covered her body with his own, pausing only to reach for a condom. Nicole stayed his hand.

"No condom," she said. "I want whatever naturally comes next in our lives and I don't want any more barriers between us."

"Are you sure?" he asked, his body rigid beneath her hands as she stroked his buttocks with a featherlight touch and then traced her fingers up the muscles that bracketed his spine. She relished the strength of him, loved that he was all hers.

"Certain," she whispered as she lifted her mouth to his, claiming his lips in a kiss that imbued everything she felt at that moment, and when he slid inside her she knew she'd made the right decision. Nothing had ever felt as good as this contact between them, heat to heat, nothing but him and her.

Nate started to move and she met him, stroke for stroke, her cries of pleasure intensifying as he pushed them over the edge of sanity and into another realm where only the two of them existed.

Afterward, they lay still locked together as one. As their breathing slowed and returned to something approaching normal, Nicole lifted a hand and traced the outline of Nate's face. He had never been more precious to her than he was at this moment.

"Do you think we'd have ended up like this without our parents' falling out?"

Nate smiled. "Who knows? I'd like to think so. I

know there's no one out there in this world for me, but you."

She snuggled against him. "Why do you think she did it?"

"She?"

"My mother. Why do you think she lied to my father for all those years? She drove a wedge between everyone without a second thought."

"You know that for sure?"

"Dad didn't tell me all of it, but he did say that her lie was responsible for what happened."

Nate shifted onto his back, pulling Nicole with him. "I suspected she instigated it all. I couldn't imagine anyone else but her having that power over them. Maybe she resented the time Charles put into the business—who knows—but it's no wonder he reacted the way he did to what he perceived as the ultimate betrayal from his best friend."

"But for her to have let it go on this long...I just don't understand it. Why would she do that?"

Nate closed his arms around Nicole and held her tight against him, making a silent vow that nothing would ever separate them again. "She was obviously a very unhappy woman. I'm sorry she never got to have what we have, but we can't let her spoil it for us, either."

Nate pressed a kiss to the top of Nicole's head. "I'm so sorry for everything I did to you, Nicole. I kidded myself that if I gave you everything I thought you wanted that you'd be happy to stay with me. I should have realized you deserved so much more."

"Good thing you got it right this time, then, hmm?" Nicole murmured as she shifted and raised herself above him. "Because I'm going to expect a whole lot of this loving."

"I think I'm man enough for the job." He smiled from beneath her, his body hardening inside her as she rocked gently against him. He gripped her hips with his hands, stilling her motion and his eyes grew serious. "Nicole, I mean it, though. Can you forgive what I did to you?"

"Of course I can, Nate. I already have. We both did things we regret."

"There's one thing I'll never regret," he said, continuing to hold her still. "And that's meeting you. You taught me to open my eyes and to love with all my heart. No conditions, no strings. You will marry me, won't you?"

"Yes," she replied. "I love you, Nate Hunter Jackson, and I will marry you."

"That's good," he replied, "because I'd hate to have to kidnap you all over again."

She laughed, her inner muscles tightening around him as she did so. She'd never felt this happy, or this complete before in her life. She belonged with him, as he did with her. All the security, love and recognition she'd craved all her life lay here with this incredibly special man. Their road together hadn't been smooth so far, but nothing worthwhile in life came easily. She knew that to the very depths of her soul. She also knew she loved him, and that her future would be all the better for having him at her side.

* * * * *

THE HIGH PRICE OF SECRETS

BY
YVONNE LINDSAY

This book is dedicated to my wonderful readers and fans who give me a reason for writing every single day. Please know I appreciate you all.

One

"What do you mean you quit? It's only four and a half weeks to Christmas! We're so busy with guests and functions that we can barely move. Look, let's talk about it. If you're not happy, we can work around that. Find you something else to do."

Tamsyn sighed inwardly. Find her something else to do. Sure, that would solve how she felt right now—not. She couldn't blame her brother, Ethan, for wanting to make things right for her. He'd done it all her life, after all. But this situation was beyond his fixing. That was why she'd needed to get away.

A holiday was something she'd been thinking about for a while. Working at The Masters, which in addition to being their family home was a vineyard and winery with luxury cottage accommodation on the outskirts of Adelaide in South Australia, hadn't given her any satisfaction for a very long time. She'd been restless, feeling as if she didn't really fit in anymore—at work, at home, in her family, even in her engagement.

The debacle of the night before had only proven just how right she was.

"Ethan, I can't talk about it. I'm in New Zealand."

"*You're in New Zealand?* I thought you were staying here in Adelaide with Trent last night," Ethan's incredulity was clear as it transmitted through the hands-free kit in her rental car.

Tamsyn counted slowly to ten, letting her brother continue to let off steam before replying.

"I've ended our engagement."

There was the briefest of silences as her words sunk in.

"You what?" Ethan sounded as if he wasn't certain he'd heard her correctly.

"Long story." She swallowed against the pain that had lessened to a persistent dull throb deep in her chest.

"I have ears."

"Not now, Ethan. I c-can't." Her voice broke and tears spilled uncontrolled down her cheeks.

"I'm going to hurt him," Ethan growled from far across the Tasman Sea with his characteristic brotherly protectiveness.

"No, don't. He's not worth it."

Her brother sighed and she could feel his concern and frustration in that single huff of air. "When are you coming back?"

"I…I don't know. It's kind of up in the air at the moment." She didn't think that now was a good time to tell him she'd only bought a one-way ticket.

"Well, at least you trained your assistant to take over when needed. Is Zac up to date with everything?"

Even though she knew he couldn't see her, Tamsyn shook her head and bit her lip.

"Tam?"

"Um, no. I fired him."

"You wh—?" Ethan fell silent as he started to put two and two together, coming up with his usual four. Even so, he couldn't keep the incredulity from his voice. "Zac and Trent?"

"Yup," she said, her throat almost paralyzed and strangling the single word.

"Will you be okay? I'll come over. Just tell me where you are."

"No, don't. I'll be fine—eventually. I just need…" She drew in a shuddering breath. She couldn't even find the words to say what she really needed—she had to simply tell him something he'd understand. "I just need some time alone. Some space so I can think things out. I'm sorry about leaving like this. Everything is in my computer, you know the password, and the bookings are all duplicated on the wall planner as well. Worse comes to worst, they can phone me if they need to."

"We'll take care of it, don't worry."

Her big brother's firm conviction wasn't as good as being right there with him, but in terms of comfort it came close.

"Thanks, Ethan."

"No problem, but Tam? Who's going to take care of you?"

"*I* will," she said firmly.

"I really think you should come home."

"No, I know what I need to do. It's important to me, now more than ever." This part, she had to share with him— even though she knew he wouldn't like it. "I'm going to find her, Ethan."

Silence, then another sigh. "Are you sure now is the best time to go searching for our mother?"

It had already been a few months now, but the shock of discovering their mother—who they'd long been told was dead—was alive and living in New Zealand still reverberated through her mind almost every moment of every day. Learning after his death that their father had lied to them all this time was one thing, discovering the rest of their family had supported him in the lie was another—but realizing that their mother had chosen to remain apart from them, to never even try to make contact, well, that had raised so many questions in Tamsyn's mind they'd begun to define everything about the way she saw herself.

Tamsyn grimaced and shook her head slightly. "Can't think of a better time than now, can you?"

"Yeah, actually, I can. You're hurt, you're vulnerable. I don't want you to get let down again. Come home. Let me put an investigator on to it so that you know what you're going into when they find her."

She could picture him right now, the frown on his forehead, the thinned line of his lips as he worried from afar.

"I want to do this myself. I need to. Look, I'm not far from that address you gave me a couple of months ago. I'd better go," she said, checking the distance on the screen of her GPS.

"You're just going to show up, no warning?"

"Why not?"

"Tam, be sensible. You can't just arrive on someone's doorstep claiming to be their long-lost child."

"Except I'm not *lost,* am I? She knew where *we* were all along. She's the one who left and didn't come back."

She couldn't hide the hurt in the words. A hurt that warred with resentment and anger and sorrow and so many unanswered questions that Tamsyn had hardly had a full night's sleep since she'd heard the news that her mother still lived. That the woman she'd quietly fantasized about, a mother who'd loved her and cared for her too much to ever leave her behind, didn't exist. She had so many questions and she had convinced herself that she was strong enough now to face the answers. She needed to so she could move forward with her life, because what she'd believed up until now had been based on lies and fabrication. Trent's betrayal was the final straw. She didn't even know who she was anymore. But she was ready to find out. Ethan's voice broke into her thoughts.

"Do me a favor, find a motel or somewhere and sleep on it before you do anything you might regret. We can talk in the morning."

"I'll let you know how it goes," Tamsyn replied, ignoring her brother's plea. "I'll call you in a few days."

She disconnected the phone before Ethan could say another word and listened carefully as the disembodied voice

on the GPS carefully enunciated that her turn was coming
up in five hundred meters. Tamsyn's gut clenched tight. She
had to do this. As irrational and out of character as it was
for her, the woman who usually planned everything out to
the finest degree, she *needed* to do this.

Carefully, Tamsyn turned in at the imposing stone-wall-
lined entrance to a long driveway. She drew the car to a halt
and closed her eyes for a moment. This was it—soon she
could be face-to-face with her mother for the first time since
she was three years old. A shudder passed through her body
as her adrenaline levels kicked up a notch.

The past twenty-four hours had been a roller-coaster
ride. One that had alternately left her giddy with anticipation or sick to her stomach. Tamsyn opened her eyes and
took her foot off the brake. The car began inching forward,
rumbling loudly over the cattle guard beneath the tires and
along the long straight stretch of driveway that gently inclined up the hill.

To the left and the right of her, regimented lines of grapevines grew, their foliage lush and green and the early signs
of fruit could be seen hanging on the vines. Considering it
was only late November, Tamsyn's experienced eye could
see that this vineyard was in for a bumper crop.

She continued along the long driveway. It snaked up a
steep incline until finally, after a particularly tight hairpin
turn, she saw the house ahead of her. The sprawling two-
story building, crafted in stone and cedar, dominated the
crest of the hill. Her lips set in a firm line of disapproval.
So it clearly hadn't been a lack of money that had kept her
mother from staying in touch, she thought cynically. Was
this how Ellen Masters had used the money her husband
had sent her for the past twenty-odd years?

Tamsyn used that cynicism to propel her out of her car
and toward the front door. It was now or never. Taking
a deep breath, she reached for the iron door knocker and

lifted it, only to let it drop with a solid clang. A short time later she heard footsteps echo from inside. Her stomach tied in knots as every last ounce of her resolve suddenly fled.

What the hell was she doing here?

Finn Gallagher opened his front door and had to force himself not to take a step back. He recognized the woman standing in front of him with a surety that went soul deep. Ellen's daughter.

So the little princess from Australia had finally decided to visit. Too little, too late, as far as he was concerned. Far too late.

The pictures he'd seen of her over the years, hadn't done her justice, though he had the sense he wasn't seeing her at her best. His sweeping gaze took in the mussed long dark brown hair that cascaded over her shoulders and the dark bruises of tiredness that stained porcelain skin under wide-spaced brown eyes. Eyes that reminded him so much of her mother. The woman who, together with her partner, Lorenzo, had mothered him when his own family had disintegrated.

Her clothes were creased but still stylish, and clung to her curves in a way that drew his eye to the opening of her blouse and especially to the tempting swell of creamy skin exposed there. Her skirt skimmed her hips and down her slender thighs to end just above the knee. Not long enough to be dowdy and not so short as to be inappropriate, but somehow still enticing.

It all spoke to the privileged upbringing she'd enjoyed. He found it difficult not to feel bitter when he knew how hard her mother had scraped and worked for a decent life. Clearly the Masters family had looked after their own—they just didn't look after those who walked away from them. Those who didn't conform.

His gaze drifted back to her face where he noticed her full lips tremble slightly before pulling into a nervous smile.

"H-hello, I was wondering if Ellen Masters lives here?" she said.

Her voice was tight, as if her throat was constricted and in the late-afternoon sun that slanted across her face he could see telltale signs of tear tracks. Natural curiosity rose from inside him but he quelled it with his usual determination.

"And you are…?" he asked, knowing full well what the answer would be.

"Oh, I'm sorry." She held out a delicate hand. "I'm Tamsyn Masters. I'm looking for my mother, Ellen."

He took her hand in his, noting instantly the coolness of her touch, the fragility in the bones of her fingers as his larger, stronger ones closed around hers. He struggled against the instinct to go into protection mode. There was something very not right in Tamsyn Masters's world right now, but, he reminded himself, that wasn't his problem.

Keeping her away from Ellen was.

Two

"There's no Ellen Masters here," he replied, letting go of her hand. "Was your mother expecting you?"

She had the grace to look shamefaced. "No, I kind of hoped to surprise her."

Surprise her? Yeah, he just bet she did. Without sparing a thought to whether or not her mother would, or could, see her. How typical of her type, he thought angrily. Pampered, spoiled and thinking the world spun for her delectation. He knew the type well—unfortunately. Too well. They were the kind who'd always expect more, no matter how much you gave. People like Briana, his ex. Beautiful, seemingly compassionate, born into a life of opportunity—but in the cold light of day as grasping and as single-minded as Fagin in *Oliver Twist*.

"Are you sure you have the right address?" he asked, tamping his fury down.

"Well…I thought…" She reached into her handbag and pulled out a crumpled sheet of paper and read off the address. "That's right, isn't it? I'm at the right place."

"That is my address, but there's no Ellen Masters here. I'm sorry. It looks like you've had a wasted trip."

Before his eyes, every particle in her body slumped. Her eyes suddenly brimmed with unshed tears and a stricken look froze her delicate features into a mask of sadness. Again that urge to protect her welled within him—along with the compulsion to tell her of the well-concealed and unsealed driveway she'd have passed on the road here. The one that led to the cottage where Ellen and Lorenzo had lived for the past twenty-five years or so—but he just as determinedly pushed the impulse back.

He knew for a fact Tamsyn Masters had legally been an adult for ten years. What whim had finally driven her to seek out Ellen now? And, more important, why hadn't she reached out to her mother sooner, when it could possibly still have made a difference to the other woman's happiness?

"I—oh, well, I'm sorry to have bothered you. My information can't have been correct."

She reached into her handbag for an oversize pair of sunglasses and shoved them none too elegantly onto her face, hiding her tortured gaze from view. As she did so, he caught sight of the white band of skin on the ring finger of her left hand. Had the engagement he'd read of over a year ago come to an end? Had that been the catalyst to send her searching for her mother?

Whatever it was, it was none of his business.

"No problem," he answered and watched as she walked back to her car and turned it around to drive back down the driveway.

Finn didn't waste another second before reaching for his cell phone and punching in a number. It went straight to voice mail and he uttered a short sharp epithet in frustration while listening to the disembodied voice asking him to leave a message.

"Lorenzo, call me. There's been a complication here at home."

He slid his phone back in his pocket and closed the front door of his house. Somehow, though, he had the feeling he hadn't completely closed the door on Tamsyn Masters.

As Tamsyn steered down the driveway, disappointment crashed through her with the force of a wrecking ball. The tears she'd battled to hold back while talking to the stranger now fell rapidly down her cheeks. She sniffed unevenly, trying to hold in the emotion that had been bubbling so close to the surface ever since she'd left Adelaide last night.

Why on earth had she thought it would be simple? She should have known better. Should have listened to Ethan, even, and tackled this another time—another day when she was in a stronger frame of mind. Well, she'd done it now, she'd gone to the address her late father's solicitor had used to send her mother all those payments through the years and it had been the wrong one.

Disappointment had a nasty bitter taste, she'd discovered—not just once, but twice now in the past twenty-four hours. It just went to prove, that for her, acting out of character was the wrong thing to do. She wasn't made to be impulsive. All her life she had weighed things up long and carefully before doing anything. Now she fully understood why she'd always been that way. It was safer. You didn't get hurt. Sure, you didn't have the thrill of taking a risk either, but was the pain you suffered when things went wrong worth it? Not in her book.

Tamsyn thought about the man who'd opened his door to her at the top of the hill. Over six feet, she'd been forced to look up at him. He'd had presence—being the kind of guy who turned heads just by entering a room. A broad forehead and straight brows had shadowed clear gray eyes the color of the schist rock used on the side of the house that was very definitely his castle. A light stubble had stippled his strong square jaw, but his smile, while polite, had lacked warmth.

There'd been something in his gaze when he'd looked at her. As if...no, she was just being fanciful. He couldn't have known her because she knew full well she'd never met him before in her life. She would most definitely have remembered.

The sun was sinking in the sky and weariness pulled at every muscle in her body as all her activity, not to mention crossing time zones, over the past day took its toll. She needed to find somewhere to stay before she did something stupid like drive off the road and into a ditch.

Tamsyn pulled the car to the side of the road and consulted the GPS for accommodation options nearby. Thankfully there was a boutique hotel that provided meals on request about a fifteen-minute drive away. She keyed the phone number into her mobile phone and was relieved to find that while the room rate was on a par with the accommodation at The Masters, yes, they had a room available for the next few nights. Booking made, Tamsyn pressed the appropriate section of the GPS screen and followed the computerized instructions, eventually pulling up outside a quaint-looking early-1900s single-story building.

With the golden rays of the early-evening sun caressing its creamy paintwork, it looked warm and inviting. Just what she needed.

Finn paced his office, unable to settle back down to the plans that were sprawled across his wide desk. Plans that were going to go to hell in a handbasket if he couldn't buy the easement necessary to gain access to the tract of land he wanted to use for this special project. He shoved a hand through his short hair, mussing it even more than usual.

The chirp of his phone was a happy distraction.

"Gallagher."

"Finn, is there a problem?"

"Lorenzo, I'm glad you called." Finn settled in his chair and swiveled it around to face the window, allowing the vista spread before him to fill his mind and relax his thoughts into a semblance of order. Thoughts that had been distracted all too thoroughly by his earlier visitor.

"What is it, my boy?"

Despite Lorenzo's years in Australia, followed by the past couple of decades in New Zealand, his voice still held the lilt of his native Italian tongue.

"First, how is Ellen?"

The older man sighed. "Not good, she is having a bad day today."

After Ellen began to show signs of kidney and liver failure, she and Lorenzo had relocated to Wellington, where she could receive the specialized care her advancing dementia required.

"I'm sorry to hear that."

He could almost hear Lorenzo shrug in acceptance. "It is what it is. I have asked Alexis to make plans to return from Italy."

"Ellen's that bad?"

Alexis was Lorenzo and Ellen's only child and had been working overseas for the past year. Currently, she was visiting with Lorenzo's family still living in Tuscany.

"*Si,* she has no fight left in her anymore. If she recognizes me at all it is a good day, but they are few."

Finn could hear the pain echoing in the older man's voice before Lorenzo took another deep breath and continued.

"Now, what did you call me for?"

Choosing blunt statement over trying to find an easy way to say what he had to, Finn said, "Tamsyn Masters showed up here today wanting to see Ellen."

"So, it has finally happened."

"I told her Ellen Masters doesn't live here and sent her on her way."

Lorenzo gave a short laugh, the sound crackling like autumn leaves. "But you didn't tell her that Ellen *Fabrini* does, I assume?"

"No," Finn admitted. He hadn't told an outright lie when he'd spoken to Tamsyn. Though Lorenzo and Ellen had never formalized their union, she'd always been known as his wife and had gone by his last name the whole time they'd lived in New Zealand.

"You say she left again?"

"Yes, hopefully to return to Australia."

"Hmm, but what if she doesn't leave?"

Finn's lips firmed in a line as he considered Lorenzo's statement. "What are you thinking?"

"You know I have no love for that family after what they did to my Ellen. I lost count of the hours she spent crying over letters she wrote to those children. It broke her heart a little more every single time. And did they ever write back, or even try to contact her when they were older? No. Yet as much as I would wish them all to Dante's inferno, I know how much Ellen loved them and if she was to stabilize, if her mind was to clear just a little, she might benefit from a visit from her daughter."

Finn fought to keep the incredulity from his voice. "You want me to keep her from going home?"

"Do not chase her away just yet. But, if you can, keep her in the dark about where Ellen is—about all of us, if you can. With things the way they are…" His voice cracked and he took a moment to recover.

"I understand," Finn soothed.

His heart broke for the man who'd stepped into the role of father figure when Finn's own father had died, and his mother suffered a complete nervous breakdown. Finn had been only twelve and Lorenzo, his father's business partner, and Ellen had taken him into their hearts and their home. The couple had been his rock through his turbulent adolescence and his teens. Their unwavering support, together with their careful guardianship of the land his father had owned, had ensured stability and, eventually, a good living for them all. Finn owed them everything.

"I'll take care of things. Don't worry," he assured Lorenzo as they completed their call.

Exactly *how* he was going to take care of things was another matter. First, he had to find out whether Tamsyn had left the area. Given how exhausted she'd looked hovering on his doorstep, he doubted she'd have gone far. It only took a few calls to find her and he wasn't at all surprised to discover the Aussie princess had chosen one of the most expensive accommodation providers in the area.

Okay, so now he knew where she was, what was he going to do next? Finn leaned back in his chair and steepled his fingers under his chin, rocking the leather chair back and forth slightly as he stared back out the window again.

Encroaching twilight began to obscure the Kaikoura ranges in the far distance, narrowing his world to the acres that surrounded him. His acres. His land. His home. A home he wouldn't have today but for the determination of Lorenzo and Ellen all those years ago. What was he going to do? Whatever they needed him to—even if it meant befriending the woman who'd caused Ellen so much suffering over the years.

Growing up, he'd heard occasional tales about Ellen's other children—the ones she'd been forced to leave behind once her marriage had irretrievably broken down. Even then, he'd seen the pain that abandoning her children had caused her, how she'd sought solace in alcohol that had eventually led to her current illness, and over the intervening years he'd wondered about the children themselves and why they hadn't done a thing to try to get in touch with the mother who'd loved them with all her heart.

As soon as he'd been old enough, and computer savvy enough, he'd done a little research and discovered the favored lives Ethan and Tamsyn Masters lived on their family vineyard estate, The Masters. They'd grown up wanting for nothing and had had every opportunity to excel presented to them on a platter. Not for them the hard graft of after-school jobs and backbreaking weekend work, just to get ahead. Not for them the millstone of student loans and expenses.

Finn didn't mind admitting he'd felt some resentment toward Ellen's other family, they'd had it so easy while she, on the other hand, had made do with so little—secure only in the love of the man she'd walked away from her husband and children with.

A man who continued to stay by her side as she'd battled her alcoholism and as eventually her body and mind broke down around her. Ellen's health was so precarious right now that Finn feared that even if she recognized Tamsyn, should she manage to track her mother down, at the sight of her, Ellen could slide into a place in her mind from which she would never return.

After all, hadn't his own mother's death occurred after he had finally been allowed to visit her following her breakdown? Hadn't seeing him been a reminder of what she'd given up on when the sudden death of her husband had forced her to retreat into the supposedly safe reaches of her mind? And hadn't her shame pushed her deeper into her mind, never to emerge again? Even now, those memories had the power to hurt. He pushed them forcibly away.

Tamsyn Masters—she should be the focus of his thoughts right now, and his plans to get her to stay in the area without letting her find out the truth about Ellen. Finn thought again what he knew about the young woman who'd turned up at his house today. She was twenty-eight years old, five years younger than himself. Last he'd heard, she was engaged to marry some up-and-coming lawyer in Adelaide. Clearly she hadn't been wearing her ring today. It could mean anything. Maybe she had taken it off to get it cleaned or resized. Or maybe she'd taken it off when she'd washed her hands and had forgotten to put it back on again.

Another idea occurred to him. One that sparked his interest. Maybe, just maybe, it meant she might be in the market for a bit of rebound romance. A bit of light flirtation perhaps—some enticement to stay in the Marlborough district? If she was as shallow as he'd found her type to be in the past it would be all good fun—no chance of emotional involvement or hurt feelings, just an opportunity to keep her very carefully under observation while making sure she found out nothing about Ellen.

It would take some doing, sure, but he was confident he could handle it. A buzz of anticipation hummed through his body. Yeah, he was definitely the man to do it, and along the way he'd find out as much as he could about the perplexing Ms. Tamsyn Masters.

Three

Voices echoed down the wide paneled hallway of the hotel as Tamsyn walked toward the dining room. She still felt a little tired, but last night's light meal, warm bath and a comfortable night in a good bed, had all gone a long way toward restoring her equilibrium.

Last night she'd all but decided to head to the airport this morning and book a flight back to Auckland. But she'd woken filled with a new sense of purpose—more determined than ever to make the most of her time here. Her mother had to be in the area somewhere. As far as she and Ethan were aware, checks were still being sent to her from their father's estate—and none of the checks had ever been returned to sender. Last night she'd been too tired and too disheartened to remember that vital detail. Today was another matter entirely and she was thinking far more clearly. A call to Ethan would confirm the address her father's lawyers used.

First order of the day though, after breakfast, was a trip to Blenheim to purchase some new clothes and luggage. She'd left Adelaide in such an all-fired hurry she'd arrived here in New Zealand with only the clothes she stood in and her handbag. Despite making use of the iron and ironing board stashed in her room's wardrobe, her clothing was definitely looking the worse for wear.

She couldn't wait to rid herself of her underwear, either—the pieces so carefully chosen to titillate and entice her then fiancé. Despite the fact she'd had to rinse out, dry and then rewear them twice now, she wouldn't be happy until she'd seen them thrown into the trash.

They were yet another reminder of how foolishly naive she'd been—and how the people she'd trusted had let her down. Bile rose in her throat as she remembered how eager she'd been to surprise Trent just two nights ago. How she'd planned a romantic dinner and evening for two culminating in the slow and sexy removal of said lingerie. But the surprise had been all hers when she'd discovered him in bed with someone else—her personal assistant, Zac.

Once the hurt had begun to recede she'd felt such a fool. What kind of woman didn't know her fiancé was gay? Worse, that he'd been prepared to marry her and simply string her along as a mask of respectability so he could continue his steady rise through the ranks of the old-school law firm he worked for.

She'd known that she only had to go home to have her family surrounding her, consoling her—but the thought had failed to comfort her. Her family had lied to her, too, had hidden things from her that she'd had the right to know. Her father, her uncle and aunts—they'd all known that her mother was alive, and they'd kept it from her. Even Ethan had hidden the truth from her once he found out, after their father's death. Suddenly desperate to get away from the secrets, the evasions and the betrayals, she'd headed to the airport, determined not to return until she found some answers for a change.

So far, it was going dreadfully.

She swallowed against the burning sensation in her throat. Maybe breakfast wasn't such a good idea after all.

"Here she is," the voice of her hostess, Penny, greeted her as she reached the doorway of the dining room. Penny rose from a small table set in the bay window that looked out over a delightfully old-fashioned garden. "Good morning, Ms. Masters, I trust you slept well?"

"Oh, call me Tamsyn, please. And yes, my room is very comfortable, thank you."

Tamsyn's eyes flicked to the man who sat opposite Penny and who now rose to his feet in welcome. The man from yesterday—and absolutely the last man she had expected to see this morning. Courtesy demanded she acknowledge his presence and she gave him a short nod, just the barest inclination of her head.

He stepped forward and held out his hand in a greeting. "We didn't get to exchanging names yesterday. Finn Gallagher. Pleased to see you again."

She gave him a weak smile and briefly shook his hand. The warmth of his broad palm permeated her skin, sending a curl of awareness winding up her arm and through her body. She pulled her hand free.

"Really, Mr. Gallagher? I had the impression yesterday you were only too pleased to see the back of me."

Amusement lit his cool slate-colored eyes. "Ah, you caught me at a bad time, I'm afraid. I'm here to apologize."

Tamsyn's mind scattered in a hundred directions. How had he tracked her down?

"Isn't that a bit stalkerish?" she said without thinking.

"We're a close-knit bunch around here," he explained with an apologetic smile that made Tamsyn's stomach do a tiny loop-the-loop. "I was concerned after you left. You looked tired, and being unfamiliar with the area...well, let's just say tourists have a bad habit of wandering off the road here and there. I called around a few places and I was relieved when Penny assured me you'd arrived safely."

It all sounded plausible, she thought, but it didn't explain what he was doing here right now. As if he could read her mind, he continued speaking.

"I didn't want to leave you with the impression that we're rude around here and thought I'd offer to show you around, if you'd like. Take you on a tour of the district. You will be staying a few days now you're here, won't you?"

He said the last few words with subtle emphasis, almost as if he was willing her to stick around.

"Yes, I will," she admitted, reluctant to tell him that her time here had no specific expiry. "But there's no need for you to show me around. I can make my own way." Besides, she wasn't really here for the sights. She just wanted to find her mother.

"Please, at least allow me to take you to lunch or dinner to make up for my abruptness yesterday."

An ember of warmth lit deep in her belly. Maybe she was being overly suspicious. He certainly seemed sincere enough. She studied him briefly, taking in the short spiky hair, the clear gray eyes that appeared to be imploring her to give in to his politely put demand. His body language was open, nonthreatening, and dressed as he was in a pair of jeans and a tight-fitting T-shirt, he clearly wasn't hiding any weapons. Except his charisma. She couldn't deny he exuded oodles of magnetism, today at least, and there was no doubting that he was one beautifully put-together piece of manhood. What would be the harm in enjoying his company for a few hours? Despite what she'd just been through with Trent, Finn Gallagher was pinging her receptors. And then there was that smile that played around Finn's lips, the expression on his face that suggested he found her attractive and actually wanted to spend time with her. Something her fiancé had not been so wont to do. The thought was like water on a drought-stricken land.

Penny interrupted her thoughts. "If you're worried about Finn, I can vouch for the fact that he's a complete gentleman. He's also a much-loved local-born philanthropist. Honestly, you couldn't be in better hands."

"I…"

Tamsyn's eyes dropped to those very hands, eyeing his broad palms and long tapered fingers. The ember flared to a flame and spread, her breasts suddenly feeling full, her nipples tight, as she involuntarily imagined those hands touching her. With a sharply indrawn breath, she dragged her eyes up to his face, where he clearly awaited her response.

"I don't want to be any trouble," she said lamely, feeling a flush of color heat her cheeks. "Besides, I have plans to do some shopping today—I came a little underprepared for this trip."

Underprepared. As if that wasn't the understatement of the year, she thought scathingly.

"No problem. Why don't you do your shopping this morning, Penny will be able to direct you to where you need to go, and I'll pick you up around lunchtime, say one o'clock, back here? Then I can show you around a bit and deliver you back this evening."

She couldn't refuse. He'd made the plan sound so reasonable. Penny had given her approval as well, and somehow Tamsyn knew the older woman wouldn't have been so forthcoming if she hadn't been certain Tamsyn would be safe with Finn.

"Then, thank you, I'd like that."

"Excellent. I'll leave you to your breakfast and I'll see you later today. Thanks for the coffee, Penny."

"You're always welcome, Finn. I'll see you out. Tamsyn, please help yourself to the breakfast buffet. If there's anything else you'd like, just ring the bell on the sideboard and one of the kitchen staff will be along to take your order."

Penny smiled and then preceded Finn from the room. Finn gave Tamsyn a wink before following.

"I'm looking forward to this afternoon," he said, his voice lowered for her hearing only and sending a shiver of anticipation down Tamsyn's spine.

She smiled in response, a nervous, almost involuntary action, and then he was gone. Tamsyn stepped over to the chafing dishes on the antique sideboard and lifted the lids. Nerves danced like butterflies in her stomach. What had she let herself in for? she wondered as she took a small serving of scrambled egg with a few fried button mushrooms and half a grilled tomato.

She placed her plate on a table and turned back to the sideboard to pour a cup of coffee from the silver carafe warmed by a single candle in a holder beneath it. Everything here was modern and comfortable yet still exuded old-world charm with these touches of elegance from a bygone era. Much like back at home, at The Masters.

For just an instant she was almost overwhelmed by a wave of homesickness, by the desire to quit this search of hers and go home and pick up where she'd left off. But she couldn't go back, not yet. Not until she'd gotten some answers. After everything that had happened, she felt so lost, as if she didn't know who she was anymore. She needed this trip, this quest, to help her find herself again.

Tamsyn forced herself to lift her fork and spear a mushroom, bringing the morsel to her mouth. The burst of flavor on her tongue reminded her that she might be down, but she wasn't out yet. Not when there were still things in this life to enjoy, to savor. Things that proved life went on as surely as the sun rose each day.

"Ah, excellent, you've helped yourself," Penny said, walking briskly back into the room. "Is everything to your liking? Perhaps there's something else I can get for you?"

"Everything is lovely, thank you. I'm fine for now."

"I'm glad," the other woman said, bustling over to clear the table where she and Finn had been sitting when Tamsyn had come into the dining room. "Finn seems quite taken with you. You can't go wrong there. He'll show you a wonderful time."

Was it Tamsyn's imagination or was there a hefty dose of double entendre seasoning Penny's words?

"You didn't mention you met him yesterday," Penny probed.

"I'd been given an address to go to. It turned out to be his and not the person I was seeking."

"Well, if anyone around here can help you find someone local it'll be Finn," Penny said with a warm smile. "Come and see me in my office before you head out to the shops and tell me what you're looking for, and I'll point you in the right direction."

What she was looking for? Well, there was an opening she couldn't ignore. Finn himself had said they were a close-knit community. Surely her mother had to be known by someone.

"Actually, now that you mention it, I was wondering… have you ever heard of an Ellen Masters?"

Penny halted midstride and the cups she'd just cleared from the table wobbled a little in their saucers.

"Ellen Masters, you say?" She pulled her mouth down into a small frown for a second before reverting to a bright smile that didn't feel quite as genuine as it had a moment before. "No, can't say I've ever heard that name. Well, I'll leave you to your breakfast. Remember to ring if you need anything else."

Tamsyn watched as Penny left the dining room. She must be getting overly sensitive because for a minute there she thought she'd seen a spark of something on Penny's face. Tamsyn took another sip of her coffee and shook her head slightly. She was probably just jet-lagged and perhaps a little overtired still. Imagining things that weren't there simply because she wanted them to be.

Still, she refused to be cowed. Someone in the district had to know where her mother was and as soon as she crossed paths with that someone, she would know, too. A person didn't just disappear off the grid without leaving a trace somewhere, did they?

Four

After her shopping expedition into Blenheim, where she found all the basics she needed, as well as a few things she didn't but were fun to buy anyway, Tamsyn continued back toward her accommodations. Certain she could navigate her way without her GPS, she was surprised when a wrong turn brought her out into a small but bustling township.

She wondered briefly, as she pulled up to halt on a street peppered with cafés and boutiques and art stores, why Penny hadn't directed her here first for her shopping. With a shrug she got out of the car and locked it before strolling the length of the main street down one side and back up the other before going into one of the clothing boutiques to browse.

"Hello, are you looking for a special outfit?" the older woman behind the counter asked with a welcoming smile.

"Not particularly, but I love this," Tamsyn said, pulling out a sleeveless dress in vibrant hues of purple and blue for a better look.

"That would look lovely on you with your coloring. The fitting room is just to your left if you'd like to try it on."

"Oh, I don't think…" About to refuse, Tamsyn hesitated. Why shouldn't she indulge herself? This morning's shopping had been mostly about function—jeans, T-shirts, a pair of shorts and a few sets of underwear, together with some trainers. Her hand stroked the fabric, relishing the texture of the hand-painted silk. It would feel divine on. "Okay, I'll try it," she said before she could change her mind.

A few minutes later she turned this way and that in front of the dressing-room mirror. The dress was perfect, as if it had been made for her. If only she had the right shoes to go with it, she'd be able to wear it to lunch with Finn. Not that she was setting out to try and attract him or anything but a girl needed her armor, didn't she? And the way this dress made her look and made her feel was armor indeed.

"How does it feel on?" a disembodied voice asked from outside the curtain.

"Fantastic but I don't have the right shoes with me."

"Oh, maybe we have something here. We carry a few styles and sizes. You're what, a size seven?"

When Tamsyn murmured her assent the woman replied, "I'll be right back."

Tamsyn took a minute to study her reflection again. She loved the dress, loved the softness of the silk as it fell around her legs, as it caressed her body. It made her feel feminine, desirable.

Was that what her need for armor was all about? Had Trent's betrayal left her feeling so unappealing? Questioning her femininity so much? Not surprising, given how he'd deliberately misled her throughout their relationship. The sting still smarted. And looking at her reflection now, thoughts of her former fiancé made her angry, too. Her reflection in the mirror looked beautiful and sexy—why had she let Trent make her feel any different? Why had she agreed to marry a man who never made her feel irresistible?

Tamsyn was more certain than ever that this trip was exactly what she needed. She had to get away from the perceptions and expectations everyone had of her back home and figure out who she really wanted to be. She just hoped her mother would want to be part of that—part of her life.

"Here we are!"

Tamsyn pulled aside the curtain.

"Oh, my," the assistant said, "that dress is really you. You look wonderful. Here, try these on with it."

She held out a pair of sandals in shades of purple, blue

and pink, and with a ridiculously high heel. They were perfect, Tamsyn thought as she slid off the trainers and socks she'd been wearing and slipped her feet into the sandals, bending down to fasten the dainty ankle strap.

"Come on out into the store, we have a full-length mirror just over by the counter. You'll have more room to twirl," the woman said with a wink.

Tamsyn couldn't help but smile in response. She actually felt like twirling when she saw her reflection in the larger mirror.

"I'll take it," she said impulsively. "The dress and the shoes. Do you mind if I wear them now?"

"Why would I mind?" The assistant smiled in response. "You're the perfect walking advertisement for one of our local designers—Alexis Fabrini."

"I love what she's done with this dress, do you have more of her clothes here? I'd really like to come back when I have more time."

The assistant just smiled and spread her arm to encompass an entire wall of garments. "Take your pick," she said, smiling. "Let me bag up your other things and take off those price tags and you'll be good to go."

Tamsyn paid for her purchases just as a Shania Twain song came onto the speakers in the store. She smiled to herself, agreeing with the lyrics. She really felt like a woman right now and was actually looking forward to lunch with the enigmatic Finn Gallagher more than she realized.

"Are you just passing through town?" asked the store clerk. Tamsyn looked at her, suddenly struck by the realization that the woman was probably around the same age as her mother. In fact, there were so many people around—on the street, in the shops—who were all around that age. Surely, amongst them, would be some of her mother's friends.

"I'm here a few days at least, although I might stay longer

if I can. I'm…" She hesitated a moment and then decided, in for a penny, in for a pound. If she didn't start asking every person she met if they knew her mom, she'd never find out, would she? "I'm looking for my mother. Ellen Masters. Do you know her?"

The other woman shook her head slowly and pursed her lips. "Hmm, Ellen Masters…no. Can't say I've met anyone by that name around here, but I'm fairly new in the region and I'm still getting to know all the locals."

"Never mind," Tamsyn said pasting a smile over the pang of disappointment that tugged at her heart. It was a numbers game. Eventually she'd find someone who knew her. Didn't New Zealanders pride themselves on the fact that there were only two degrees of separation between them and a fellow Kiwi? "It was a wild shot."

"Well, good luck finding her and do come back soon!"

Tamsyn gathered her things and started to walk back to her car. Even with this small latest setback she still felt more positive. Just before she reached her car she stopped and perused the window of a real estate office that appeared to double as a letting agency and an idea occurred to her. If she found a place to rent she could set herself up more permanently here and could use the property as a base from which to widen her search. She scanned the listings in the window and an address caught her eye. It was on the same road as Finn Gallagher's property, fairly close, too, if the street number was any indicator.

A coil of something she couldn't quite identify curled tight in her stomach as she read the details. It was a short-term lease on a week-by-week basis. She could see why it was still available. Not many people would want the insecurity of week-by-week rental, but it suited her just perfectly and as a bonus it was fully furnished. All she'd need to do was feed the cat and the chickens on the property. She could do that. She pushed open the door to the agency, coming out twenty minutes later with an agreement in one hand, a key in the other and an excitement roiling in her she barely knew how to contain.

A late-model Porsche Cayenne, a Turbo S model, she noted with some appreciation, stood in the driveway when she returned to the hotel. No doubt Finn's, she thought as she took a quick look at the dashboard clock on her rental. The side trip to the property agency had made her late, but right now she didn't care. From tomorrow she had somewhere of her own to stay. Things were falling into place and who knew? Maybe the next person she saw would be someone who could tell her where to find her mother.

Finn watched from the office window as Tamsyn alighted from her car. Even from here he could tell she was excited. There was a light and energy about her now that had been missing yesterday and this morning. It served to make her even more beautiful.

He tamped down on the shiver of desire that threatened to ripple through his body. If he was going to control this situation he'd have to start by controlling himself. Errant physical attractions would only complicate things. And as complications went, getting a call from the leasing agent handling Lorenzo and Ellen's cottage to say a certain princess from Australia was interested in taking up the short-term leasing option was a big one.

As tempting as it had been to say an absolute and re-sounding no when the agent had queried him about the lease, especially as the leasee had no references, he'd been mindful of Lorenzo's wish to keep Tamsyn close for Ellen's sake. How much easier would it be to keep an eye on her if she was just down the hill from where he lived?

Of course, he reminded himself, there was the bonus of him not having to feed Ellen's man-eating black cat, Lucy— short for Lucifer. A singularly appropriate moniker Finn had always privately thought. He hadn't had a morning yet where the feisty feline hadn't delivered him a scathing hiss or a barbed paw.

Plus, he knew for a fact that Lorenzo and Ellen's personal effects and identifying items had all been packed away in Alexis's old bedroom and a new lock put on the door to ensure that while renters made use of the house, their private things remained just that, private. He'd done it himself after Lorenzo had accompanied Ellen to Wellington. What harm could come from having Tamsyn literally under his eye?

"Looks like she's been shopping," he commented as he watched Tamsyn pull several shopping bags and a small wheeled suitcase from the trunk of her car.

"And not just in Blenheim. That pink bag, that's from a local store," Penny commented from behind him.

"Damn. I thought you directed her to Blenheim for what she needed."

"I did, but honestly, Finn, you can't expect to control her every movement."

Oh, can't I? "More's the pity," he growled, stepping away from the window before Tamsyn could see her spying on him.

Penny laughed. "She obviously found our nearby center all on her own, and from the look of things she's boosted the local economy in the bargain. I'm pretty sure that's one of Alexis's designs she's wearing right now and you and I both know they don't come cheap."

Finn stifled a groan. What were the odds that Tamsyn Masters would walk out the door here this morning and come back wearing a dress designed by her half sister? A sister she didn't even know she had—and probably wouldn't, ever, if he succeeded in keeping Tamsyn in the dark as he'd promised. He needed to hold it together, for Lorenzo's sake. The man had stepped in and helped him when his whole world shattered apart when he was only twelve years old. Now Lorenzo's world was imploding and it was up to Finn to return the favor.

At the sound of her heels clicking on the polished wooden hall floor he spun away from the window and went out to greet her.

"Oh, hello!" Tamsyn said, coming to an abrupt halt as he exited the office right in front of her.

A waft of her fragrance drifted around him. Something with flowers, fruit and a hint of spice. Something that sent reason fleeing from his mind and a crazy desire to lean forward and inhale more deeply driving through his body.

"Sorry I'm late," she continued, oblivious to the tug-of-war going on in Finn's mind, not to mention the tug of something else far lower down in his body. "I'll only be a minute. Just let me put these things in my room and I'm all yours."

All his? Somehow he doubted that. But it certainly promised to be interesting finding out, he thought with a smile as he watched her graceful departure.

Gone was the wounded creature who had been at his front door last night. Gone was the troubled but determined young woman who'd arrived in the dining room this morning. In her place was charming, confident sex on legs, and very beautiful legs they were, too, he admitted as he admired the slim turn of her ankle and the slender, yet shapely, calf muscles heading in the opposite direction on a pair of colored icepicks that defied logic and gravity in one, literally, easy step.

He shook himself out of his daze as she disappeared from view. Just as well, he thought, or he might even have been tempted to follow her.

True to her word, she was back in only a few minutes, delivering him a shy smile as she returned.

"All ready?" he asked, his mouth drying as he studied her anew.

The purple of the dress did something striking to her

brown eyes, reminding him of pansies. Bold, yet fragile at the same time. *God,* he groaned inwardly. What the hell was wrong with him? Next he'd be acting like some crush-struck teenager.

"I certainly am," she replied, falling in alongside him as he headed for the door. "Where are we going?"

He named a vineyard and winery that was only a fifteen-minute drive away. "Their restaurant is immensely popular for lunches and their wines are world renowned."

Tamsyn rubbed her flat tummy and laughed. "I certainly hope you're right. I'm famished after all that shopping this morning."

"You won't be disappointed," he assured her.

He kept up a bland running commentary on the surrounding countryside and their destination, to fill in time as they drove to the vineyard.

"This place sounds a lot like home," Tamsyn commented. "We run a similar operation with cellar door, restaurant and winery. It'll be fun seeing how they do things. I could almost tell myself it was work if—" Her voice broke off.

"If?" he coaxed.

"If I hadn't resigned and walked away from it all," she said with a brittle smile that didn't quite reach her eyes.

"Oh? Sick of the daily drudge?" he probed, curious to know her answer.

If she was the spoiled princess he'd always imagined her to be, then his guess would fit right in with that. He used that thought to quell his firing libido.

"Something like that," she answered noncommittally and turned her head to stare out the window.

Something like that. Huh. What he wouldn't give to find out what that "something" was. Then maybe he could resolve his conflicted feelings. On the surface, Tamsyn Masters had proven true to form. She'd turned up at his doorstep unannounced, which, if it had been Ellen's home, could have had devastating consequences. She spent money like water, which made him wonder if she'd ever had to work hard for a single thing. And, by her own admission, she'd simply walked away from the family business and whatever responsibilities had been hers while she was there.

All in all, her actions made her appear to be an unappealing package—a package not unlike Briana had proven to be.

So why on earth did he find her anything but?

Five

Tamsyn woke the next morning filled with a renewed vigor to face the day. Lunch with Finn had been delightful, far better than she'd anticipated, although the setting had sharpened her homesickness for The Masters. Her host, however, seemed to read her mood instinctively and had distracted her with his knowledge of the immediate district. It was obvious he cared about the area and the people within it, and several other diners had stopped by their table at the restaurant to give their regards.

While Finn had introduced her politely to each and every person who had spoken with him, he'd made it subtly clear at the same time that he didn't want additional company. She'd been a little surprised by how efficiently he'd closed people out. She'd also been frustrated as she'd wanted to ask each of them if they'd heard of her mother. Despite that, by the time they were enjoying their coffee and a shared apple tarte tatin for dessert Tamsyn had begun to feel more relaxed than she had in a very long time.

And there was something else. She'd felt protected, almost cherished, which was weird considering she'd only just met Finn, but his behavior toward her was caring and solicitous. She'd thrived under his undivided attention. It was a luxury she couldn't remember experiencing in a very long time.

After a delicious leisurely lunch, their sightseeing had taken them well off the beaten track and away from populated areas. Tamsyn had fallen in love with the amazing vistas that looked out over the Marlborough Sounds and then the stunning valleys and hills on the journey home that led them back to the river plains and her hotel.

As lovely as yesterday afternoon had been, today promised a different and perhaps more challenging agenda. Moving into the cottage. She understood it had been vacant for a couple of weeks. Hopefully that didn't mean it would be musty and in need of heavy cleaning when she arrived.

"Are you all set?" Penny asked as Tamsyn wheeled her new gleaming blue suitcase containing her recently acquired possessions toward the front door.

Tamsyn had told her hostess last night that she'd be checking out in the morning. Penny hadn't been able to keep the surprise from her eyes when Tamsyn had told her where she'd be staying but had swiftly covered that with an offer to provide her with some food supplies to take with her.

"Yes, I am, and thank you so much for a lovely stay."

"You're welcome, any time," the other woman smiled. "Are you sure you want to go out to a place on your own? You'll be a bit isolated there."

"You know, my life has been so frenetic lately, I think I'm going to relish the peace and quiet of being on my own. To be honest, I don't think I've ever just had to bear my own company. I'm actually looking forward to it."

"Well, don't be a stranger, feel free to pop in for a cuppa if you're passing," Penny invited.

Tamsyn drove to the address the letting agent had given her, missing the entrance completely the first time. After executing a U-turn she inched back along the road until she saw the slightly overgrown access to the driveway. It was obviously a good place to go when you didn't really want to be found, she thought as she drove up the dusty unsealed track and toward a small cottage nestled at the bottom of the hill. The very hill, in fact, that was crowned by Finn Gallagher's opulent stone-and-cedar palace.

She hadn't realized she'd be this close. She could hop a

fence and walk through the vineyard that stretched up the hill and be at his place in little more than a vigorous ten- to fifteen-minute walk. It was both unsettling and reassuring at the same time. At least knowing someone was close in case she needed help was a bonus...but Finn Gallagher?

As attractive as he was, and as immediate as her reaction was to him, he still unnerved her on some levels. His attentive behavior since their not-so-friendly first meeting definitely was appealing, as was the way he looked at her as if she was all woman, but coming so close on the heels of her broken engagement she still felt nervy, distrustful. And while it was flattering at the time that he'd obviously wanted to keep her company all to himself yesterday, when she'd thought about it late last night she'd started to get the niggling feeling that he had some ulterior motive for doing so.

Maybe she was just overreacting. After all, it wasn't every day a woman had to accept that she'd been efficiently lied to for the better part of two years by a man she'd trusted enough to want to marry. The dull ache that seemed to permanently reside in her chest intensified.

In the clothing store, wearing a beautiful dress and anticipating an afternoon with a handsome man, it had been easy to lay the mess of their shattered engagement entirely on Trent's shoulders...but deep down she felt it had to be her fault. How could she not have seen Trent and Zac's interest in one another? How could she never have suspected a thing? Sure, her relationship with Trent had been cool, their sex life minimal, but she'd put that down to the type of man he was. And she'd loved him—believed they had a future together. Just went to show what a rotten judge of character she really was, she told herself with a rueful glance in her rearview mirror.

She pulled her car to a halt outside the front of an old detached garage next to the cottage and got out. Maybe she was just being paranoid. Actually, more than maybe and that

wasn't necessarily a bad thing. Her experience with Trent
had been a rude and very unpleasant awakening. It wouldn't
do her any harm at all to be a little less eager to salve her
mortally wounded pride with the company of a handsome
man, even if he did have the power to make her heart skip.

The cottage was old, probably circa early 1900s, but very
well maintained by the look of things. A large deep veranda
stretched invitingly along the front of the house and around
to one side. She hoped the interior was as appealing. Tamsyn grabbed the plastic bags Penny had enthusiastically
filled with what she'd deemed to be the essentials to see her
through the next day or so. Tam had been overwhelmed by
the other woman's generosity, even more so when Penny
had refused any payment for the items. As a result, Tamsyn
doubted she'd need to make her way into town for supplies
for several days, given the fresh meat, milk, eggs and other
items the hotelier had given her.

The key slid smoothly into the front door lock and turned
easily. Feeling almost as if she was trespassing, Tamsyn
stepped inside.

Dust motes floated on the gilded rays of morning sun
that streamed in through windows to her left, but aside from
that, the place looked well kept. Almost as if the owners
had stepped outside for only a moment.

"Prrrrp." She jumped at the sound as a sleek black cat
followed in through the front door behind her, eyeing her
carefully with its golden eyes before winding in and out of
her legs and purring.

"Well, hello," Tamsyn said, bending down to stroke the
cat. "I guess you're one of my responsibilities while I'm
here, hmm? What a shame no one thought to tell me your
name."

The letting agent had mentioned that a neighbor had been
caring for the animals at the house, but that they'd be her re-

sponsibility for the duration of the tenancy. How hard could it be, right? A few chickens, a cat. It wasn't rocket science.

The cat looked up at her and blinked slowly before lithely jumping up onto the windowsill and grooming itself in the sun. For some reason, the animal's presence made Tamsyn feel more at home. She took her supplies through to the compact and slightly old-fashioned kitchen and put them in the refrigerator. Through the window over the kitchen counter she could see a vast, somewhat overgrown, vegetable garden.

She wrapped her arms around herself and squeezed tight. It shouldn't be so exciting to have this—temporary—home of her own. After all, she'd grown up on an amazing estate. But it was her *family's* estate, never solely hers. She'd never truly been on her own. It was surprising how much she liked it. She really was pretty self-sufficient for the next few days. If she didn't want to, she needn't go anywhere. But how would she find her mother if she didn't keep going out into the community and asking around?

Tamsyn groaned aloud as another thought came to her. The internet. Of course. Why hadn't she thought of that?

Because her mind had been too distracted with other thoughts—thoughts of Trent and, more so, thoughts of the tall, enigmatic man who lived at the top of the hill—she'd completely discounted using her smartphone to do an internet search for her mother. As soon as she'd unpacked she'd get right onto it.

Tamsyn turned on her heel and nearly screamed when something brushed against her leg. The cat. Oh, God, her heart was racing. Living on her own, albeit with a resident feline, was going to take some getting used to.

The cat rubbed against her, twining in a figure eight between her legs and purring loudly before stalking toward a cupboard with its tail in the air. Sitting in front of the cupboard, it began to scratch.

"Oh, no, don't do that," Tamsyn said, hastening over.

She pushed the cat away from the door, but it determinedly moved back in front and began scratching again. Curious, and not a little fearful that perhaps there might be a mouse inside, she opened the cupboard. A sigh of relief flooded through her when she saw the bag of dried cat food sitting on the bottom shelf of what was obviously a pantry.

"You're hungry, that's what it is, isn't it, Puss?"

She looked around for a bowl and spied a small plastic mat on the floor near a glass-paned door, an empty bowl and a water dish sitting side by side. The cat purred its obvious approval as she collected the empty dishes and rinsed them out at the kitchen sink before drying them and refilling them with cat biscuits and water.

"There you go," she said, putting them back on the little mat and running her hand down the cat's black furry back.

Feeling well-satisfied with herself, Tamsyn went back out to her car and grabbed her suitcase. This time, she turned to her right as she came back in. The bedrooms had to be down this way, she thought as she tried each door as she got to it. There were two bedrooms to choose from, one bathroom and one door that was locked. Tamsyn chose the smaller of the two bedrooms and unpacked her meager belongings. It was hardly worth the bother, she thought as she hung up the couple of things she'd bought and stuffed her small collection of underwear into a drawer. Compared with her walk-in closet at home, she had majorly downsized.

Home. Another wave of homesickness washed over her. She should call her brother, reassure him she was okay and tell him of her plans. Before she could talk herself out of it, she pressed the quick dial for his mobile number.

"I was beginning to think I'd have to send out a search party for you," he answered.

While there was a teasing note in his voice, Tamsyn could hear the underlying concern.

"I did say I'd call in few days. I'm fine, by the way," she assured him. "Thanks for asking."

"Ready to come home yet?"

"Not anywhere near it, Ethan. How are you managing without me?"

"We're coping surprisingly well. Aunt Cynthia has really come into her own taking over for you, you'd be impressed."

Tamsyn felt his words like a physical blow. Sure, she'd walked out on them, but couldn't they have missed her—even just a little bit? Nobody had missed her, it seemed. She hadn't even had so much as a text or email from Trent. Not that she wanted to hear from him, but they'd been engaged over a year and had gone out for several months before that. Surely she'd warranted something from him, some explanation, *anything*. She quashed the thought. She'd walked away from him and his lover, and everything associated with them. That was her choice, as was her mission to find her mother. It was time to stop looking back and to keep her sights firmly fixed on her new future.

Forcing a smile to her lips, she said, "Hey, can you check something for me?"

"Name it."

"The address Mom's checks are sent to—can you give that to me again?"

"Sure, just give me a minute to find the email," her brother replied.

In the background she could hear him using his usual hunt-and-peck keyboard skills to pull up the information. She smiled to herself. Computers were a necessary evil in Ethan's book—he'd much rather be blending his world-famous wines and watching over their production as if they were his children heading out to a first day at school. While he was busy, Tamsyn scrabbled in her handbag for a pen and notebook.

"Found it," he said a moment later. He rattled off the address.

"That's weird," Tamsyn replied, chewing on the end of her pen. "That's the address I went to on Saturday, but the man there said he hadn't heard of Mom."

"Let me check with Dad's solicitor and get back to you. Could be someone made a mistake somewhere."

Or it could be that someone was lying to her. The thought echoed around in her mind. Could Finn be deliberately keeping information about her mother from her? Surely not. What would be the point? It's not as if he stood to gain anything by it.

"Okay, thanks. Send me a text or email when you know, okay? In the meantime, I've decided to take a short-term lease on a cottage here. I want to spend more time poking around, see if I can bump into anyone who might know her and how I can find her."

"Tam, are you sure you're doing the right thing? Maybe if she's hard to find it's because she doesn't want to be."

"It's not about what she wants anymore," Tamsyn said with uncharacteristic firmness. "This time it's about what she owes me. I deserve to know why she left us, Ethan. I *need* to know."

She heard her brother sigh in frustration. "By the way," Ethan said, "I talked to Trent. He told me what happened."

Tamsyn felt as if a fist had closed around her heart and her lungs burned, reminding her to draw in a breath.

"R-really? Ev-everything?" she stuttered.

"With a little coaxing." The steel in Ethan's voice left her in no doubt that her brother had not been his usual urbane self when approaching her ex-fiancé. He continued before she could gather her thoughts together. "I don't blame you for needing some time out. He duped us all, Tam. Led us all to believe he'd love you the way you deserved to be loved. He was promising something he couldn't deliver. No matter his orientation, what he did to you was wrong on every level. You deserved better than that and you still do. Isobel's so mad I had to physically restrain her from heading into town to deal with him. I just wanted you to know, we're in your corner. Whatever you need from us right now, it's yours."

Tears throbbed at the back of Tamsyn's eyes and she stared up at the ceiling in a vain attempt to force them back. If she let go now, she didn't know if she'd be able to stop, and if Ethan heard her crying he'd be here faster than she could blink. This was her mission, her goal. She had to do it for herself. For once in her life she wasn't doing something to please someone else, this was all about her.

She focused, instead, on the idea of Ethan's fiancée, Isobel, and the very idea of the tiny blonde going head to head with Trent in a fight. It was enough to calm her—to almost make her smile.

"Thank you," she managed to whisper then drew in a steadying breath, one that made her voice stronger. "I'll be in touch when I learn anything, okay?"

"It'll have to be okay," Ethan conceded. "And I'll check that address and get back to you later today."

Tamsyn said goodbye and severed the connection, feeling a little as if she'd cut off a lifeline. She was grateful for the distraction when the sound of tires on the graveled driveway drew her attention out the window. She watched as a now-familiar SUV pulled in next to her rental. An all new tightness replaced the pain that had been in her chest only moments ago as Finn stepped down from the vehicle and started toward the house.

Ignoring her body's sudden and unsettling awareness of him, she examined the question that now hovered foremost in her mind. Did some of the answers she sought lie with Finn Gallager?

Six

Finn approached the open front door not entirely sure what he was doing here. Lorenzo had asked for updates, but even that wasn't enough of a reason to be virtually stalking Tamsyn Masters the way he was.

She moved into the doorway just as he raised his hand to the frame to knock. Today she was dressed simply in strategically faded, snug blue jeans and a deep V-necked white T-shirt that hinted at the shell-pink bra she wore beneath. The soft swells of her breasts pushed against the fine cotton above the cups of her bra.

Finn forced his eyes upward to her face. With her hair pulled back into a ponytail she looked younger, the dark marks under her eyes were a little more faded than they'd been the day before.

"Hi," he said. "I was just passing and thought I'd see if you needed anything in town."

A slow sweet smile pulled at Tamsyn's lips.

"That was thoughtful of you, but Penny's actually given me quite a few things to take care of me for the next few days."

"Okay, great. That was good of her." He searched for something else he could say to prolong the conversation. "Oh, and I thought I'd give you my number in case you need any help with anything around the house."

He yanked his card holder from the back of his jeans pocket and slid out a business card, handing it to her. She took it carefully, but her fingers still lightly grazed his. A flare of sudden and instant heat burned up his arm at her touch.

"Thank you, although on first glance around here I don't think I'll need help with anything. Your neighbors appear to have been very self-sufficient."

"Yes, they are."

"Have you been the one feeding the animals?" she asked.

"Yeah, the chickens are easier than that feline monster."

The monster in question padded down the hallway and sat down at Tamsyn's feet, eyeing him with a baleful glare.

"This one?" she asked, bending down to tickle it behind the ears. "Do you know its name?"

"Lucy, short for Lucifer. In name and in nature. They thought she was a boy when they first got her and had to shorten her name when they discovered she was carrying a litter."

Finn watched in surprise as the wretched animal began to purr and nudge its head against Tamsyn's hand.

"Lucifer? For this cutie?" Tamsyn laughed. "That's a touch harsh, don't you think?"

Maybe he'd misjudged the animal. It had only ever barely tolerated him. He bent down to give it a pat only to have Lucy's ears flare back and her teeth bare as she hissed her displeasure at his presumption.

"Nope, not harsh at all. Funny that she's so tolerant of you. She usually only lets her owner and her daughter touch her."

As soon as the words were out of his mouth Finn wished them back. Of course Lucy would connect with Tamsyn. She was Ellen's daughter, too.

"Maybe she just prefers female company," Tamsyn commented, oblivious to Finn's discomfort.

"That's probably it."

"Did you want to stop in for a cup of coffee or something? I'm not quite sure where everything is yet, but I'm sure I can find it all."

Should he? Sure, why not. It was neighborly, after all.

"That'd be great. While I'm here I can check the hot water is turned on for you. I know the property manager was going to take care of it, but they may not have gotten around to it yet."

"Oh, would you? That would be wonderful. I'd love nothing better than a long soak in that fabulous old bath tonight."

Finn's body hardened at the visual image that flooded his mind. It took no stretch of the imagination to envisage the drape of her lean arms along the sides of the old claw-footed tub he knew resided in the bathroom. Or the delicate curve of her shoulders and the sweep of her collarbone glistening with scented bath oil.

"Right," he said, pulling himself together abruptly. "I'll get onto it then."

"I'll go and put the jug on," she replied, stepping back from the doorway and ushering him inside.

Lucy gave another short hiss at him before springing away and settling herself on the windowsill of the large front bay window.

"The cylinder is in the old laundry off the back porch," Finn said by way of explanation as he followed her through to the kitchen.

He unlocked the back door and stepped through the small porch to the door on the other side, reaching above the door frame for the key. He was as familiar with this house as he was with his own face in the mirror each morning. Lorenzo and Ellen had provided him a home here and despite his offers to build them something newer and more comfortable, they'd insisted they were happy in their small cottage, especially now that Alexis's business was taking off, leading her to spend much of her time working from overseas.

By the time he'd checked the cylinder he could hear the jug beginning to boil, the sound accompanied by Tamsyn's light humming as she moved around the kitchen finding coffee and mugs.

"You just have your coffee black, right?"

He was impressed she'd both noticed and remembered. Her attention to detail was good—he needed to remind himself of that, and not to slip up the way he had earlier when he'd nearly mentioned Ellen and Alexis by name.

"That's right," he answered, locking the laundry door behind him and returning the key to its spot.

"You seem to know your way around here pretty well."

"We've been neighbors a long time. Plus, I've been watching the animals the past few weeks."

She gave a short laugh. "It's a good thing that Lucy could tolerate you feeding her then."

"Cupboard love," he commented in response. "Cats are well known for it."

"I wouldn't know," Tamsyn replied as she added sugar and milk to her coffee. "We never had pets growing up."

"Not at all?"

"No, our father didn't think they had a place in our household. Occasionally a feral cat would have kittens on the property, but Dad always made sure they were rehomed before we could adopt any of them."

Finn thought of the farm dogs his father had always had, even after he'd downsized the stock running on the farm and begun to change his primary business over to growing grapevines. The animals had been as much of an extension of his life as Lorenzo and Ellen had been after his father died. Add to that his mother's and Ellen's procession of cats over the years and he couldn't imagine growing up without a pet. He'd always imagined he'd have a couple of dogs when he finished building the house, but Briana had insisted she was allergic and since her departure, a year ago, he'd been too busy to do anything about it.

"So where did you grow up that pets weren't considered a necessary part of family life?" he asked, forcing a smile to try to soften his words.

"It's a property similar to where we lunched yesterday, although possibly a bit bigger. We have a vineyard and winery, restaurant and wedding venue, plus luxury cottage accommodation. Of course, when I was little it was just the vineyard and winery and on a much smaller scale. Dad's family were still working really hard to reestablish what they'd lost after a devastating bushfire when he was in his early twenties. The whole family had to start from scratch."

"Sounds like hard work."

"I guess it was. We didn't know any different, though, growing up. And all of us, my brother and my cousins, we all knew we'd be a part of it one day. Each of us has had their place in the family business basically grow around them and their interests."

What she said didn't quite gel with the image he'd always had of her. He'd imagined her living off the luxury, not working hard to be a part of bringing it about. It roused his curiosity even further.

"And you? What about your place and your interests?"

Tamsyn picked up her spoon and began absently stirring her coffee.

"That doesn't matter now," she said, her voice empty of emotion.

Clearly she didn't want to talk about it, which only served to make Finn all the more determined to find out why. Even he knew when not to push, though. Softly, softly would be the best approach, he decided, taking a sip of the instant brew Tamsyn had poured for him.

He pulled a face. "Remind me to show you how to use the espresso machine," he said.

"It's bad, isn't it?" she admitted with an uncharacteristic giggle. "I'm not even sure it's coffee."

"If you don't mind, I'm going to tip this out," Finn said, brushing past her on the way to the kitchen sink.

She'd moved toward the sink at the same time and his

arm grazed the side of her breast. Not a deliberate move on his part but he wasn't sorry, especially not when he saw her nipples pebble behind the lacy bra she was wearing and thrust against her shirt. This close to her, he heard her breath catch in her throat. Knowing she was just as affected by his touch as he was by hers was gratifying.

Her eyes were dark pools of confusion, her mouth still slightly parted on that gasp. It would only take a second to lean forward and capture those lips with his. To test their softness, to tease a response from her. The air thickened between them. Outside, he was aware of the rasp of cicadas in the garden, the lazy buzz of bees around the flower beds. Inside, he could hear nothing but his rapid heartbeat whooshing in his ears.

Too soon. It was far too soon. She was a timid thing. Tentative, almost wounded. She needed to be drawn in slowly, to be tempted to take him as bait. He took one step back, then another, his body instantly mourning the nearness of hers.

"I'll be off then," he said with as much control as he could muster. "I'd say thanks for the coffee, but…"

She gave a nervous laugh. "Yeah, I know. Thank you for coming over and checking the hot water for me."

"No problem. If you like, I can call in tomorrow and show you how to use the espresso machine."

"I'd like that," she replied, following him as he went out the front door.

She stayed there on the front veranda, her hands shoved into the pockets at the front of her jeans, watching while he executed a neat turn and headed down the driveway. A sense of anticipation stole over him. Getting to know Tamsyn Masters better was proving to be more challenging than he'd anticipated. And more appealing. Far, far more appealing.

Seven

Tamsyn waited until Finn's car was out of view before turning and going back into the cottage. The place felt still and empty without his presence. She chided herself for being fanciful as she went around the house opening windows to let in fresh air. Lucy had disappeared again, clearly off on an agenda of her own, which pretty much left Tamsyn to her own devices.

Speaking of devices, she retrieved her mobile from her handbag and, after pouring herself a glass of water, she settled down on the front porch in a sagging wicker arm chair to see if her mother's name came up in any local searches.

An hour later she was feeling intensely frustrated. The only search information she'd turned up to date all related back to when her mother still lived in Adelaide, the most recent being her wedding announcement way back over thirty years ago, together with a grainy photo of her parents standing in the entrance to the church, followed by brief birth announcements in the newspaper when Ethan and Tamsyn were born. After that, nothing. Tamsyn stared at the wedding photo on her cell phone screen. The quality of the photo was poor, blurring their features into near obscurity. A bit like the dearth of information about Ellen Masters since. It was truly bizarre. Almost as if, in marrying John Masters, Ellen had dropped out of society and circulation and ceased to exist.

Tamsyn scoured her memories for any hint of her mother that went past a vaguely remembered cuddle. The best she could muster was the sound of peals of laughter infused with the scent of freshly cut grass and the heat of summer sun. She gave up with a curse that startled the birds that had been pecking at the lawn. They lifted to the nearby trees with a flurry of wings and squawks of indignation.

This was hopeless, she decided, closing the applications on her phone and picking up her glass to take it back inside. Clearly she needed a face-to-face approach. She wondered if there was somewhere local where she could view an electoral roll or something like that. Perhaps the nearby town's information center might be able to head her in the right direction.

Tamsyn went back into the house and grabbed her keys. Eschewing closing all the windows again, she locked the front door and headed for her car.

The drive into town was quiet; in fact, she hardly saw another vehicle on the road until she got within town limits. She eased her car into a space on a side street, near the boutique where she'd shopped yesterday, and got out. She vaguely remembered seeing an information center sign posted near the end of the main street and she struck out in that direction.

It looked as if she was headed toward a small town hall. This was probably the hub of the immediate district's social life in its day. Judging by the activity milling around there now—a mixed age group of people wearing loose clothing and carrying yoga mats, spilling out the front door—it was still equally well used. A large notice board out front attracted her attention and Tamsyn was surprised to see the list of activities available on various days. A bright notice stuck to one side caught her eye. It was an advertisement for a volunteer seniors' activities coordinator to provide temporary cover one day a week in the lead-up to Christmas. Applicants were bidden to apply at the office.

Tamsyn mulled over the notice. Once a week for five weeks? She could easily commit to that. It might take her that long to find her mother at this rate. Even if she found her sooner, she'd certainly want to spend time with her before going back to Adelaide.

If she went back at all.

The thought wasn't as unsettling as it should have been. Instead, a kernel of excitement began to cautiously unfurl within her at the thought of truly starting over fresh. She reached out to take the notice from the board and walked up the steps leading to the front of the hall. Nerves assailed her as she lifted her hand to knock at the door marked Office. This was the first job she'd ever actually applied for. In the past she'd always worked at The Masters in one field or another. Odd jobs while she was at school, and subsequently, during her semester breaks while she was at university. Once she graduated, she took over developing and managing the accommodation cottages, eventually expanding to special events and weddings. She'd never once had to face rejection in the course of her work.

What if she applied for the job and they said no?

She swallowed against the fear that threatened to paralyze her. She'd never had to second-guess herself before. Trent's lies and subterfuge had totally done a number on her head, she realized. Especially coming on the heels of discovering the secret her family had been keeping from her. Now she was so shaken up she was second-guessing her ability to apply for a casual position doing something she knew in her heart she could do virtually blindfolded.

She forced herself to knock on the door before she could give in to the anxiety.

"Come in if you're good looking!" a gravelly voice answered.

The words brought a smile to her face and she opened the door.

"I'm here about the coordinator's job?" she said as she stepped into the chaos that was the hall's office.

Papers were strewn on every available surface, together

with an array of multicolored empty coffee cups. Behind the desk sat a woman who was probably anywhere in age between fifty and eighty. Her wiry hair stuck out in all directions and an unlit cigarette hung from her lips as she looked up in response.

"An Aussie, huh? What makes you think you can do the job?" she barked.

Tamsyn fought to keep her face impassive. She took a deep breath. "I have a degree in communication, majoring in event management, and I've worked the past seven years coordinating events on both small and large scales, from company dinners and product launches, to weddings and anniversary celebrations."

"The job's not paid."

"I'm aware of that. Money isn't an issue."

"Hmmph. Nice for some. You know it's only for five weeks—only four probably because no one will want to come on Christmas Eve."

"Five weeks is fine."

"Damn-fool woman who normally does it tripped backward last week over a carpet bowling ball and broke her leg. I guess you'll give the old codgers something new to look at. You're hired."

Tamsyn looked at the woman in surprise. "Just like that? Don't you want references?"

"Do I look like I need references?" The woman peered at Tamsyn over her half-lens glasses. "What I need is a cigarette, but we're not allowed to smoke in a council-affiliated building anymore."

Just privately, Tamsyn thought that given the tsunami of paper throughout the small office, it was a good thing the woman wasn't allowed to light up.

"Okay, when do I start?"

"Next session is Wednesday this week. Runs from ten-thirty until one. People bring their own lunch. Here's the ring binder with the weeks' activities set and the roster of who does what. Don't lose it."

"Thank you. I'm Tamsyn Masters, by the way."

"Gladys. I run this joint because no one else can. Got any questions, ask me. Just not now. Damn bingo caller for tomorrow night has laryngitis and I need to get someone else. I don't suppose…?" Gladys looked at Tamsyn who firmly shook her head. "Hmmph, you better give me your number in case I need to call you."

Tamsyn gave her cell phone number. "Okay if I take a look around?"

"Feel free. And don't lose that binder, whatever you do."

"I won't," she promised, tucking the item firmly under one arm and walking back out of the office.

Well, she thought as she carried on into the main hall, that had to be the shortest job interview in history. She laughed out loud. What on earth had she been worried about? She stopped and looked around.

Sash windows with half-lowered black-out blinds lined the hall on both sides. A raised stage stood at one end with ancient dark red velvet drapes hanging on either side. Tamsyn felt as if she'd stepped into a time warp. As if she could just close her eyes and reopen them to a wartime dance, or a seventies disco.

Folding tables were slanted against the wall on one side, stacking chairs on the other. Tamsyn pulled out one of the stacking chairs and sat down to study the folder she'd been given. Despite Gladys's curt demeanor and seeming disorganization, everything in here was neatly compiled and ordered. Activities were basically the same each week, with an occasional out-of-town trip organized to see a movie in Blenheim or to visit a restaurant.

Basically, all she had to do was oversee each week and ensure that the door takings, a gold coin per member each meeting, were given to Gladys to bank by the end of each session. It'd be a walk in the park. Even so, the prospect left her feeling more enthused than she'd felt in a very long time. She itched to share her news with someone. Finn, maybe?

She put a clamp on her wayward thoughts. Tomorrow would be soon enough to tell him, when he came to show her how to use the espresso machine. It wasn't as if they were friends or anything.

Tamsyn thought back to this morning's meeting, to that moment when she'd thought he might kiss her. He'd been so close, his gray eyes—dark as storm clouds before torrential rain—fixed on her lips. Her whole body had gone on high alert from the instant he'd brushed against her, all her feminine sensors pinging at that merest of touches. She lifted her fingers to her lips. What would it have felt like, she wondered, if he'd followed through on what she thought had been clear intent in those tempestuous eyes?

A thrill rippled through her body as her imagination took hold, and she closed her eyes, lost in the moment.

"Are you planning to nap there all day? I've got somewhere to go to, even if you haven't."

Gladys's raspy voice jarred her out of her reverie.

"I'm sorry, I'll be out of your way in a minute," Tamsyn said, lurching to her feet and stacking the chair back where she'd found it.

Accompanied by mutterings of "young people these days," she headed back out the main door and onto the street. Behind her, Gladys activated an alarm, clanged the front doors closed and methodically locked them.

"You still here?" the old woman asked as she reached the pavement.

"I was wondering if you could tell me where I can find the information center."

"That'd be me," Gladys said crustily.

"Oh, okay. Maybe you can help. My mother is from here and I'm trying to track her down."

"Hmmph. I thought you had a familiar look about you. Your mother a local, is she?"

"I…I think so. Ellen Masters, have you heard of her?"

Gladys fossicked through her voluminous crocheted handbag before extracting a lighter and applying it to the cigarette still hanging from her wrinkled lips. She sucked long and hard on the filter, an expression almost close to happiness spreading across her lined face.

"Can't say as I have. Maybe she doesn't want to be found."

The old woman's statement hung on the air between them. Tamsyn was initially at a loss for words but pressed on.

"Well, do you know where I can view an electoral roll?"

Gladys took another long pull at her cigarette, the smoke filtering out between her lips as she spoke. "Library could be your best bet. Ask for Miriam, tell her I sent you."

"Thank you. Where can I find the library?" Tamsyn answered, but she was talking to thin air.

For an old lady Gladys sure did move fast, and she was barreling down the pavement toward the local pub as if she was on a deadline. Frustrated and unsettled by the comment about her mother, Tamsyn pulled out her phone and keyed in a search request. Ah, there it was. The library should be just around the block from where she stood now. Given that the blocks were tiny, she was there in five minutes, only to find the doors closed.

She gritted her teeth as she studied the opening hours on the neatly hand-printed notice stuck on the inside of the glass door. She'd just missed them. She jotted a note on her phone with the hours and promised herself she'd be back on Wednesday before she attended her first day as the seniors' coordinator.

For now, there was nothing for it but to head back to the cottage and take out her frustration for a few hours on the weeds growing through the garden. Her car was hot from sitting in the sun and she waited a while with the windows open for it to cool down before starting the engine. She looked around the township from where she sat. The place was quaintly idyllic. Everywhere she looked people greeted one another with a cheerful smile and a wave or a toot of their horn.

So, if everyone was so darn friendly why was it proving so hard to find anyone who'd met her mother? What was it with this place? Was everything and everyone conspiring to prevent her from finding her?

Eight

The garden looked as if a whirlwind had torn through it, Finn realized as he stepped out of his car the next morning. Clumps of weeds lay in piles here and there all over the slightly overgrown lawn. He made a mental note to drag out the ride-on mower and run it around the grass sometime soon. But what Tamsyn had done with the untidy garden was nothing short of spectacular.

"Good morning!" she called, stepping out onto the veranda to welcome him.

She was a sight for sore eyes today, dressed in shorts and a tank top that already showed the efforts of her labors, stained as they were with a combination of perspiration and dirt.

"You've been busy," he said, getting out of the Cayenne.

"I started yesterday and kept going this morning. I'm not used to sitting around doing nothing, and I hate leaving a job unfinished," she said. "It's enough to drive a woman to drink."

And wasn't that exactly what had driven her mother to the bottle back in Australia? Finn thought privately. Being forced to sit around, doing nothing, just being decorative? Always at Tamsyn's father's beck and call, but only getting attention from him in dribs and drabs? Even the children, he'd heard, had been mostly raised by nannies.

He pasted a smile on his face and pushed the stories he'd heard from Lorenzo to the back of his mind.

"Would an espresso do?" Finn offered.

Tamsyn gave a heartfelt groan of appreciation. "I'd do anything for one."

Deep down, Finn's gut clenched tight. Oh, yeah, he was doing well so far. Not. Less than five minutes in her company and he was already fighting a hard-on. Willing his errant body back under control, he stepped up onto the veranda.

"I'm sure your boyfriend wouldn't like you going around making that offer," he finally answered.

"No boyfriend at the moment. I'm off men."

"Off men?" Finn reached for her left hand, his finger stroking the white line on her ring finger. "This the reason?"

Her hands, despite the grime from the garden, were soft. Tamsyn looked down at where he touched her. Finn watched as a gamut of emotions played across her expressive features.

"Yes," she said abruptly, tugging her hand free. "I need to rinse off. You know where everything is, I take it?"

Ah, so she didn't want to talk about that either. Had the Aussie princess met her match in her former fiancé? Was that why she was so intent on finding Ellen? he wondered. Was she looking for affection now that her fiancé was no longer in her life?

Finn told himself not to jump to conclusions. He needed to understand her in order to keep a lid on this situation. To control it and to guide Tamsyn away from trouble. Trouble, in this case, being finding out anything to do with Ellen whatsoever.

He went through to the kitchen and pulled out Lorenzo's favorite coffee cups and the imported Italian-branded coffee beans the older man swore by. Putting the required scoops in the grinder, Finn set the machine to work.

"My own personal barista, how did I get so lucky?" Tamsyn said a few minutes later from behind him, startling him with her arrival in the kitchen.

She'd taken a very quick shower, judging by the fresh

soapy scent of her, and changed into the jeans she'd worn yesterday, teamed this time with a pale pink T-shirt.

"Well, the luck stops here. You're doing the rest. I'm here to show you how, remember?"

She shrugged. "No problem. Let's start with how many beans you measured into the grinder."

Finn went through the steps. She was a quick learner, grasping the use of the machine easily.

"Let's take these out the front and enjoy looking at your efforts in the garden," he suggested when the cups were poured.

"It's been a while since someone has worked in it, hasn't it?" Tamsyn asked as they settled into a pair of cane-and-wicker chairs.

He just nodded, not really trusting himself to speak. The garden had always been Ellen's domain, but in recent years it had become too much for her. Lorenzo, busy overseeing the staff who tended the vines on the joint property he shared with Finn, had little love for working in the rambling cottage garden Ellen had created and had done the barest minimum to keep the weeds at bay. Finn had frequently suggested they employ someone to help out around the house, but his business partner had adamantly refused.

Considering he and Ellen were still only in their late fifties it was an emotional outburst, but Finn respected that it couldn't be easy for Lorenzo to slowly see the woman he had loved for so long slowly wither away physically and mentally. Lorenzo hadn't wanted to admit that Ellen could no longer handle the tasks she'd once loved, like gardening. The early onset of her dementia had been devastating news for them all.

Finn and Tamsyn settled into an easy silence together, broken only when she finished her coffee and placed her cup back on its saucer on the small glass-topped cane table between them.

"That was pure gold. I feel like a new woman," she declared with a happy sigh.

"Something wrong with the old one?" he queried, always ready to delve into what made Tamsyn Masters tick.

"A few things, but I'm working on them," she answered vaguely. "I got a job, by the way. Not paid work, but I'm volunteering in town at the hall."

"Seriously? Gladys is letting you help her out?" Finn's eyebrows rose in tandem with the incredulous note in his voice.

Tamsyn laughed, the sound plucking at his chest. God, he loved it when she laughed.

"Oh, no, as tempting as it is to set her office to rights, I wouldn't dare trespass on her domain. No, they needed someone to fill in for the seniors' program coordinator. She hurt herself last week, apparently, and won't be back until the new year."

"You're planning to stay here that long?"

Finn was surprised. Surely she intended returning home long before Christmas?

"I don't have any other demands on my time."

"But your family? They'll expect you back for Christmas, won't they?"

Tamsyn shrugged. "As far as my immediate family goes, it's only Ethan and me and he's recently engaged. I think it would be nice for him and Isobel to enjoy their first Christmas together without having to worry about me tagging along. The rest of my family is big enough and noisy enough not to miss me too much. Besides, I'm *needed* here now." She gave him a bright smile that didn't quite reach her eyes.

There was a note to her voice it took him a moment to place—she was feeling lost and vulnerable. He didn't doubt for a second that her family would miss her over Christmas, but she obviously felt they didn't need her. If anything, she needed the voluntary position here in the community more than they needed her.

The realization knocked his impression of her back a couple of notches. No matter which way he turned it, she was looking less and less like the spoiled little princess he'd built up in his mind. Had he been so determined to see the worst in her that he hadn't opened his eyes to the person she really was? Obviously the scars that Briana had left had gone far deeper than he'd thought if he was incapable of seeing the good in a person anymore.

After all, he thought, looking out over the garden, would someone who didn't understand hard work or dedication have worked so diligently to expose the carefully cultivated loveliness behind the weeds?

"I'm sure the old guys at the center will be thrilled to have you. You're far easier on the eyes than their usual co-ordinator."

"Oh, I'm sure the novelty will wear off soon enough," she said, brushing aside his comments even as a delicious blush spread up her chest and neck before tinting her cheeks with a delicate pink.

"Well, I had better get back to work," Finn said, rising to his feet.

"What is it you do exactly?" she asked, getting up to lean on the railing that skirted the edge of the veranda.

"This and that. At the moment I'm developing a new idea."

"Oh, hush-hush, is it? Tell, and you'd have to kill me, is that it?"

Finn chuckled. "No, nothing like that. I used to be in I.T.," he said, downplaying the company he'd established on the internet and then sold for several billion dollars a few years ago. "Nowadays I dabble in all sorts of things, including the vineyards around us. The owners here and I are partners in this lot."

He opened his arms to encompass the surrounding land.

"I'm impressed," Tamsyn answered with a smile. "I'll bet this is a lot more fun than being lashed to a computer all day."

"Different strokes. What I did was fun at the time. Leaving it was even more so as it gives me the freedom now to do what I please, although I'm more of a silent partner with the vines. We grow for supply to the local wineries and it turns over a good living."

He started to walk toward his car, Tamsyn following him.

"I enjoyed the coffee," she said, "and the lesson in how to make it. Thank you for coming over."

"No problem. Say, are you busy for dinner tonight? I was wondering if you'd like to come up the hill and eat with me. Beats eating alone."

"Are you sure I won't be any bother?"

"One steak or two on the grill, it makes no difference to me."

"Okay, then," she agreed. "I'd like that. How about I bring a salad and something for dessert?"

"I've got dessert covered, but if you'd like to bring a salad that'd be great. See you around six?"

"Sure." She nodded eagerly, her dark eyes glowing. "I'm looking forward to it already."

Nine

The afternoon dragged interminably. Tamsyn dusted and polished and vacuumed the cottage feverishly. She'd had to keep busy to keep her mind off the dinner ahead.

Over and over she'd told herself it was just a neighborly gesture, but she couldn't forget that moment yesterday when they'd almost kissed. Of course, she'd castigated herself several times over for a fool for even contemplating kissing another man. It had only been a matter of days since she'd broken her engagement. But had it been a true engagement?

She'd thought so at the time, even though their relationship had been low on intimacy and high on society events. Looking back, she realized that Trent had been grooming her to be his very public partner right from the start of their relationship—introducing her to the senior partners of the law firm where he worked at his earliest opportunity. She could see now that she'd been a smoke screen to hide the parts of himself that his conservative bosses wouldn't have liked, and now that the shock was receding, she was angry. Angry at him for using her so badly and, even more so, angry with herself for not realizing she was being used.

Perhaps if she hadn't had such a sheltered upbringing at The Masters. Perhaps if she'd traveled widely, like her soon-to-be-sister-in-law, Isobel, or been more outgoing or... well, anything—it might have saved her from making herself into the biggest fool in her family's history. Whatever, she'd grown up the way she had, made the choices and decisions that had led her to Trent and now here. She had nothing to be ashamed of.

Yet, if that was the case, why did she feel she had so

much to prove? Why was it so important to her that a man like Finn Gallagher find her attractive? She'd be stupid not to have seen the way he looked at her. She'd done a fair bit of looking herself—he was, after all, gorgeous, and he made her feel almost gorgeous herself. Maybe a fling with a man like Finn Gallagher was exactly what she needed.

She was going to dinner with an attractive man. One who'd asked for her company. One who she'd seen every day since she arrived here. That had to count for something, surely. He'd chosen to seek her out, chosen to spend time with her. The idea gave her a happy buzz and she went out to the vegetable garden with a spring in her step.

Bringing a salad for tonight's meal might not be much of a contribution, but she'd make sure it was the best salad Finn Gallagher had ever seen. After picking the salad greens and some early ripe cherry tomatoes, and pulling a couple of fresh radishes from the plot, she took everything inside to wash and drain. Afterward, she went for another brief shower and decided on what to wear tonight. Jeans just felt too casual and she'd already bundled up the skirt and blouse he'd seen her wear on Saturday for recycling—never wanting to ever wear them again. Given her limited options, that pretty much left the purple-and-blue dress she'd worn on Sunday.

Well, why not, she decided, pulling it off the hanger and slipping it on over her head. She loved it and she might as well get the use out of it. She brushed her hair out thoroughly until it crackled beneath the bristles then swept half of it up into a loose knot, leaving the lower section to tumble down her back and over her shoulders. Glancing at herself in the mirror she found herself smiling. Yeah, she liked the effect.

A quick application of the limited cosmetics she'd had in her handbag when she'd boarded the flight to New Zealand and she was ready.

Putting the salad together only took a few minutes and the colorful combination of the vegetables and tomatoes was both appetizing and attractive. A quick glance at the carriage clock on the sideboard in the dining room confirmed it was five minutes to six. Perfect. She covered the bowl with cling wrap and, grabbing her keys from the hall table, she locked up and went out to her car.

Lucy lifted her head briefly from where she lay curled up on one of the wicker chairs at the front.

"I'm off on a hot date, Lucy," Tamsyn called to her. "Don't do anything I wouldn't do while I'm gone."

Inside the car, Tamsyn closed her eyes and took a deep breath, trying to settle her nerves, with little success. Her hand shook slightly as she reached to put her key in the ignition.

This was ridiculous, she thought as she finally managed to insert the key and set the engine to life. It was dinner. That was all. Nothing more. Nothing less. If that was the case, then why did her heart beat so fast and why were her cheeks lit with a flush of anticipation?

Because she was being stupid, she told herself sternly as she guided her car up the hill toward Finn's residence.

Once again she was struck by the majesty of his home as she pulled up outside. The imposing entrance, with its cathedral style two-story ceiling, made her feel small and insignificant as she got out of her car and started toward the door, bowl in hand. She felt as if she should be bearing a gift of more significance—not merely a salad.

She lifted, then dropped, the heavy iron door knocker and waited. When the door opened, Finn literally took her breath away. Hair still wet from his shower, jeans slung low on his hips, he was still buttoning his shirt, giving her a glimpse of a hard ridged abdomen and a broad muscled chest. Words failed her.

"Sorry, I'm running a bit late, I had a phone call," he said as he finished his buttoning. "I'm not usually this disorganized. Here, come in."

"Here's the salad," Tamsyn managed to say past a throat that had been temporarily paralyzed with longing.

"Great, it looks delicious. Follow me, I'll take it through to the kitchen."

Tamsyn followed behind, noticing that Finn had bare feet that hardly made a sound on the polished wooden floors. God, even his feet were sexy, she thought as her inner muscles clenched involuntarily. She dragged her eyes upward, focusing instead on a point just between his shoulders in an attempt to drag her contrary hormones under some form of control.

"Take a seat while I check on the marinade," Finn said, gesturing to a set of solid-wood high-backed bar stools at the edge of a large granite breakfast bar.

"Thanks. Do you mind if I take my shoes off?" Tamsyn asked, feeling just a little overdressed.

"Make yourself at home." He smiled in response before applying his attention to the dish he had on the countertop and turning the meat inside it.

Tamsyn was assailed with the aromas of ginger and garlic and felt her mouth begin to water.

"That smells great," she commented.

"It's going to be," Finn said with a conspiratorial wink that did weird things to her stomach all over again. "Can I offer you a glass of wine?"

"Sure, that'd be nice."

"Red or white?"

"How about you surprise me," she answered, all capability of making any rational decisions gone in his company.

"Okay," he said. "I'll be back in a minute. Unless you'd like to see my wine cellar?"

She laughed. "Does that fall under the same category as seeing your etchings?" Heat flamed in her cheeks as she realized what she'd just said and she clapped a hand to her mouth. "Oh, I'm so sorry, I didn't mean anything by that, it just slipped out!"

Finn laughed, his eyes crinkling at the corners in genuine amusement. "It's no problem and, for the record, no, this isn't in the same category at all. The cellar is through this way," he said, reaching for her hand.

Tamsyn tried not to think about the way his warm dry hand encapsulated her own or how the sensation of his palm against hers sent her synapses into meltdown. Instead, she focused on her breathing as they walked through a door off the kitchen and down a couple of stairs before continuing along a short tiled corridor.

"The cellar is built into the side of the hill," Finn said as they went down a couple more stairs before stopping at a door. "Obviously it's easier to keep it temperature controlled this way."

He opened the door and Tamsyn couldn't stop the captivated sigh of appreciation as she saw the shelved walls open up before her.

"This is impressive," she said, stepping forward and checking the labels on some of the several hundred bottles of wine on shelves that crisscrossed the walls. "Ethan would love this."

"Ethan?" Finn asked, raising one brow.

"My brother. He's our head winemaker at The Masters."

"Maybe he'll visit sometime," he said blandly before selecting two bottles from the shelves. "Here we go. How about a pinot gris to start and then a pinot noir with dinner?"

"Sounds great," Tamsyn agreed and turned to precede him out of the cellar and back to the kitchen.

While Finn opened the white wine and poured two glasses, Tamsyn drifted over to the wall of French doors that opened out onto a wide patio.

"This is quite a house you have," she said as she accepted the glass of wine Finn brought over to her.

"It's big, yeah, but it's home," Finn said, reaching past her to open the glass door and guided her outside onto the patio. "Take a seat," he invited. "I'll just get some appetizers."

Tamsyn perched on the edge of a comfortably padded patio chair and waited for Finn to return. Her eyes widened in surprise when she saw him return with a tray laden with antipasto.

"Wow, you put all this together?"

"One of my many talents," he answered with a smile. "A…close friend of my father's taught me to appreciate life with all its flavors. These are just some of them."

"Sounds like a great friend to have."

Finn took a sip of his wine before nodding. "The best. When my dad died and my mother became unwell, he stepped up and provided me with a home. I'll always be grateful to him for that. I owe him a lot."

Tamsyn heard the subtext behind Finn's words. Whoever this man was, he'd obviously been a big influence in Finn's life.

"You were young when your father passed away?"

"Twelve. Mom got sick soon after."

"That must have been hard. I'm really sorry," Tamsyn said with her heart behind every syllable.

"It was a long time ago." Finn sat staring out at the ranges for a while before leaning forward and lifting the antipasto platter toward her. "Here, try some."

"This is really lovely," Tamsyn said, taking a piece of artichoke and lifting it to her lips. "You have an amazing setting here."

Finn nodded. "I love it. I could never imagine living anywhere else."

"I used to feel that way about The Masters…" Tamsyn let her voice trail away.

Right now she wondered if she'd ever feel it was home again. She felt so disordered, as if her life was so jumbled that she might never feel settled again.

"Used to?"

"Things change," Tamsyn said with a shrug, thinking of both the lie her father had perpetuated for most of her life—letting her and Ethan think their mother had died—and Trent's duplicity. "People frequently turn out to be someone different to what you thought."

There was more to it than that. The lies had driven her away...but with the perspective that came from distance, she realized that she hadn't been happy, even before she knew the truth. She'd always felt safe at The Masters—sheltered and protected. But she'd never felt truly, fully alive. Nothing about her job had her deeply invested; nothing in her personal life made her deeply happy. Perhaps she'd outgrown "safe and sheltered." Maybe she needed something more.

"Sounds deep. Want to talk about it?"

Tamsyn sat silent for a moment or two. Did she want to talk about it? She wasn't sure. She certainly didn't want to spoil what had started out to be a lovely evening by delving into her doubts and questions.

"Not really," she decided out loud. "I'll deal with it in my own way."

"If you ever need an ear or a shoulder—" he tapped himself on the chest "—you can apply here."

They turned their discussion to generalities about the area and Finn soon had Tamsyn in stitches over some of the stories about Gladys from the hall office from when he was a boy. Seems she'd been old even then. Mind you, Tamsyn mused, maybe some people were just born old.

Finn suggested they return inside after he'd grilled the steaks. He turned perfectly baked potatoes onto their plates together with their steaks and took them to a casual dining table just inside the French doors. He put her salad onto the table, poured them each a glass of red wine and sat down.

By the time they finished, it was growing dark. They lingered over their wine, Tamsyn mindful that she still had to negotiate the driveway and a small section of road before she reached home tonight.

"You know," she said, gesturing to the darkening vista spread before them, "where your house is reminds me a lot of Masters Rise. It was our family home before it was destroyed by bushfires nearly forty years ago. But it had an outlook like this, over the vineyards."

"It must have been a struggle for your family rebuilding after the fire."

"Yeah, it was. I think that's part of the reason our father was so distant with us as kids. He was focused on re-creating what the old days had been like for the family. Between him, his brother and my aunt, they have all had a hand in restoring the vineyards and the family business. It was pretty demanding."

So demanding that the man hadn't had time for his wife, Finn thought angrily. He'd been eight years old when Lorenzo and Ellen had arrived here and he still remembered the incredibly fragile woman Ellen had been. One thing had been constant for her, though. Her love for the children she'd been forced to leave behind. And now one of them sat here, with him. Finally making an effort to reconnect with a woman for whom it was all very possibly too late.

Finn forced his attention back to his guest.

"And your mother, where did she fit into all this?" It was hard to keep his emotions out of his voice.

"You know, I barely remember her. Sure, I have snippets of memories here and there, but I was just turning three when she left. I wonder, sometimes, what kind of woman just walks away from her children."

"There are always two sides to every story."

Finn reached for his wine and took a deep swallow. He ached to defend Ellen, but he couldn't, not without betraying Lorenzo's trust.

Tamsyn laughed. A sound that totally lacked humor, however, and bordered on the satirical.

"In our case I think there are way more than two sides. I grew up thinking my mother was dead. It was kind of a shock to find out she wasn't."

"Dead?"

Finn felt a chill seep through him. What had happened? Had John Masters been so intent on ensuring his wife walked away with nothing from their marriage that he'd even lied to their children? What kind of father did that to his kids? And what did that do to the children when they grew up and learned the truth?

Ten

"Ethan and I only found out recently, after our father died. If Ethan hadn't queried some financial statements in the estate we still wouldn't know."

"Tell me what happened," Finn urged, suddenly reminded of his own words that there were two sides to every story. So far he'd only heard Ellen's version of events through Lorenzo's protective filter.

"All I know is my mother tried to leave my father. Apparently she had Ethan and me in a car with her. She'd…she'd been drinking and lost control. Ethan and I were briefly hospitalized. Dad told our mom she could go if she wanted, but she wasn't taking us with her. He agreed to pay her a monthly sum if she'd stay away. And she did. She just left. Dad had been making payments to her all this time. She accepted money to leave us behind."

"And that's why you want to find her now? To find out why?"

Tamsyn turned her wineglass around and around in her hands and he watched her as she stared at the ruby liquid inside the crystal bowl, her face pensive.

"Yes," she said decisively, putting her wineglass down on the table with an audible clink. "I think I deserve to know why I had to grow up without a mother."

There was still a raw pain echoing in her; Finn could feel it as if it were a tangible thing in the room with them. He felt his earlier assumptions about Tamsyn Masters begin to crumble.

It can't have been easy for a little girl to grow up with a

distant father and no mother, no matter how efficient her nannies must have been and no matter what other family she had around her. Kids needed their parents, both of them. He'd been lucky, at least for the first twelve years of his life and then, subsequently, with the love and support given to him by Lorenzo and Ellen.

"Don't get me wrong, I didn't want for anything at all growing up. Ethan and I were close, he's always been so protective of me, Dad loved me in his way and I've always been tight with my cousins. I just want to know why she left us. Why we were so unimportant to her that she could just walk away."

Finn ached to tell her there was so much more to Ellen's story than that, but it wasn't his information to share.

"I hope you get to find your answers," he said softly, at a loss as to what else to say.

"Yeah, me, too." Tamsyn gave him a wobbly smile.

"So, about dessert," Finn said, injecting a lighter note into his voice. "Are you ready for some?"

"Sure, bring it on. I've already eaten way too much this evening, what're a few more calories. The seniors at the center are probably going to work it all off me tomorrow anyway."

He reached out and took her plate. From what he could tell, she'd eaten hardly enough to keep going. Still, it wasn't his place to harangue her into stuffing herself. Instead, he retrieved the container of hokey-pokey ice cream from the freezer and dished it up into two bowls. Putting them on a tray and reaching for a container of chocolate sauce, he carried them over to the table.

"Ooh, ice cream!" Tamsyn exclaimed.

"Not just any ice cream," Finn said with a mock-stern expression on his face. "New Zealand's finest."

Tamsyn lifted her spoon and scooped up the tiniest mouthful. "Oh, is that toffee inside it?"

Finn smiled at the expression of sheer delight on her face. "You haven't lived until you've tried it. It's better in a cone, but I thought we should be civilized for our first dinner together. Here," he said, extending the chocolate sauce to her. "Try this on top."

She tried the new combination, the chocolate sauce freezing to a hard crust as it drizzled over the ice cream. A deep sound of appreciation hummed from her throat, sending a jolt of lightning-hot desire straight to his groin. He'd been able to hold it together most of tonight, to keep her at arm's length. But right now he wanted to do nothing more than lay her on the table and eat dessert right off of her. He shifted uncomfortably in his seat.

"Oh, that's good," she said, taking another spoonful. "I can't believe I've lived this long and never tried it."

Finn scooped up a generous mouthful and shoved it in his mouth. Maybe the icy concoction would chill his fiery libido. Difficult to achieve success on that score, he noted, while watching Tamsyn savor every mouthful of her own. Her tongue swept out and traced her upper lip, seeking and finding a tiny trace of chocolate that had lodged there. He closed his eyes briefly, trying to rid himself of the urge to find out what that dainty tongue would feel like on his body. Jeez, he needed to get a grip here.

It wasn't until Tamsyn's spoon fell with a clatter in her bowl that he realized she'd finished. Heaving a sigh of relief, Finn reached for her plate.

"Here, let me take that for you," he said, pushing his chair back.

"Oh, I can do that," Tamsyn insisted, taking both his bowl and hers out of his reach and rising also. "You've already done so much for me this evening. Can I do the dishes before I head off?"

"That would be a definite no," Finn said, following her

into the kitchen. "Besides, that's what dishwashers are for, right?"

"If you're sure…"

"I am," he said, taking her hand and leading her away from the kitchen. "Can I offer you some coffee? My machine isn't as flash as yours, but it makes a good brew."

Tamsyn shook her head. "No, I'd better get going. I want to be fresh for tomorrow. Thank you for tonight. It was really lovely."

"You're welcome, I enjoyed it." *I enjoyed you,* his mind reiterated. He lifted her hand to his lips, pressing a kiss to her knuckles. "I'm glad you came."

"I—um, me, too," she said, suddenly flustered.

As disconcerted as she was, she made no effort to pull away, so Finn did what naturally came next. He leaned forward and kissed her. The instant their lips touched he forgot everything he'd ever thought about her—all the nastiness, all the subtle envy he hadn't even realized he'd allowed to build up over the years. In their place, he allowed himself to be lost in her softness.

Her lips felt like warm petals against his. While a clawing need deep inside him demanded he plunder their tender surface, a voice of reason warned him to hold back, to tease instead, to coax, and when her lips parted on a swift rush of warm breath, he took advantage. He gently sucked her lower lip between his, tentatively tracing his tongue along the tender inner edge.

The shudder that went through her body at his touch saw him step closer. Saw him wrap one arm around her waist, drawing her slender form against his strength, molding her against him. He deepened their kiss, his mind a fog of need and want, and yet beneath it all lay an overpowering urge to cherish.

Her arms snaked around his waist, her hands pressing

flat against his back. Finn fought back a groan of satisfaction as her lips began to move against his, as her tongue boldly followed where his led. She tasted intoxicatingly sweet and he knew, even with this one kiss, he would be addicted forever.

He was shaking when he pulled away. Aware that what they'd shared wasn't enough, would never be enough, but also aware that he didn't want to frighten her away. He could sweep her off her feet…but he'd so much rather she come to him when she was ready.

The pupils of Tamsyn's eyes all but consumed the dark velvet brown of her irises and her lips were slightly swollen from the intensity of their kiss.

"I…I need to go."

"Yeah, I know."

He took her by the hand again and led her through to the front entrance and to her car. He opened her door for her and watched as she settled herself behind the wheel. She reached out to pull the door closed and gave him a small wave before sending her car down the driveway. As Finn watched her taillights disappear down the hill, he wondered how, just a few days ago, he'd ever actually *wanted* to see her drive away.

Tamsyn could barely remember the short drive back to the cottage. Her emotions were in a crazy jumble It had been just a kiss. One normal everyday kiss between two consenting adults. So why had it left her feeling like this? How had a simple caress suddenly become so intense, so complicated, so layered with feeling?

Her entire body vibrated with sensation. When Finn had leaned forward to kiss her she'd expected it to be nice. Nice? She snorted in disgust with herself. She should have known a man like Finn didn't do *nice*. No, he did earth-shattering, mind-blowing, skin-searing fantastic. Not once, with Trent, had she ever experienced a kiss like that. With Finn, her entire body had turned molten, her brain scrambled and then reassembled with one purpose in mind.

And then he'd pulled back. It had left her feeling way off kilter, suddenly fearful that perhaps he hadn't felt the same way as she had. But she'd seen the turbulence in his eyes. Eyes that had darkened to the color of rainwashed slate. Her heart had thrilled to the knowledge that he wanted her with as much force and need as she wanted him. That knowledge, however ephemeral, was balm to her wounded soul.

It shocked Tamsyn to realize that if Finn had suggested they take their embrace further, she would have wholeheartedly thrown caution to the winds and let him take her to bed.

She pulled her car to a halt outside the garage, turned off the engine and sat in the dark, mulling over the enormity of what had happened between them. Where did they go from here? Did he want to take things further? They'd known each other only a few days and yet…

She started suddenly, a small scream erupting from her throat as a dark shape landed on the hood of her car.

"Lucy! You scared me half to death," Tamsyn scolded as she got out of the car and scooped the cat up in her arms.

Lucy merely bunted Tamsyn's chin with her head and began to purr loudly. Inside the house, Tamsyn made sure that the cat was fed and watered and went through to her bedroom. Her mind still raced and, despite all her activity in the garden this morning, she felt totally wired and ready to do something, anything, rather than go to sleep.

Anything? she thought to herself. *How about Finn Gallagher?*

She giggled, earning a quizzical look from Lucy, who after completing her supper, had jumped up onto Tamsyn's bed and begun grooming herself.

The chirp of her phone distracted her from her thoughts. Who could be ringing at this hour?

"Hello?" she answered cautiously.

"It's me, Finn. I just wanted to check and see if you got home safely."

Warmth spread through her body in response to his rich deep voice.

"I did, and thank you again for tonight. I enjoyed it." She hesitated a moment before adding, "All of it."

She could hear the smile on his lips as he answered. "Me, too. By the way, I still have your salad bowl. Okay if I drop that around to you tomorrow?"

Her heart leaped in her chest. Okay? Of course it was okay. She couldn't wait to see him again.

"Sure, I'll be home after one."

"I'll be around shortly after, then. Good night, Tamsyn."

"Good night," she whispered, suddenly reluctant to lose the all-too-brief connection between them.

She felt like a teenager waiting for the other person to hang up first, not prepared to be the one to do it herself. She heard the beep as he disconnected the call and finally hit the end button on her phone.

Well, clearly her silly rush to leave after their embrace hadn't put him off wanting to see her again, Tamsyn thought as she brushed her teeth and readied herself for bed. Later, as she lay between her lavender-scented sheets and absently stroked Lucy, who had curled up by her waist, she played the evening back in her mind.

Relived that all-too-brief kiss. A kiss that had ignited a passion she'd feared she was incapable of igniting—both within herself and within a partner. A passion that had been unequivocally reciprocated. The realization was both empowering and terrifying in equal proportions.

She sighed in the dark, squirming a little against the mattress as her body started that slow burn all over again,

aching and wanting. Tamsyn shifted position and tried to
rid her thoughts of anything to do with Finn Gallagher.
God, she thought as she finally began to drift off to sleep,
if a single kiss could leave her this flummoxed, what would
she be like if they ever made love?

Or maybe she should be asking herself, *when* they made
love?

Eleven

Tamsyn made it into town early after a surprisingly deep sleep. It seemed that a delicious meal and good-night kiss from a supersexy man was enough to chase the doubt demons away. She really should do it more often, she thought with a cheeky smile at herself in the rearview mirror of her car.

She parked near the hall and then made her way to the library, determined today to find the librarian, Miriam. The library doors stood open as she approached, always a good sign, and when she entered, she saw that it was doing a brisk business. As she mounted the stairs to the entrance, several people gave her a second glance—something she was beginning to get used to around here. Perhaps they treated all newcomers that way.

An older woman, with hair an interesting shade of pale blue, was busy checking out books at the front desk. Tamsyn waited until the line receded before stepping forward.

"Excuse me, I'm looking for Miriam. Gladys sent me."

"Oh, you must be the new seniors' coordinator," the woman said brightly, her pale blue eyes sparkling through the lenses of her pink wire-framed glasses.

"Yes, temporarily at least." Tamsyn smiled. "Are you Miriam?"

"Yes, dear, I am. How can I help you? Looking for a specific title?"

The woman changed windows on the computer in front of her and looked expectantly at Tamsyn, her hands poised over the keyboard.

"I'm looking for my mother, actually. Ellen Masters. I

was wondering if I could view the electoral rolls to see if she's still a resident in the area."

"The electoral rolls? Did Gladys send you here for those?"

"Well, she did say you'd know where I could find information about people living in the area."

"Hmm." Miriam slipped her glasses off her face and chewed thoughtfully on the tip of one arm. "Well, the electoral rolls aren't kept here. They used to be at the post office, but since all the smaller ones were closed down some years ago, your best bet for that information would be in Blenheim, or even Nelson. What did you say your mother's name was?"

"Ellen Masters, have you heard of her?"

Tamsyn held her breath, hoping against hope that Miriam would smile and tell her that of course she knew her mother, but her hopes were dashed as the older woman shook her pale blue head.

"I don't know anyone of that name."

Tamsyn forced a smile to her face. "Thanks anyway."

"You're welcome, dear, and good luck for today."

"Today?"

"With the oldies," Miriam said with a conspiratorial wink.

"You think I'll need it?" Tamsyn said, this time with a genuine smile.

"Some of those old men can be a bit of a handful. Mind you, most of them always were. You'd best hurry on then. You don't want to be late on your first day."

Miriam hadn't been kidding, Tamsyn realized later on. Every man there, whether he be in a wheelchair or ambulatory, was an incorrigible flirt. By the time twelve-thirty rolled around she'd received no less than three offers of marriage and a few offers of other things she wouldn't touch with a barge pole. It was all in fun, though, and as she took the box with the door takings to Gladys she felt as if she'd been a part of something worthwhile for a change.

Her life had become so superficial, she realized as she said her goodbyes to Gladys. She'd lost touch with the simpler things, the ones that made her feel valuable and valued. At The Masters, her work had become a daily treadmill of boosting sales for their luxury accommodations and winning business for functions and weddings, together with all the various, and sometimes outrageous, requests those events demanded. Even events that should have been meaningful lost their warmth and humanity when they became that grand and elaborate. Her work had stopped being personally satisfying a long time ago.

Today had been a much-needed shot in the arm. A reminder that a little effort, a little care, went a long way. Tomorrow she would go into Blenheim again and find those blasted electoral rolls and, if she had no luck there she'd also go to Nelson.

Gladys was on the phone and just waved at Tamsyn to put the box with the takings on her desk. Tamsyn did so and then walked to her car. She wound the windows down to let out the accumulated heat and checked her phone. In her email, she saw a forwarded mail from their father's lawyer confirming the address she'd been given was the correct one.

She struck her steering wheel in frustration. It was like being caught in a continual loop, each time ending with Finn Gallagher. Surely if he knew anything about her mother at all, he would have said something by now? It just didn't make any sense. Still puzzling over the situation, she started her car and headed back to the cottage.

Tamsyn kept the car windows down on her drive, hoping the breeze whipping through would help clear her mind. As she turned up the driveway, she heard the roar of a mower.

It grew louder the closer she got to the house. Her eyes widened in appreciation as she espied the source of the noise.

Dressed in jeans and rubber boots and with a pair of earmuffs bracketing his head, Finn Gallagher rode a mower across the tangled lawn, making short work of the piles of weeds she'd left the other day as well as the overlong grass. The sweet scent of freshly cut grass hung in the heated air, but it was nowhere near as sweet as the view of raw male that presented itself to her.

Sweat gleamed across the tanned surface of his back and she watched the muscles at his shoulders bunch and shift as he turned the wheel. A deep throb built inside her body, sending heat and moisture of a different kind to pool at the juncture of her thighs. Finn executed a neat three-point-turn and began to drive the mower toward her, his hand lifting in acknowledgment as he saw her standing there.

She was grateful she didn't need to speak because right now, with him driving toward her, shirtless, she doubted she'd be able to form a single comprehensible word. Lines of sweat gathered in the ridges of Finn's taut abdomen. It seemed the more moisture collected on his body, the dryer her mouth became.

He cut the engine on the mower and braked to a stop in front of her.

"H-hello," she said hesitantly.

"Hello yourself."

The effect of his smile curled all the way to her toes.

"I finished my work early this morning and came down to return your salad bowl. I've left it at the front door," he said and gestured to the veranda. "Since I was at a loose end, I thought I'd surprise you with the lawns."

Oh, he'd surprised her, all right.

"You look…hot," she said, feeling a fair amount of that heat radiating all over her body.

"I wouldn't mind a drink of water."

"I'll get you some."

She shot away, more as a measure of self-preservation than anything else. In the kitchen she sloshed cold tap water into a jug, sliced a lemon and threw the pieces into the water together with some ice from the freezer and a sprig of mint from the plant at the back door, then put the jug and two glasses on a tray. Several deep steadying breaths later, she carried the tray out onto the veranda.

"Here," she said, pouring a glass of water for Finn and handing it to him.

"Thanks."

He took the glass and downed it in a couple of long easy swallows. Tamsyn was mesmerized by the muscles working in his throat and forced herself to look away.

"Another?" God, was that her voice? That weird strangled sound?

"You read my mind," Finn answered, handing her his glass.

Thank goodness he wasn't reading hers, she thought quietly. She swiftly poured him another glass of water and handed it to him, this time determined not to watch as he drank it. But where did that leave her to look? At the breadth of his bare shoulders? The small dark brown nipples that lay flat on his chest? Or maybe she should watch the trail of a bead of sweat as it trickled over those too-perfect abs and down past the waistband of his jeans.

She'd be needing to tip a glass of water over herself if she continued like this. Instead, she picked up her glass and drank.

"How did your first day go?" Finn asked, leaning one hip against the veranda railing.

"It was good, thanks. The women were a little wary of me to begin with, the men hopeless wannabe Romeos, which was sweet. Overall I think I held my own. Next week will probably be easier. At least, I hope so."

"They didn't scare you off?"

"It'd take more than that to put me off. When I commit to something, I like to go all the way."

The words hung in the air between them, her unintended double entendre assuming the proportions of a six-foot-high neon sign. Tamsyn wished the wooden floor could just open up and swallow her whole.

"I'm pleased to hear it," Finn said, putting his glass on the wide veranda railing and fixing her with his gaze.

A flutter started in her chest and she knew they weren't talking about the community work anymore. The fine hairs on her forearms rose in a prickle of awareness and heat flooded the lower regions of her body. Her fingers curled tight around her glass. Any minute now there'd be steam rising, she thought. If she reacted like this to just a look, how would she feel when he touched her—really touched her?

She couldn't wait to find out.

"I'd better get back to the lawns," he said, breaking the spell that bound her in its sensual haze. "I'm heading out tonight and will be away until Friday afternoon. Will you be okay until then?"

"Okay? Of course. I should be fine." Tamsyn smiled to hide the disappointment that flooded her at his words. It shocked her to realize just how easily she'd become dependent on these moments they'd shared each day. "It'll give me time to do some more research in my hunt for my mother."

Was it her imagination or did Finn's face suddenly harden? No, it had to just be the effect of the sun slipping behind a cloud, casting him into a pocket of shade, she decided.

"How's that going?" he asked, picking up his glass and bringing it over to put it on the tray beside her.

He smelled delicious. Warm and slightly sweaty, but with a freshness about him that made her wish she could press her nose against his bare flesh and inhale more deeply. I she knew him better, more intimately, she'd close that final distance between them, lay her hand on the broad plane of his chest—feel the hardness of his strength, the nub of his nipple, beneath her palm.

"Tamsyn?" he asked, jerking her from her suddenly inconvenient daydream.

"Um, not so well, actually," she said, trying to gather her scattered thoughts together. It was about as easy as hunting down the free-range eggs the chickens on the property seemed to delight in hiding all over the place. "But I'm going to go to Blenheim tomorrow to see if I can find her on the electoral roll. It'll be a start. What I don't understand is why Dad's lawyer is certain that your address is the right one for her. It's where they insist they've been sending her mail. You're not hiding her somewhere, are you?"

Tamsyn laughed but didn't miss the change in Finn's body language. He angled himself away from her and she felt a definite cooling in the air between them.

"I'm certainly not hiding anyone at my house," he said firmly.

She put a hand out, touched his forearm. His skin was moist and hot, his muscles bunching under her fingertips.

"I didn't mean to offend you, Finn."

He moved away. "You didn't. I'm going to finish the lawns and then I'm heading back up to my place. I'll put the ride-on back in the shed when I'm done."

"Thanks, and thanks for doing the lawns for me. I was getting around to it."

"No problem," he said, stepping down off the veranda and striding toward the mower.

The roar of its engine precluded any further attempt at communication. What had she said to make him so reserved all of a sudden? She played their conversation over in her mind. The only thing she could think of was her allusion to him hiding her mother. Had there been some truth to her question? No, there couldn't be. If there was, why would he have denied her mother's being there right from the start? Tamsyn couldn't quite figure it out. But one way or another, she was going to.

Twelve

Finn shoved the earmuffs back onto his head and steered the mower around the back of the property. Irritation burned inside his gut. Irritation at himself, at Tamsyn, at Lorenzo—hell, at the whole world. It was crazy having her stay here right in Lorenzo and Ellen's home. She was bound to discover the truth eventually, yet Lorenzo was still adamant that Finn do whatever he could to ensure she be kept in the dark. Lorenzo was lucky that the network of friends they had in and around town were equally as protective of Ellen's fragile peace of mind as he was. So far no one had let anything slip.

But every day she stayed here, every day she went into town, the odds increased that Tamsyn would stumble over something or someone that would lead her to her mother. And what if, for some reason, she gained access to the locked room? He knew the deadlock on the door was a good one—he'd installed it himself and had the only key on a hook in a cupboard in his office, but it still made him uneasy to think of how many secrets were separated from Tamsyn by only one door.

He executed a line and turned to come back the other way, constantly aware of Tamsyn's presence inside the cottage. She was going to be devastated when she found out the truth. And furious with him. Lorenzo had put him in an untenable position, one he planned to discuss with the older man tomorrow morning when he caught up with him in Wellington.

Finn had to meet with some business associates during his time in the capital city, but he planned to spend as much time as he could at the hospital with Ellen, too. He needed to see for himself if she'd be capable of withstanding a visit from the daughter she'd left so long ago.

He tried not to think about what had happened with his own mother. About how her mental state had been so fragile that when her medical team had finally deemed her well enough to have a visit from her only son, it had tipped her completely over the edge instead. All the twelve-year-old Finn had known at the time was that he was somehow responsible for what had happened. That seeing him, a younger version of his father, had made her elect to give up resuming her old life. That it would make her choose to opt out of life altogether.

He couldn't let that happen to Ellen. Couldn't let that happen to another mother figure in his life. But he couldn't stand the thought that choosing to protect Ellen set Tamsyn up to be hurt instead.

Finn finished the lawns and rode the mower toward the implements shed. He grabbed his T-shirt from the shelf where he'd thrown it and tugged it on. He hadn't been oblivious to Tamsyn's unmasked appreciation of his body. If he hadn't been so determined to tread softly with her he might have done something about it today, but her casually thrown out remark about him hiding her mother had hit just a little too close to the mark.

He *was* hiding Ellen from her. Maybe not physically, but he was definitely keeping the truth from her. A truth he was struggling now to justify keeping to himself. He forced himself to clear his mind. To focus instead on his visit to Wellington and the decisions he would make after he'd seen Ellen for himself. And the fight he would no doubt have with Lorenzo when he made them.

Friday rolled around all too slowly. Tamsyn had been achingly aware of the empty house up on the hill the whole time Finn had been away. It had left her unsettled, especially as they'd parted on what she thought were less than good terms. She hoped to rectify that today and had already left a message on his voice mail inviting him for dinner at the cottage tonight. Depending on how his trip had gone, she hoped he'd prefer an evening where he didn't have to fend for himself. Even so, her voice had been a little on the wobbly-nervous side when she'd left her message.

Yesterday's trip into Blenheim had been another wasted effort and today's to Nelson was no better. She was beginning to wonder if her mother had even lived in the region at all. It was hard not to just give up on it all and walk away.

She reminded herself that today marked only the seventh day since she'd arrived in New Zealand. It was still way too early to call it quits. Maybe she needed some professional help in her quest, though. Next week she might look into hiring a private investigator.

Somehow, though, she was reluctant to turn the search over to someone else. This was her journey, her need to find her mother. She wanted so much to have control over it. Her father had taken away her right to know her mother. Trent had taken away her right to expect happiness and a future through their relationship. She'd worked too hard for too long to please men who, in the end, had chosen what was best for themselves with no genuine regard for her feelings or needs.

So where did that leave her with Finn? She sank into a worn easy chair in the sitting room of the cottage and stared out the bay window. Lucy, as usual, sat in pride of place, her eyes drifting closed in the sun now her toilette was complete.

Finn hadn't made her any promises. He'd just been here. Available—except for the past two days. He hadn't pushed her when they'd kissed on Tuesday night, a kiss she still relived in all its sensation-soaked glory each night when she went to bed, leaving her sleep fractured and her body unrested and aching with unresolved tension. She'd tried physical exertion around the cottage to wear herself out each afternoon and into the early evening, but it had only served to add more aches upon the pains. Even a soak in the large tub each evening hadn't been enough to ease them away.

Tamsyn let her eyes drift closed, let her senses relax, her body sag into the chair. Outside she could hear the birds and the drone of the bumblebees that favored the flowering plants she'd revealed among the weeds. It wasn't long before she'd drifted off to sleep.

She woke with a start about an hour later. Her phone was ringing. Where the heck had she left it? She staggered to where she'd left her handbag.

"Hello?" she answered groggily.

"Did I wake you?"

Finn's voice filled her ear, warming her from the inside out.

"Caught me napping, guilty as charged," she answered, trying to keep her voice light, especially considering the awkwardness that had developed between them the last time they spoke.

"I'm jealous."

It sounded as if a faint smile played around his lips. Tamsyn hugged one arm around herself and leaned against the wall, imagining his face as he spoke.

"Don't be, I've given myself a crick in the neck."

"Maybe I can help you out with that later on," he said smoothly. "I'm told I have good hands."

A flush suffused her body. She just bet he did. Broad palms, long capable fingers. Her legs weakened just at the thought.

"I got your message," he continued, "and yes, I'd love to come for dinner tonight. What can I bring?"

"How about a nice bottle of wine from that impressive collection of yours," she suggested. "Something white. I'm doing chicken. Nothing fancy."

It was one of the few things she could cook successfully. Growing up at The Masters they'd had staff for just about everything, something she'd learned to appreciate when she'd gone to university and had had to fend for herself in the kitchen of the small flat she'd shared.

"Anything I don't have to cook and prepare myself sounds great. What time do you want me?"

Want him? Oh, about 24/7, to be totally honest. She gathered the raveled strands of her mind together and gave them a swift tug into submission.

"Sixish suit you?"

"Perfect. See you then."

He ended the call, leaving her standing there like a lovesick teenager still holding the phone to her ear. The disconnect signal beeping in her ear galvanized her into action. It was four o'clock, and she still had so much to do. She swept into the kitchen and grabbed the two chicken breasts she'd put into the fridge last night to defrost. Still a bit on the icy side, she realized, and put their plate on the countertop to finish defrosting, covering them carefully so Lucy wouldn't be tempted to check them out.

Okay, what was she going to do with the chicken? Stuff it? She mentally went over the range of ingredients she had at her disposal and decided on a carpetbag-style concoction that had been popular with her flatmates. She even had some frozen scallops in the freezer to stuff the chicken with. She put them on a separate plate to defrost, making a mental note to replace them the next time she shopped for groceries.

Boiled baby potatoes, seasoned with parsley butter, and asparagus spears would be a perfect accompaniment to the chicken. Moving swiftly, Tamsyn prepared a marinade for the meat, throwing the almost-defrosted breasts into a dish with lemon juice, tarragon, some finely chopped garlic, salt and ground black pepper and covering it again.

The baby potatoes were easy. She grabbed the box she'd bought at a grocery store on the way back from Nelson and rinsed a few under the kitchen faucet before popping them in a saucepan with water and a dash of salt and setting them on the stove to cook later. The asparagus she rinsed and snapped and put in a dish ready to steam in the microwave just before serving. She wished she'd paid more attention at home when the cook had prepared hollandaise sauce with their asparagus dishes, and contemplated looking up a recipe on the internet. In the end she decided against it. What if it didn't work? She'd rather have a practice at it first before dishing it up to Finn, who had served her such a delicious dinner, himself. She badly wanted to impress him.

She sobered for a minute, the wild excitement of planning and preparing her meal deserting her. Insecurity trickled its icy fingers into the corners of her mind. What, in all honesty, was she trying to prove? Was she so desperate for male approval that she was prepared to put herself through hoops again already?

Tamsyn stepped away from the kitchen counter and walked out the back door, sinking onto the wooden steps that led down to the vegetable garden. She pulled her knees up under her chin, growling at herself under her breath. She needed to get a grip, to stop defining herself by the men in her life.

She'd invited Finn to dinner because she enjoyed his company and, frankly, enjoyed the way he made her feel. She wanted to know if that feeling could go further, that was all. And, whether it did or it didn't, she would handle it like an adult.

They would enjoy a nice meal together, then a nice evening together. What happened next…well, she shrugged and pushed herself back up to her feet again. What*ever* happened next, just happened.

She went back into the kitchen and turned the chicken. She had the main course planned, which left her with a question. What was she going to do for dessert? She opened the refrigerator and studied its contents again. Cheese and crackers with some fresh sliced fruit? It would have to do, she decided. She was no Cordon Bleu cook by any means. Which left predinner nibbles… She hoped he liked crudités with hummus. She could slice some carrot sticks and celery as well as a red bell pepper and arrange them all on a plate.

Right, the food was sorted, which just left her. What the heck was she going to wear? She thought for a minute then decided on the gypsy-style skirt she'd bought yesterday from the boutique in town. Another item by the same designer as her purple-and-blue dress, it had cost a pretty penny, but the swirl of color, in shades of coral over a sumptuous midnight blue, and the sheer femininity of the item had filled Tamsyn with delight. She'd team it with a blue silk knit singlet and a pair of navy ballet flats that she'd picked up while in Nelson today.

Satisfied she'd done all she could for now in the kitchen, Tamsyn quickly zoomed through the sitting room, clearing away old newspapers and tidying the stack of magazines on the shelf under the coffee table. There, tidy, but not staged. She groaned. Who was she kidding? She was staging everything in anticipation of Finn being here tonight. It didn't matter how sternly she talked to herself, deep down it mattered to her what he thought.

Acknowledging that was a freedom in itself and allowed her to make a decision about another question that had been playing around the back of her mind. She went straight to the linen cupboard in the passageway and grabbed out fresh linen for her bed.

She was going to be prepared for every eventuality tonight. Come what may.

Thirteen

Finn approached the cottage slowly. His visit to Wellington had gone well, businesswise, but not so well when it came to Ellen. For the first time, she hadn't recognized him. He'd expected it, thought he'd been prepared for it, yet when it happened it hurt far more than he'd ever anticipated.

Lorenzo had been apologetic, Alexis understanding, but none of it made up for the fact that Ellen was slowly but surely slipping away from them all—and that included Tamsyn. She was running out of time to meet her mother. It put him between a rock and a hard place. Lorenzo remained adamant that Tamsyn be kept from finding Ellen.

In some ways Finn totally agreed. He knew that the woman Tamsyn would see was not the mother she had hoped to find. Ellen was far past the point of being able to answer the questions Tamsyn carried. Perhaps it would have simply been easier for everyone if Tamsyn continued to believe her mother had passed away. Rare now were the days when there was even a glimmer of understanding in Ellen's faded brown eyes.

Lorenzo was never far from her side, constantly on the alert for the opening of those precious windows in her mind—each one a gift beyond price. While Finn warred with Tamsyn's right to at least see her mother, could he honestly deny Lorenzo those moments? What if seeing Tamsyn sent Ellen hurtling away into the far reaches of her dementia? Her last days would be nothing more than hours of emptiness for those who loved and cared for her. Finn couldn't do that to another human being.

He pulled his SUV to a halt at the end of the driveway

and pulled himself together. He probably shouldn't have accepted Tamsyn's invitation tonight. He doubted he'd be good company, but when he'd heard her voice mail issuing the offer, he knew he couldn't deny himself the respite of her company.

Finn grabbed the wine carrier, with its two chilled bottles of wine nestled inside in one hand, and the bunch of tulips he'd bought at the florist's after getting Tamsyn's call in the other. The soft pink long-stemmed blooms reminded him of her—their exquisite smooth petals a perfect shield for their additional beauty when they opened to the sun. She was just like that. Guarded smooth walls of perfection on show to the rest of the world, and yet when she was given warmth and affection she flourished.

He nudged the car door shut with his hip and covered the distance to the house in long strides. Now he was here, he was eager to see her again. She opened the door before he could juggle his items and knock.

The sight of her knocked the breath clean out of his lungs. She had her hair up in some twisted knot on top of her head, exposing the slender arch of her neck and making her look divinely feminine and impossibly fragile at the same time. Every male hormone in his body rose to the occasion, making him ache to be her knight—to be that one man to protect her from all wrongdoing, from all sorrow. He swallowed hard. No woman had ever made him feel this way, so desperate to be her valiant defender. The sensation was primal and dark, yet uplifting and filled with warmth at the same time.

"Good evening, are those for me?" she asked, reaching for the tulips that he'd forgotten the instant he'd laid eyes on her.

"Yeah, I hope you like them."

"I love them, thank you so much. Come inside."

She stepped aside to let him in and as he walked past her

he caught a whiff of her fragrance. Subtle, like her, like the way she'd inveigled her way into his psyche, the blend of sweetness and spice wound around him in a sensual spell of promise.

"I'll pop these in some water right away. Can I take the wine through to the kitchen for you?"

"It's okay, I'll do that," he said, still feeling a little awe-struck.

She'd done something with her makeup that made her dark eyes look huge and warm, and the fresh pink lipstick she wore made him itch to lean forward and kiss it all off. And there was something different about her tonight—a soft confidence that radiated from her. It was there in the smile in her eyes and in the way she walked. He liked it, he decided. He liked it very much.

In the kitchen Finn automatically reached for the champagne flutes on the hutch dresser and extracted a bottle of a locally made sparkling wine. The second bottle, a sauvignon blanc, he put into the refrigerator.

"Are we celebrating?" Tamsyn asked, noting the label on the bottle. "Oh, I've always wanted to try that."

"It's very good. It's been made here in Marlborough since the late 1980s. They blend seventy percent pinot noir with thirty percent chardonnay. Here," he said, passing her a glass filled with the rapidly bubbling straw-colored liquid. "Try it."

"I can't do that without a toast," she said with a secretive smile. She raised her glass toward his. "To new friends."

He liked that, although right now his feelings toward Tamsyn Masters went way beyond friendly. He clinked glasses. "Indeed, to new friends."

Their eyes remained locked together as they sipped their wine. He'd never be able to drink it again without thinking of this moment—of her.

"Mmm, that is lovely," she said, flicking her tongue over

her lower lip as she set her glass down on the countertop and picked up the vase of flowers. "Can you bring my wine while I take these to the sitting room?"

Finn reached for the glass, and followed her through. She was as enticing from the rear as she'd been face on. The sway of her hips as she walked made the fabric of her skirt swing gently from side to side, caressing her thighs and the backs of her calves. He'd never been envious of a skirt before. It was a new and distinctly unfamiliar sensation.

He could not, in all honesty, say that his growing feelings for Tamsyn were normal. Not in his experience, anyway. These feelings were consuming. Invading his concentration and disturbing his usually short but fully restful sleep at night.

"Crudité?"

He looked up as Tamsyn passed him a small platter decorated with vegetable sticks and one of those dips females seemed to like so much.

"Sure," he said, helping himself to both.

It was tasty, the garlic and lemon tang in the hummus leaving a fresh aftertaste in his mouth. Maybe there was something to the dip after all.

"How was your trip away?" she asked, settling herself on the sofa and slipping her feet out of her ballet slippers to tuck them up beside her.

He took the chair opposite, not trusting himself to sit closer.

"Ah, yeah, Wellington. It's a beautiful city."

"And your business? It went well?" she continued.

"It did."

"But something's still bothering you, isn't it? You looked…I dunno, worried, when you arrived. Is everything okay?"

Damn, did it show that much? He decided sticking close

to the truth was better than fabricating a whole bunch of lies that he might struggle to remember.

"I spent some time visiting a good friend in the hospital. It was hard to see them so unwell."

"I'm really sorry to hear that," Tamsyn said softly, her voice filled with genuine sympathy.

"Thanks."

Finn took a long drink of his sparkling wine. It served as a good way to stop himself from giving her any more details about exactly who he'd been seeing. As if sensing he didn't want to talk about it further, Tamsyn shifted the conversation to what she'd been doing the past couple of days while he'd been gone. He felt a tug of relief when he heard she had gotten no further in her search for Ellen, but that tug was tempered with a powerful sense of guilt over her very evident disappointment.

She worked her way past it though and the conversation soon shifted to books they'd recently read. She had a very sharp wit and they enjoyed many of the same authors. By the time she served cheese and crackers and fruit back in the sitting room after dinner, Finn was feeling very relaxed. Due in part to the glasses of wine they'd shared, but mostly due to her company. He'd enjoyed entertaining her at his house a couple of nights ago, but he loved watching her in this environment too. She was more in control here, adapting this place to her own patch. Now, as they sat side by side on the sofa, he was looking forward to seeing more.

"You never mentioned you were such a great cook," Finn said, slicing a sliver of ripe Brie and placing it on a lightly flavored rice cracker.

"That was the sum total of my expertise. Ooh, could you pass me one of those, please?" she said with a cheeky smile, and leaned forward to accept it from him as he changed its trajectory from his lips to hers.

Her teeth bit into the cracker, her lips brushing the tips of his fingers just as he started to pull away. The butterfly-soft sensation of her skin on his set up a chain reaction through his body and he suddenly found himself craving the feel of her lips everywhere.

"More?" he asked, his eyes fixed on her face as she clearly relished the morsel he'd fed her.

"Yes, please," she answered. "More."

A tremor rippled through him. He hoped she meant what he was thinking she meant. He went through the motions again, spreading some of the ripe cheese on a cracker and taking it to her mouth. This time she lightly grasped his wrist, held his hand in front of her parted lips. When she took the cracker she lingered over the action. Her lips, this time, deliberately grazing his thumb and forefinger.

Finn's body went from semi-aroused and languidly comfortable, to rock hard and aching in a nanosecond. A crumb from the cracker fell to the top of the curve of her breast. All night he'd been treated to the enticing shadow of her décolletage, but now he had fair reason to explore further. Without wasting a moment, he bent his head and licked up the crumb. Beneath his mouth her skin contracted and a flush of color spread across its surface.

She tasted like more. Like sunshine and heat and warmth and woman. He was starving—for her. He traced his tongue on her skin again, heard her moan, felt her drop her head onto the back of the sofa, exposing the tantalizing line of her throat. He welcomed the invitation and nuzzled the point where her shoulder curved up to the side of her neck and pressed his mouth into the hollow just above her collarbone.

Her gasp of pleasure urged him on and he continued his journey up, to the fine contour of her jaw, to the corner of her lush lips. Then, finally, to capture those lips with his once more. She was no quiescent participant this time around, instead she was heat and fire all focused on that point where their bodies fused and melded.

It wasn't enough, it could never be enough. Finn raised shaking hands to her waist and began to tug at her top even as he felt her fingers working his shirt buttons. He yanked the stretchy material up, exposing the soft curves of her belly—the striations of her rib cage, the swell of the underside of her breasts fettered inside flimsy lace—to his ravening touch. Still, he wanted more.

Fourteen

Tamsyn squirmed against him, frustrated by the barriers of their clothes. She wanted to feel—him, everything—like she'd never felt before. Her fingers fumbled on his buttons and impatiently she tugged even harder, barely noticing as she ripped the remaining fastenings from the cotton of his shirt.

Finally, she could do what she'd wanted to for what felt like so long. Her hand spread upon his heated skin, sweeping across his chest, her fingers lingering to gently pinch his nipples into even tighter nubs. In answer to her actions, she felt his teeth at her neck—a gentle-enough nip, but one that made every internal muscle in her body clench on a white-hot wave of sensation. She felt as if she could melt right here on the spot.

Her singlet was bunched at the top of her breasts and she lifted herself forward, holding on to his torso as he pulled the garment up and over her head.

"God, you're so beautiful," he groaned against her skin, his mouth hot and wet against her.

She shifted, offering herself toward him in aching invitation. Finn continued to torment her, his tongue lightly tracing the contours of the lace of her bra. Why, oh why, had she worn one? The rasp of his teeth through the lace sent a jolt of electricity spiraling into her body. Her nipples pebbled into painfully taut beads, the texture of her bra near unbearable as she waited for his touch.

"There, oh please, there," she begged, threading her fingers through his short cropped hair and holding him to her.

She felt his hand reach around behind her, felt the clasp

of her bra fall undone and her flesh become exposed as he peeled the garment away. Hot breath tantalized, her heart now beating a frantic tattoo as she anticipated what came next. She wasn't disappointed. Closing over her peak, he drew her into his mouth, his tongue drawing her in deep, his teeth a gentle scrape against oversensitized skin.

Something pulled deep inside her, as if the two most sensitive parts of her body were joined by one glorious shimmering thread.

Finn shifted his attention to her other breast, eliciting the same penetrating response. She was panting, her mind fracturing as sensation after sensation poured through her body. He pulled away from her and she murmured in protest, her hands reaching for him.

"Let's take this to the bedroom," he said, his voice uneven.

He rose to his feet and offered her his hand to help her up. She was grateful to him for that as her legs felt like water, almost incapable of holding her up. As if he knew, he swept one arm behind her back, the other behind her knees, and lifted her into his arms. Instinctively she burrowed her face in his chest. Her lips caressing the smooth skin, her hands now clasped around his neck.

"Which one?" he asked, his breathing barely changing as he carried her.

"Second on the right," she whispered.

When they reached the door, he slid her to her feet, stabilizing her with his solid presence. She reached up, cupping his face between her hands and, going up on tiptoe, she kissed him—long and deep, leaving him in no doubt that she wanted every second of what was yet to come.

Outside it was growing dark and she pulled away to close the bedroom drapes. Even though there was no chance anyone could see them from the roadside, she wanted to close them in, to cocoon them in their own little world. He sat on the bed and toed off his loafers and shed his socks as she moved around, lighting the candles she'd placed throughout the room—just in case tonight would end this way.

"Come here," Finn said as he sat with his legs spread wide on the edge of the bed.

Tamsyn moved between them, resting her hands on his shoulders. He flicked one nipple lightly with the tip of his finger.

"A man could be forgiven for thinking he's being seduced," he said with a knowing smile.

"A man could," she agreed with a laugh, loving that even as her body wound tight as a drum, they could still find humor in their situation.

"Should I be asking what your intentions are?"

"Only if you're man enough to hear them," she teased, lifting her hands up to pull the pins from her hair, one by one, until it tumbled over her bare shoulder, tendrils teasing her breasts.

She reached behind her to unzip her skirt, let it drop in a cascade of color and softness and kicked it away from her feet. Finn's eyes roamed her body as she stood there, dressed only in a scrap of café au lait–colored lace and satin. The appreciation, the marvel on his face gave her a strength she'd never known she was capable of possessing.

Emboldened, Tamsyn skimmed her hands over her belly and up over her rib cage, until she cupped her breasts in both hands. His eyes darkened, his tongue swept out to moisten his lips and she saw a tremor rock through him as she squeezed her nipples between thumbs and forefingers. Moisture pooled, hot and slick, at the apex of her thighs— a steady throb building there as she tweaked and pulled, caught in the spotlight of his stare.

Finn's hands went to the belt of his jeans, making fast— if unsteady—work of the buckle.

"Too damn many clothes," he said through clenched teeth, his eyes never straying from her body.

In seconds he had unbuttoned his fly and shoved his jeans and boxers down over his hips. His erection sprang free, the rigid flesh jutting proudly from a nest of dark curls.

"Man enough for you?" he asked, a tiny smile playing around his lips.

She smiled in return, moving forward to straddle his thighs, her hands at his shoulders. She felt his length twitch against her.

"Oh, I think you'll do," she answered, shifting so she could reach one hand between them.

She wrapped her fingers around the thick, hot shaft and stroked him from base to tip, then shifted slightly so she could reach the small box she'd secreted under her pillow after remaking her bed today. "I think we need to move on to the next step."

"I think you're right and I see you're prepared."

She tapped herself on the chest with one finger. "Event manager, I'm always prepared."

He started to speak, but his words were lost on a hiss of air as she began to apply a condom, adroitly smoothing the thin sheath over his penis.

"I'm an event?" he asked, keeping things light even though his voice was strained.

"No," she corrected him, moving her hips so he was positioned at her entrance. "*We* are."

Banter ceased the instant she began to slide down, to accept him into her body. Tiny shocks zapped her as her muscles accommodated his size. She moaned in pleasure, unable to hold back as he filled her, stretched her, completed her. Finn's hands gripped her hips and he lifted her slowly, hesitating for what felt like an aeon before inching her down again.

She gripped his shoulders as they found their rhythm,

then increased in tempo, spiraling into a cacophony of sensation. Until they peaked together in a penetrating awareness of pleasure that swamped them in forceful waves.

Finn fell back onto the bed, pulling her on top of him. Beneath her cheek she could feel his heart hammering in his chest, feel the answering thud of her own. One of his hands traced up and down her spine, while the other held her firmly to him, anchored at the hip as if he couldn't bear to let her go. She could still feel his pulse inside her, felt the answering squeeze of her own.

"As events go, I'd say that was a resounding success," he said against the top of her head.

She chuckled, filled with a sensation of well-being. She'd never had a relationship like this, one where you could banter and have mind-blowing sex at the same time.

"I'd have to agree," she said, lifting her head and nipping at his chin.

He rolled to the side, finally allowing their bodies to disengage. "Let me get rid of this, I'll be right back."

She watched his taut buttocks and long legs appreciatively as he stepped across the hall to the bathroom and stretched languorously across the bed. She ought to move, to pull the covers down and make the bed comfortable for them both. Unless, now that they'd made love, he planned to leave?

Insecurity flooded her, making her dash across the room to where she'd slung a robe over an easy chair. She shrugged herself into it and knotted the sash, like a barrier across her body.

"What's wrong?" Finn asked as he reentered the room.

"Nothing," she insisted.

He walked straight up to her and gathered her in his arms. "You having regrets?"

"None," she answered as firmly as she could, but even so, she couldn't meet his eyes. "You?"

She tensed, waiting for his reply.

"Same, so why the frown?"

He traced twin lines between her eyebrows with his fore-finger and she forced herself to relax the muscles.

"I—I guess I just don't know what happens next. It's been a while since I...since..." She shook her head in frustration, struggling to find the words she needed to say.

"Since you've been in a new relationship?"

She sagged against him. Was that what this was to him? A relationship? A tiny light of hope flared in her chest. Logically she knew it was far too soon for her to even think about embarking on a new relationship with someone. It had been a week—just one week—since she'd walked in on Trent and Zac. A week since she'd given Trent back his ring and walked away from her old life.

But why shouldn't she grasp this, whatever it was, with Finn while she could? Grasp it and hold it tight, and ride it for what it was worth. It went against her nature, went against every instinct that told her to play it safe...but last time her "safe" choice of boyfriend hadn't been enough to keep her from getting hurt. What did she have to lose by taking the risk?

"Yes," she replied. "And it's not that long since my last one."

"I figured as much. Do you want me to leave?"

"Not at all!" The vehement response was out of her mouth before she could censor it.

Finn laughed. "It's okay if I stay then?"

"Do you want to stay?" There was still that kernel of doubt niggling at the back of her thoughts.

"I do. Very much."

His big warm hands slid up her back and to the back of her head, his fingers sending tingles through her scalp and releasing the tension she had there. When he bent to kiss her it was gentle, reassuring. Not the crazy heady kiss they'd shared earlier, but one that started a mellow simmer that radiated from her core. Between them she could feel his arousal stirring, felt an answering response in her.

She slid her hands around his waist, relishing the taut muscles that played beneath her fingers, relishing the fact he was here, for her and her alone. This was right, for now at least, and, reminding herself of her earlier vow, she meant to make the most of it.

This time their coming together was slow and languid. Each touch a measured stroke, each kiss lingered. When he slid inside her she was hit with that feeling of rightness, and when his long strokes drew them both to climax she tumbled over the precipice knowing she was safe and secure in his arms.

Knowing she could trust him.

Fifteen

Finn lay awake in the predawn hours, Tamsyn sprawled across his chest, her leg across his hips. He'd never been a snuggler, but somehow this felt right. So right he hadn't wanted to lose a moment of it in sleep.

She was so vulnerable, so innocent in all this. He felt like the lowest of the low deceiving her—deliberately holding her back from what she sought. She would never forgive him when she found out, and he didn't doubt that one day she would. The district was too close-knit for Ellen's whereabouts to remain a secret forever.

But for now he had her in his arms, and maybe, just maybe, now that they'd crossed this bridge into intimacy together, he'd be able to keep a closer eye on her—find a way to keep the secret and still protect her for a bit longer.

His fingers curled around her as he thought about the truths she'd shared in the dark, about how she'd happened upon her fiancé and his lover, a man who was *her* PA no less, in bed together. How she'd been betrayed by the two men she'd had every right to trust and expect loyalty from. It made his blood curdle when he heard that her ex had brushed off his affair, still expecting her to carry on as if nothing had happened, as if she deserved no better than to be second best in their life together.

It must have been made even harder for her with the timing—finding out about her fiancé so shortly after discovering the truth behind her father's lie that her mother had died. She had come here to get away from the lies, and the expectations, and the falseness that seemed to fill every aspect of her life. She'd come to find her mother and learn the truth…and instead, she'd found him—master betrayer of them all.

His gut clenched painfully at the thought of the hurt he would inflict on her, of the guilt he carried with him. Another mantle to bear, he realized with a deep breath that filled his senses with her special scent. She stirred in his arms, a small cry erupting from her mouth as she startled awake.

"Finn?" she mumbled, sounding disoriented.

"You okay?"

"I had a bad dream. I couldn't find you."

"I'm right here," he assured her, tightening his arms around her again. "Go back to sleep. I've got you."

For now, he thought as he felt her body relax against his again. But for how much longer?

Tamsyn woke feeling extraordinarily refreshed. She couldn't quite wipe the smile off her face. She'd woken after nine, and couldn't remember the last time she'd ever slept so late. Mind you, she couldn't remember the last time she'd spent half the night making love, either. She stretched against the sheets, wondering what Finn was up to.

The scent of a rosebud perfumed the air and she turned her head toward the source. As she did so, a whisper of paper on the pillow beside her caught her attention. She lifted first the rose, then the sheet of paper, that happy smile widening as she read its contents.

Finn apologized for not being there when she woke and said that business had called him away for the day. He'd be back late that night but hoped to see her again on Sunday. While Tamsyn knew she'd miss him, at least she knew she'd be seeing him again soon. She held the rose to her face, deeply inhaling the heady fragrance, touched that he'd thought to pick it for her and leave it with his note.

Her insecurities of the night before had faded into nothing. She'd never thought she'd ever share with another person, outside her family, what had happened with Trent, but confiding in Finn during the night had been cathartic. He'd listened without judgment and, afterward, he'd made love to her again as if she was the most precious creature on the planet, wiping away any lingering doubts about her attractiveness or femininity.

He was a skilled lover and had driven her body to heights she'd never experienced before. Heights she was looking forward to experiencing again. Hopefully, tomorrow.

Over the next few days they fell into a pattern of sharing meals, and nights, together. For the first time since she'd discovered her mother still lived, Tamsyn's need to find her softened. Oh, she still knew she wanted to track her mother down, but the urgency had faded, and exploring Finn's likes and dislikes held more immediate appeal.

Maybe she was in avoidance mode, as it had occurred to her that she might not like what she discovered. Her mother had chosen not to be part of Tamsyn's life years before. Did she really want to risk the pain of an in-person rejection when she could, instead, focus her time and attention on a man who made her feel so cherished? Being part of a two-some with Finn Gallagher had brought her more happiness in the past week than she'd known in a long time and she reveled in it. Plus, this week at the hall with her community group had gone exceptionally well. Every day, she felt more comfortable and at home in this town.

All in all, life was sweet, she thought as she prepared a meal for one the following Friday night. Finn was away again. He'd been distracted the past couple of days and she had the distinct impression that something was worrying him, but when she'd pressed him, he'd said he was fine.

The wind had come up today and thick black clouds, heavy with rain, banked up in the sky. It looked like it could be a rough night. Tamsyn didn't mind a storm, it was always good for blowing away the cobwebs, but this would be the first time she'd weathered one on her own.

"Prrrp!" Okay, so not completely on her own, she smiled to herself, bending down to stroke Lucy, who wound around and around her legs.

"It's just you and me tonight, Luce," she said before straightening and looking outside.

She'd have to try to round up the chickens into their coop if the weather kept deteriorating. She didn't look forward to the experience but figured with some chicken feed she should be able to tempt them into safety.

After her meal, she did just that, finally settling the last of the birds just as the first big fat drop of rain hurtled from the sky and hit her smack in the forehead. As if it had given carte blanche to the clouds to simply open up, the drops increased until the rain was bucketing down. Tamsyn raced to the house, struggling as the back door was almost torn from her grip by a particularly vicious gust of wind.

She got inside and slammed the door closed. Locking it behind her for good measure. It had only taken seconds but she was drenched to the skin. A long soak in a warm bath with a good book was just what she needed. Lucy curled up on the bath mat beside her as she lit the last candle in the bathroom, shed her wet and now-cold clothing and tested the temperature of the water.

"Perfect." She sighed as she sank into the enveloping warmth and reached for the glass of chardonnay she'd poured to enjoy with her book.

The lights overhead flickered, then brightened.

"Uh-oh," she said to the cat, who appeared unperturbed by the glitch in the electricity. "That doesn't look promising."

The words were no sooner out of her mouth than another massive gust of wind hit the house, causing the lights to flicker again before going out, this time completely. Tamsyn sat upright in the water and waited for them to come back on, but she waited in vain. Deciding she could do nothing about it for now, she dropped her book on the floor next to the bath and sank back in the water. At least she had light, thanks to the candles she'd lit earlier. As for the blackout, well, it would be a good excuse to have an early night.

Her sleep was fractured, punctuated by the crash and boom of thunder as the storm built through the night. Even ducking under the covers and pulling them up over her head did little to block the noise. The time gap between flashes of lightning and the explosive rumbles that followed got shorter and shorter until they seemed to land one on top of the other.

What a night for Finn to pick to be away, Tamsyn thought as she fought the rising fear that clawed at her throat. Even Lucy had deserted the top of the bed and was, Tamsyn suspected, cowering under it instead. She wished there was room enough under there to join her.

Bang! Cr-a-ck! Tamsyn jumped out of her skin. That was too close for comfort, the report sounding as if it was right on top of the house. Should she find a coat and check for damage? Another flash of lightning, followed a few seconds later by an almighty clap of thunder, warned her of the stupidity of that idea. She burrowed back under the covers, pulling her pillow over her ears for good measure. Tomorrow would be soon enough.

Morning dawned, as it so often does after a storm, with a fresh new promise of a beautiful day. Thankfully, at some time during the early hours, the power had been restored. Tamsyn was bleary eyed as she drank her morning coffee and waited for the caffeine to hit her bloodstream. Once she'd finished, she'd borrow a pair of rubber boots from the laundry and inspect outside. Even here from the kitchen window she could see there was some damage from the storm. Plant debris scattered through the vegetable garden and she could see she'd have to tie up the tomatoes again.

Coffee finished, she found the boots and clumped outside. The back of the house didn't look too bad, she thought, gathering up the detritus of leaves and small branches into a wheelbarrow from the implements shed as she went. It wasn't until she was close to the front that she saw the shattered window with a broken tree branch resting half in and half out of the room.

A Venetian blind swung drunkenly in the morning breeze, attached at only one end and, from the looks of it, bent and damaged beyond repair. This had to be the locked room, she thought as she moved closer. The owners wouldn't be happy about this. She'd have to call the property manager and see if they could get someone out to repair the window and contact the owners about replacing the blind. In the meantime, she'd see if she could find something to board the broken window up.

Before she went back to the shed to see if they had any plywood and nails stored there, she moved over to the house. Thankfully, the deep eaves on the property had kept most of the rain out. Broken glass littered the windowsill and, from what Tamsyn could see by jumping repeatedly, the floor of the room inside.

She started to turn for the shed, hoping to return with a stepladder and a saw in addition to plywood and nails. As she did so, the curtain billowed out of the window. She caught a glimpse of what looked to be a framed photo on the opposite wall. Tamsyn turned over the wheelbarrow and stood on it for a better look. The woman in the photo looked familiar....

In fact, she looked very much like the face that greeted Tamsyn in the mirror each morning.

A cold trickle started at the base of her neck and ran a rivulet down her spine. She had to get into that room to make sure she wasn't imagining things. Jumping down from the wheelbarrow, she jogged to the shed and spotted the ladder she needed hanging on the wall, together with a set of leather gardening gloves nearby that would protect her hands from the broken glass.

The rubber boots were going to be too clumsy to wear going up the ladder and through the window frame so, after lugging the ladder and a saw across the lawn to the house, she dashed inside and pulled on the runners she'd bought a couple of weeks ago. Once she was level with the window, she could see the room was stacked with boxes and the walls and the dresser top appeared to be the repository for every framed photo that had probably adorned the rest of the house before the owners went away.

Tamsyn worked determinedly at the branch with the saw until one end fell down into the garden. The other rested just inside the window frame and down onto the glass-strewn floor. Swiping away the broken glass from the sill with a gloved hand, Tamsyn pulled herself up and through the window, feeling like nothing more than a burglar. She told herself not to be so stupid. She was being a fastidious tenant, ensuring that the damage inside wasn't severe, that's all. Once inside, she pushed the drapes wide open, letting light flood into the room.

Ignoring the crunch of broken glass beneath her feet, she crossed the room and lifted the photo frame off the wall. It was like looking at a picture of herself in another five or ten years' time. That chill ran down her neck again as she studied the woman in the photo more closely, mentally comparing it to the wedding photo she'd found on the internet. She and Tamsyn were a lot alike, from the shape of their face to their figures. While the photo was somewhat faded, Tamsyn could make out the color of the woman's eyes. Dark liquid brown, just like her own, except rather than being fresh and bright, the woman's were sad and slightly unfocused.

In the photo, a man with light brown hair and a sun-weathered face stood beside the woman, just slightly taller and bearing a look of pride that beamed out to all and sundry that he was well satisfied with his world. She had no idea who he was…but she was increasingly certain that she knew the woman. There had to be more photos, maybe even some papers that might confirm who the woman was.

She turned and ripped open one of the boxes and found it filled with albums all neatly dated on the spines. She ran her hand over the dates, choosing one from about three years after her mother had left. Sliding down onto a clear space on the floor, Tamsyn began to turn the pages. With each one she became more and more certain that the couple pictured were her mother and Ellen's partner, who seemed very much in love with her.

There was more. Several pictures had a young girl in them, aged about two or three years old. Honey blonde but with the same dark brown eyes as her mother, she looked to be a happy child and always had a coloring pencil in one hand and paper in the other—either that or she was dressing a doll in all manner of garments.

Tamsyn turned another page and felt a wave of shock hit her fair smack in the stomach. She blinked away the black dots that began to swim before her eyes, closing them briefly—unable to believe what she saw before her. She took a steadying breath, then another, before opening her eyes again.

The picture swam before her and she blinked once more to clear her vision. Yes, it was still the same as before. The shock of it was fading, but the image's ramifications were no less devastating. There, right in front of her, stood the woman Tamsyn believed to be her mother, with the man and an older version of the little girl…and with a young boy aged about twelve. A young boy with brown hair and gray eyes.

A young boy who looked very much like Finn Gallagher.

Sixteen

Finn Gallagher knew her mother!

He'd lied to her all this time. Confusion warred with anger inside her until, with a bubbling rising fury, anger won. How dare he? He'd known she was looking for her mother and yet he'd never given the slightest indication he knew her mother at all. In fact, he'd deliberately and calculatedly told her Ellen didn't live there. Well, didn't live up on the hill at his house, maybe, but that was splitting hairs.

Tamsyn slammed the album shut and staggered to her feet, unsure of what to do next. The sound of a car coming up the driveway gave her her answer. It could only be one person.

She turned to the door and easily unlocked the deadlock from inside—it was, after all, designed to keep people out of the room, not in it. She left the door ajar as she strode down the hallway toward the front door. Finn stood there in all his God-given glory, fresh and handsome in a pale gray suit, white shirt and tie.

"I heard about the storm, are you all right? You look—"

She jabbed him in the chest with her forefinger, taking him completely by surprise. "You knew!" she shouted, unable to contain her anger a second longer. "You knew all along and you lied to me! Why?"

For a second he almost looked as if he was about to deny her accusation, but then a cold, calm expression settled over his face, his eyes turning arctic.

"I never lied to you."

"You did," she insisted, fighting back the burning sensation that began to sting her eyes. Be damned if she was going to cry in front of him. He didn't deserve her tears after the way he'd taken her trust, her fragile heart and stomped them under his feet as if she was nothing. "You deliberately withheld the truth from me when you could have told me from day one where I could find my mother. Worse, you let me *trust* you."

"Look, I told you that Ellen didn't live at my house. That's the truth."

"But you never thought to tell me that she lived here." Tamsyn uttered a bitter laugh. "Oh, I bet you had a good old chuckle about that when I took on the lease. What a freaking joke. Tamsyn Masters living in her mother's house and not even knowing it. I suppose the whole town has been having a roaring time at my expense. Tell me, does everyone know?"

His silence told her everything.

"How could you do that to me?" she asked brokenly, the anger suddenly leaving her in a rush, leaving behind an awful hollowness.

"How did you find out?"

"Is that all you can say?"

Tamsyn stood and waited for his response, but he simply continued to stare her down. The generous lover who'd left her bed yesterday morning was a far cry from the man standing before her now.

"The storm did some damage, broke a window in the room with the locked door. I was trying to clear it up a bit from outside when I saw a picture on the wall."

"Show me."

She turned and went back up the hall, standing outside the now-open door and gesturing inside. Finn stood next to her as he surveyed the damage, the twisted blinds, the remnant of tree branch still dangling from the window frame.

"You broke into the boxes? Into their personal effects?" he asked.

"Wouldn't you?" Tamsyn defended herself and pushed past him to pick up the album that had held the damning evidence that showed his complicity. "Who is this?" she demanded, stabbing at a photo of the blonde girl.

"That's Alexis."

The name was familiar. Yes, the designer. "Alexis Fabrini?"

"She's your half sister."

Tamsyn wobbled on her feet, her legs suddenly as weak as if she'd emptied a flagon of wine straight down her throat. It was only the solid presence of the doorjamb that kept her upright. She had a sister? She looked at the photo again, this time noticing the similarities between them, the things they'd both inherited from Ellen.

"Is there anything else you're not telling me?" Her voice was weak, thready with shock. She let out a bitter laugh. "Why am I even bothering to ask? I've got no reason to believe anything you tell me anymore—or ever again."

Finn tried to ignore the clawing pain in his chest. He had known this would come to pass, that he'd hurt Tamsyn immeasurably. He'd just hoped to stave it off for longer, for Ellen's health to rally and for Lorenzo to perhaps agree to let Tamsyn visit her mother in the hospital. Then he could have told her the truth himself—broken it to her gently. He'd never wanted her to find out like this.

"Look," he said, shoving a hand through his hair, "Ellen is a much loved member of this community. If people didn't talk about her it's because they wanted the best for her—to protect her."

Pain streaked across Tamsyn's face, leaving it even paler and more drawn than it had been seconds ago.

"Protect her from me? Her own daughter? Why, Finn? Why wouldn't I be considered to be the best for my mother?"

His arms ached to reach out and comfort her. Finn closed

his eyes and wished fiercely that he could turn back time, could avoid the trip that had taken him away from Tamsyn and left her alone when she was exposed to the truth.

"I guess most people feel that you took your time trying to find her." The words sounded lame, even to his ears.

"But you know I only found out this year that she was even still alive. She walked away from us, Finn. She left her two children in the hospital—injured in an accident she caused—and never looked back. Abandoned us, for what? So she could be with her lover?" Tamsyn stabbed her finger now at a picture of Lorenzo. "I didn't know where she was, Finn, you know that and I know that. Ellen, however, knew exactly where Ethan and I were and she never tried to contact us. I want to know why. Don't I deserve to know why she left us and why she never came back? Why was she happy to be dead to us?"

Finn put out a hand to touch her but she flinched away from him. It cut him to his core to know he'd irreparably damaged the relationship they'd begun to develop. Damaged? Hell, he'd destroyed it, crushed it like a bug, pure and simple. He'd done it for Lorenzo, for Ellen—people he'd do anything for. But, God, how he wished he'd never had to do this.

"I can't tell you that, but I'll do what I can to see you find out."

She looked at him from eyes bruised with disappointment and grief. "That's it? That's all you're going to do? You're not going to tell me where she is?"

"I can't promise any more than that, Tamsyn. I'm sorry, but they're not my secrets to tell."

"So, at least you admit that you've been keeping secrets from me."

"I have, and I regret it. If I could—ah, what's the point?" He cursed under his breath. "I'll do what I can, and I'll get someone on to that window, too."

He turned and walked down the hall, painfully aware of her gaze drilling steadily into his back as he left.

Tamsyn watched him go—a stranger to her now. She'd thought Trent's betrayal had cut her deep, but this was something else. She stalked down the hall and slammed the front door shut, then slid down the wall into a heap on the floor. Shock and anger had rendered her numb for the time being, but even through the numbness she could feel waves of pain building.

She daren't open her mouth for fear of the scream she knew would come out. Instead, she clenched her teeth, wrapped her arms around her body and rocked in silent agony.

Her mother left her. Check. Her mother didn't try to stay in touch. Check. She'd been let down by her mother. Check. She'd been lied to and let down by—oh, let's see—her father, her extended family, her ex-fiancé, her personal assistant, Finn. Check, check, check, check and double check.

At the last she began to feel her tentative control break. What did it matter to her that Finn had added his name to the illustrious list? It wasn't as if they'd known each other long or as if they'd promised undying love for one another. It wasn't as if she even *should* have thought she could trust him. Hadn't there been that tiny niggle in the back of her mind for some time that he was hiding something?

Instead of listening to her instincts, she'd allowed him to play her for a fool. She'd been so pathetically desperate to be spontaneous, to be carefree, to be happy that she'd let herself be blinded to the truth. A man like Finn, he was no better than the rest. Worse, even, for having used her pathetic need for acceptance against her like that. For having inveigled his way into her day-to-day existence so that she'd come to rely upon him, need him. Love him.

No! Not that, never that. Tamsyn squashed down so hard

on the thought that her head began to throb with pain. It had been attraction. Pure and physical. Okay, very physical, she amended as she burrowed her face into her hands. She didn't love Finn, she couldn't. Her senses had been seduced by his attention, that was all it was. She'd have to have been both blind and stupid not to find his attentiveness appealing. It had been a salve to her wounded pride like nothing else could be. And look where that had left her, she thought bitterly.

Tamsyn pushed off the wall and went to the door to the previously locked room. She ought to pick up the broken glass, set the boxes back to rights, but she couldn't summon the care or the interest required to do so. Instead, she went back to her bedroom, kicked off her shoes and pulled the covers up over her. She felt as if she'd been hit by a freight train—physically and mentally. She craved oblivion, even if only for a couple of hours. Then she'd be able to cope, to figure out what she had to do next, because right now it all seemed far too hard.

The sun was low in the sky when the constant chirp of her mobile phone woke her. Tamsyn groggily reached out to the bedside table for the device.

"Hello?"

"Ms. Masters? It's Jill from the letting agency."

"Ah, yes, about the damage—"

"I've talked with the property owner, Mr. Fabrini, today and he's asked that you move out."

Move out? While a pane of glass was being replaced?

"I beg your pardon? That seems extreme." Tamsyn forced her sluggish brain to function. "It's only a pane of glass that needs to be replaced. Surely I can remain while that's done?"

"I don't think you understand me, Ms. Masters. Mr. Fabrini has requested you vacate the property permanently."

The words slowly sank in. "What? Vacate the property? But the lease—"

"Is a week-by-week agreement that can be terminated at any time by any party without notice. You will be refunded for any overpayment."

"Yes, yes, I'm aware of that." Tamsyn had thought the rental conditions to be very unusual at the time, but they'd suited her so she hadn't questioned it. Of course, she'd assumed she'd have at least a week's notice of the owners' intention to return before being asked to vacate.

"Then you'll make other arrangements?"

"Of course. I don't suppose you have any other properties on the books at the moment that might be suitable?"

"I'm sorry, no. There's a festival in the area and all our casual rentals are completely booked out. Have been for some time."

"Oh, I see. Well, if you could just give me a few days until I find something—"

"Ms. Masters, I'm sorry. Obviously I didn't make my client's wishes clear. Mr. Fabrini wants you out of the cottage today."

Seventeen

"Today?"

"He was most insistent."

She just bet he was. What was it Finn had said before he left? That he'd do what he could? Well, it appeared he'd done it, all right. He'd obviously spoken with this Mr. Fabrini and her eviction was the result. Anger slowly began to replace the hollow pain that had consumed her this morning.

"Fine, I'll be a couple of hours."

"That will have to do, I suppose."

Too damn right it would, Tamsyn thought, severing the connection without saying goodbye. She pushed up off the bed and methodically stripped the sheets, taking them through to the laundry and throwing them in the machine together with the towels from the bathroom. She had half a mind to leave them in there, wet, but her own standards wouldn't let her slide that low no matter how badly she was being treated. Or by whom.

Methodically she went through the motions of setting the house back to exactly how she'd found it—pushing the vacuum cleaner through, remaking the bed, laying fresh towels in the bathroom and clearing the perishables from the fridge. By the time she'd finished, and her case was packed, she felt completely empty inside. Not surprising, she realized, as she'd eaten nothing all day. Still, the thought of food was the furthest thing from her mind. More pressing was the need to find somewhere to stay tonight. And the next. Mr. Fabrini probably wanted her to leave New Zealand, too, but that wasn't happening. Not today. Not until she found her mother—no matter who stood in her way.

After feeding Lucy, and shooing her outside and locking up the house, she drove into town to leave the key with the letting agency. Then she stopped in a local café. Christmas decorations hung in a jaunty display of festivity in the window, and the sound of carols greeted her as she went inside. Feeling more like a modern-day Scrooge than anything approaching Christmas cheer, she ordered coffee and a slice of quiche to eat while she searched on her smartphone for local accommodations.

Starting with Penny's place, she began calling around. Half an hour later she was no nearer to finding a roof to put over her head. Everything in town, and beyond—even the local motor camp—was booked solid. At this rate she'd be sleeping in her car.

At least the rental car company hadn't canceled her contract on that, she thought cynically, using her fork to push the now-cold quiche around her plate. She knew she should eat, but her appetite had deserted her.

"There you are. I've been looking for you."

Finn towered over her table, forcing her to crick her neck to look up at him.

"What, not finished lying to me yet?" she replied, determined not to show any sign of weakness to this man who'd proven as two-faced as all the rest of them.

"I heard what Lorenzo did. I want you to know I didn't have anything to do with that."

"You really expect me to believe you? Goodness, and when you've been so honest and forthcoming with me already." The sarcasm fairly dripped from her tongue. "You'll have to excuse me. I've had my full quota of unpleasantness today."

She picked up her bag, grabbed her car keys and rose to her feet, determined to head back out to her car and put a decent amount of distance between her and Finn. She'd no sooner gotten out of her chair when a wave of dizziness hit her, sending her straight back down again. She rested her head in one hand, her elbow on the table, as she waited for the world to right itself again. Finn's hand descended on her shoulder.

"Are you all right?"

She gave a strangled laugh. "Of course, I'm fine. I have a mother who is determined to hide from me, a friend who betrayed my trust, a landlord who's evicted me and a dearth of places to stay tonight. Things couldn't be better, thank you."

"Come with me. Stay at my house."

She lifted her head and stared at him incredulously. "You have to be kidding me, right?"

His eyes bored straight back into her. "Why not? I have plenty of room. I won't touch you, if that's what you're worried about."

Of course she wasn't worried about that. There was no way she was letting Finn Gallagher touch her ever again.

"I'd rather sleep in my car."

She got up to leave again, but that same dizziness sent her reeling, making her drop her keys. Finn's hand shot out to steady her.

"You're in no condition to drive anywhere. What were you thinking of doing? Settling down for the night here on the main street?"

She shot him a malignant glare. "If I must."

"Not happening. You're coming with me. We can pick your car up tomorrow."

He swiped her keys from where they'd fallen on the table and called out to the man behind the café counter. "Hey, Bill, could you park the blue hatchback around the back for me for tonight? We'll be back tomorrow for it."

"Sure, Finn, no problem."

Finn tossed the keys to Bill then wrapped his arm around the back of Tamsyn's shoulders and pulled her into his side. She resisted for as long as she could, but then found herself sagging into him. The rough stormy night combined with the morning's revelations and the eviction had completely done her in. For now, it was easier to simply let him take charge. Tomorrow, however, would be another story altogether.

Tamsyn woke the next morning to the sound of someone coming into her room. She jolted upright in bed, clutching the covers to her.

"What do you want?" she demanded as Finn settled a cloth-covered tray on the bed beside her.

"I thought you might like breakfast." He whipped the cloth off the tray. "And we need to talk."

"Unless you're going to tell me where my mother is, I have nothing to say to you," she said.

Her mouth watered as she looked at the freshly buttered toast and preserves he'd laid out on the tray, and her nostrils twitched at the enticing coffee-scented aroma borne on gentle wafts of steam coming from a white porcelain mug.

"Then maybe you can listen." He sat down on the bed and repositioned the tray across her thighs. "Eat," he commanded.

Figuring that if her mouth was full she wouldn't have to talk to him, Tamsyn spread some orange marmalade on a slice of toast.

"I talked to Lorenzo last night."

"That was good of you," she conceded mockingly around a mouthful of toast. "And what did the illustrious Mr. Fabrini have to say? Did he rescind his eviction order?"

Finn's mouth twisted. "No, he was adamant he didn't want you staying at the house any longer."

"Tell me, what did I ever do to him to make him hate me so much?"

"It's not you, it's—look, I can't say. I gave my word I

wouldn't tell you and I'm honor-bound to hold to that. I owe Lorenzo a lot."

"I see," she said before taking a sip of her coffee. "And your honor doesn't extend to telling me anything that he doesn't want me to know—which means anything about him or my mother, is that right?"

"I'm sorry."

"That's it? You really expect me to accept that as an apology?"

Finn sighed. "No, I don't. But I can't give you what you want so, it will have to do." He stood up and started walking to the door, hesitating in the entrance a moment. "You're welcome to stay here for as long as you need to. I'll try again with Lorenzo. He's pretty angry right now."

"Well, that makes two of us."

"You'll stay?"

"I don't have much choice, do I?"

He inclined his head in acknowledgment. "I'll be in my office. If you need me, go downstairs, to the end of the gallery then turn right."

He was gone before she could think of an appropriate rejoinder.

After she'd finished eating, Tamsyn got up and showered and dressed—grudgingly grateful that Finn had removed her suitcase from her car and brought it with them when they'd returned to his home. She needed armor, and that meant feeling good in what she was wearing, so she chose the gypsy skirt and blue tank top again. Before slipping on the skirt, she studied the label. Alexis Fabrini was embroidered in silver cursive script on a dark purple satin background.

She thumbed the silky material. Her sister—her half sister to be more precise. Was it strange that her sister's talent had appealed to her so much or was it simply a connection they'd shared without knowing? Either way, it was strange to discover that out there, somewhere, was another sibling. Another connection, forged in blood. Another secret exposed. She'd have to tell Ethan, eventually, but right now that was low on her priorities.

How many more secrets would she have to uncover before she could find her mother? She had absolutely no idea and the prospect was more daunting than it had seemed a few weeks ago.

She'd always lived her life with purpose, careful and measured. Each step meticulously planned, each outcome virtually assured. Until she'd tried to surprise Trent, until she'd decided to find her mother and turned her back on every security she'd ever known and trusted. And look where those decisions had led her. Straight down the barrel of heartbreak and disappointment. One thing she knew for sure—unexpected and spontaneous decisions weren't for her. Not anymore. Not ever again.

From now on, she vowed, she'd go back to her old ways. To being careful, considered and safe. She should have taken Ethan up on his suggestion to use an investigator to do the hard work first instead of racing off with no obvious plan other than to just show up. She hadn't been thinking clearly, not since she'd been told that her mother still lived. But now everything was crystal clear. Her mother didn't want to see her. And Tamsyn wasn't going to go back to Australia until she did. Once she'd cleared away all the lies, all the secrets, all the evasions...then and only then would she go home.

She finished dressing, collected the tray from the bed and took it through to the kitchen. Still slightly hungry, she grabbed an apple from the fruit bowl and went to find Finn. She wanted her car and she needed him to help her go and pick it up. She hoped the café was open on a Sunday because she'd be annoyed if she had to wait, at Finn's and the café owner's convenience, a day more than necessary for her link to independence.

The interior gallery shared a stone wall with a court-
yard outside. Even so, long windows shed ample light to
showcase the works Finn had spread along the wall. Local
scenes mostly, by the look of them, although one in particular made her breath catch in her throat. Painted from the
bottom of a valley, with its outlook stretching up a hill, it
featured a looming ruin—a dark brooding stain on a clear
blue sky. She knew that ruin, had viewed it virtually every
single day in living memory.

Masters Rise, the original home of her family, destroyed
by bushfires. Too expensive to rebuild and refurbish, the
ruin remained on the ridge of the hills overlooking The
Masters, her family's vineyard estate and business, a constant reminder of how far they'd fallen and how far they'd
come to fight back to where the family flourished today.

But what was the painting doing here? She peered at the
artist's signature, surprised to see the letters E and F inter-
twined in the corner. Ellen…Fabrini? No wonder she hadn't
been able to find her if she'd changed her name.

This was her mother's work? Tamsyn studied the picture
again, in particular how her mother had captured the old
ruin. It looked menacing, forbidding even. Was that how it
had felt to Ellen living there at the base of the hill? As if she
was being watched and perhaps found wanting?

Tamsyn could only speculate. Without access to her
mother, she certainly wasn't going to hear it from Ellen's
point of view, was she? Maybe she was imbuing too much
into Ellen's interpretation of her home, there on the wall. Yet
she couldn't keep from feeling that the painting was helping her understand a little better why her mother had chosen to leave. Tamsyn had known from an early age that the
presence of the ruins was what motivated her father every
day. He'd told her that it reminded him that he wouldn't be
beaten by the elements, that he would prevail and ensure
his family prevailed along with him.

Everything he'd done, every decision he'd made, had all been with the one purpose of ensuring the Masters family remained great. Granted, it had meant he was entirely driven, focused more on his work and its output than on his growing children. Had Ellen struggled with that? Was that why she'd sought a lover? Left her home, her family, her children?

Tamsyn groaned in frustration. The questions were simple, the answers probably equally so. But when would she have the chance to hear them, to judge for herself or, alternatively, to heal and forgive her mother for what had happened?

She turned away from the work on the wall, determined not to let it mess with her head a second longer.

Directly ahead of her was a door, and she opened it without thinking, surprised to find a very-well-set-up home gym inside. So, that explained Finn's impressive physique. A lick of heat started, but she quelled the sensation before it could take hold. He might be physical perfection, he might be the best lover she'd ever enjoyed sex with, but he was just another liar, she resolutely warned herself.

She left the room, closing the door behind her with a snap and turned down the hallway toward what she hoped was Finn's office. A door was open just ahead of her and she could hear Finn's voice. Her steps slowed as she made out what he was saying. She paused where she was, unashamedly eavesdropping and thankful that the soft soles of her ballet flats hadn't announced her coming. He sounded very worked up. Was he…could he be talking to her mother?

Eighteen

"Yes, of course she's staying with me. I couldn't very well let her sleep in a roadside layby, now, could I?"

He sounded frustrated. Tamsyn wished she could hear the words on the other end of the line.

"What were you thinking kicking her out of the cottage like that?" Another pause. "Yes, yes, I know she went into the room, but she was merely checking the damage, not outright snooping. Look, I really think you should talk to her yourself."

Tamsyn's stomach coiled into a knot and the bite of apple she'd taken as she walked down the hall stuck in her throat.

"Lorenzo, calm down. I know how you feel about the whole Masters family, but Tamsyn was just a little girl when it happened. She and her brother were told Ellen was dead. She only found out the truth this year, after her father died."

Her whole body tensed, poised for what she hoped would come next. Clearly, Lorenzo Fabrini was her mother's gate-keeper. If she could only get past him.

Finn's sigh echoed down the hall.

"Yeah, yeah, I know. You only want what's best for Ellen, and I agree it could be upsetting for her to see Tamsyn." Tamsyn's stomach sank. She should have expected it…but it still hurt to hear that no one, not even the man who'd been her lover just a few nights ago, was willing to put her feelings first.

"While you think about it," Finn continued, "hopefully Tamsyn will stay here. I've left it open to her to stay as long as she needs, but she's not my prisoner. It would have been easier for her to remain at the cottage and keep herself busy there... Okay, okay, enough already. Call me tonight."

A sharp expletive rent the air as Finn ended the call. Tamsyn rocked back on her heels and thought about what she'd just heard. She still didn't understand why everyone seemed to think it would be bad for her mother to see her. And she certainly didn't understand why it had been necessary to lie to her all along. But she had to admit, Finn had seemed truly interested in helping her, as much as Lorenzo would let him. She wasn't ready to trust him or even forgive him yet, but it did take the edge off her anger.

She waited a minute before continuing the short distance to his office. He wheeled around to face her as she gently knocked on the door and entered the room.

"Hi," she said awkwardly. "Any chance we can pick up my car this morning?"

"After lunchtime will be best, the café will be busy with a crowd after the morning church services in town."

She nodded, accepting that she could do nothing without his assistance. She ached to ask him about the phone call, but that would mean admitting she'd overheard part of his side of the conversation. Tamsyn very much doubted he'd be happy about that. She finished her apple, tossed the core into a small trash bin and then wandered over to the window. In front of it was a large table with a three-dimensional plan of a set of buildings next to a painted lake.

"You're into development?" she asked, studying the layout of the buildings carefully. They looked similar in design to Finn's house, making the most of the natural contours and features of the molded land.

"For this, yes."

He came and stood beside her. Even though he was a good few inches away, she was acutely aware of the heat of his body, of the answering heat of her own. On the pretext of examining the board from a different angle, she moved away.

"What will it be?"

"Well, if I ever get decent road access to the property, it will be a respite center for families with a loved one suffering from mental illness."

"Why a respite center?"

"Personal reasons." He swung away from the model and went back to his desk.

"More secrets or is this actually something you can tell me?" Tamsyn pressed. They had time to kill before going to collect her car—he may as well fill it for her since he'd put her in this position.

"I've seen from personal experience, the strain it puts on a family to care for another family member undergoing mental health treatment—it's especially tough on kids. I think it's important for them to have a safe place to go, to chill out, where the people around them really do understand what it's like. I'm hoping to build family chalets, as you can see. Each one would be private from the others but still near enough for a sense of community for people. Also, I'd like to see children's camps run there too—in those buildings on the other side of the complex. Have camp counselors, trained in dealing with the issues that arise for kids with parents or siblings under care, that sort of thing."

Tamsyn came and sat down opposite Finn's desk. "It's an ambitious project. What was that you said about needing road access?"

He pointed to a gray ribbon of road that came down from the hill. "I can create it by rebuilding my driveway as a two-lane road and then going down here from the top of the hill, where the house is. As you can see, to make a decent and safe road, it would have to cut into the contour of the land considerably and would have quite a few twists and turns to it. If I can get access here—" he gestured to a level tract of land that butted up to the lake and then stretched back to the main road "—I can put in a straighter road that will make it easier for everyone—suppliers, contractors, visitors and staff."

"So what's holding you back?"

"This piece of land is owned by a trust and, while I've tracked the trustee company to a firm of lawyers in Auckland, I haven't been able to get a response out of them with respect to a partial sale of the land. It would just be an easement, right on the boundary of our two pieces of land and I'm prepared to build the road so they'd have access from every point along here if they so desired. But so far, I've heard nothing."

"Frustrating," Tamsyn commented. "What will you do if you don't get the easement?"

"I'll still go ahead, but it will mean a bigger investment into the road construction and less into the complex itself. We'd have to do the complex in stages. Perhaps start with the children's camp and move on in a few years to building the chalets, or vice versa. I'm still hoping we won't have to make that decision."

"You mentioned personal experience...your family?" she probed carefully.

"My mother. She was—" He broke off and his lips firmed into a straight line, his eyes becoming unfocused for a moment. "Fragile, I guess you could say. She probably should never have been a farmer's wife, but she loved my father with a passion that knew no bounds. She lived for the very moment when he'd walk through the door each evening and she died a little every time he went back out again in the morning. Dad was shifting stock one day, his last herd. It wasn't long after he and Lorenzo had formed a partnership, converting part of Dad's farmland into a vineyard and amalgamating it with the Fabrini land where Lorenzo had already begun growing. Dad's quad bike rolled, and he was crushed beneath it. Lorenzo and I found him late that night, guided by one of his farm dogs barking. The dog had stayed with him the whole time. But by the time we found him, there was nothing anyone could do."

His succinct telling of the story didn't diminish the flash of pain in his eyes. A rush of sympathy filled her. Hard enough to lose a parent, but to be one of the people who discovered him? Grim didn't even begin to describe it.

"Finn, I'm sorry. That must have been awful. How old were you?"

"Twelve. Mum was devastated. At first she coped, barely, but I ended up having to take on more and more of the duties around the house—on top of school, on top of doing Dad's chores around the farm. Eventually it got to be too much and it showed. I got into some trouble at school when some kids started teasing me about falling asleep in class. My teacher came over to talk to Mum one day—they'd known each other when they were younger. When she saw how bad the situation had gotten, she called the authorities."

Finn rubbed his eyes and got up from his chair. He opened a nearby cupboard, which turned out to be an integrated bar-fridge door. "You want water or a can of soda?"

"Water, thanks." Tamsyn accepted the bottle he passed her and screwed off the cap. "What happened then? Did you get help around the farm?"

He ripped the tab off the soda he'd pulled from the fridge and took a long swallow before answering. "We were both put into care. Me into a foster home in town, Mum into a secure facility outside of Christchurch. I didn't know it then but she'd begun self-harming. I couldn't see her for a long time. Lorenzo and Ellen approached social services about providing a permanent home for me and eventually I moved in with them. With Lorenzo's help, the farm was slowly converted to what you see today—one of the most prolific and high-yield vineyards in the district. While we've never produced our own wines, we get a certain satisfaction when the wineries we supply produce another gold medal winner."

She could see now why the bond between Lorenzo Fabrini and Finn was so strong. The older man had been a father figure to him, a mentor, a savior. But it still didn't explain his not telling her where Ellen was. If Ellen didn't want to see her, why not simply tell her that and spare her the wild-goose chase? And for that matter, were they being honest with Ellen either? Did she even know that Tamsyn was looking for her, or had her menfolk simply circled the wagons and kept her in a state of oblivion? She couldn't bring herself to ask.

"So, you want to establish the respite center in your mother's memory?"

"She's part of the reason," he agreed. "The other part is I have a whole lot of money sitting around doing nothing and I feel the region has a need that I can fulfill. I want to give back. If it's successful, I'd like to develop centers all around the country."

Tamsyn sat back in her chair and deliberately took another sip of her water. She had no words to say. Finn's philanthropic nature appeared in total contrast to the way he'd treated her. Which man was the real Finn Gallagher? She was inclined to believe that it was Finn the philanthropist. The one the entire township knew and obviously had a very high regard for. The one who'd been helpful and solicitous even while hiding her mother's whereabouts from her at the same time. So why had he done it? What secret was he still holding back that would explain the rest of the puzzle?

"After we've collected your car, would you be interested in visiting the site?" Finn surprised her out of her reverie.

"Visiting the site? You have access now?"

"It's a rough track, still, but we can do it on the quad bike." At her look of concern he hastened to add. "I'll take it easy. We'll be quite safe."

She took only a moment to make up her mind. "Okay, that sounds like a great idea. I'd like to see it. I guess jeans and runners would be more in order than this," she said, gesturing to her skirt.

"Definitely." He flicked a glance at his watch. "How about you get changed now, and we can head into town and get your car. On the way back I'll check on Lucy and the chickens and then meet you back here."

A twist of anger flared in her chest as he mentioned Lucy and the chickens. If Lorenzo wasn't being so unreasonable she'd be there now, tending to her responsibilities. She nodded to Finn in answer and rose from her seat.

"Give me five minutes," she said.

"Sure, I'll be out front in the car."

Finn rubbed his hand over his face again as Tamsyn left the room. That had been close. The call from Lorenzo hadn't gone as he'd hoped. When it came to protecting Ellen from what he saw as the terribleness of the Masters family, he was almost rabid. It didn't seem to matter what Finn said, Lorenzo's mind was made up.

Added to his overprotective nature was his fear, because no matter what the doctors did, no matter how hard Lorenzo fought to hold Ellen here, she continued to deteriorate. He was desperate to safeguard what he saw as his last weeks with her.

Finn understood why Lorenzo was so scared. Talking about his mother, remembering how it felt, day in and day out, trying to hold everything together around the farm, trying to support his mom through her grief while virtually having to ignore his own, had left deep scars.

There'd been days when he'd resented her deeply, had wished she'd been more like other mothers—loving and capable, present in the moment instead of locked inside some awful living tomb. Then, of course, he'd be assailed with guilt and shame. She missed his father—they both did—

and without his father's booming, happy presence, it was up to Finn to fill the gaps.

But he'd failed. He'd failed her then, and he'd failed her later by insisting on going to see her before she was ready to see him again. By forcing her to face him, he'd forced her to face her own failures as a parent, and that had been enough to make her withdraw from reality completely. She refused to eat, refused to leave her bed—eventually dying in her sleep. Lost in her anguish. Alone.

He'd been responsible for his mother choosing death over life and, all guilt over keeping Tamsyn from seeing her mother aside, he'd be damned if he visited that responsibility onto Tamsyn as well.

Nineteen

Riding the rutted track on the quad bike, with Tamsyn's arms reluctantly secured around his waist, was bittersweet. With every bump in the road he felt her press against him—the softness of her breasts, the involuntary thrust of her hips. She'd started the journey determinedly holding on to the back of the seat, but as the track had grown rougher she'd been forced to relinquish her hold and cling to him like a limpet.

He released a breath he hadn't realized he was holding when they reached the flat and she didn't let go. The going was easier but still she held on, her slender arms like a band around his waist. He allowed himself to enjoy it while he could, certain it wouldn't last long.

She'd barely said a word to him since he'd returned to the house after their jaunt into town. She was still mad about the cottage, he knew. Mad about the secrets he was still keeping, mad about the whole situation. He didn't blame her, but there was nothing he could do. Nothing but to try and distract her in the meantime.

Fire lit his groin at the thought of various sensual ways he could distract her but he fought himself back under control. For now he needed to earn her trust back. He'd wounded her, he knew that, and it hurt with an almost physical pain to admit it.

He opened the throttle some more and swiftly covered the remaining few hundred meters to the lake's edge where he'd optimistically begun to peg out the buildings a couple of weeks ago. The sooner they dismounted the quad bike the sooner he'd be able to rid himself of the sensation of her fastened against him, and of how right it felt.

"This is a beautiful spot," Tamsyn commented as she got off the bike and walked over to the lake's edge. "You didn't want to build down here for yourself?"

"My parents' house used to be over there." He pointed to a stand of trees where a crumbling chimney and fireplace were all that remained of his former home. "A wiring failure one night led to it burning down after I went into foster care. I always said I'd rebuild there, but as I grew older I began to appreciate that it was probably better to make a new start. Besides, I love the outlook from my home now."

"King of the castle and master of all you survey?" Tamsyn said dryly.

"Hardly," he answered with a small frown.

Was that how she saw him? Autocratic and wanting to control everything?

"I think it's the freedom of the space that appealed to me most up there. The sensation of not being boxed in. Plus, it was symbolic of a new start for me after I sold my business. Fresh horizons and all that."

She nodded and started to walk along the waterline, her hands shoved in her pockets. He followed her a few steps behind.

"I thought this trip to New Zealand would be a new horizon for me," she said softly.

He could feel the pain in her voice.

"You know, I think I would have been better off not knowing that my mother is still alive. Alive and, from the looks of things, not wanting to see me." She huffed a humorless laugh. "Not wanting me, period."

Finn reached out and grabbed her arm, spinning her around to face him. He had to tell her something, give her *something* she could hold on to.

"Your mother has loved you all your life. I've known

her for much of mine and she never stopped thinking about you or your brother. *Never*. Believe me or not, but it's true."

He pushed as much honesty into his words as he could. She had to believe him. He knew he'd failed when he saw Tamsyn's expression cloud over, saw anger make her eyes turn hard.

"Well, if she has, she sure has a funny way of showing it. I've been here, searching for her, for weeks with not a word from anyone to tell me where to find her. They kicked me out of their house. There's no way they're ever going to want to see me, is there?"

He couldn't lie. "That's something you might just have to come to terms with, Tamsyn. As hard as it is, as awful as it is, it's out of both our hands."

He let his hand slide down her arm, his fingers tangling with hers. She didn't resist and he couldn't help but feel a surge of triumph that she didn't pull away.

"C'mon, let me show you where I've pegged out the chalets and main buildings. It's not far from the jetty over there." He pointed with his free arm. "My dad and I built it and it's still solid. We used to have so much fun here at the lake. That's what I want to give the families that come here. A chance to play together again. To create good memories." He wanted desperately to give *her* good memories of her time in New Zealand—something to take away the sting of the situation with Ellen. But would she let him?

The sun beat down on them as they walked the perimeter of the proposed respite center and Tamsyn felt a trickle of perspiration run down her spine. Jeans had obviously been the practical choice for the quad bike ride and walking in the long grass but, oh boy, did they make a person hot. She lifted her hair off the back of her neck, allowing the breeze to cool her ever so slightly. The lake looked cool and inviting.

"Thirsty?" Finn asked, as if he could read her mind.

"Yeah, although I wouldn't say no to a swim either. Shame we didn't bring bathing suits."

"We don't need suits."

She snapped her head around to look at him.

He gave her a nonchalant look in return. "It's totally private here. I can't even see this edge of the lake from my house, so if you want to take a dip, go for it."

"But…"

Whatever she was going to say flew from her mind as he tugged his T-shirt loose from his jeans and yanked it up over his head. Her eyes were drawn like magnets to his naked torso, to the play of muscles across his chest and lower. He reached down to undo his trainers and slid them and his socks off before his hands went to the waistband of his jeans.

"What are you waiting for?" he asked, a cheeky gleam in his eyes. "Last one in is a rotten egg."

The band of his boxer briefs was already showing. Not one to be left behind, Tamsyn slid her tank top off and toed off her runners while rapidly undoing her jeans. Jeans and socks came off in a smooth movement and she shoulder-barged him as she went past, putting him completely off balance and sending him to the ground in a tangle of jeans and limbs.

"Cheat!" he called after her.

He was only seconds behind on the wooden planks of the jetty and she squealed as she heard his rapid footsteps gaining. She was about a meter from the end when she felt his arms close around her waist, felt him lift her in the air, take another long step and twist to fall back backward into the lake.

Freezing cold, the water closed over her head and shocked the air out of her, but she didn't panic, didn't squirm. Instinctively, despite everything, she knew she was safe. Finn's arms were locked around her like a band and she felt his strong legs kick them back toward the surface. And that wasn't all she felt. His body was responding to hers and he wasn't trying to hide it.

Their heads broke the water and he released her.

"Man, that feels good," he said with a grin that went ear to ear.

She couldn't help but agree. The sweltering heat that had made her so uncomfortable before had been driven out of her body. But rather than chilling her to the bone, the water felt like silk stroking against her skin—making her aware of each of her nerve endings as they responded to the sensation, and to the nearness of the almost-naked man treading water beside her.

"Sometimes during the school holidays, when Dad would come back to the house at lunchtime, we'd race each other off the jetty. I lived for those moments. Mum would bring a picnic lunch for us and we'd all sit together afterward until he had to get back to work."

"It sounds like you guys had a great relationship," Tamsyn said, adopting a lazy breaststroke to swim in circles around him.

"We did. I'm lucky. Even though he died, I still have so many great memories. You missed out on that, didn't you? Doesn't seem from what you've told me that your father took time out with you kids."

"No, he didn't, but we didn't miss out altogether. We grew up with our cousins, Judd, Raif, Cade and Cathleen. We were always off on one adventure or another, when we weren't working on the estate somewhere."

Although she'd quietly envied her cousins their mothers while she was growing up, she'd still had a pretty carefree childhood. Ethan had seen to that. Protective, inclusive— he'd been her rock, and still was in so many ways. And her dad had been there, too, in his own gruff workaholic way, along with her uncle and aunts. But there had still been that vital component missing for her.

The water began to feel chilly again and she gave a little shiver.

"Let's get out," Finn suggested, obviously noticing her discomfort. "We can dry in the sun and have something to eat."

"You brought food?"

"And wine," he admitted. "Or you can have juice or water if you prefer."

"Wine would be nice," she said, striking out for the ladder on the side of the jetty.

She was acutely aware of Finn's presence behind her as she started up the ladder. It kept her from concentrating as she should on the slippery rungs. Her foot shot off the bar and she started to fall, only to be halted by warm hands at her hips steadying her. The feel of Finn's hands on her body had her senses reeling and heat flashed through her.

"You okay?" he asked from slightly below her.

"Y-yes, I'm fine," she said through gritted teeth.

Slowly and determinedly she made her way up the ladder, out of his reach—but only for a moment as a hunk of wet, dripping male came up the ladder right behind her.

He'd have had a good eyeful of her backside, she thought as she finally put her feet onto the wooden jetty and began to walk to where they'd tossed their clothes. She picked up her things and held them in front of her like a shield as he drew closer, suddenly feeling vulnerable in her dripping, clingy underthings.

Finn's gaze swept over her like a blast of hot air and she clutched her garments closer to her wet chest.

"Here," he said, grabbing his T-shirt up off the ground. "Wear this if you'd be more comfortable."

"But I'll make it wet," she protested, even as she accepted it from him.

He shrugged. "It'll dry, it's only lake water." He picked up his jeans and shook them out. "You want to turn your back a second?"

Color rushing to her cheeks, Tamsyn did just that and heard the wet plop of his briefs hitting the ground followed by the sound of him easing denim up long damp legs.

"It's safe to look now," he said, and she turned slowly.

Safe? He had to be kidding. With his hair all wet and spiky, his skin gleaming and his jeans slung low on his hips he was anything but safe.

"Um, perhaps you'd like to do the same for me?" she asked, her voice betrayingly husky.

"Sure. In fact, I'll set up our meal by the old fireplace. Join me when you're ready."

He shoved his socks inside his shoes and, tying the laces into a knot together, he hooked them with a finger and began to head back toward the bike. She watched as he increased the distance between them. Something pulled deep in her belly, as if there was an invisible thread that lay between them. A thread that tightened a notch at a time as he took each step away.

She shook her head. This was ridiculous. She was still angry with him, he'd lied to her. But he'd also made sure she had a roof over her head and food in her belly. And, from what she'd overhead in his conversation with Lorenzo Fabrini earlier today, he was trying to get the older man to agree to her seeing Ellen.

The sun slipped behind a cloud and a breeze off the lake caressed her skin, reminding her that she was standing here chilled, almost naked. Tamsyn lifted Finn's shirt up to her face, checked to ensure he still wasn't looking and inhaled. His scent filled her, consumed her almost. Spice and wood and quintessential Finn. It made her whole body ache for him.

He'd reached the quad bike and was lifting a large box off

the back. With his back still toward her, he headed toward the ruins of his old home. Secure in her privacy, Tamsyn quickly unsnapped her wet bra and pulled his T-shirt over her head before shimmying out of her wet panties. Instantly she felt warmth begin to seep through her, as if she'd been enveloped by the man himself. How did he do that? How did he make her feel so secure and yet so vulnerable at the same time? It wasn't fair.

Her hair still dripped down her back and she twisted its length to one side, wringing out as much excess water as she could before lifting it and, in lieu of having a band to tie it with, twisting it in a damp knot at the top of her head. A small twig, about the length of a chopstick, shoved through the knot held it from slipping in wet coils down her back. Satisfied she was more comfortable, Tamsyn followed in Finn's wake.

He'd spread a blanket on the grass and was taking out some pots of food as well as a pair of wineglasses.

"Better?" he asked as she drew closer.

"Thanks, yes." She spread her bra and panties in the sun on the bricks of the old fireplace and sank to her knees on the blanket.

"You must be hungry. It's ages since I brought you breakfast."

"I am a bit," she admitted, realizing now that she was ravenous.

"Help yourself while I pour the wine."

Tamsyn eyed the spread he'd laid out—smoked chicken, coleslaw, fresh bread rolls as well as olives, baby gherkins and sundried tomatoes. Her mouth watered. "It looks great," she commented, filling the plate he handed her. "I suppose you just threw this together?"

"Ha! I wish I could take the credit. No, I asked Bill at the café to put this together for us." He looked at her, his features softening. "You remind me a lot of her—Ellen."

"I do?"

"Yeah. You look like her, of course, but it's also the way you move, the way you sit. It reminds me of when she used to declare dinner a picnic, even in the middle of winter, and we'd sit around on the floor—Ellen, Lorenzo, Alexis and me—eating with our fingers off the plates. She'd laugh, how she'd laugh."

At first his words hurt, opened wider the gap between what she'd had and what she'd lost when her mother had left her. But then she felt a different sensation, almost tenderness, as a similar picture flooded her mind. Of her mother and Ethan and herself as a small girl, sitting in front of the fireplace at The Masters, rain pelting against the side of the house and yet they were cozy, together—enjoying a meal as if it was the simplest and most fun thing in the world. And she could hear her mother's laugh echoing through her memories; sense the touch of her mother's fingers on her face as she brushed away a clinging scrap of food from a cheek.

Tamsyn swallowed against the rise of emotion that clogged her throat.

"Damn, Tamsyn, I didn't mean to upset you. I just thought—"

"No, you haven't upset me," she choked out, "not at all."

"Then why are you looking so sad?"

"I just had a similar memory. Just a snippet, but I know it was real." She reached across the short distance between them. "Thank you," she said in all sincerity.

"For what?" He curled his hand over hers.

"For sharing her with me. Even just that little bit."

He lifted her hand to his lips and pressed them against her knuckles. "I wish I could do so much more for you, Tamsyn."

"I know," she answered, and she did. It still stung a little that she was being prioritized last, but she understood why his loyalty to Lorenzo went deep. And really, he was doing everything he could for her that didn't directly challenge that loyalty. That had to mean something.

He took her empty plate with his free hand and stacked it with his. Tamsyn's heart rate skipped a beat as he turned his gaze back to her. He still held one hand in his, and with the fingers of the other he traced the contours of her face—his touch so gentle, almost reverent.

"I want to make love to you again," he said, his voice a soft growl. "Will you allow me that honor?"

Twenty

Tamsyn felt the shiver of desire run from the base of her spine and all the way up into her clouded brain. She could refuse him, pull her hand free and withdraw from his request. He'd respect her decision, she was certain. For all that he'd withheld truths from her, she understood he was an honorable man. But her body had its own demands and try as she might to hold on to her anger with him, she couldn't resist him.

"Yes," she answered, her voice a whisper taken on the breeze that nuzzled and eased around their bodies.

His irises widened and she heard his breath hitch just that little bit. Enough for her to know he'd been anticipating a no from her. Enough to know what it meant to him that she'd said yes.

"Thank you," he said, pulling her toward him and meeting her lips with his own.

His kiss was tender at first, a soft play of his lips against hers—sucking, teasing kisses that enticed and tempted. Her nipples tightened beneath the cotton of his shirt, pressing against the fabric with an ache that spread all the way down to her core. A soft moan fled her mouth as he traced her jawline with his mouth, sucking softly at the sensitive skin of her throat.

Tamsyn hitched herself against him, her legs falling on either side of his, her rapidly dampening center pressing against the ridge that told of his body's own silent entreaty. Finn's hands were at her waist, pushing up the fabric of his shirt, tracing her ribs and slowly, oh so tormentingly slowly, moving higher to cup the fullness of her breasts.

His thumbs grazed against the tight nubs that peaked at their tips and she shuddered, pressing harder against him. He squeezed and rolled the taut beads between thumb and fingertip and in response she arched her back, flexed her hips against him, against his straining erection. Finn's mouth traced a blazing trail of wet heat to the fullness of her breasts until he took first one, then the other nipple in his mouth, rolling them with his tongue, suckling and grazing them with his teeth.

Her hands gripped his shoulders, her nails embedding in his skin as with each pull of his mouth he sent a spear of sensation to her aching core. She needed him—inside her, outside her, everywhere…all the time. Acknowledging that fact was a pleasure-pain that drilled into the back of her mind. This was no fling for her, not anymore. Somehow they'd crossed the invisible boundary of simply being lovers. Somewhere on this journey, she'd fallen irrevocably in love.

A sharp pang resonated through her as the truth hit home. Was she forever destined to fall in love with men who'd put others' needs before her own?

Now wasn't the time to reach for the answer to that question. Now was a time to take, to share, to give in return. And she did. They shed their clothes until they lay on the blanket, bare in the glorious sunshine, dappled by the shadows of the tree on the outer perimeter of the ruins. How symbolic, she thought, that their coming together like this, right now, should be within the confines of a home, a life, ruined by fire. Hadn't it been so with her own family? Hadn't they then risen from the ashes, stronger and better than before?

She could only hope that what she shared with Finn would be the same. That it could withstand the elements that battered against it. That they could rise together in the aftermath. A unit rather than two individuals. And so she gave herself over to the rhythm of their lovemaking, and when he slid his length inside her, she cried out in welcome, closing around him, holding him there as if she wished she need never let go of him again.

Afterward they lay together, legs entangled, his body half across hers. Their heartbeats hammering crazily in their chests as perspiration dried on their skin. Ripples of pleasure still ran through her body, each one gentling in its turn as her breathing slowly returned to normal. A deep lassitude spread through her body. If only they could stay here, like this, forever. No worries about the outside world, about the people within it or the decisions they made.

The sun slid behind a cloud, sending a change through the air. Nature's reminder that nothing remained in a state of suspension forever. She thought about Finn's earlier words, about coming to terms with the fact that she might not see Ellen, ever. Could she settle for that? Could she let go of the need to ask the questions that only her mother could answer and still be happy, still move forward with her life?

Only time would tell.

Back at the house, Finn asked Tamsyn to move into his room and heaved a sigh of relief when she agreed. He might not be able to offer her what it was she wanted most, but he could openly give himself as much and as often as she'd have him.

Over the next two weeks, they settled into a pattern together, one interrupted only by her volunteer work in town. For the rest of the time, he'd invited her to help him with the early planning stages of the respite center.

Her experience at The Masters proved surprisingly useful as they discussed the construction and outfitting of the family chalets. Her work in restoring and converting the old laborers cottages on their family property into luxury accommodation gave her insights and ideas that he found integral moving forward.

They made a terrific team. So terrific that he could barely

sleep at night, wondering when it was all going to fall apart. What would Tamsyn do when she found out the last secret—that Ellen had not chosen to bar Tamsyn's access to her after all but was, instead, dying...and that he'd known it all along? Would she ever forgive him when the truth came out? Was there any way he could keep from losing her?

Christmas loomed in just ten days' time. He'd half expected Tamsyn to at least want to head home for the holiday but she'd shown no inclination to want to be with her family. Instead, she'd teased him into buying a tall tree and festooned it with lights and decorations, some of which were ones his mother had carefully collected, spared in the house fire since they'd been stored in the detached garage.

He'd forgotten he had them, to be honest, until she'd started in about the tree. Decorating it with her had brought happier memories back to the surface in his heart. Memories of times with his parents when they looked forward to the festive season and made a huge fuss over him. Memories of Lorenzo, Ellen, Alexis and him sharing Christmas meals and the spirit of giving.

Each night he and Tamsyn had begun their own ritual, turning on the tree lights as soon as they finished their work, even though dark didn't come until closer to eight-thirty in the evening. Before they prepared their evening meal together, they'd share a glass of wine and share stories as they sat by the tree, his peppered with vignettes of life with Ellen and Lorenzo, as well.

Tonight, though, she'd become quiet before eventually asking him to stop talking about Ellen.

"I'll never find my peace with the fact she doesn't want to know me if I'm constantly wishing for what I never had—for what she gave to you."

Her words had cut him to the bone, scourging him anew with guilt. He wondered whether the gift he'd chosen for her for Christmas, the one he had yet to place under their tree, was still the right thing. A self-portrait, Ellen had done the painting about ten years ago. It was one of his favorite pictures of her and he'd believed Tamsyn would appreciate having it. Now, he wasn't so sure. Would it just reinforce the loss she felt all over again?

He had quietly cursed Lorenzo's dictates and his own promise to the man who'd raised him from adolescence into adulthood. But he'd held his tongue, and would keep his word to both Tamsyn and Lorenzo inasmuch as he was able.

One thing he knew above all others now, though. He loved Tamsyn. She'd inveigled her way into his life, but he'd welcomed her into his heart and his home, and now he never wanted her to leave. How they could work that out going into the weeks and months ahead was a problem.

Finn drifted to sleep no closer to finding an answer today than he'd been in all the days and nights before.

The subtle buzz of his mobile phone on the bedside table roused him from sleep a few hours later. Carefully, so as not to disturb Tamsyn, he slid out of bed and left the room, answering the call only when he'd closed the bedroom door securely behind him.

"Finn?"

Lorenzo's voice was different. More strained than usual.

"Lorenzo, are you okay? Is Ellen—?"

"She dying, Finn. She's letting go. Each hour, each minute, a little more. The doctors…they say it won't be long now."

The older man's voice broke and tears burned at the back of Finn's eyes, a massive lump fixed in his throat. All along, Lorenzo had been strong for Ellen, strong for Alexis, too, when she'd returned home from Italy. Now he was crumbling and he needed someone else to lean on as he faced the biggest loss of his entire life.

"I'll be there as soon as I can," Finn promised, blinking

back the tears and biting back the fear that he might be too late to be of any help to anyone.

"Whenever you arrive, my boy, it cannot be too soon," Lorenzo said, confirming Finn's worst fears.

"If I have to charter someone to take me there, Lorenzo, I'll be there. I promise."

He ended the call and made his way to his office, settling in the chair and, waking up his sleeping computer, he punched the appropriate keys to bring up flights and availability from Blenheim to Wellington. The first flight out was at 7:05. He flicked a glance at his watch: 5:00 a.m. Allowing for the half an hour preboarding check-in and the half hour or so to get to the airport, he'd need to leave soon. He booked himself on the flight, printed his ticket and boarding pass and headed back upstairs toward his bedroom so he could gather some things together.

Tamsyn.

The thought of her stopped him in his tracks. All he wanted to do was protect her from the inevitable pain ahead. What should he tell her? What *could* he tell her?

The answer came in a resounding echo in his head. Nothing. He could tell her absolutely nothing.

Twenty-One

Tamsyn sleepily rolled over, her arm reaching out beside her. The sheets were cold. Instantly awake now, she sat up and listened. Finn wasn't in the en suite bathroom. A glance at the clock confirmed it was still early, only a quarter to seven. So where was he?

She slipped from the bed and draped her robe around her. In the kitchen there was still no sign of him. The coffeepot was cold and no breakfast dishes lurked in the sink. Even his office was empty. She racked her brain to remember if he'd said something last night about having to go away, but nothing came to mind.

Her phone, which she'd left on the kitchen counter, buzzed to life and she snatched it up, recognizing Finn's number on the caller I.D.

"Finn? Is everything okay?"

In the background she could hear engine noise and the sound of lots of people.

"I'm sorry, but I got called away again. I'm not sure how long I'll be gone. Look, they're doing the last call for my flight. I have to go. Take care, okay?"

"What about Lucy?" she thought suddenly.

It still grated that Finn went daily to the cottage to feed the cat and spread feed for the chickens. If she'd been allowed to stay there... She shook her head. It didn't pay to dwell on the issue.

Finn uttered a short expletive. "I forgot about that. Are you okay doing it?"

"Yes, of course I am," she answered. She knew where he kept the key, so that wasn't going to be an problem. "I'll take care of it. You had better go. I'll see you when you get back. I'll miss you."

"I'll miss you too," he said. "We'll talk when I get back. I've been thinking…about the future. *Our* future."

"Our future?" Tamsyn's heart fluttered in her chest.

Her love for Finn grew stronger every day. To hear him mention a word like *future* was a light in the darkness. A shred of hope that things would come right.

"I—hell, I didn't want to say this the first time over the phone, but I need to. I love you, Tamsyn. I'll be back soon."

He cut the link between them before she could answer but it didn't stop her continuing to press the phone to her ear as if doing so could extend their contact a few moments longer. Eventually she put the phone down and wrapped her arms around herself as joy built from deep inside. She danced a little jig around the kitchen island, hugging herself tight until she threw her arms out with a squeal of happiness. Everything was going to be all right. She just knew it.

It was a week before Christmas and the crowd for the end-of-year Christmas potluck meal at the seniors' center was swollen with extras Tamsyn had never met before. Given the greetings that flew back and forth, several had been away or unwell and unable to attend, but all had made a monumental effort to attend this last get-together for the year. The tables groaned with the bring-a-plate offerings and the Secret Santa gifts under the artificial tree Tamsyn had erected and decorated quickly this morning were plentiful.

This was going to be a great day, she thought as she watched everyone's happy faces. She moved through the crowd, ensuring all the guests had what they needed. As she did so, she picked up snippets of conversations that made her smile. Grandparent rivalry was thick in the air, from all accounts. One conversation, though, made her pause as a name hung in the air.

"Did you hear how Ellen is doing?" one of the new faces asked one of the regulars.

"Still in hospital from what I heard," the regular responded with a dour look on her face. "And it's not looking good."

"Oh, dear, that poor woman. Poor Lorenzo."

Her mother was in hospital? Was that why Lorenzo was being so protective? All the air drove out of Tamsyn's lungs.

The new woman continued. "So is she still local? Can we visit?"

"No," came the reply. "She's in Wellington. They airlifted her there weeks ago. Heart, kidneys, liver—all failing. Tragic, just tragic."

The other woman nodded in understanding. "So sad."

Tamsyn wheeled away from the group, desperate for a quiet place where she could think for a moment—process what she'd just heard. She'd hoped, eventually, for a snippet of information to come her way and lead her to her mother, but she'd never anticipated it being anything like this.

A gnarled hand on her arm, accompanied by the reek of stale cigarettes, made her flinch.

"You heard that, didn't you?" Gladys rasped. "Are you all right, lovey?"

Tamsyn could only shake her head.

"'spected as much. It was only a matter of time before someone let something slip."

"I have to go," Tamsyn finally managed to say through numb lips.

"I'll take care of things," Gladys said with a look of understanding in her rheumy eyes that was just about Tamsyn's undoing. "For what it's worth, we're all very sorry about your mum."

Afterward she didn't remember actually driving from town back to Finn's house. All she remembered was sitting in his office, the office of the man who'd known all along that her mother was in a hospital in Wellington, dying, and who had kept that information from her. Honor? Promises? Love? They could all be damned. This situation went beyond a vow, beyond loyalty to another man.

Anger kept her from falling apart as she methodically checked every hospital in the book until she struck pay dirt. Her glow of success was short-lived, hitting a wall when the patient-inquiries staff wouldn't give her the status of her mother's health, insisting she was not on the authorized list of family members.

More research turned up a flight to Wellington that would take a half hour. She sank back in the chair. All this time her mother had been just across Cook Strait, a short hop in a plane. Determination saw her book the last seat on the next flight out, and kept her sane as she drove to Blenheim airport.

"I'm sorry, miss, but we cannot disclose the patient's details." The young woman behind the patient-inquiries window was sympathetic but adamant.

"Can you at least tell me if she's still alive?" Tamsyn pleaded.

"Please, I will be forced to call security if you don't leave. I've told you all I can."

"But you've told me nothing! She's my mother and she's dying. I just want to know if I'm too late to even see her one last time. Is that too much to ask?"

Tamsyn's voice bordered on the hysterical and the clerk reached for her phone, her hand hovering over one quick-dial button in particular.

"Miss, I understand this is distressing for you, but my instructions are quite clear."

Tamsyn tore herself away from the window, utter dejection dragging down every cell in her body. She looked toward the elevator bank and weighed the prospect of visiting every floor in the hospital, trailing through each ward searching for the room that had her mother's name on the door. She'd begun to move toward the elevators when the doors of one car opened and her heart jumped in her chest.

Finn. All the breath in her lungs disappeared on a *whoosh*. There was an older man with him, she noticed, and a woman perhaps a little younger than herself. Lorenzo Fabrini and his daughter, Alexis. Chills ran through Tamsyn's body as she recognized them both from the photos at the house, as she laid eyes on her sister in person for the very first time.

Alexis lifted a tissue to her eyes with one hand, wiping fiercely; the other was tucked firmly into the crook of her father's arm. From here, Tamsyn couldn't be sure who was supporting whom. Suddenly the ramifications of what she viewed struck home. The older man's eyes were red-rimmed, as were Finn's, and Alexis still wept. It was still visiting hours—they wouldn't have left Ellen entirely alone unless…unless…

Was she too late? Had she come this far only to fail? The awful possibility hit her in the chest with the weight of a well-aimed sledgehammer and she staggered, the movement attracting attention from the self-contained group that approached.

Lorenzo's dark eyes bored straight through her for a moment before he turned to Finn, anger suffusing his haggard features.

"I thought you were keeping her away," he said, the words sharp and clear on the air.

"Papa!" Alexis remonstrated, tugging at his arm.

But the words were said. Damning words that confirmed that Finn had not just been withholding information from her, he'd actively ensured she didn't find her mother's location. Hurt piled upon hurt.

"I'm my own person," Tamsyn said shakily, stepping up

to the small group. "You can't keep on pushing me away, hoping I'll just disappear. I want to see my mother."

"You're too late," Alexis said softly. "Our mother passed away two hours ago. I'm sorry. If I'd known you were here—"

"If you'd known, nothing!" Lorenzo spat. "She's a Masters. You know what they did to your mother, how they broke her spirit."

"Enough!" Finn said firmly, stepping between Tamsyn and Lorenzo. "Now isn't the time for recriminations. Alexis, take your father back to the hotel. I'll look after Tamsyn."

Tamsyn stood there, numb and disbelieving. Her mother was dead? Every opportunity she'd had over the past four and a half weeks was irrevocably lost. Every question she'd ever want answered, every story she'd ever want told—gone. Forever.

She couldn't even summon a reaction as Finn took her arm and led her out toward the taxi rank. The journey to his hotel was swift and, before she knew it, she was in his room, a slug of brandy in a short tumbler thrust into her hands.

"Drink, you've had a shock," he insisted, cupping his hands over hers and lifting the glass to her lips.

Automatically she obeyed, automatically she swallowed the burning liquid, felt its trail from her lips to her tongue and down to her stomach where it hit and spread, infusing her frozen senses with some sense of warmth.

"Why?" she asked, her voice cold and empty. "Why did you keep me from her? I wouldn't have hurt her. I just wanted my mother!"

Her last words rose to a pained peak and tears brimmed in her eyes before they began to roll, one swiftly after the other, down her face.

"It wouldn't have made any difference, Tamsyn. Whatever you wanted from her, you wouldn't have been able to get. I'm sorry, she was too sick."

"How can you say that? You never even gave me a chance."

Finn sighed and sat in the chair opposite her, his forearms resting on his knees, his head dropping between his shoulders for a minute before he lifted it and faced her.

"For the last ten years Ellen has been battling early-onset dementia. It progressed dramatically in the past year. Coupled with that, she had underlying health problems created and subsequently exacerbated by her alcoholism. Her life has been a battle for a very long time. One she fought bravely." He shoved a hand through his hair, making the ends spike in disarray. "Ellen wouldn't have known you, Tamsyn. She didn't even know Lorenzo or Alexis these past few weeks. She disappeared into a part of her mind where she could hide until she had to face the end."

"And you knew this all along?" Pain edged every word she uttered.

"Yes." The single word made her shudder. He started to reach for her, but his hand stopped halfway, clearly sensing his touch would not be welcome. "It wasn't my choice to keep you in the dark. Not once I got to know you, once I understood that you hadn't been deliberately staying away."

"Deliberately? What are you talking about?"

"We always thought you knew she was still alive."

"But I told you the truth ages ago."

"I know that, and from that time forward I begged Lorenzo to let you see her—maybe not visit her, but at least see her—but he was adamant." Finn dropped his head again.

"Why not let me visit her?"

"You have to understand, Tamsyn. After my father died, my mother couldn't cope with what she saw as her failure to be a good farm wife, to be a good mother. I wasn't allowed to see her for months, but when I did I was a reminder of all that she'd failed at. After my visit, she was so ashamed of herself that she stopped eating, stopped getting out of bed—until eventually she stopped living.

"*I* did that to her. I know what it feels like to be the catalyst for something so awful it was beyond my comprehension at the time. Seeing you? Well, if Ellen *had* recognized you, given how traumatic her departure from Australia was—leaving you and Ethan behind—and how it's colored her entire life since, who knows what would have happened? If she had recognized you it might have only caused her more pain, more guilt, more regret. It could have driven her to her death sooner.

"I didn't want you to go through what I went through. I didn't want you to feel the same guilt, to have to live with that all your life."

Tamsyn pushed up from the chair and moved over to the bottle of brandy on the bureau against the opposite wall. She sloshed another generous measure into the glass and sipped it slowly before responding.

"So that's why you didn't want her to see me. But you never told me that, never explained. You just kept me from being able to see her. That wasn't your decision to make."

"No, it wasn't. The decision to keep you away from Ellen was Lorenzo's. Mine was in agreeing with him for, I believed, all the right reasons. Believe me, Tamsyn, you wouldn't have wanted to remember Ellen the way she was before she died. *She* wouldn't have wanted you to see her like that."

"I'll never know now, will I? And you'll have to forgive me," she said, sarcasm beginning to color her voice an unpleasant shade, "if I find it difficult to believe you when you say you did any of this for me. From day one you lied to me. Tell me, was our affair a deliberate choice on your part? Did you set out to seduce me to distract me from finding her? Was everything we did together, everything we shared, all based on a lie?"

Finn locked gazes with her and she saw the damning truth reflected back at her.

"In the beginning, yes. But not later, Tamsyn. Definitely not later."

It didn't matter to her now. His intent from the outset was clear. The lies aside, the hurt aside, he'd just confirmed to her that she was worth nothing—just as her father had done, just as Trent had done. Without another word, she carefully placed her glass back on the bureau, picked up her handbag and walked out.

Twenty-Two

"You love her, don't you?"

Finn shot a look of surprise at Alexis, pausing in his task of handling the details to bring Ellen's body home to rest. He couldn't lie to her, not this girl who'd grown into a beautiful young woman—one he regarded as a sister.

"Yes," he answered simply, then folded the papers they'd completed and pushed them back into an envelope before handing the envelope to her to return to the undertaker.

"Then what are you still doing here?"

"What?"

"Go after her. I can cope with this, Finn. We've been expecting it a long time. I know Papa is beside himself with grief—despite the evidence in front of him he couldn't let her go, couldn't believe that one day she wouldn't get well again. I did my grieving for the mother we both remember a long time ago. I'm sad now, but I know she's finally at rest. It's been a long time coming. Too long."

Finn's throat choked up. She was right, on all counts. She didn't need his help for this. And he had to get back to Tamsyn. He hadn't had the heart to try to stop her when she'd left him today. He knew he'd done a number on her—had betrayed the fragile trust he'd painstakingly rebuilt on the backbone of a very shaky start. But he owed it to her to go after her. To apologize, to convince her—

His gut twisted. Could he convince her that his love was real? That he'd believed he was acting in her best interests as well? He wanted to believe the answer was yes…and feared that it was no. That's why he was stalling, as if he could convince himself that she was back home waiting for him, loving him, as long as he wasn't there to watch her pack her bags and leave. But sooner or later, he'd have to go home and see for himself.

"I'll head to the airport right now," he said, throwing his meager supply of things into an overnight bag and heading for the door.

He stopped briefly to give Alexis a kiss on the cheek.

"Thank you," he said simply.

"It's what I'm here for. To remind you sometimes that you're not always right."

He gave a strangled laugh. Nothing changed between them. Even though she knew he'd been a complete ass with Tamsyn, and she'd soundly told him that not five minutes ago, they still had a connection that not even their eight-year age difference could sever. Friends, family. The lines had always been blurred, but one thing was certain. They were always there for one another and were always one hundred percent up front.

"You're growing cobwebs," she said with a cocked eyebrow.

"I'm gone. Wish me luck."

"You're going to need more than that, but I'll wish it for you anyway. Now, shoo!"

He was gone.

A last-minute ticket came at a premium, but Finn didn't care. Money wasn't the issue, he'd have paid whatever it took if the ticket could guarantee he'd be able to stop Tamsyn from leaving him. He was flooded with relief as he saw her rental car parked outside the front door to his home. The trunk was open. Clearly he was just in time.

Her keys hung in the ignition and he pocketed them for safekeeping. If she still chose to leave after what he had to say, then he would have to watch her go, but in the meantime he wanted her to have to listen to him.

He found her in their bedroom shoving the last of her

things into her case. Her face was pale, her eyes holding a world of hurt as she looked up and saw him. She turned her attention back to her case, wrestling with the tab on the zipper and uttering a string of curses before the thing came off in her hand entirely. Defeated, she slumped onto the floor beside the case.

"Need a hand?" he asked, stepping closer.

"Go away," she replied, her voice tearful, shaky.

He had the distinct impression that if he reached out and touched her she'd shatter into a thousand pieces where she sat. She was clearly operating on her last reserve.

"Don't go, Tamsyn. Please?"

"There's nothing left for me here now. Do you hear me?" She turned her face to him, her beautiful lush mouth twisting as she repeated herself. *"Nothing!"*

She'd meant the words to hurt him, and they had.

"I'm sorry, so sorry."

"Empty words," she said, forcing her attention to trying to clip the zipper tab back on her case. "I don't want to stay here anymore, I don't want to see you anymore."

"I understand, you have every right to feel this way, but please stay. At least for Ellen's funeral."

She uttered a sound, a bitter ringing laugh. "Your precious Lorenzo wouldn't let me see her alive, what makes you think he'll let me be around now she's dead?"

"He was only trying to protect the love of his life, the way I was trying to protect mine."

"Don't give me that," she said, her voice cracking under the strain of holding on to her anger, of holding back the tide of her grief. He knew how it felt. He was doing exactly the same thing himself. "The choices you made right from the beginning had nothing to do with what was best for me. You were his willing puppet all along. He must have commended you on going above and beyond the call of duty. You're quite a guy."

"You deserved to see Ellen—we were both wrong to stop you. I saw that earlier on but I couldn't convince him of that. I couldn't go against him, not when I knew how much he loved her. He'd never have forgiven me if I let any harm come to her—just like I'll never forgive myself for what I did to you."

"I don't believe you. Why would you begin telling me the truth now?" She gave a small sound of satisfaction as she got the tab onto the zipper and managed to successfully close her case.

"Because I love you and because I want you to stay."

She shook her head. "Good try, but not working."

Tamsyn rose fluidly to her feet and extended the handle of her bag. Finn rose to block her way.

"Stay, at least for Alexis's sake. She wants to meet you properly."

About to step around him, he was relieved to see that his words had temporarily stopped her in her tracks.

"Alexis? She wants to talk to me?"

"More than that, she really does want to get to know you," he assured her.

Tamsyn visibly sagged. All the bravado, all the fight leeching out of her before his eyes.

"All right. For her, I'll stay, but not in here. If I didn't know for a fact that the whole town is booked solid, I'd get a hotel room. Instead, I'll use the room I had before."

"Thank you."

She lifted her head, her eyes hollow and filled with sorrow. "I'm not doing it for you."

No, of course she wasn't. He understood that as he'd understood nothing else before. But it was a small victory. She was here, still under his roof. As she walked from the room and down the hallway he closed his eyes and thanked his lucky stars he still had this much. And, he hoped, time enough to convince Tamsyn to stay for good.

* * *

Tamsyn hung on the outskirts of the throng of mourners attending Ellen's wake at Finn's house. She'd never felt more utterly alone in her life. Ethan and Isobel had tried to come but, this close to Christmas, they'd been unable to secure flights to get them here in time. As it was, with Christmas only three days away, she'd been lucky to get a flight out of Blenheim to Auckland for later this evening.

The local townspeople had done Ellen proud. The hall was used for her funeral and it had been filled to the seams—with more chairs, speakers and screens outside—with those who'd come to pay their respects. Several people came up to Tamsyn, to offer their condolences, many with apologies for their own guilt at keeping the truth from her reflected in their eyes.

Throughout the activity of the day, Tamsyn was constantly reminded that no matter how well everyone had known and loved her mother, nobody here could answer her questions. No one could explain why Ellen had abandoned her children and left them to grow up thinking she was dead. The last remaining person who could have done that was being laid to rest in the small graveyard beside the church.

She'd sat between Finn and Alexis for the service—dry eyed, stoic—and learned for the first time how others had seen her mother. Yes, she'd been flawed and, yes, she'd struggled with alcohol abuse, but in her stronger moments she had been the kind of woman that Tamsyn knew she would have wanted to know. Ellen's contributions to the district had varied and she was fondly remembered for the art classes she'd taught in the community. It reminded Tamsyn of the paintings she'd seen at Finn's house in the gallery, signed with her mother's initials. She ached to possess something of her mother's. The closest thing she had was the new sister in her life.

Alexis had been a surprise. Sunny-natured with not an

unpleasant bone in her body, her half sister was easy to be with and even, Tamsyn knew, to begin to love. That Alexis held Finn in a state of near hero worship reminded Tamsyn very much of her relationship with her own brother growing up. And, like Tamsyn with Ethan, Alexis was clear-eyed about her foster brother's flaws.

Under Alexis's less than subtle onslaught of friendship over the past five days, Tamsyn had begun to rationalize, again, Finn's reasons for keeping the truth from her, but that did nothing to ease the pain and emptiness that echoed inside her every day. And, rationalization aside, she was still angry with him. However valid he'd made his reasons seem, she'd deserved the opportunity to make the final judgment about trying to see her mother herself. Just one last glimpse, one final opportunity to hold her hand, to feel the connection that had been missing for most of her life. Her right to choose what to do had been stolen from her and she struggled to forgive that.

Distance and space to think in was what she needed most right now. She was waitlisted on several flights out of Auckland, hoping to be home in time for the twenty-fifth, where she could lick her emotional wounds among her own people.

"Miss Masters?"

Tamsyn wheeled around at the accented sound of Lorenzo's voice. He'd avoided her completely since his return to the cottage at the bottom of the hill and she couldn't mask her surprise at having him approach her now. Her eyes roamed his face. He was still a handsome man, although grief clouded his eyes and aged him.

"I would speak with you. Will you walk with me a moment?" he asked, offering her his elbow with old-fashioned courtesy.

Every instinct within her wanted to refuse the man who'd deliberately thwarted her attempts to find her mother and she opened her mouth to do exactly that.

"Please, Tamsyn, in your mother's memory, I beg this of you," he asked, his voice solemn.

They strolled away from the house in silence, to the edge of the manicured lawns where the vineyard started, and then they strolled along one long row after another. Tamsyn began to feel uncomfortable, to wonder what it was that Lorenzo wanted to talk to her about.

"I am sorry for what I did to you," he said heavily as they reached the end of a row and stopped. "I was wrong, I see that now. I was acting from a point of fear, when I should have been acting from a point of compassion. Worse, I made Finn keep his word to me even when I knew it was destroying him inside. I was a desperate, foolish old man and I hope that one day, in time, you can find it in your heart to forgive me, to forgive Finn, for what we both did. Once he got to know you, he was not a willing partner in our deception, believe me."

"I…I don't know if I can forgive, Mr. Fabrini. I really don't."

"I understand," he said, closing his eyes and bowing his head. "I have something for you. I wanted to be sure you had this before you go home to The Masters again."

He reached in his pocket and withdrew a fat bundle of envelopes tied with a length of faded ribbon. Lorenzo's thumb played along the narrow band of light purple-colored satin for a moment before he drew in a deep breath and passed the packet to her.

"These are your mother's. More correctly, they are from her to you and your brother. She wrote the letters inside over many years but never posted them. She'd promised your father she would never make contact with anyone at The Masters again, but it didn't stop her from writing what she needed to say. Here."

Tamsyn's hand shook as she took the envelopes, as she saw her mother's handwriting for the first time, scrawled in lilac-colored ink across the fine linen stationery. Tamsyn smiled a watery smile. Her childhood room had been decorated in shades of purple—that obviously had been her mother's hand at work. Knowing that now brought a flicker of warmth to her heart that had been missing for days.

"Thank you," she whispered.

"You're welcome. I hope her words can bring you some peace, show you the kind of woman she was before she became ill."

"I'll treasure them."

He nodded, his eyes filling anew with tears. He sniffed loudly and turned his head, too proud to let her see his tears fall. "I'll go sit over there in the sun. I am in no hurry to go back to that crowd up there. When you are finished, I will answer anything I can for you if you still have any questions. Take your time, eh?"

"I will," she promised. She watched as he settled himself on a wooden bench seat that gave a view over the vineyards and down to where his and Ellen's cottage nestled against the bottom of the hill.

She lowered herself to the ground and put the letters in her lap before carefully undoing the ribbon and lifting the first envelope to her face. She closed her eyes and inhaled deeply, trying to catch the scent of her mother, to see if there was anything that still remained of who she'd been.

There it was, ever so faintly. A fragrance that reminded her of childish giggles, of summer sunshine, of the warmth of a woman's embrace. Her mother's embrace.

Tamsyn lowered the envelope, slid a nail under the flap and began to read.

Twenty-Three

She cried many tears over her mother's words, words threaded with guilt that she'd failed to protect her children from her own weakness. She'd been running away from The Masters—from her marriage and the failures she'd struggled to live with—to Lorenzo, who waited for her at the airport with tickets for all of them to travel to New Zealand, when she'd crashed her car.

John, her husband, had arrived, distraught to find his children injured and furiously angry to find his wife under the influence of alcohol and sobbing on the side of the road. He'd used the weight of the Masters name to see the police suppress their evidence against her, and eventually drop all charges, on her promise that she'd leave, without her children, and never return. Plus, he'd arranged to pay her a stipend to ensure she stayed away, out of all their lives forever.

Ellen had battled with her guilt, and her drinking, for years after that, but had continued to accept the money from John Masters month after month, year after year. Lorenzo hadn't wanted Masters money to touch the life they'd rebuilt for themselves in New Zealand, so she'd saved it in a separate account, eventually using it to buy some land, which was being held in trust for Ethan and Tamsyn. While her biggest regret in life had been not fighting harder to maintain a relationship with her children, she'd at least ensured she had something to give them, something definite and valuable to remember her by.

She closed the last letter with the name of the legal firm in Auckland that oversaw her and Ethan's inheritance.

Tamsyn struggled to her feet, easing the stiffness out of her muscles as she walked toward Lorenzo, who rose to greet her.

"We don't need the land, Lorenzo," she said after explaining what Ellen had done. "It should be yours. We already have far more than we need at home, you especially should know that."

"I do know that. I worked for your family for many years and I know what your family land means to you all. This is why you should know what this meant to Ellen to give you something that is purely yours, from her. You and your brother may do with it whatever you want, but remember, it was her only way of leaving you something of her. Think on it, and make your decision once you have talked to your brother, yes?"

Tamsyn nodded. "Okay."

Back at the house, after everyone had gone, she gathered her things together for her flight away from here. Away from the pain, away from the memories, both good and bad. Finn waited at the door as she approached, a wrapped rectangle in his hands. She'd done her level best to avoid being alone with him since Ellen's death and with her spending so much time with Alexis, it hadn't been difficult. Finn, too, had been out of the house a lot—helping to coordinate the funeral as well as being a constant support for Lorenzo. Tamsyn had told herself she was relieved he hadn't had the opportunity to wear down her shaky resolve to leave, but right now she felt so raw it was as if she was bleeding inside.

"Before you go, I'd like you to have this," he said, handing her the parcel.

She looked at the bright Christmas wrappings and shook her head. "No, Finn. Please. Not a Christmas gift. We're not…I can't…"

"It's yours, you have to take it."

"Fine then," she said, grabbing it from him and shoving it under her arm as she pushed past and carried on to her car.

She wouldn't open the gift, she decided as she got into her car and, without a backward glance, drove down the hill toward the road that would take her to the airport.

Once she reached Auckland, she could have stayed with either of her cousins. Judd Wilson, who had grown up with her and Ethan at The Masters, lived in the city with his wife, Anna. So did Judd's sister Nicole, who'd grown up in her father's custody in New Zealand and who Tamsyn had only gotten to know in the past year, with her new husband, Nate. But the prospect of having to explain what she'd been through this past month or so was more than she could bear. The anonymity of a hotel was just what she needed and she'd been fortunate when a last-minute cancellation had secured her a room in one of Auckland's most prestigious hotels.

The next morning Tamsyn checked with the airlines several times. Nothing was available, not even taking a more circuitous route through Sydney or Melbourne. It seemed everyone wanted to go to Australia for Christmas. To take her mind off the unsettled feeling that she'd left something vital behind in Marlborough, she phoned the lawyers her mother had mentioned in her letter. To her surprise, she was able to get an appointment immediately.

Later, sitting in a café on the waterfront, Tamsyn sipped a latte and let the news she'd just received sink in. She needed to talk to Ethan and dialed him up immediately.

"Have you got a flight yet?" he asked as he answered his phone. "We're looking forward to having you back where you belong."

Did she really belong there, back at The Masters? Sure, it was where she'd been brought up, but she had been restless, unsettled, for a long time. That feeling had begun to lift while she'd been in Marlborough, while she'd been with Finn. She stubbornly pushed that last thought aside before answering her brother.

"No luck with flights yet but I'm on the lists. Just keep your fingers crossed, okay? In the meantime, there's something I need to talk to you about."

"What's that?"

"Our mother. She left us property here in New Zealand. Apparently she had been putting the money Dad sent her into some land close to where she was living. Once she'd paid it off, the balance went into an account that's been held in trust in both our names."

"Seriously? She did that?"

"There's more. She wrote us letters, lots of them. They explain everything."

Tamsyn gave him the full rundown on the letters' contents. There was a long pause before Ethan answered.

"And do you feel better about everything, about her, now?"

Did she? Had reading the letters brought her any closer to understanding, to making peace with the myriad of answers she'd sought?

"I think I understand her a little more. She was miserable inside, before. She made some stupid, totally wrong, decisions and she paid for them dearly. I still wish we'd had a chance to know her, but I can't pin the rest of my life on something I can never have or change. So, yeah, I do feel better, stronger even."

"Should I be scared?" he teased and she smiled in response. The first genuine smile to stretch her face in almost a week.

"Funny, Ethan, very funny. Now, about this land. Obviously I don't expect you to make a decision right now—but we'll need to think carefully about what we want to do."

"I don't think we need it, Tam. Do you?"

"I agree. I said as much to Lorenzo, but he was insistent that Mom wanted us to have it, to do with it whatever we wanted."

"Hmm. Then how would you feel about selling the land? Maybe donating the money toward a charity or something in her name, something that might help other people going through what she went through."

Tamsyn felt herself nodding. "That's a good idea. I'll put some thoughts together and we can discuss it when I get home, okay?"

They said their goodbyes and Tamsyn decided to walk back to the hotel as a vague feeling of disquiet still niggled at her. Saying "home" hadn't felt quite right. For some reason, it felt as though the vast tract of land encompassing The Masters, including the imposing ruins of Masters Rise on the hilltop, belonged to another Tamsyn, another time, another world apart from what she'd begun to think of as home now. Did she even belong there at all? Did she belong anywhere?

From her harbor-facing hotel room window she watched as seagulls lazily circled in the air. She felt displaced, and wasn't that what had led her to try to find her mother in the first place? The only time she'd felt as though she truly belonged anywhere was when she'd been in Finn's arms. The past couple of weeks, working with him, just simply *being* with him, had felt so very right.

Her chest ached with a definite physical pain. She missed him already, even though he'd hurt her, even though he'd lied. As Alexis had stressed, Finn had acted with the very best intentions—not just toward Lorenzo, but toward her, as well. Perhaps not immediately, but certainly within the first week of knowing why she was there.

On the table beside her, her phone chimed with a new

text message. Idly, she picked it up, surprised to see it was
from Alexis and contained a link to a clip in a national current affairs show.

Hi sis. Hopefully ur still in NZ. U HAVE to see this! Luv
Ax.

Tamsyn swiftly texted back asking what it was about but
only received a watch it! in response.

She thumbed the link, hoping it wouldn't be a total waste
of her data allowance, and watched as the show advertising
scrolled across the screen. The presenter's words immediately made her sit up and take notice.

"Tonight we have well known philanthropist Finn Gallagher with us, to tell us about his exciting new project. Finn,
what led you to this project in particular?"

Tamsyn watched, enthralled, as Finn filled the screen
of her smartphone, as his measured voice came from the
tiny speakers. She recognized the suit he was wearing as
one he'd had on when he'd returned from a day trip to Wellington last week, so the interview itself was very recent.

During the interview he spoke eloquently about the respite center and about the families and children he hoped
it would serve, and why. It seemed to take a toll on Finn,
putting such a public face on one of his very personal proj-
ects, which fit in with what Alexis had told her about him
and how much he supported those less fortunate in the community.

It hurt to watch him, yet it filled Tamsyn with a deep
sense of calm as well. He was, essentially, a good man with
a heart that beat for those he loved. He'd told her she was one
of those people, but with everything that had happened afterward, she'd been too angry, too wounded and too scared
of making herself vulnerable again to believe him.

Thinking back now, she remember how he'd sounded

when he'd said the words before he went to be with Ellen as she died. He'd obviously been distraught at the knowledge that the mother figure, who'd been there for him while he was growing up, was leaving them all for good, yet he'd taken the time to call Tamsyn. To give her that piece of himself.

The current affairs piece was wrapping up and Tamsyn forced her attention back to the screen.

"And do you have a name for the center?" the presenter asked.

"Yes, I do. I'm naming it for a very special woman. To honor her strength and my love and admiration for her, I'm calling it, Tamsyn's Place."

Tamsyn didn't hear whatever it was the presenter said next. All she could hear were Finn's words repeating in her head as she tried to comprehend the enormity of his action in wanting to name the center after her. She didn't deserve the accolade. She would have thought, after all they'd been through, the last thing he'd have wanted would be the constant reminder of her in his life. But it seemed she was very wrong. And if she was wrong about that, maybe she'd been wrong about other things as well.

She looked at the documents poking out from her handbag lying on the hotel bed—the copy of legal title to the land her mother had left her, and realized why looking at it caused that niggling sense of familiarity. It was the land Finn had tried to get for the easement—the one he needed for the road to Tamsyn's Place. And as she stared at the papers, she knew what she needed to do.

More, she now knew exactly where her place was. And maybe in going to claim it, she could stand to be spontaneous just one more time after all....

Twenty-Four

The persistent hammering at the front door woke Finn from his slumber on the couch where he'd collapsed last night. The racket matched the hammering in his head.

Last night, all his duties to everyone else behind him for a while, he'd done some serious damage to a bottle of whiskey and now he was paying the price. Still, it had been worth it for the brief oblivion it had given him. He mourned Ellen, but he was dying inside for what he'd done to Tamsyn and for how his choices had lost her from his life for good.

He caught sight of himself in a wall mirror and made a sound of disgust. He looked terrible. Hair unkempt, clothing slept in, face unshaven. Maybe he could just scare away whoever was at the door without having to speak—something he was sure would make his head ache even more.

Finn swung the front door open with a growled greeting and felt the world tilt at his feet when he saw Tamsyn standing there. He rubbed his eyes—clichéd, he knew, but he couldn't quite believe what he saw.

"You look like hell," she said, walking past him and into the house before he could say anything. "We need to talk."

"By all means, come in," he said, closing the door behind her and following her down the hall to the kitchen.

He stood there, saying nothing, just drinking her in as she moved around the kitchen preparing a fresh carafe of coffee. She was a sight for sore eyes and he was glad those sore eyes didn't deceive him, but what the hell was she doing here?

Once the coffee was brewed, she poured them each a mug and handed one to him.

"Drink," she ordered then went to sit at the casual dining table in front of the French doors.

He joined her and took a long draw of the life-sustaining brew. She'd made it strong. Good, he had the feeling he'd really need his wits about him for whatever came next.

"I have a proposition for you," she said, pulling a sheaf of papers from her voluminous handbag and setting them on the table.

"A proposition?"

It certainly wasn't what he'd expected to hear from her lips. He sat up a little straighter. She was a far cry from the desperately unhappy and wounded woman who'd driven away from him two days ago. Something had happened to change her, but what? Whatever it was, he was grateful it had brought her back here, to him, even if only for a short time. Grateful enough to give his full attention to whatever proposition she wanted to make, no matter how badly his head hurt.

"A business proposition, actually. I don't know if Lorenzo told you—"

"I haven't spoken to him since the funeral on Monday," he interrupted.

Tamsyn nodded. "Okay, well, it seems that my brother and I are the proud owners of this."

She pushed a copy of a title plan toward him, and her finger pointed at the acreage adjoining his own. The very acreage he needed a slice of to complete his dream for the respite center. His headache grew to new proportions. How on earth had she and Ethan gotten possession of the land? And why was she telling him this? Was it so she could have the satisfaction of rubbing his face in it, in telling him that for what he'd done to her he could wait until hell froze over before he could have that easement?

"I don't understand. I've been approaching the trustees for months with no satisfaction. How did you get hold of it?"

"Ellen gave it to us."

She lifted her eyes and stared at him, gauging his reaction, no doubt, and he didn't disappoint. The shock that hit him now was second only to the shock that had shaken him when he'd opened his front door to her just a few minutes ago.

"Ellen?"

She nodded. "It seems she bought it many years ago with money she'd saved from what my father had sent her. He paid her a lot to stay away and Lorenzo wouldn't let her use it for their new life together. I think that's why my father's solicitors had your address for mailing—did she maybe have her mail redirected to your address?"

Realization dawned. Lorenzo and his parents had shared a letter box on the road and when Finn had built up here on the hill he hadn't seen any point in changing what had worked for a couple of decades or more. He quickly explained it to Tamsyn.

"So that's why my mother's checks were coming here, except you wouldn't have known that, would you?"

He shook his head. "We just leave each other's mail in the box for whoever it was addressed to, to pick up. It's always been as simple as that."

"Ellen was determined to leave something for Ethan and me, something that had meaning to her and that she hoped would have meaning to us, as well. Ethan and I have only talked about this briefly, but we're one hundred percent on the same page about it. We both feel it's very important to honor her memory and in that vein, we want to gift the land to the respite center."

"Are you sure? I mean, you know what getting that easement is going to mean to the overall development, but—"

"Finn, you misunderstand me. We're not offering you the easement."

Confusion muddled his already aching head. He sup-

posed he deserved it if she wanted to deny him the easement, but then what had she been talking about?

"What do you mean, exactly?"

"We're offering you everything, the entire acreage."

His fingers tightened around the coffee mug. "Seriously?
The whole thing? What's the catch?"

"Just the one—well, two actually."

He wasn't entirely surprised. He sighed. "Okay, let's get
it over with. Give me your terms."

"One, I want naming rights to the retreat."

"No way. It already has a name and I'm not changing it."

She leaned back in her chair and he watched as her face
lit up, a smile pulling her lips into a gentle curve. "Oh-kay, I
can live with that, but the other condition is nonnegotiable."

"And it is?"

"That you'll let me continue to work with you on the
development."

"Are you serious? You want to stay?"

"With you, if you'll have me."

He was on his feet and pulling her from her chair before
his brain even fully assimilated what he was doing.

"*If* I'll have you? You have to be kidding me. I thought
I'd never see you again, that I'd destroyed every last chance
I could have to keep you in my life."

She lifted her hands and bracketed his face. "Finn, I
know how hard it was for you, how torn you must have
been toward the end. I've been so focused on just one thing,
finding *my* mother, for so many months now and you were
the person standing in the way. I thought that you couldn't
possibly love me because you didn't simply hand over what
I wanted. I never stopped to think, until just recently, what
that was doing to you. How it pulled at your honor, at your
heart. You didn't just lose one mother, you've lost two, and
I forgot all about that because all I wanted was mine. I
couldn't see all the ways you showed me you loved me since

I was so focused on the one thing you wouldn't do. I was single-minded and selfish and I'm sorry."

"No," he protested. "What Lorenzo and I did was wrong. I'm the one who's sorry, Tamsyn, you'll never know how sorry."

"Shh," she said, laying a finger across his lips. "We have to let it go now. Put it in the past where it belongs. We need to honor the women who brought us here, who brought us to this, to each other."

"You can forgive me?"

"I already have, Finn. Sure, I wish things could have been different, but no one can change the past. The only thing we can do is move forward."

She lifted her face to his, her lips a tender entreaty, one he accepted with every beat of his heart.

When they broke apart he shook his head. "I can't believe I was so wrong about you right from the start. I've been a total idiot."

"What do you mean?"

"From when I was about fifteen I started keeping tabs on you and your brother, on your family's lifestyle. It used to make me mad to see you guys had so much, that your life was so easy, when Ellen had so little and worked so hard. You all seemed so happy without her. I allowed those impressions, formed when I was too young to fully understand, to color how I treated you when you arrived here."

"You were pretty cold, but you've thawed out nicely," Tamsyn said with a forgiving smile he really didn't deserve.

"You thawed me out. You made me see the real you, the beautiful woman inside that perfect exterior. It's why I want to hold on to naming rights for the center."

"You really want to call it Tamsyn's Place?"

"You know about that?"

"Alexis sent me a link to the clip on TV."

He smiled. Of course she had. "Are you okay with that?"

"Well, I would have preferred to see it named after Ellen, but maybe we can do that with the next one."

"I like the sound of that. Tamsyn, I want our future to be together, planning everything together, no secrets, no lies."

"Me, too," she answered softly.

"Then, will you marry me? Will you have a family and grow old with me?"

"Oh, Finn, yes! I will."

Much later, after they'd sealed their reunion with a wealth of physical promises and lay, replete, in one another's arms, Tamsyn reflected on how she finally felt as though she'd come home. Tomorrow would be Christmas Day and while she would miss her family she knew she was exactly where she was meant to be. With this man, for the rest of her life.

Thinking of Christmas reminded her of the gift Finn had thrust at her after the funeral when she'd left for Auckland. She hadn't gotten around to unwrapping it, yet hadn't quite been able to bring herself to discard it, either.

"Finn? What was the parcel you gave me the other day?"

"You didn't open it?"

"Not yet."

"Then why don't you?" he suggested.

She slipped from the bed and pulled on his T-shirt and went outside to her latest rental and dragged her case from the trunk. Bringing it upstairs to the bedroom, she unzipped it and burrowed through her clothes to where she'd stashed the package, cushioned in the center.

Sitting cross-legged on the bed beside him, she ripped away the paper, her eyes filling with tears as she saw the image of her mother looking back at her.

"Oh, Finn. She was so beautiful."

"Inside and out, just like you," he replied, dropping a kiss on her shoulder.

"But this picture, it must have been special to you. Why did you give it to me?"

"Because you deserved to have something of her. Something you could keep forever to remember her by and something that I know she, too, was proud of."

Tamsyn carefully placed the picture on the bedside cabinet and turned to the man beside her. If she'd had any doubts whatsoever they were all banished now. She'd made the right choice in coming back to Finn, in coming home. Finally she could be secure in the knowledge that, for the first time in her life, she was finally where she truly belonged.

In his arms, in his life, and ahead of all others in his heart. Always.

* * * * *

'05

Join Britain's BIGGEST Romance Book Club

50% OFF your first parcel

MARINELLI
...nt Conquest

- **EXCLUSIVE** offers every month

- **FREE** delivery dire to your door

- **NEVER MISS** a title

- **EARN** Bonus Book points

Call Customer Services
0844 844 1358*

or visit
millsandboon.co.uk/subscriptio

BKCB3

MILLS & BOON®
are delighted to support
World Book Night

World Book Night is run by The Reading Agency and is a national celebration of reading and books which takes place on 23 April every year. To find out more visit worldbooknight.org.

www.millsandboon.co.uk